Kaleb-
Merry Christmas
2017 !
Enjoy the adventures
of Dog man!

Love,
Grandma Pat
+
Grandpa Rich

Tree-
House
Comix
Proudly
Presents

DOG MAN
UNLEASHED

WRITTEN AND ILLUSTRATED BY **DAV PILKEY**

AS GEORGE BEARD AND HAROLD HUTCHINS

WITH INTERIOR COLOR BY JOSE GARIBALDI

AN IMPRINT OF

■SCHOLASTIC

FOR Phil Falco

Library of Congress Control Number 2016936340

ISBN 978-0-545-93520-3

10 9 8 7 6 5   17 18 19 20 21

Printed in China   62
First edition, January 2017

Edited by Anamika Bhatnagar
Book design by Dav Pilkey and Phil Falco
Interior color by Jose Garibaldi
Creative Director: David Saylor

Chapters

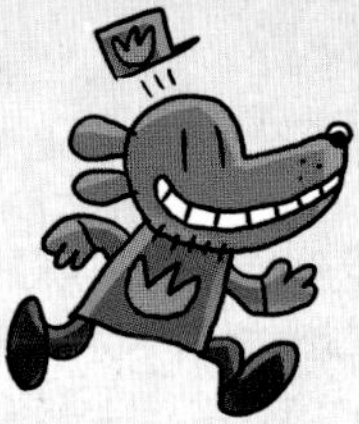

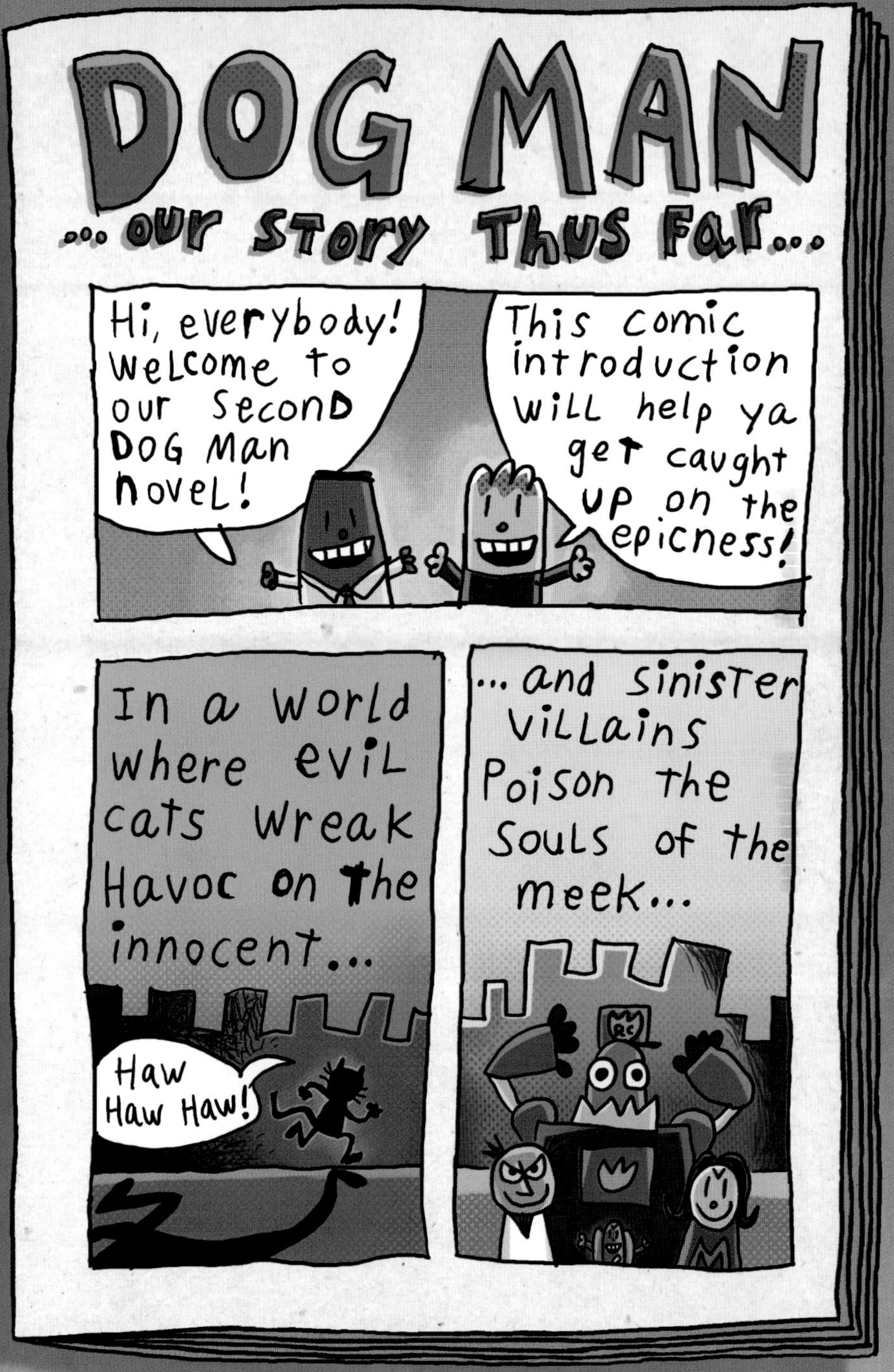
DOG MAN
...our story thus far...
Hi, everybody! Welcome to our second DOG MAN novel!
This comic introduction will help ya get caught up on the epicness!
In a world where evil cats wreak havoc on the innocent...
Haw Haw Haw!
...and sinister villains poison the souls of the meek...
RC

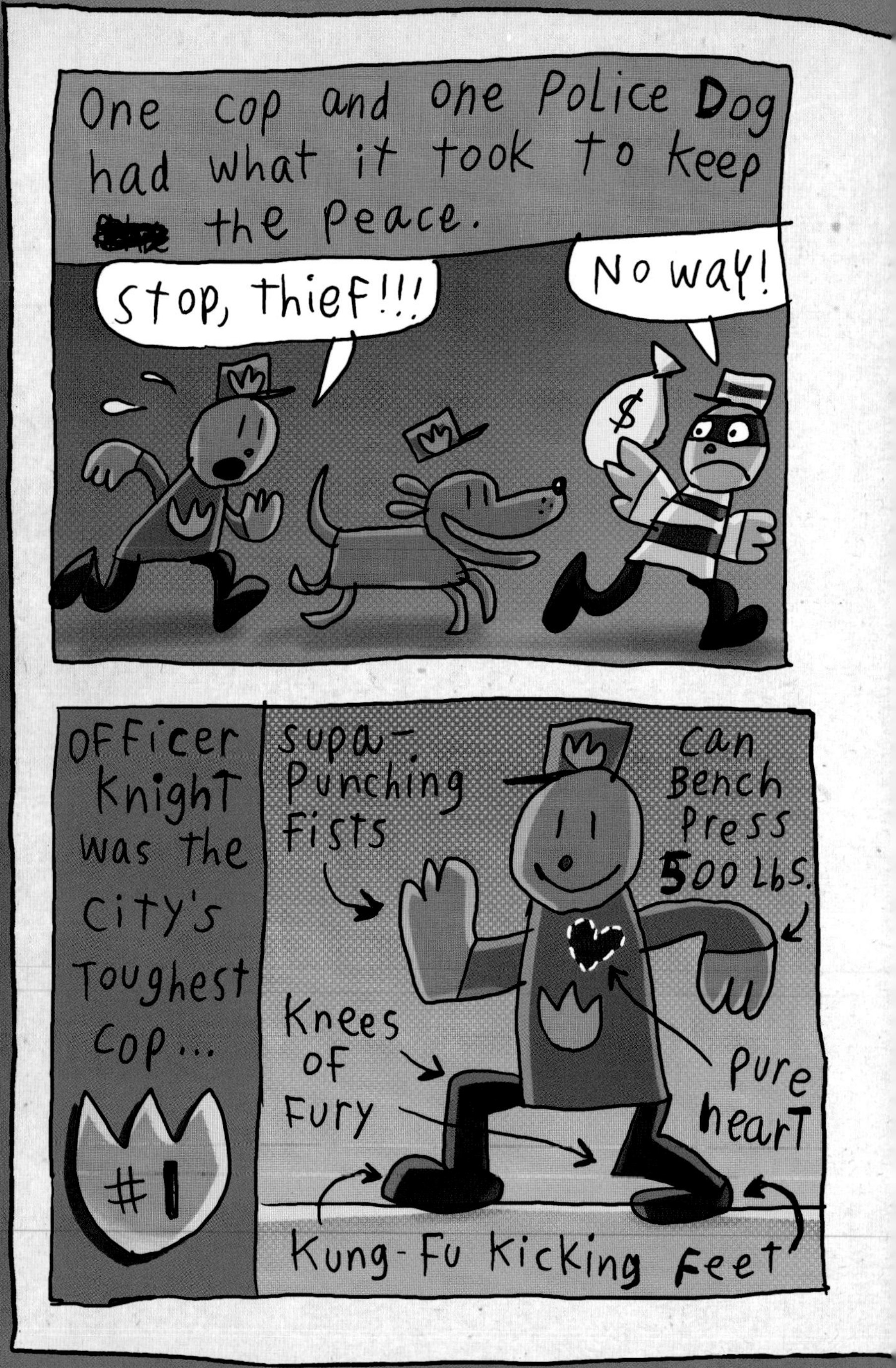
One cop and one Police Dog had what it took to keep the peace.
Stop, thief!!!
No way!
Officer Knight was the city's Toughest cop...
#1
supa-Punching Fists
can Bench Press 500 Lbs.
Knees of Fury
Pure heart
Kung-Fu Kicking Feet

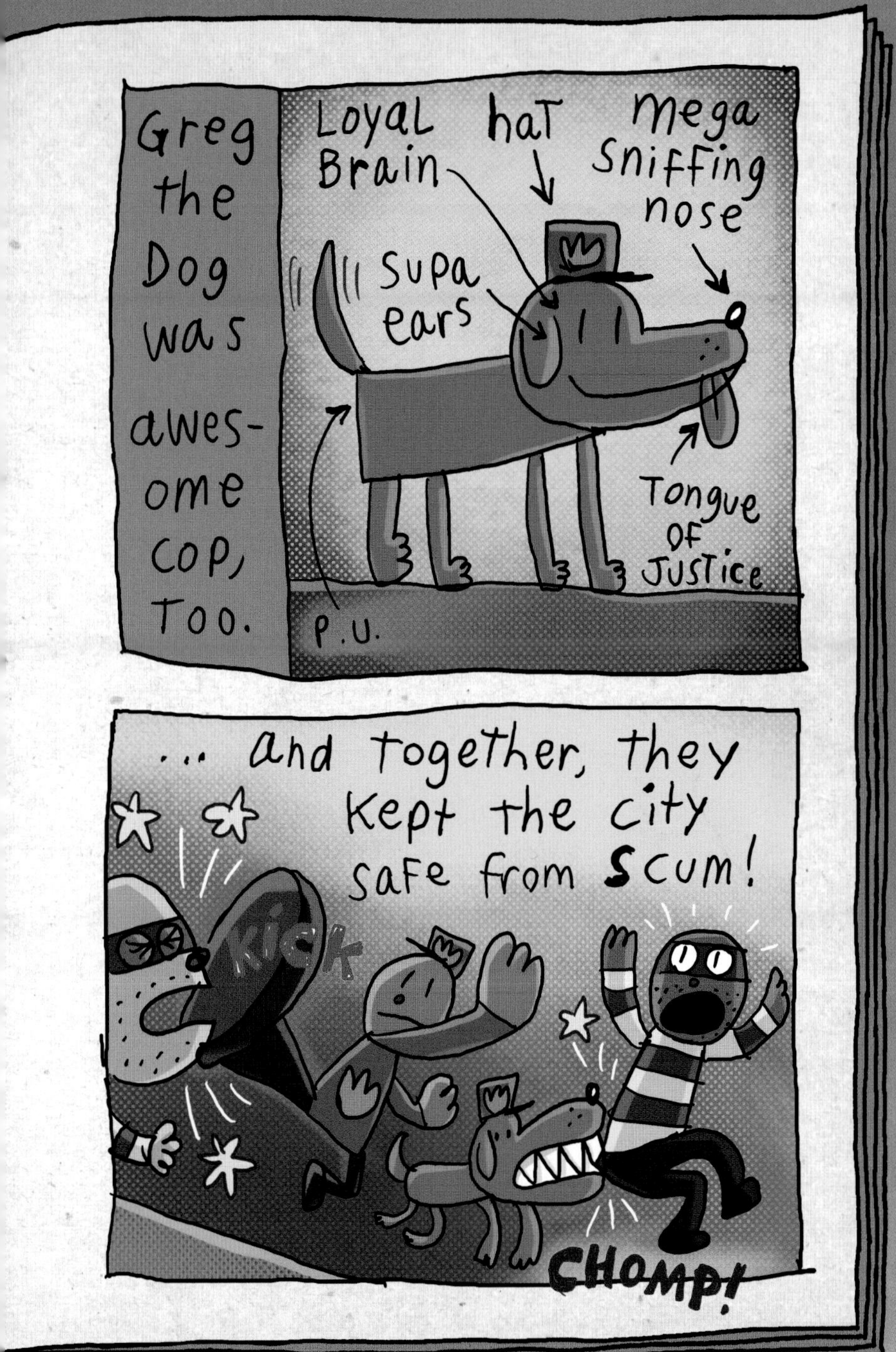
Greg the Dog was awesome cop, Too.
Loyal Brain
hat
Mega Sniffing nose
Supa ears
Tongue of Justice
P.U.
... and together, they kept the city safe from Scum!
KICK
CHOMP!

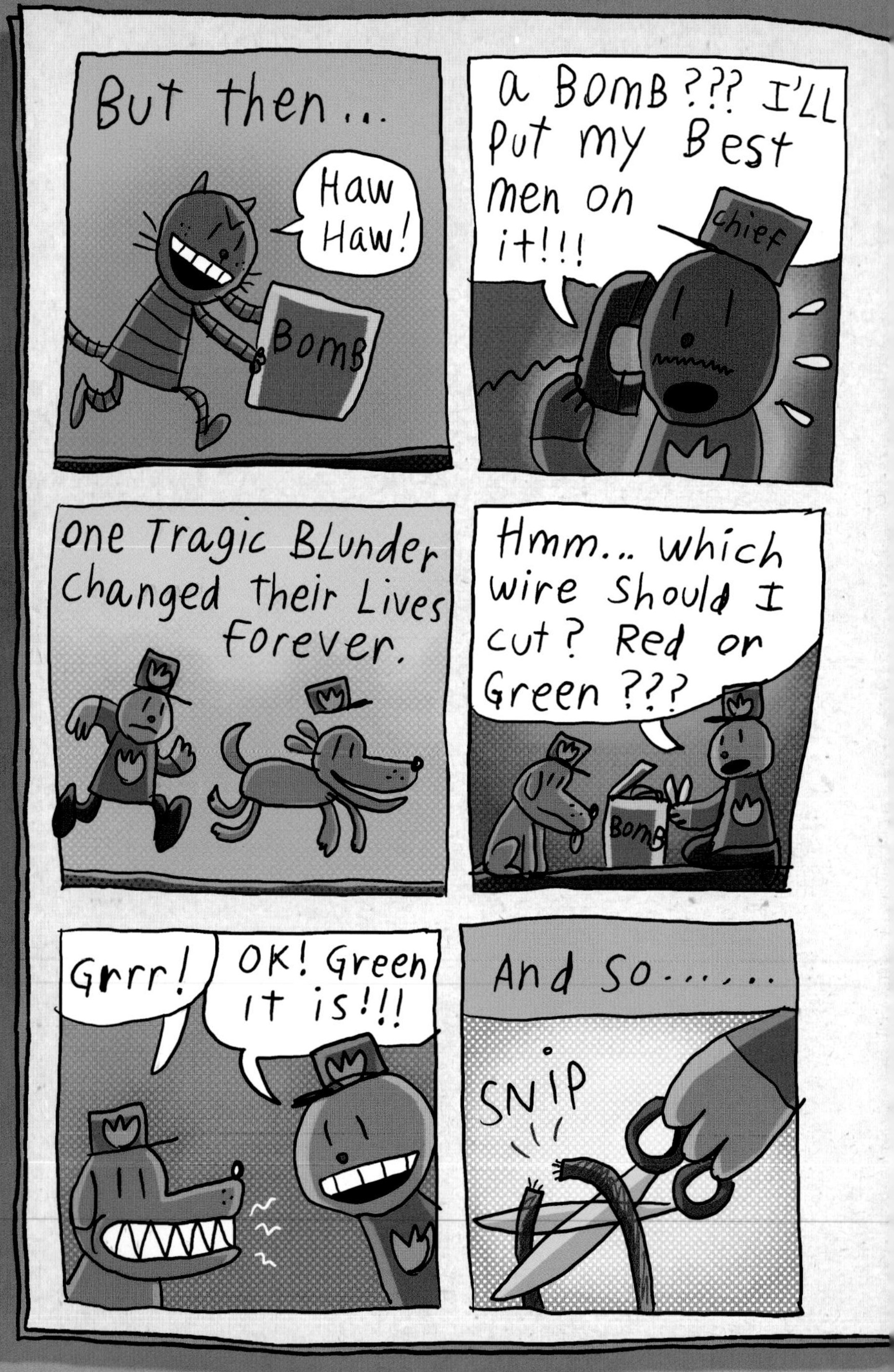
But then...
Haw Haw!
BOMB
a BOMB??? I'LL put my Best men on it!!!
chief
One Tragic BLunder changed their Lives Forever.
Hmm... which wire should I cut? Red or Green???
BOMB
Grrr!
OK! Green it is!!!
And so......
SNIP

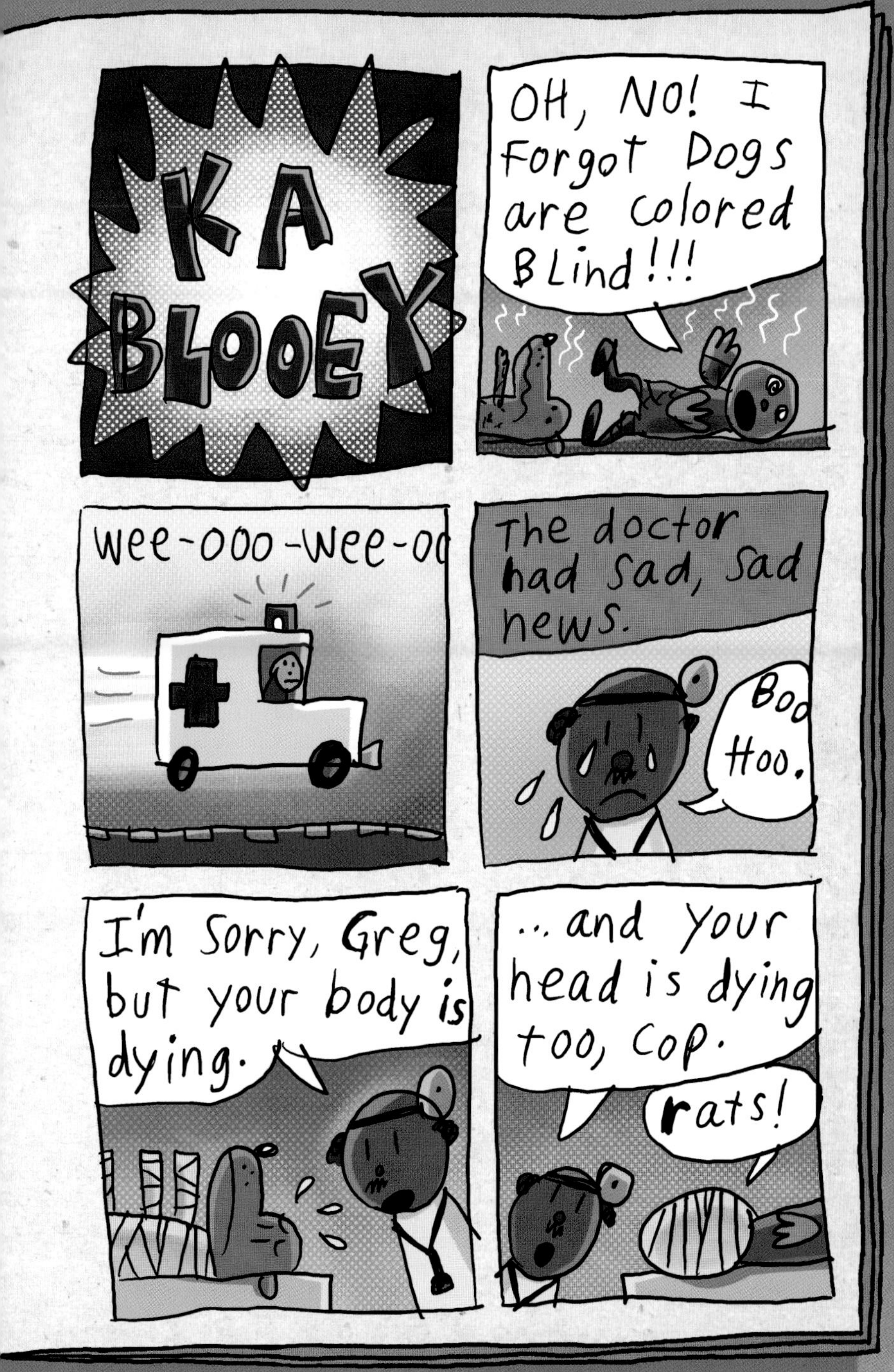
KA BLOOEY
OH, NO! I Forgot Dogs are colored BLind!!!
wee-ooo-wee-oo
The doctor had sad, sad news.
Boo Hoo.
I'm Sorry, Greg, but your body is dying.
...and your head is dying too, cop.
rats!

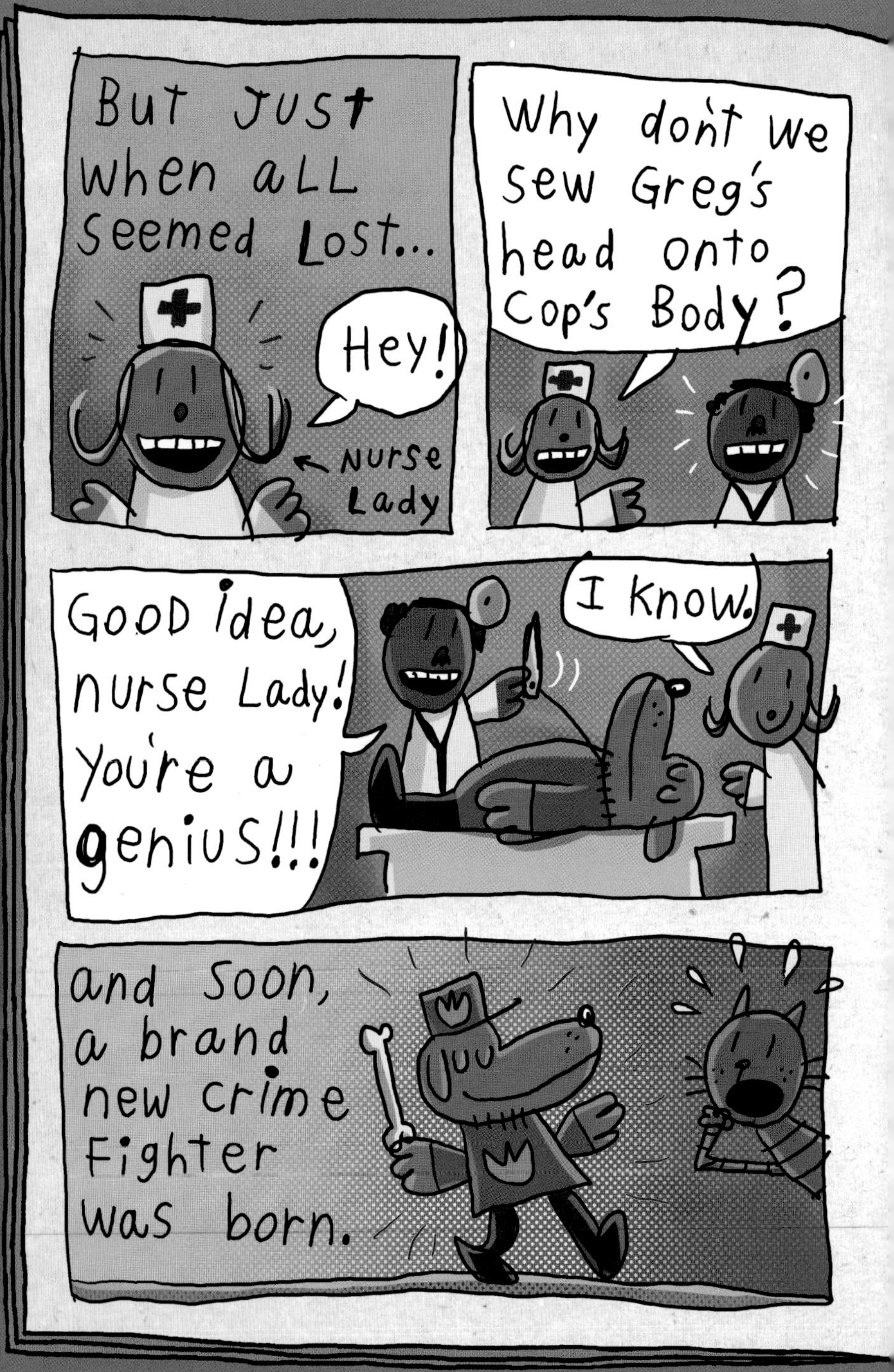

But just when all seemed lost...
Hey!
Nurse Lady
Why don't we sew Greg's head onto Cop's Body?
Good idea, nurse Lady! You're a genius!!!
I know.
and soon, a brand new crime Fighter was born.

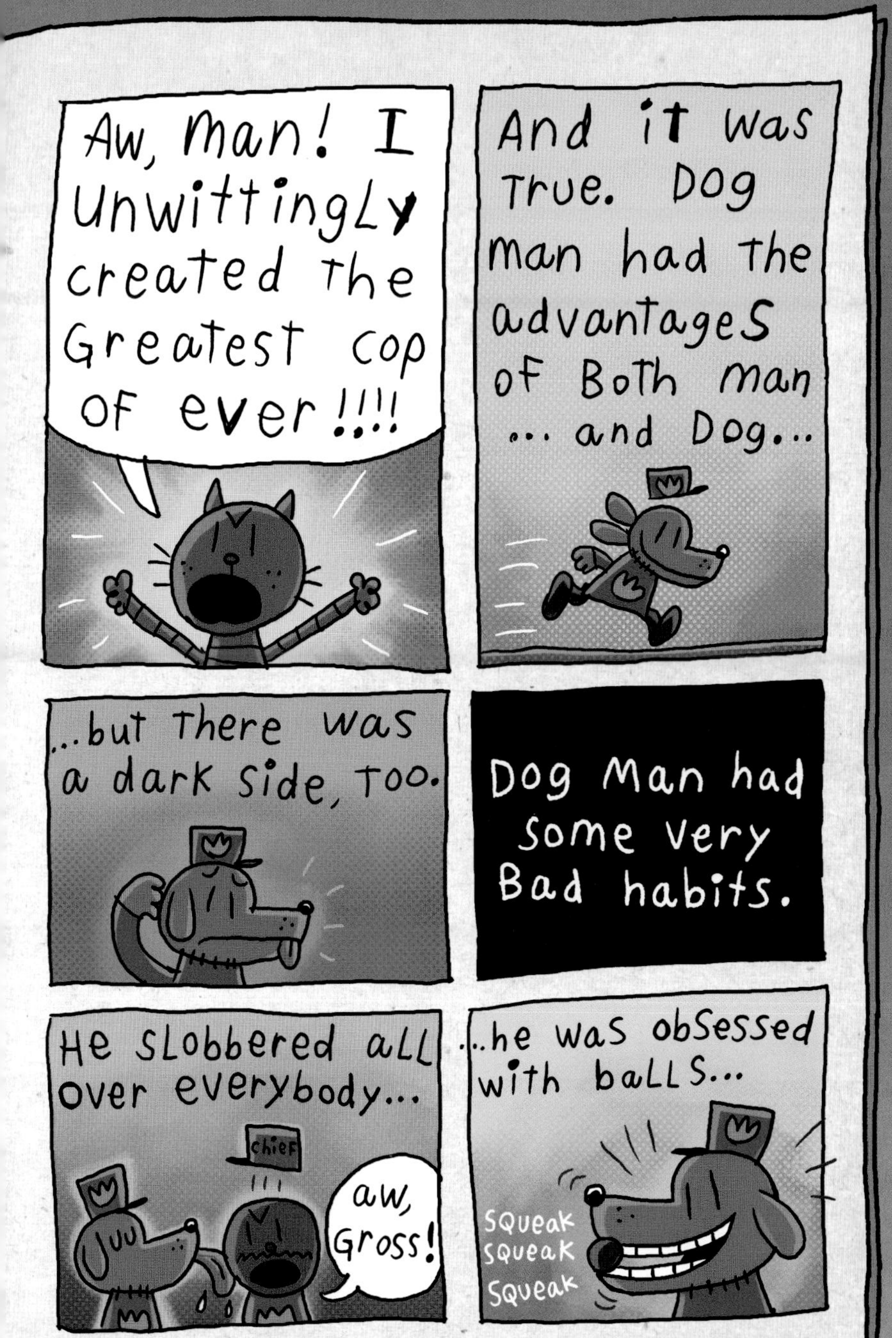
Aw, Man! I UnwittingLy created The Greatest cop of ever!!!!
And it was True. Dog man had the advantageS of Both man ... and Dog...
...but There was a dark side, Too.
Dog Man had some very Bad habits.
He sLobbered aLL over everybody...
chief
aw, Gross!
...he was obSessed with baLLS...
SQueak
SQueak
SQueak

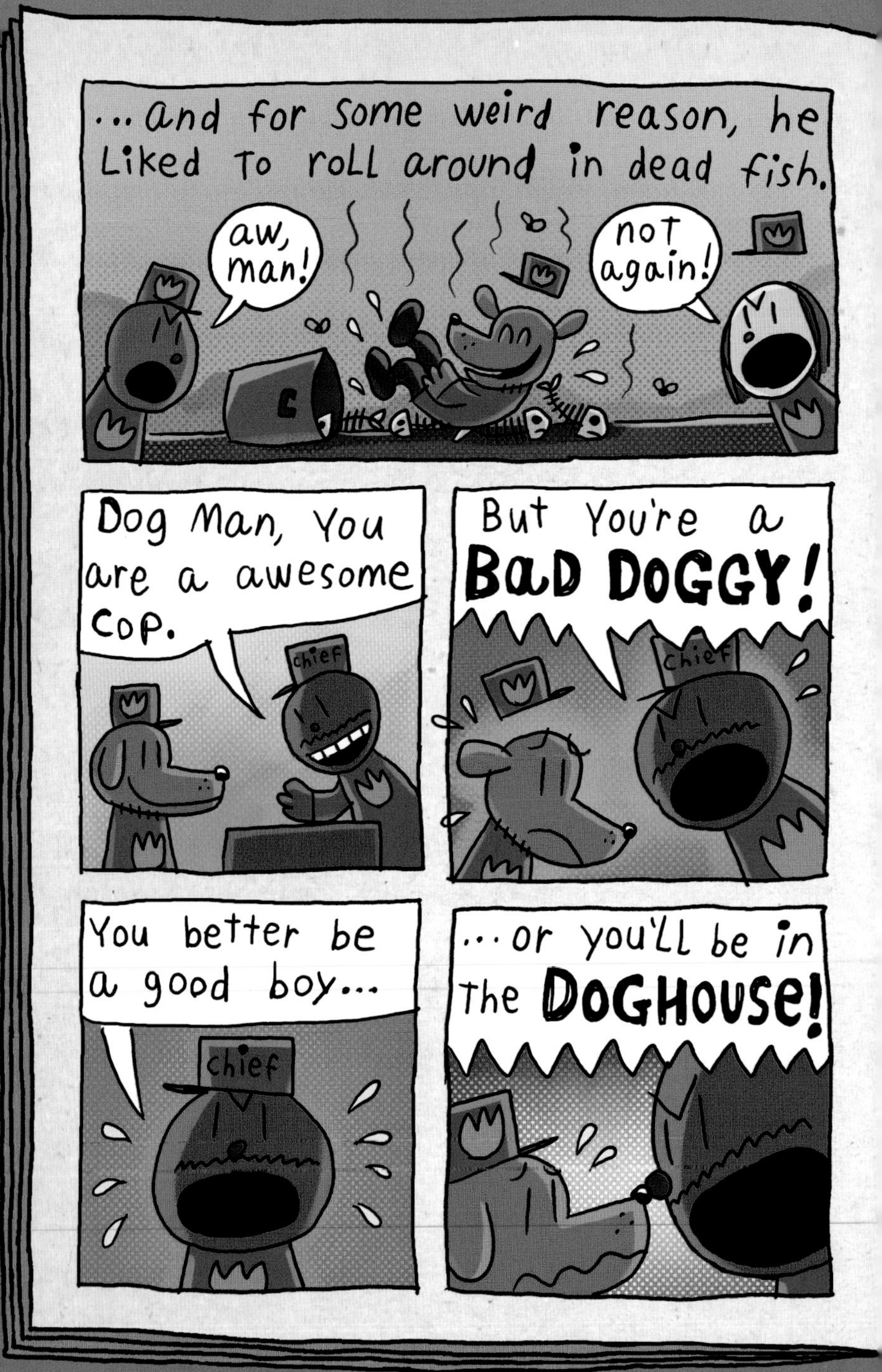
...and for some weird reason, he Liked To roLL around in dead fish.
aw, man!
not again!
Dog Man, You are a awesome cop.
But You're a BAD DOGGY!
You better be a good boy...
...or you'LL be in The DOGHOUSE!

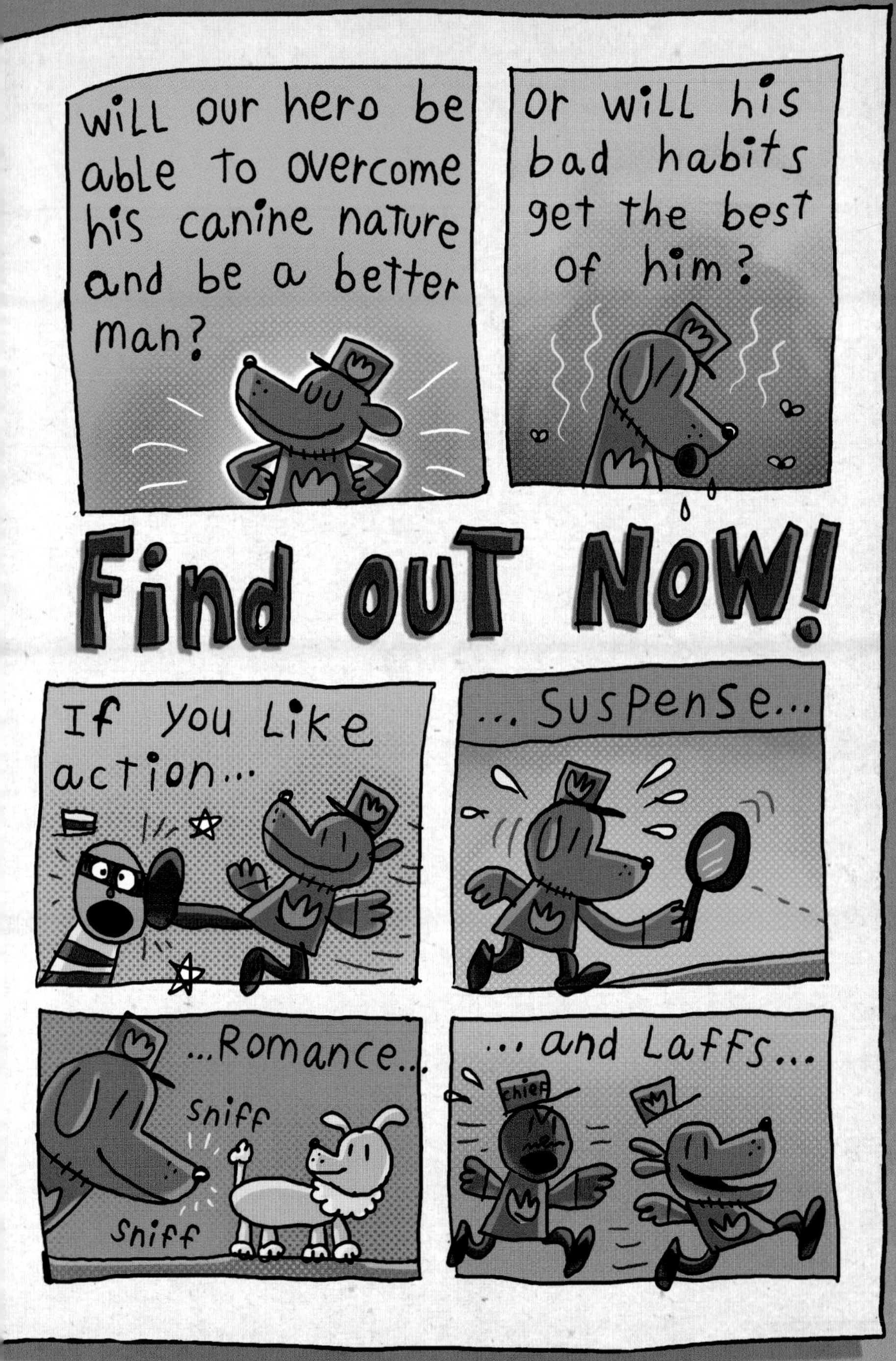
Will our hero be able to overcome his canine nature and be a better man?
Or will his bad habits get the best of him?
Find OUT NOW!
If you like action...
...Suspense...
...Romance...
sniff
sniff
...and Laffs...
chief

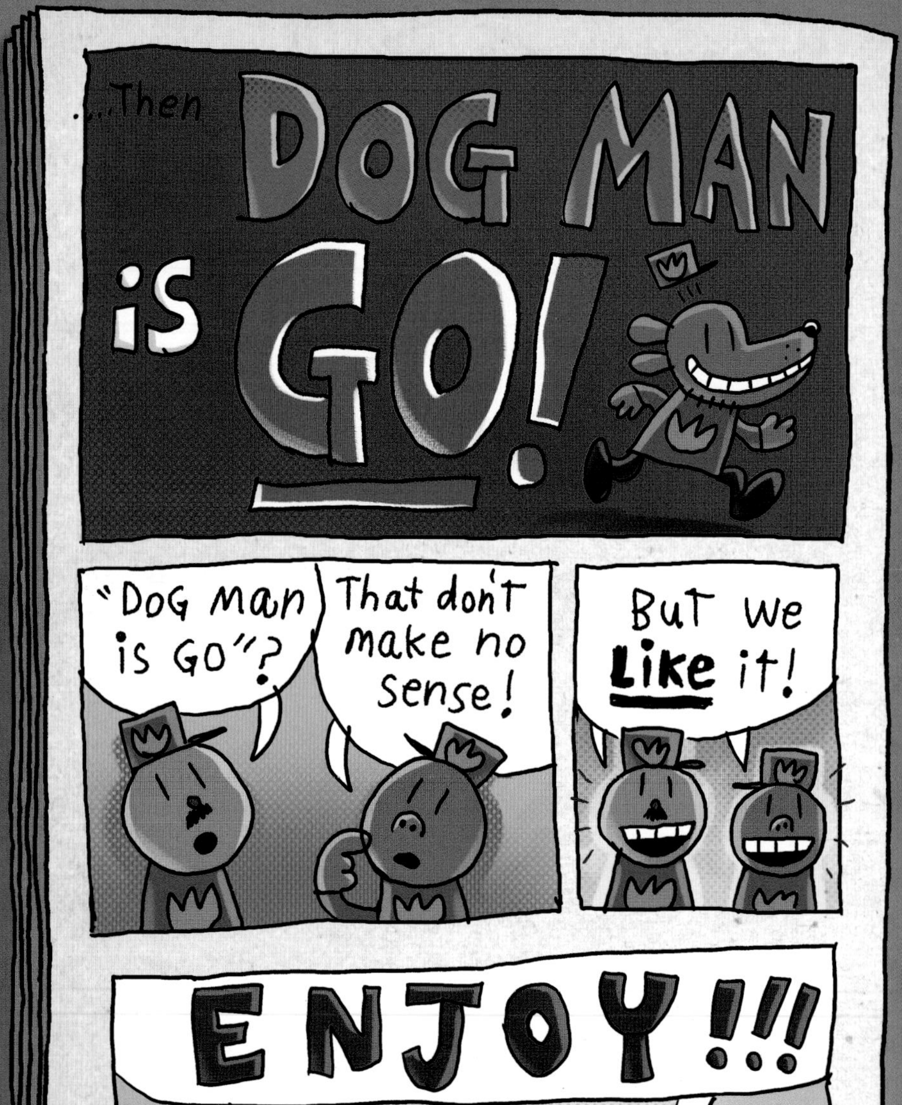
...Then DOG MAN is GO!
"DOG MAN is GO"?
That don't make no sense!
But we LIKE it!
ENJOY!!!

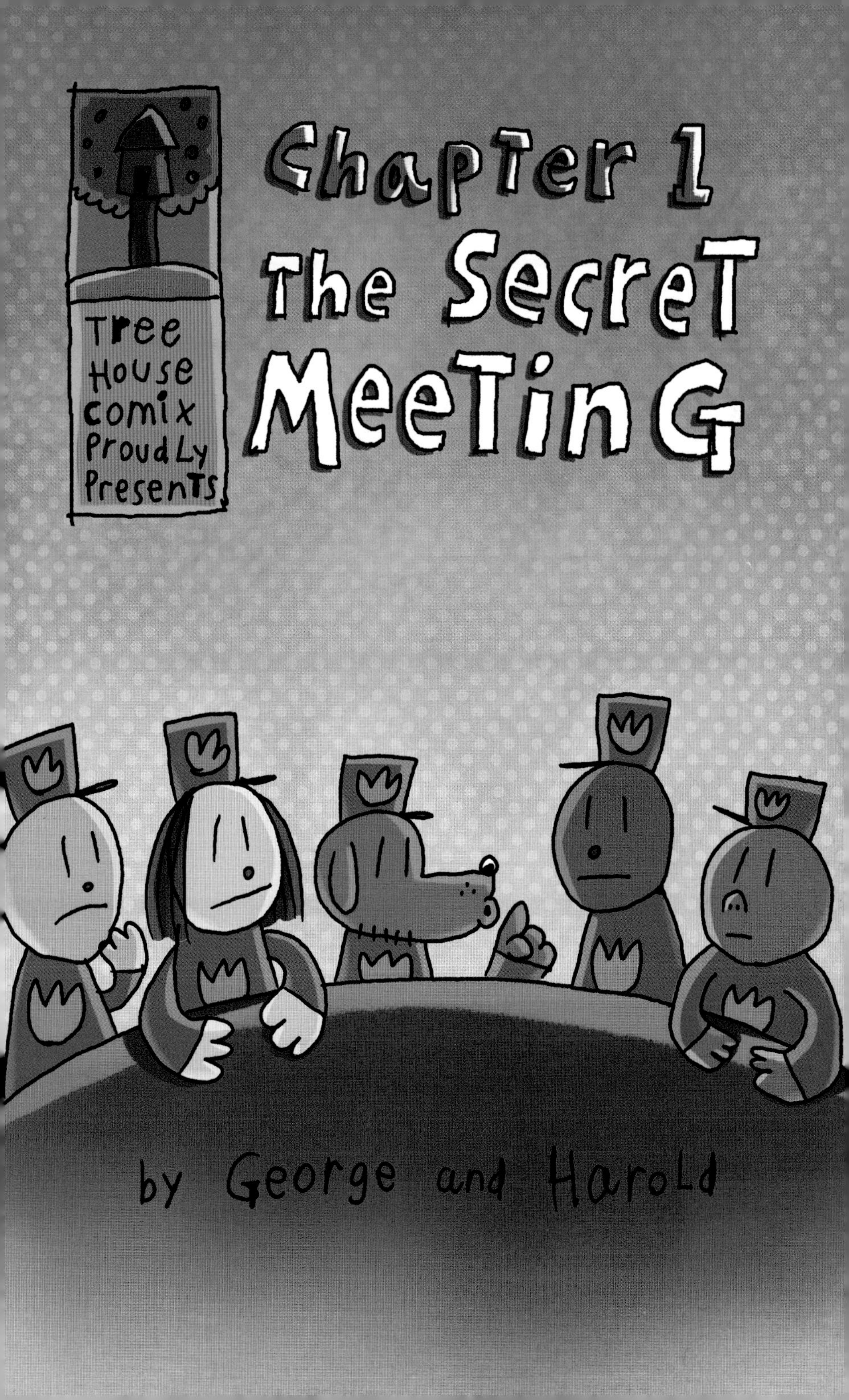

Tree House Comix Proudly Presents
Chapter 1
The Secret Meeting
by George and Harold

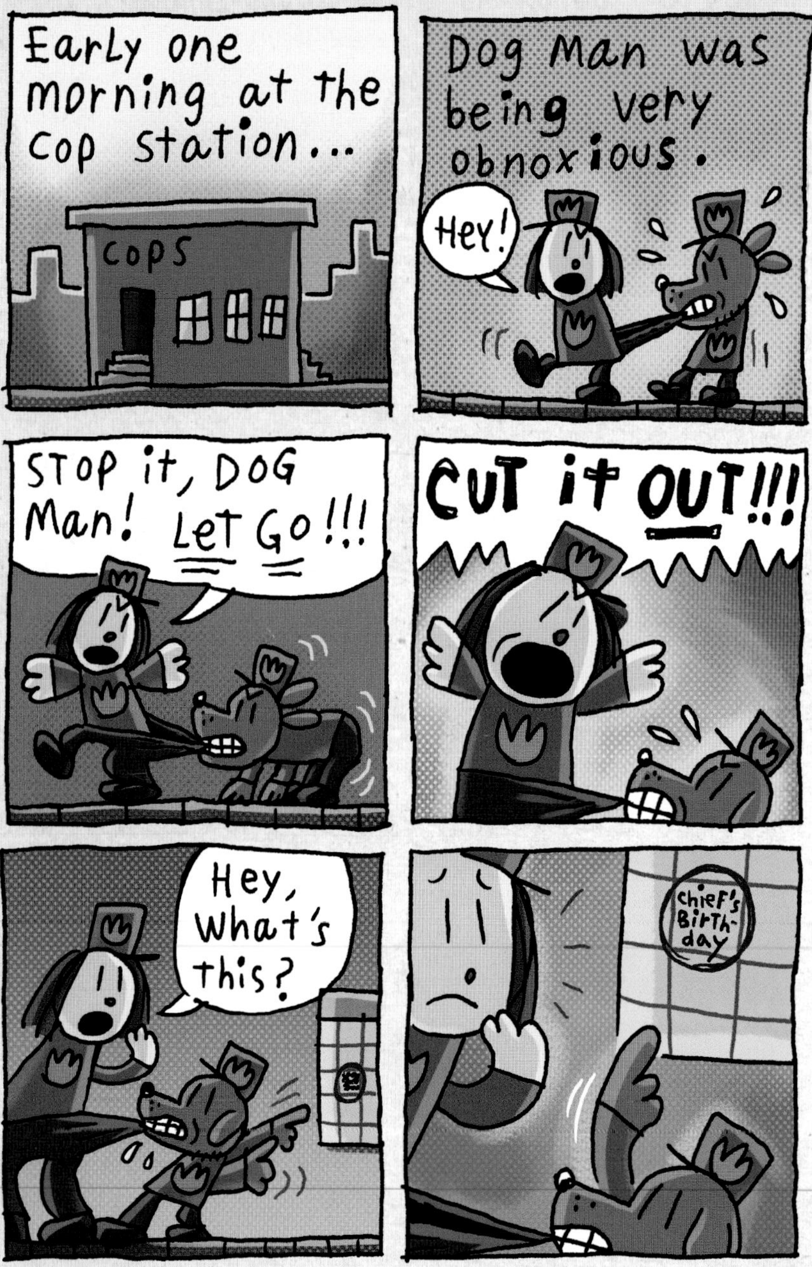
Early one morning at the cop station...
COPS
Dog Man was being very obnoxious.
Hey!
STOP it, DOG Man! LeT Go!!!
CUT it OUT!!!
Hey, What's this?
chief's Birthday

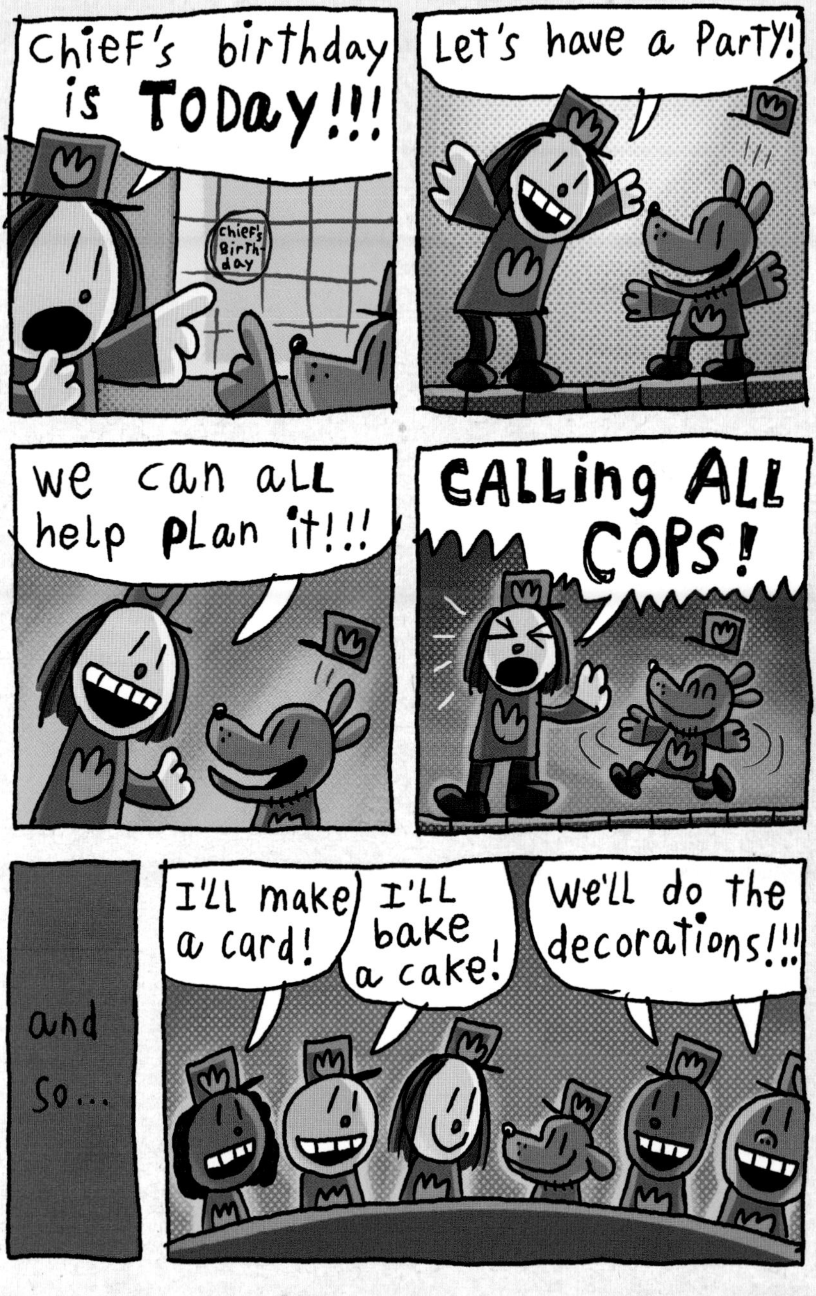
Chief's birthday is TODAY!!!
Chief's Birthday
Let's have a Party!
we can all help plan it!!!
CALLING ALL COPS!
and so...
I'll make a card!
I'll bake a cake!
We'll do the decorations!!!

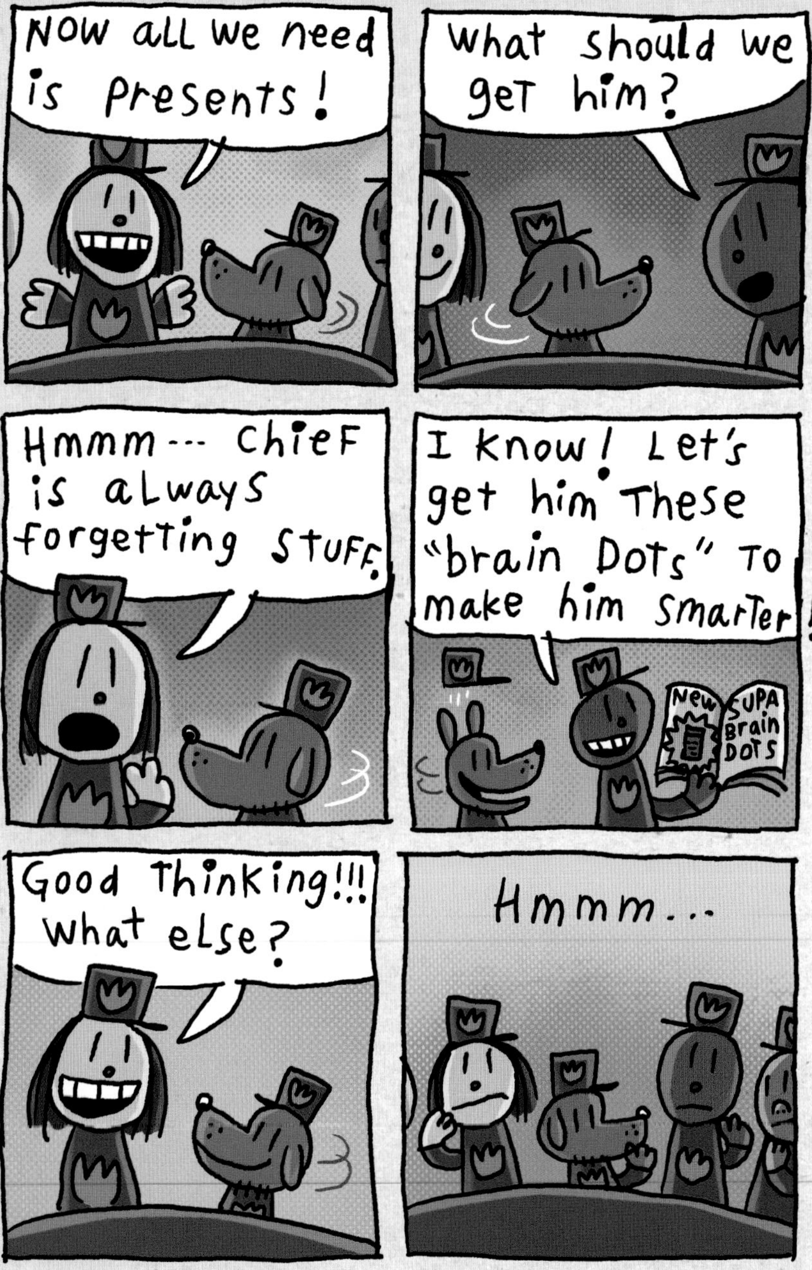
Now all we need is presents!
What should we get him?
Hmmm... Chief is always forgetting stuff.
I know! Let's get him these "brain dots" to make him smarter!
New SUPA Brain DOTS
Good thinking!!! What else?
Hmmm...

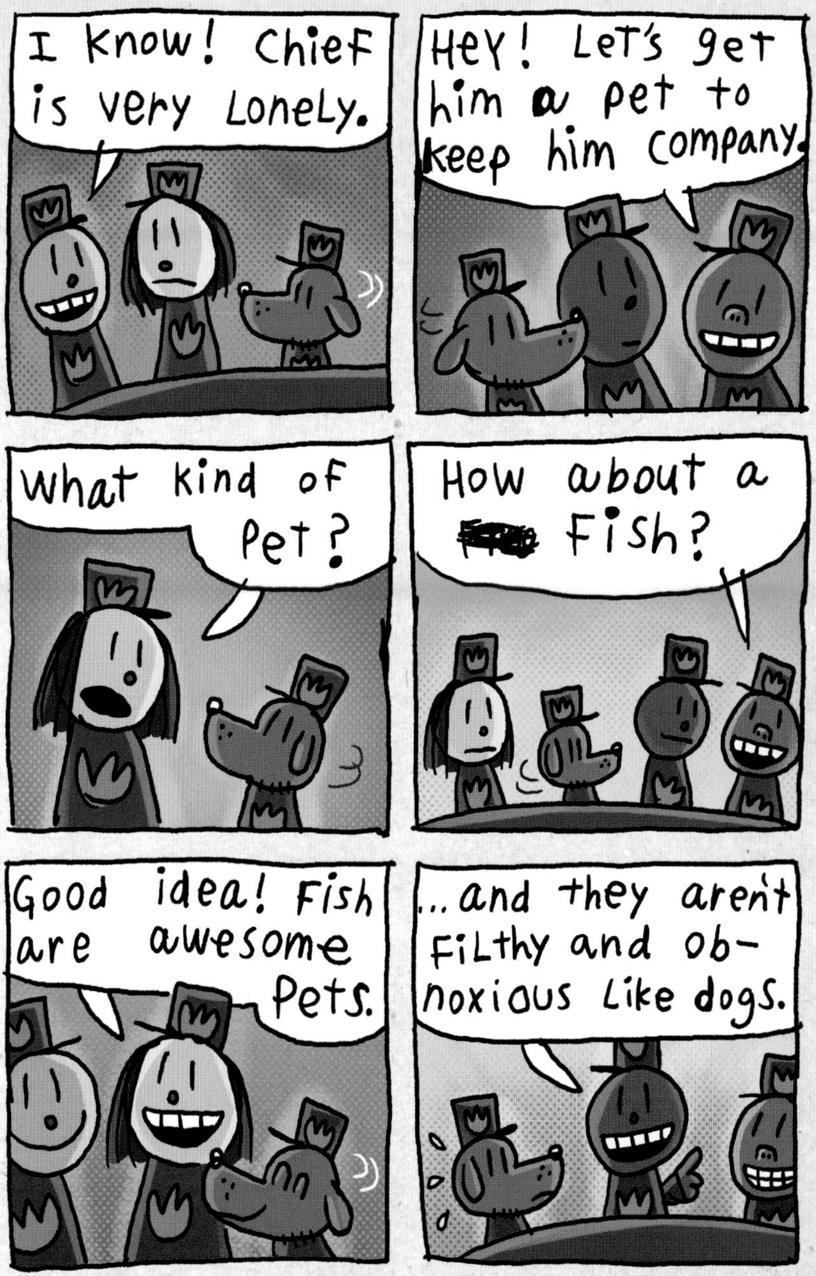
I know! Chief is very lonely.
Hey! Let's get him a pet to keep him company.
What kind of pet?
How about a fish?
Good idea! Fish are awesome pets.
...and they aren't filthy and ob-noxious like dogs.

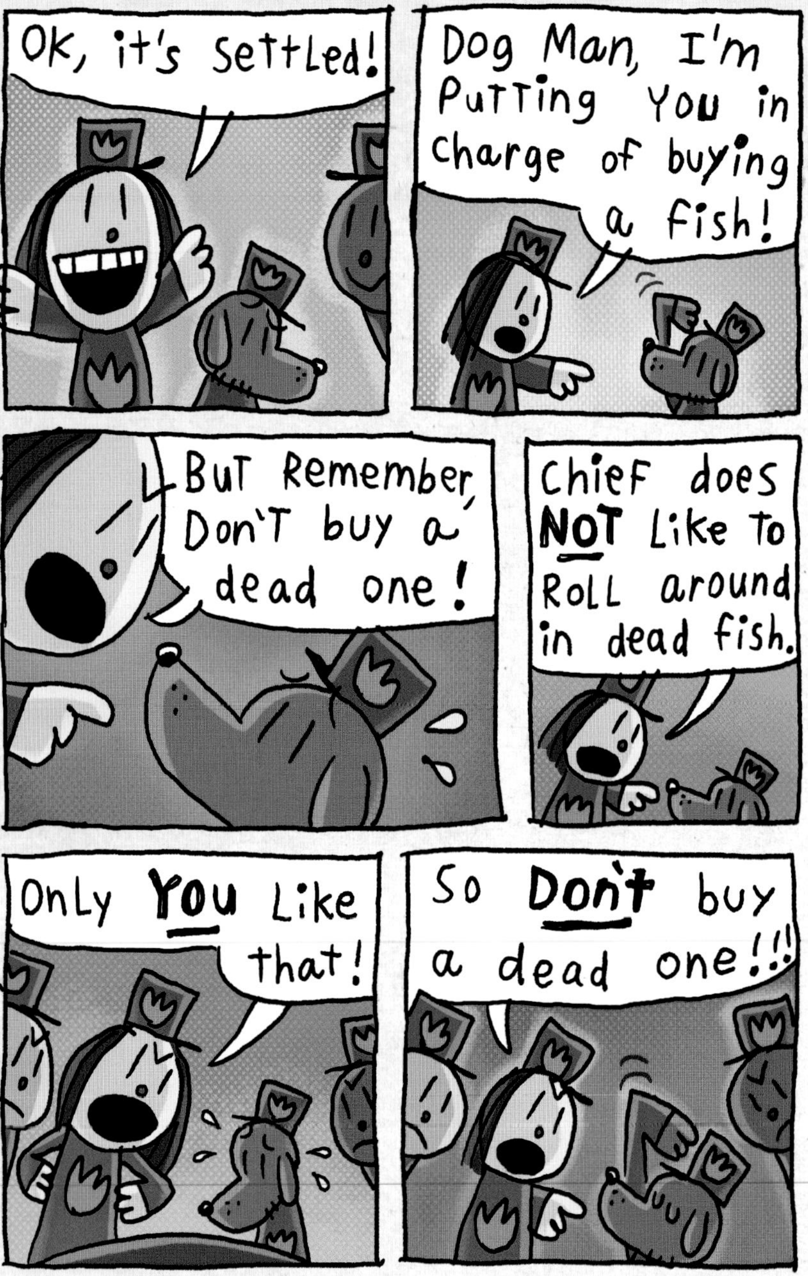
OK, it's settled!
Dog Man, I'm putting you in charge of buying a fish!
But remember, Don't buy a dead one!
Chief does NOT like to roll around in dead fish.
Only YOU like that!
So DON'T buy a dead one!!!

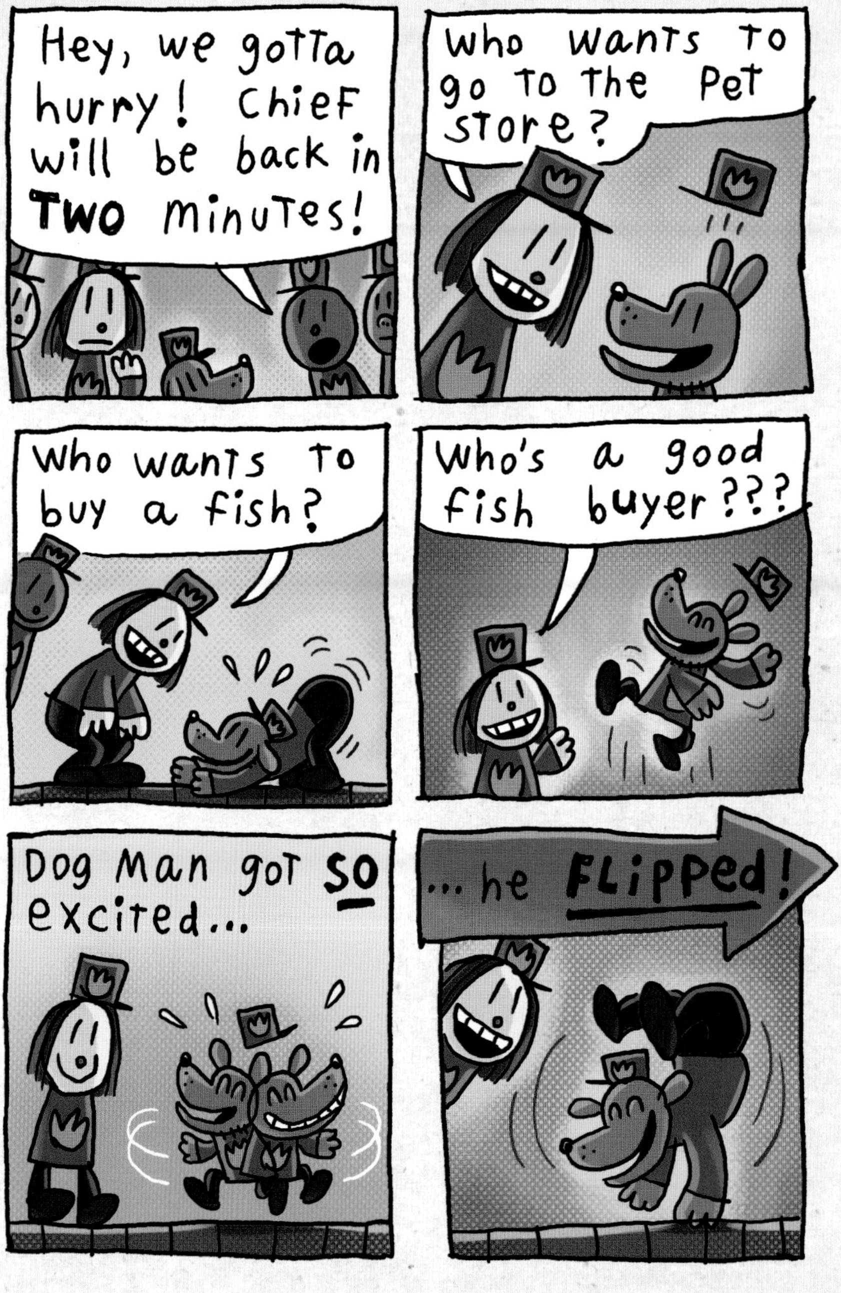
Hey, we gotta hurry! Chief will be back in TWO minutes!
Who wants to go to the pet store?
Who wants to buy a fish?
Who's a good fish buyer???
Dog Man got SO excited...
... he FLIPPED!

Introducing **FLiP-O**
Be A FLiP MASTER!

FLiP-o-rama is
Easy if you know The rules:
FLip it, don't rip it!

a haiku
by
Dog Man.

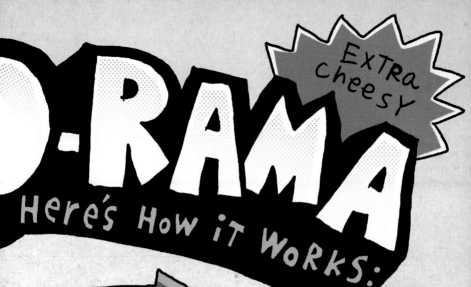

-RAMA

EXTRA CHEESY

HERE'S HOW IT WORKS:

STEP 1.
First, place your left hand inside the dotted lines marked "Left hand here". Hold the book open FLAT!

STEP 2:
Grasp the right-hand page with your thumb and index finger (inside the dotted lines marked "Right Thumb Here").

STEP 3:
Now quickly flip the right-hand page back and forth until the picture appears to be Animated.

(for extra fun, try adding your own sound-effects!)

Remember,

while you are flipping,
be sure you can see
the images on page 25
AND the images on page 27.

If you flip quickly,
the pictures will
start to look like
one **ANIMATED** cartoon!

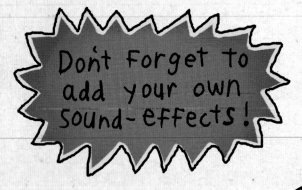

Don't forget to
add your own
sound-effects!

Left
hand here.

who wants
to go
to the
pet
store?

who wants
to buy
a fish?

Don't
buy a
dead
one!

Right
Thumb
here.

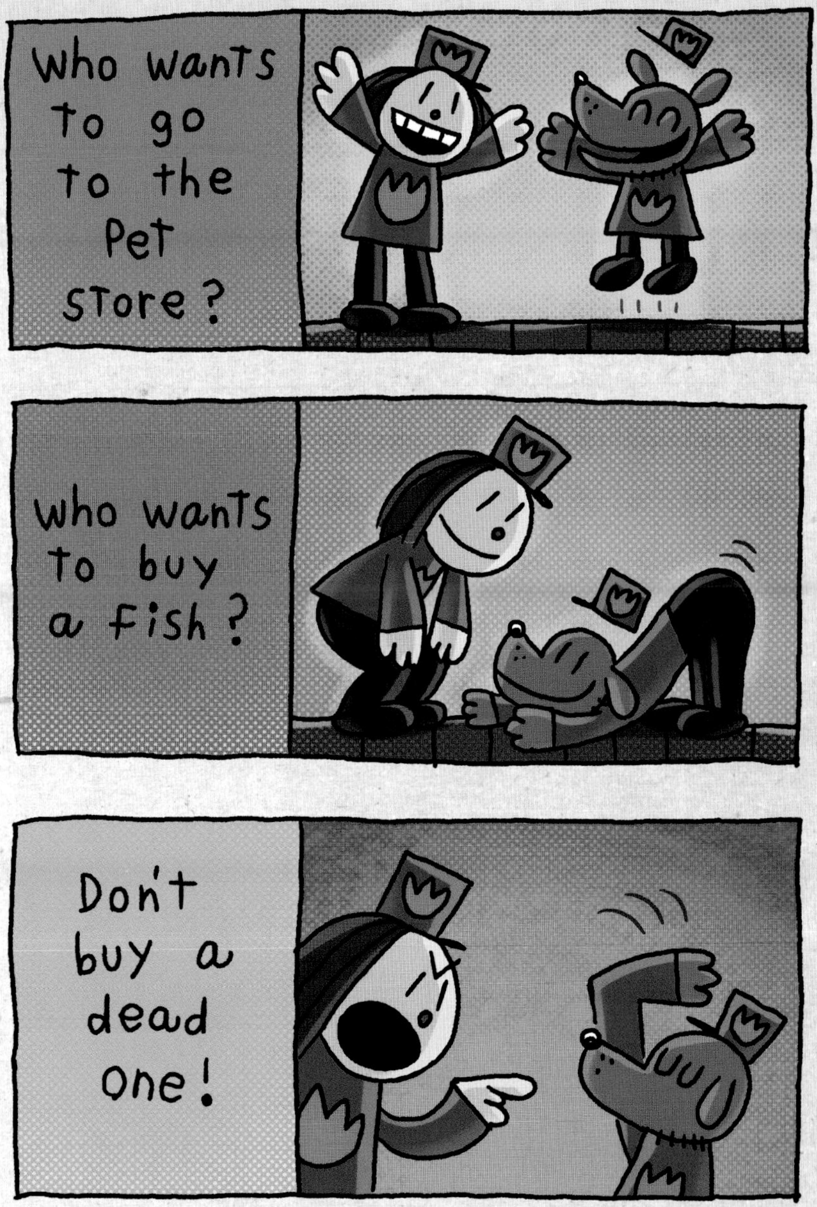
Who wants to go to the Pet store?
Who wants to buy a fish?
Don't buy a dead one!

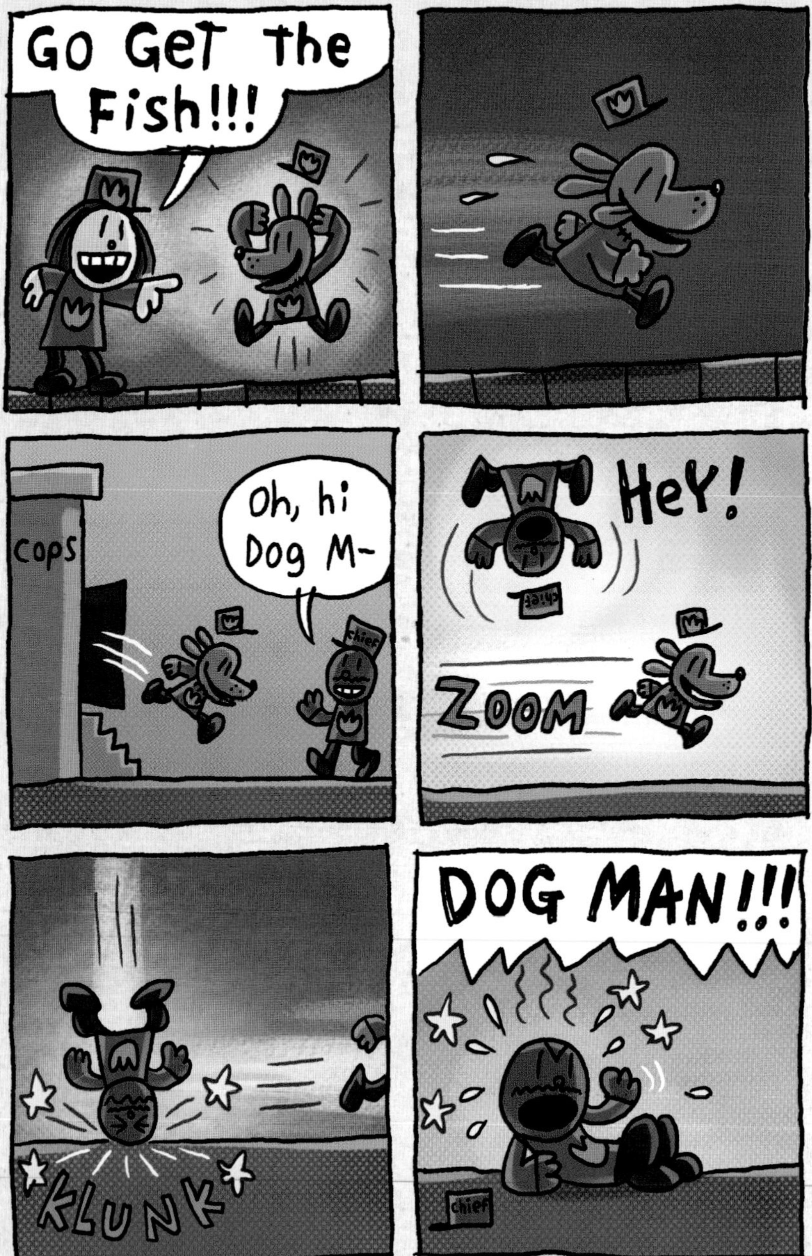
GO GET the Fish!!!
Cops
Oh, hi Dog M–
chief
HEY!
chief
ZOOM
KLUNK
DOG MAN!!!
chief

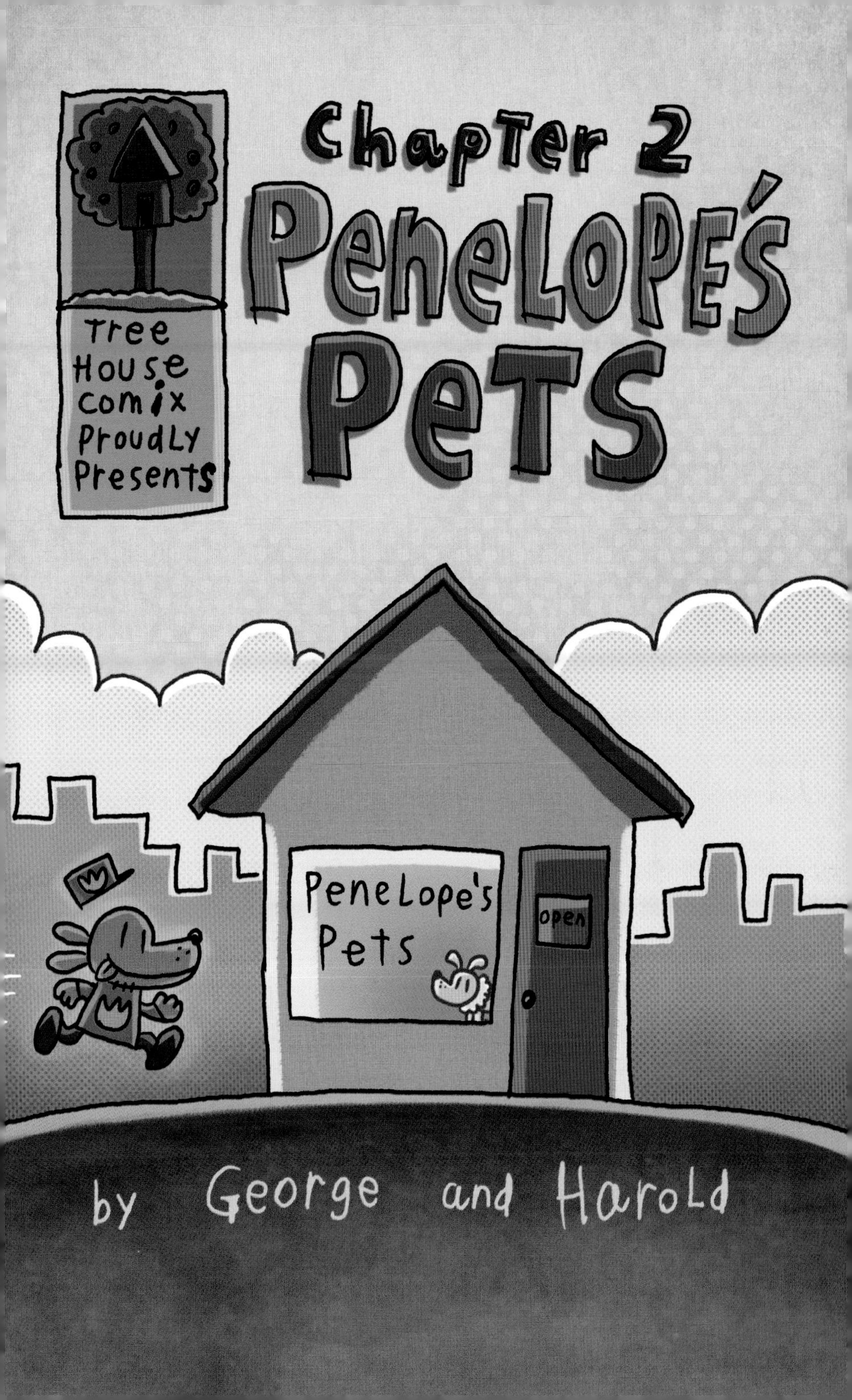
Tree House Comix Proudly Presents
Chapter 2
Penelope's Pets
Penelope's Pets
open
by George and Harold

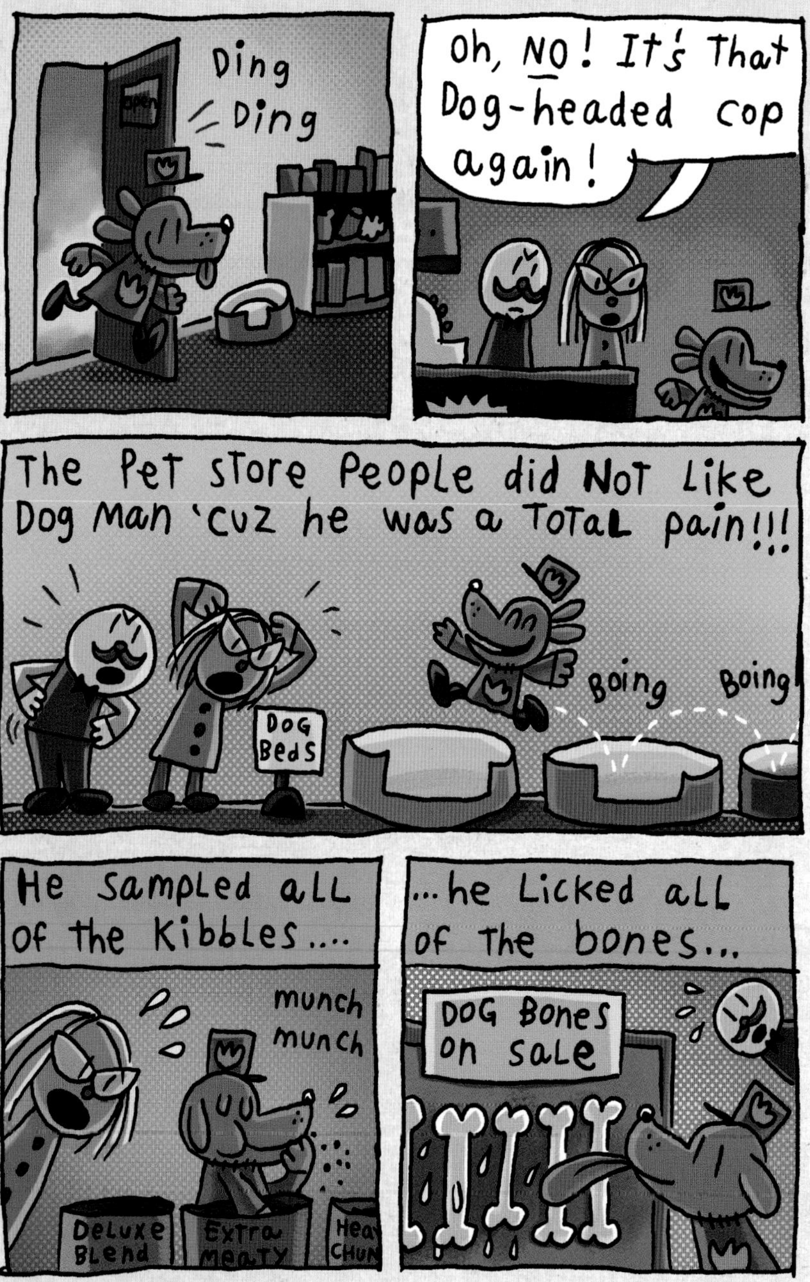
Ding
Ding
Oh, NO! It's That Dog-headed cop again!
The Pet store People did NOT Like Dog Man 'cuz he was a TOTAL pain!!!
DOG Beds
Boing
Boing
He sampled all of the Kibbles....
munch
munch
Deluxe Blend
Extra Meaty
...he Licked all of The bones...
DOG Bones on sale

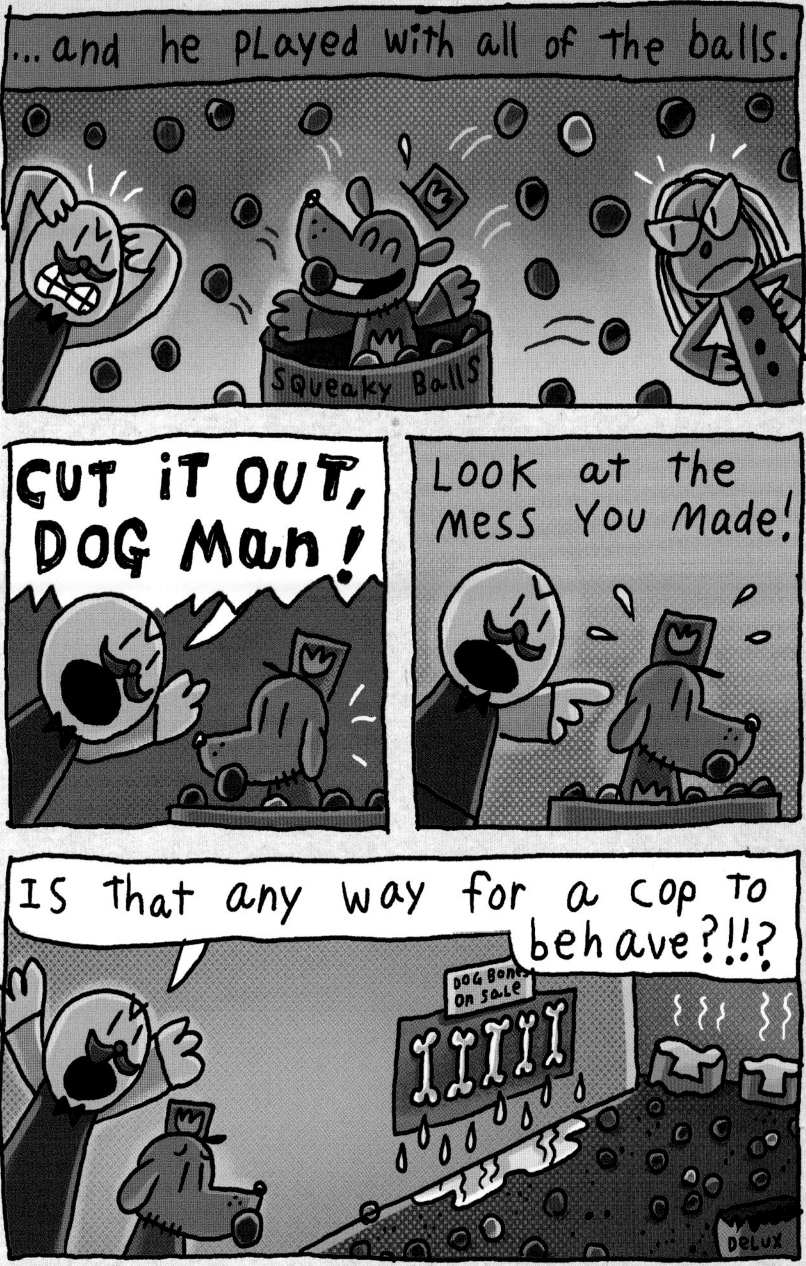
...and he played with all of the balls.
Squeaky Balls
CUT iT OUT, DOG Man!
Look at the mess you made!
IS that any way for a cop to behave?!!?
DOG Bones On SALE
DELUX

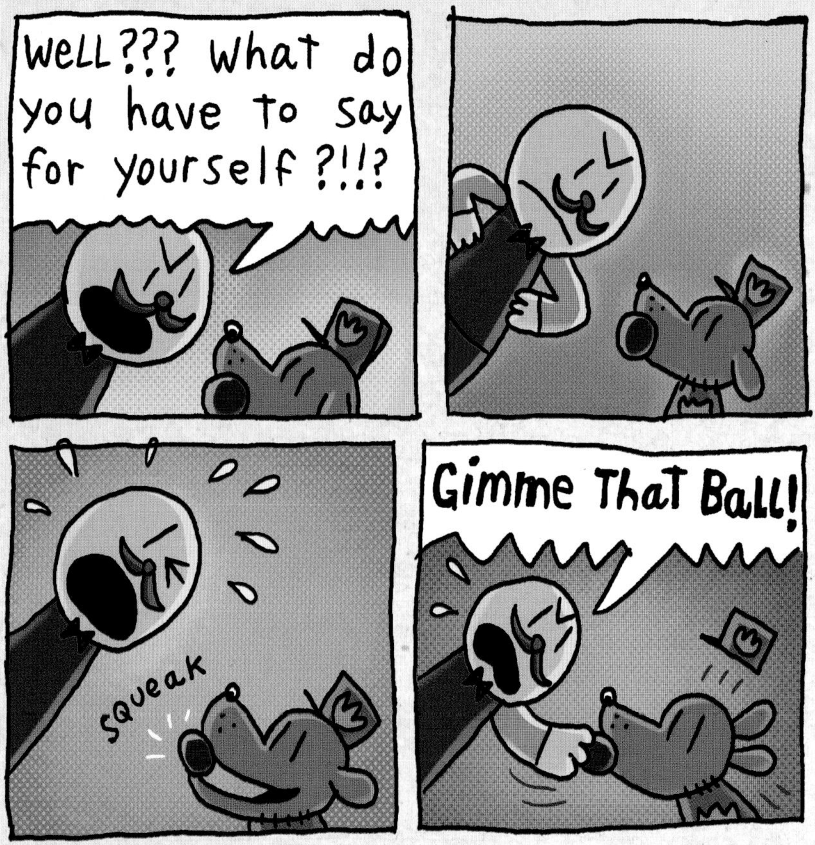
WELL??? What do you have to say for yourself?!!?
squeak
Gimme That Ball!

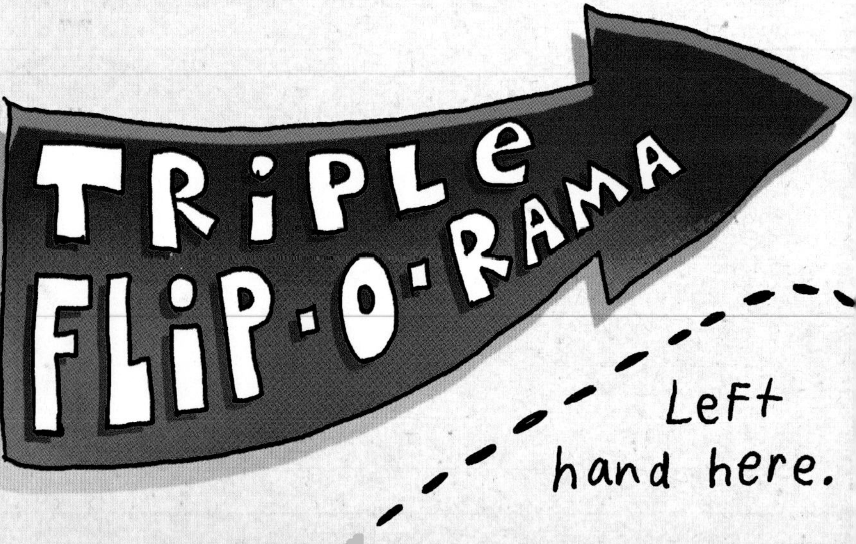
TRIPLE FLIP-O-RAMA
Left hand here.

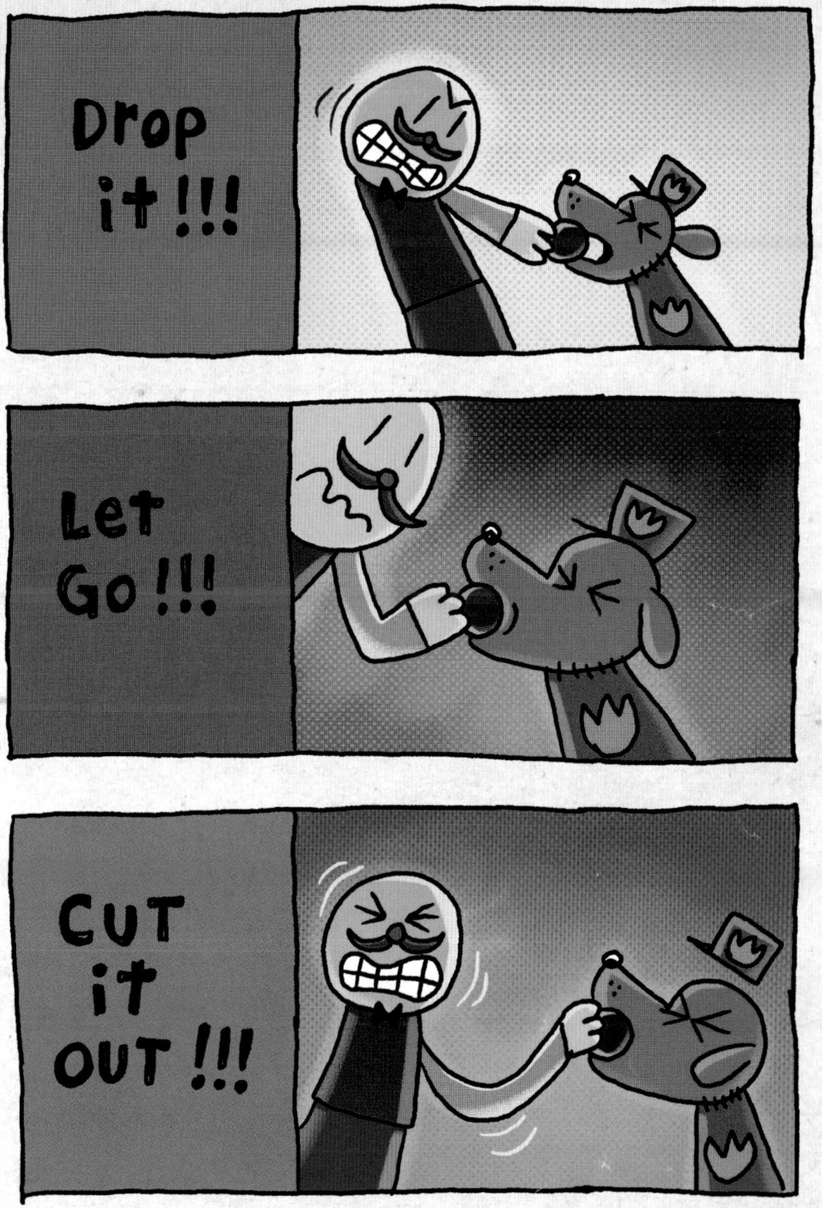
Drop it!!!
Let Go!!!
CUT it OUT!!!

Right Thumb here.

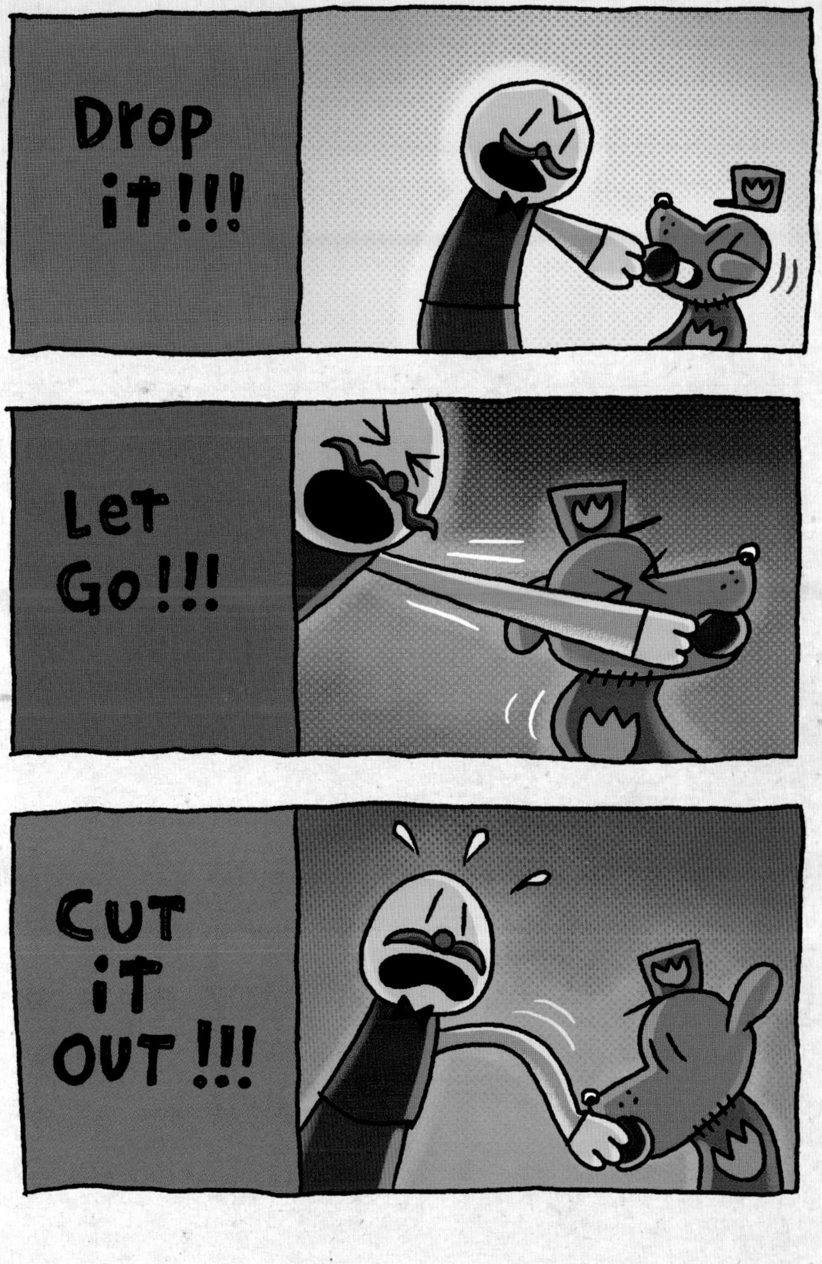
Drop it!!!
Let Go!!!
CUT iT OUT!!!

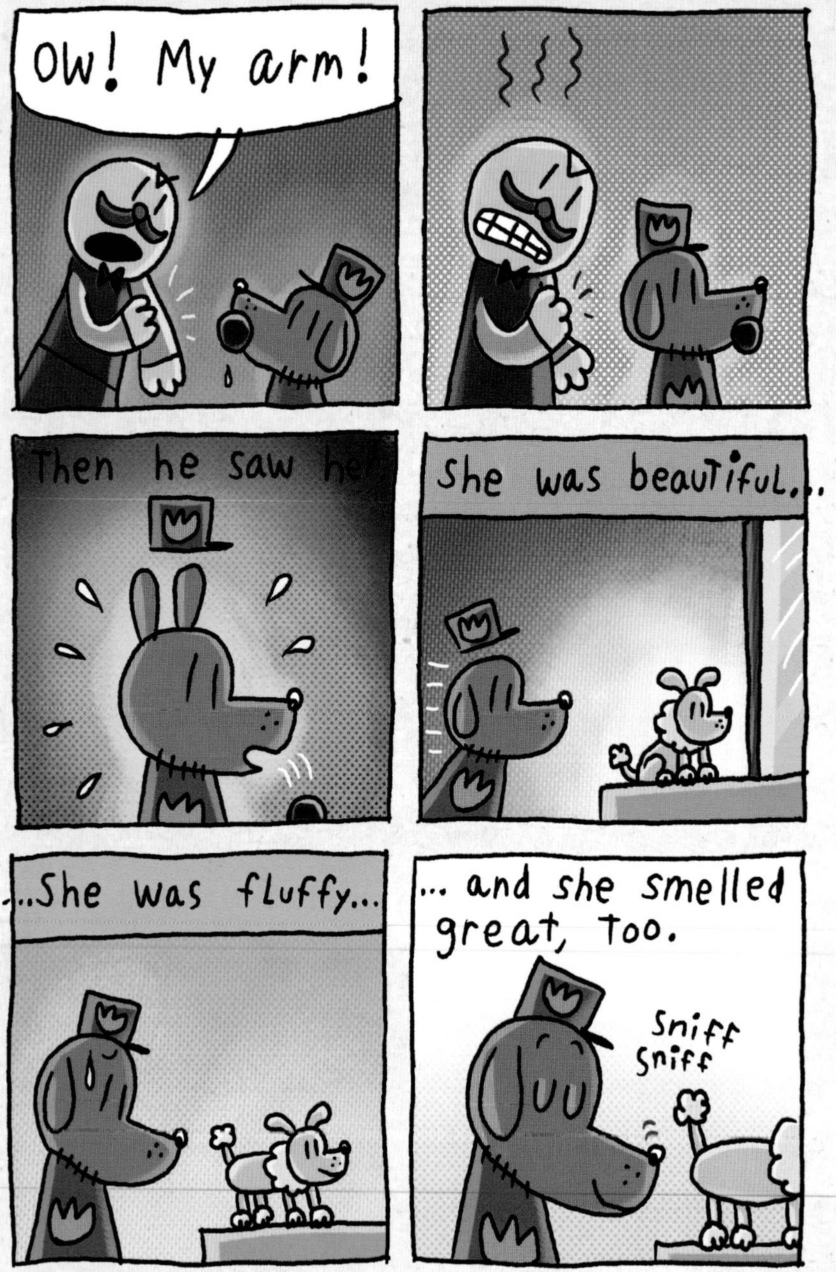
OW! My arm!
Then he saw her.
She was beautiful...
...She was fluffy...
... and she smelled great, too.
Sniff
sniff

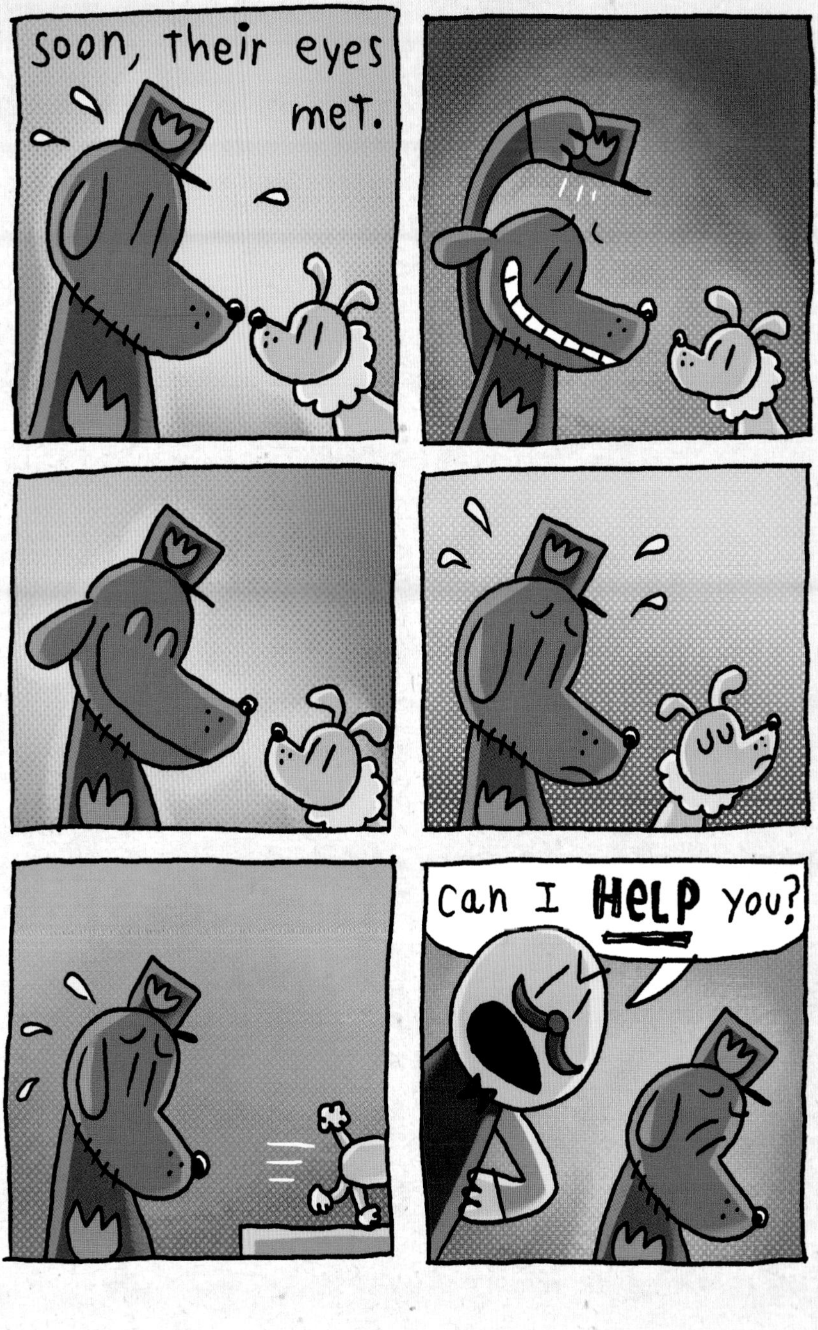
Soon, their eyes met.
Can I HELP you?

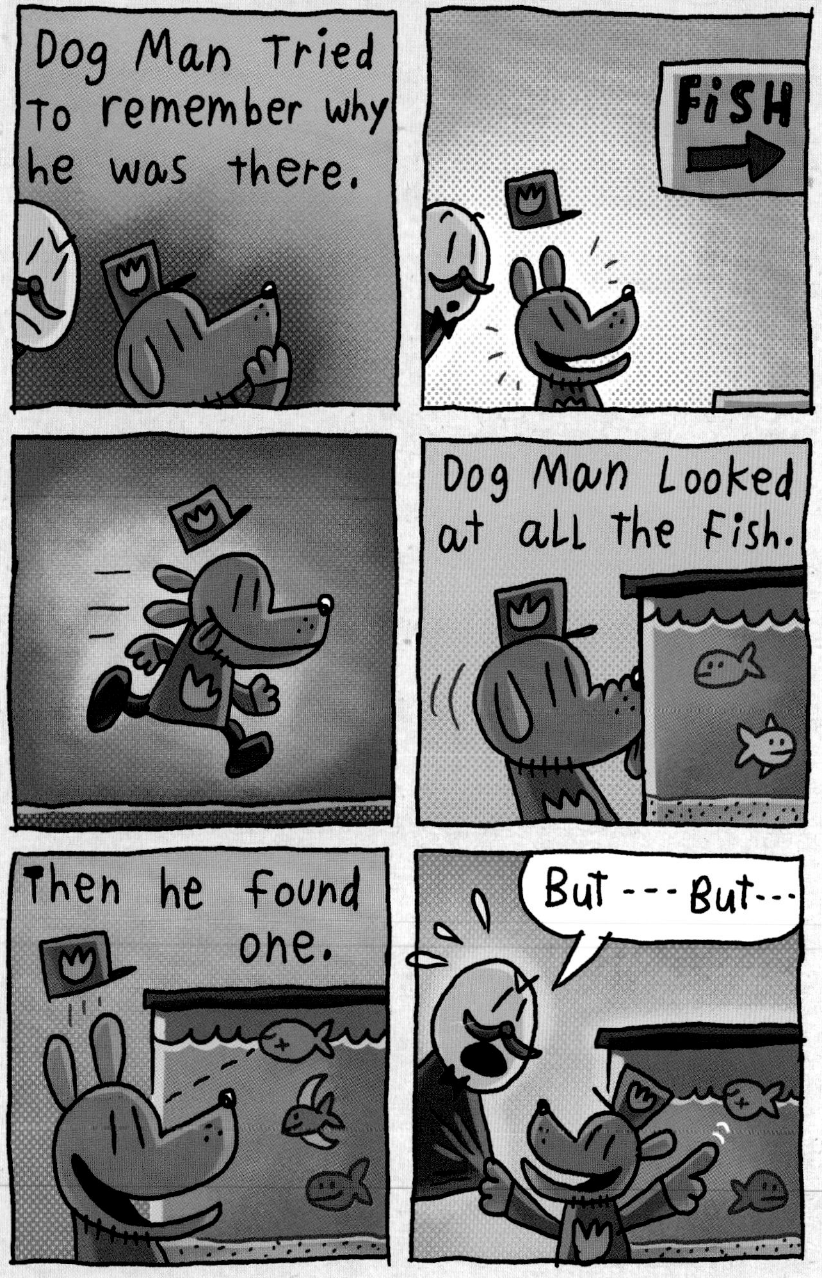
Dog Man Tried To remember why he was there.
FiSH
Dog Man Looked at all the Fish.
Then he found one.
But --- But---

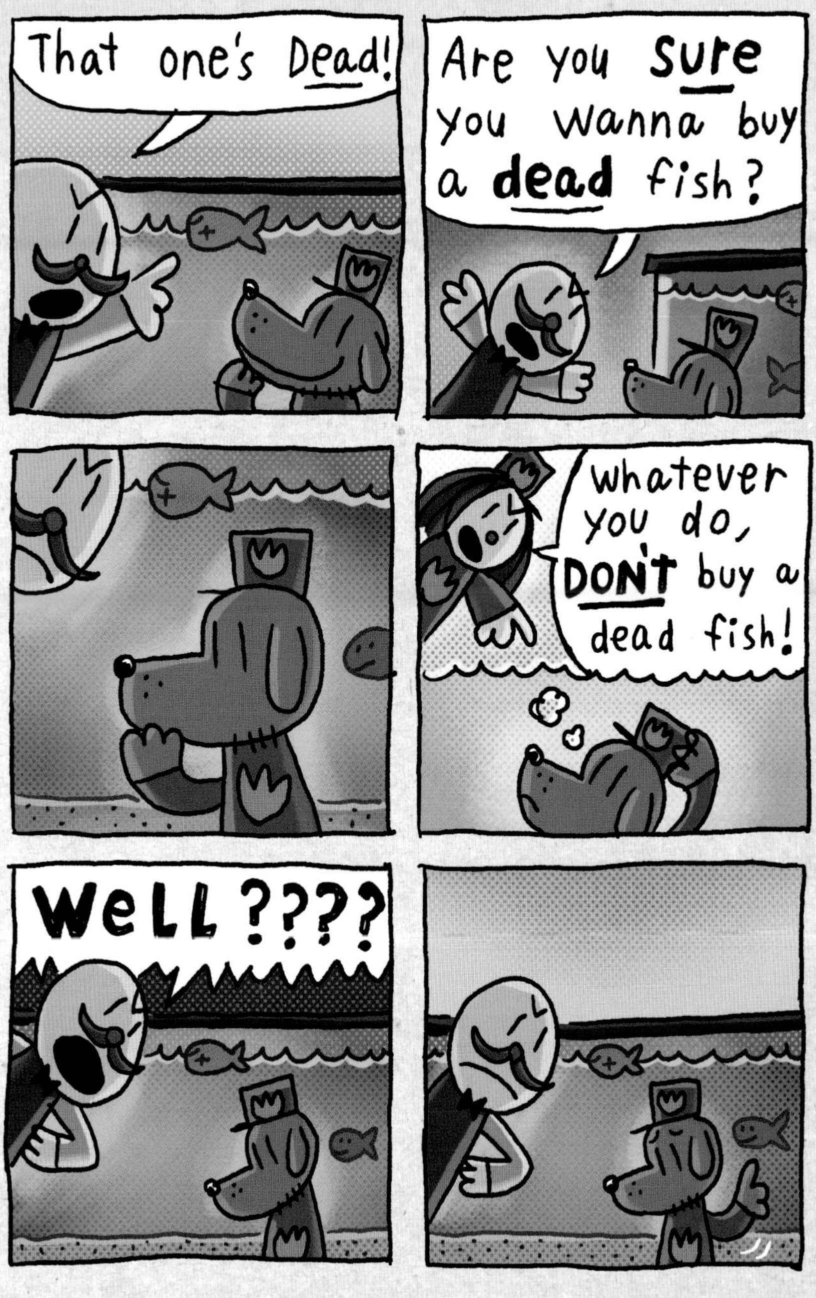
That one's Dead!
Are you sure you wanna buy a dead fish?
whatever you do, DON'T buy a dead fish!
WeLL????

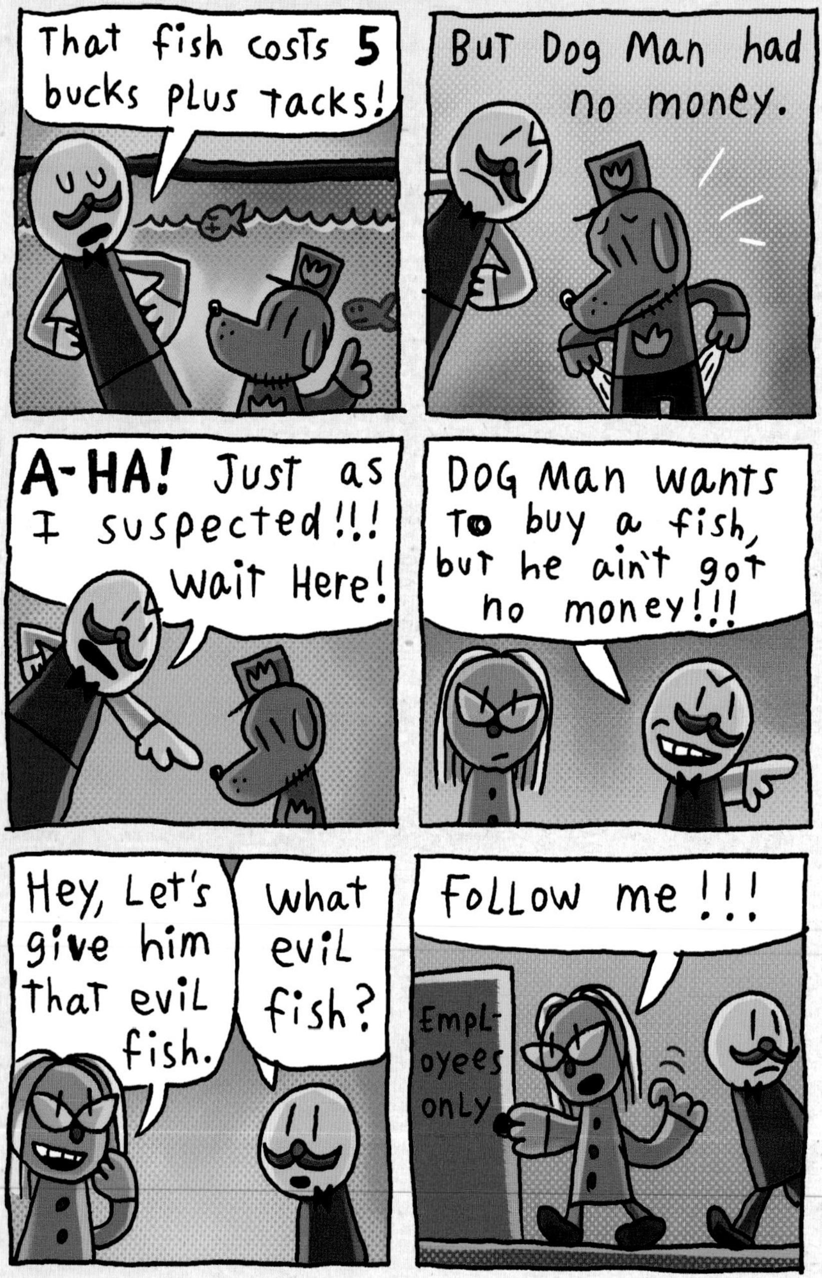
That fish costs 5 bucks plus tacks!
But Dog Man had no money.
A-HA! Just as I suspected!!! Wait Here!
DOG Man wants to buy a fish, but he ain't got no money!!!
Hey, Let's give him that evil fish.
What evil fish?
Follow me!!!
Empl-oyees only

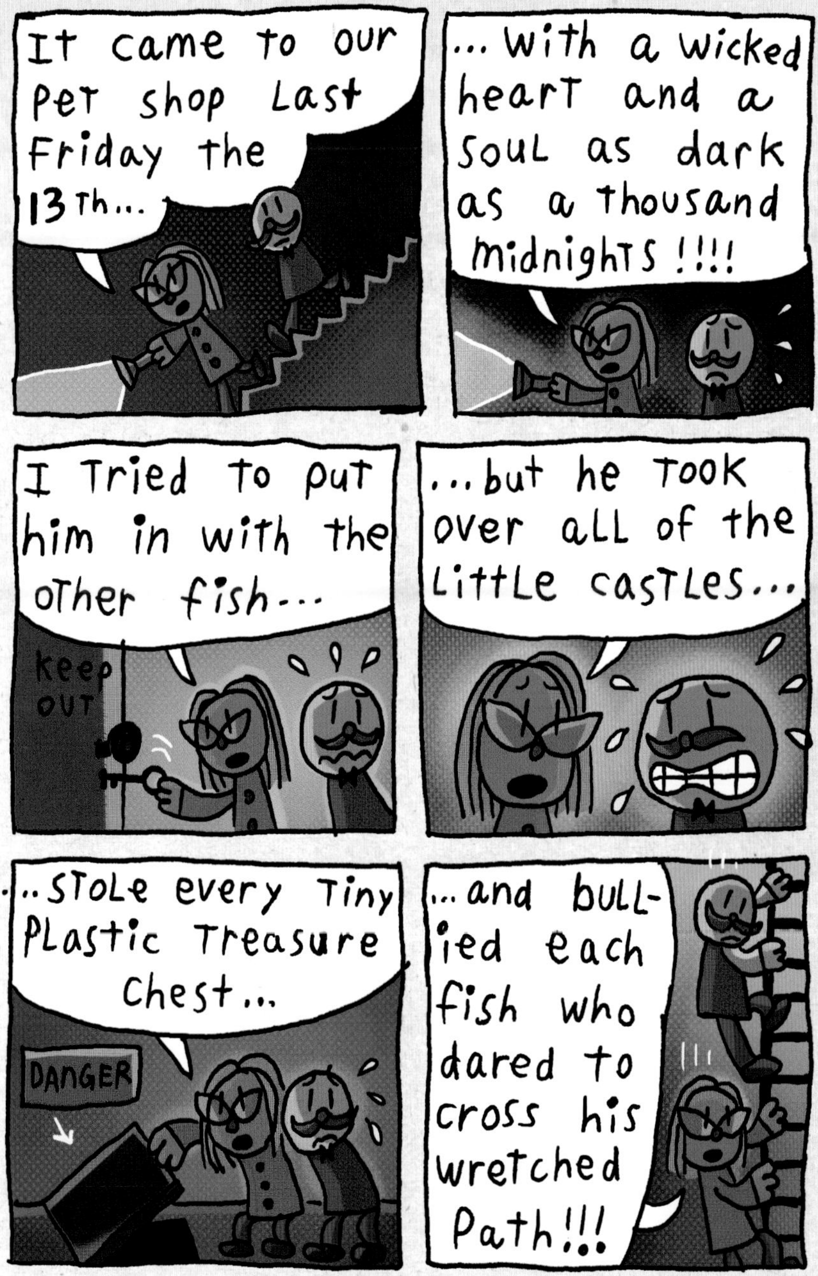
It came to our pet shop Last Friday the 13th...
...with a wicked heart and a soul as dark as a thousand midnights!!!!
I Tried to put him in with the other fish...
Keep OUT
...but he Took over all of the Little castles...
..stole every Tiny Plastic Treasure chest...
DANGER
...and bull-ied each fish who dared to cross his wretched Path!!!

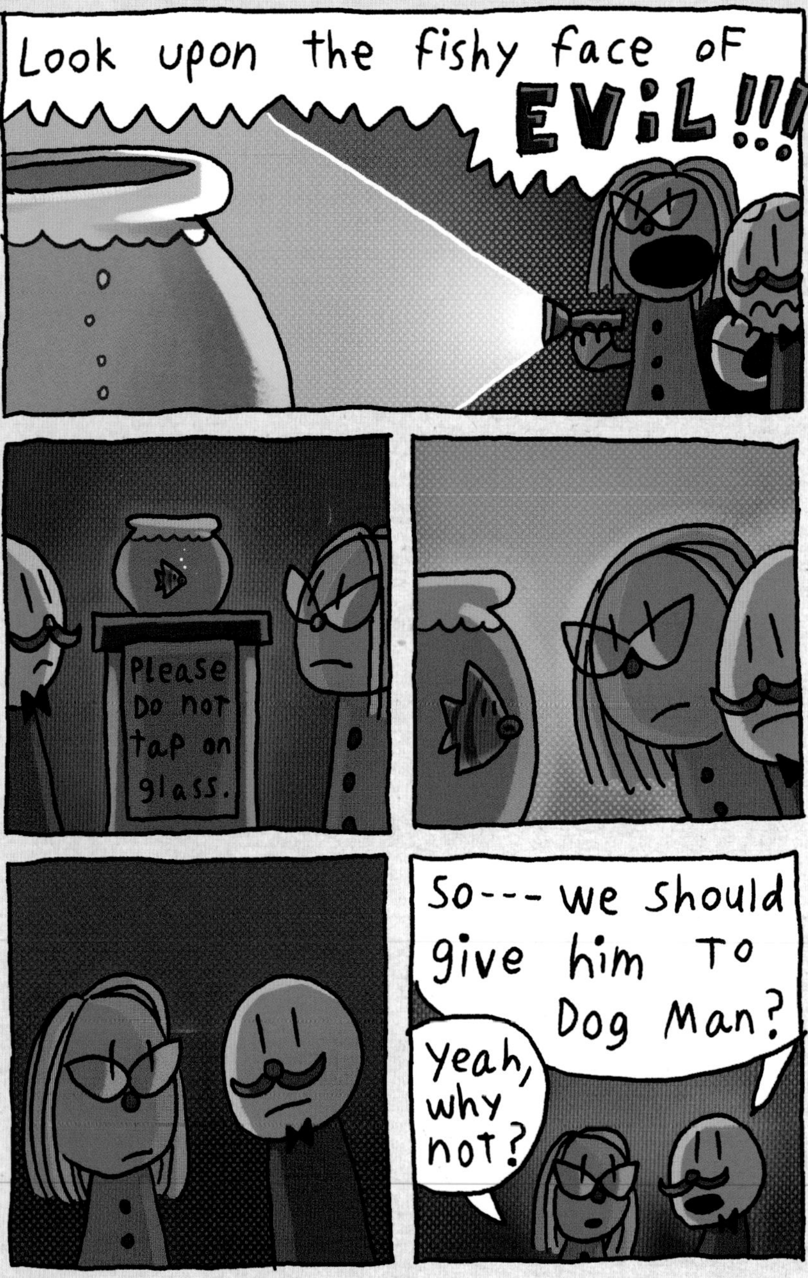
Look upon the fishy face of EViL!!!
Please Do not tap on glass.
So--- we should give him To Dog Man?
Yeah, why not?

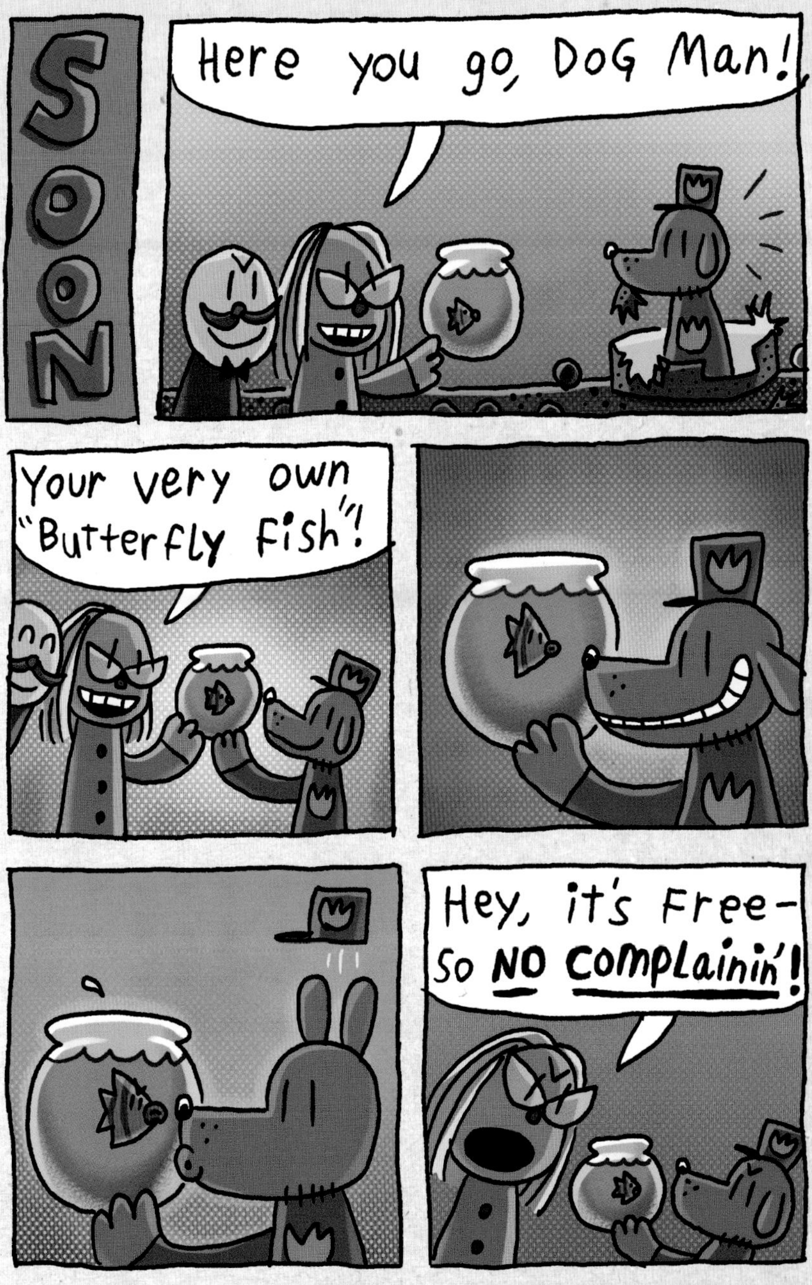
SOON
Here you go, DOG Man!
Your very own "Butterfly Fish"!
Hey, it's Free-
So NO Complainin'!

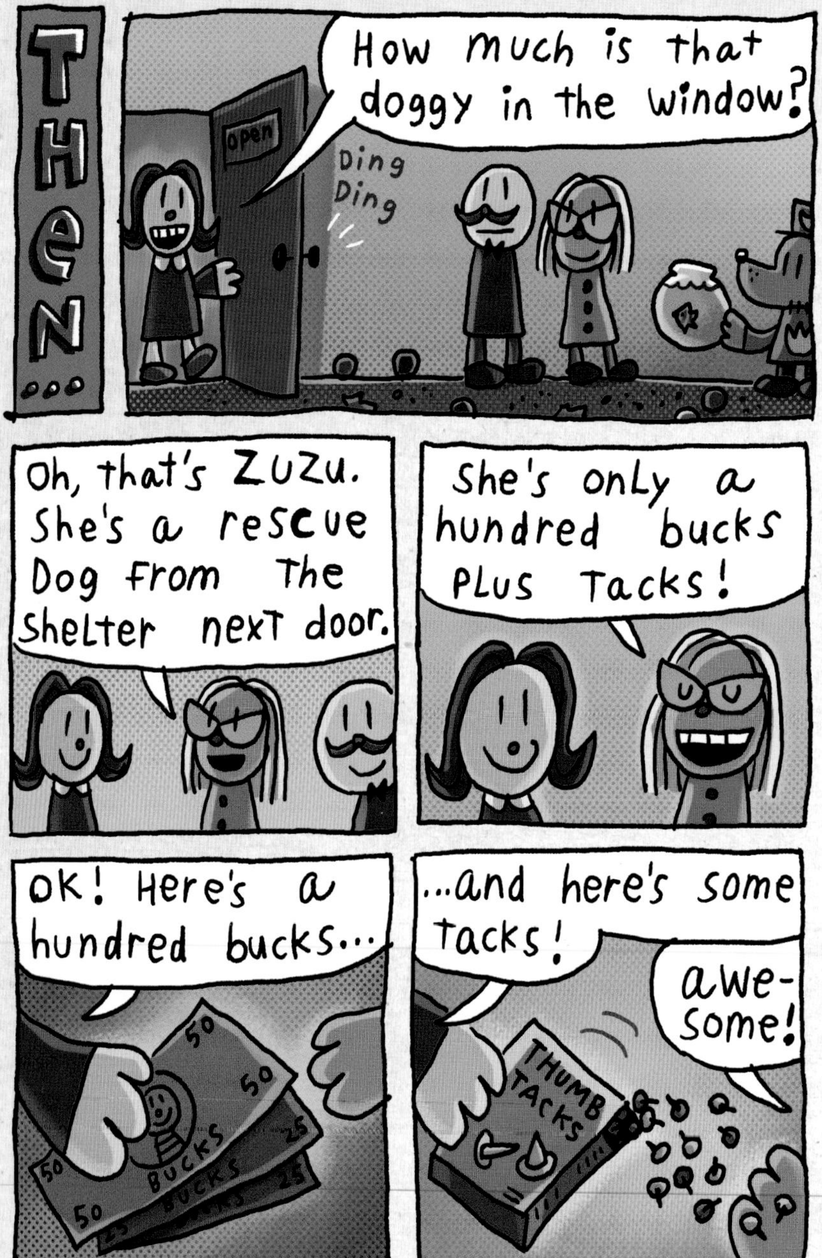
THEN...
open
How much is that doggy in the window?
Ding Ding
Oh, that's ZUZU. She's a rescue Dog from The Shelter next door.
She's only a hundred bucks plus Tacks!
OK! Here's a hundred bucks...
50
BUCKS
25
...and here's some tacks!
THUMB TACKS
awe-some!

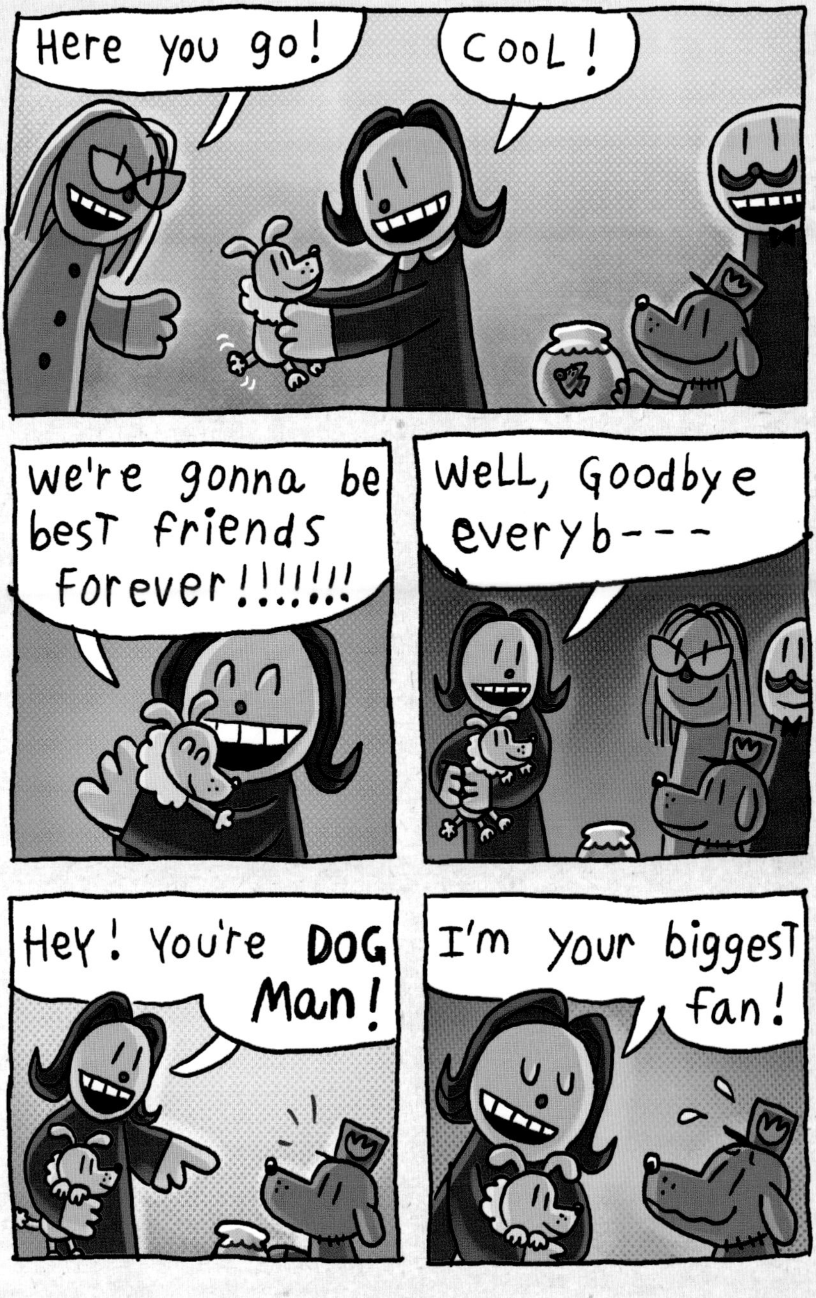
Here you go!
COOL!
we're gonna be best friends Forever!!!!!!!
WeLL, Goodbye everyb---
Hey! You're DOG Man!
I'm your biggest fan!

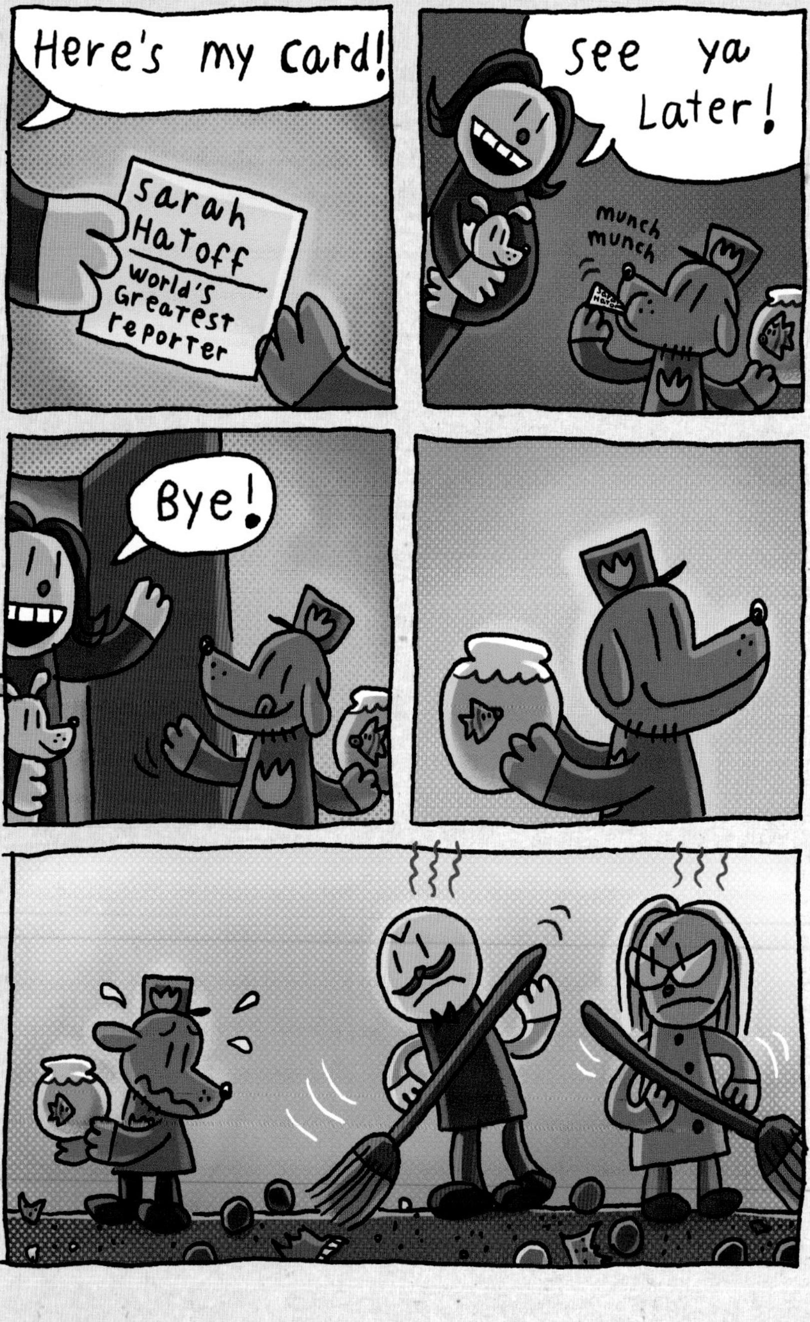

Here's my card!
Sarah Hatoff
World's Greatest reporter
See ya Later!
munch munch
Bye!

Chapter 3

Happy Birthday, Chief

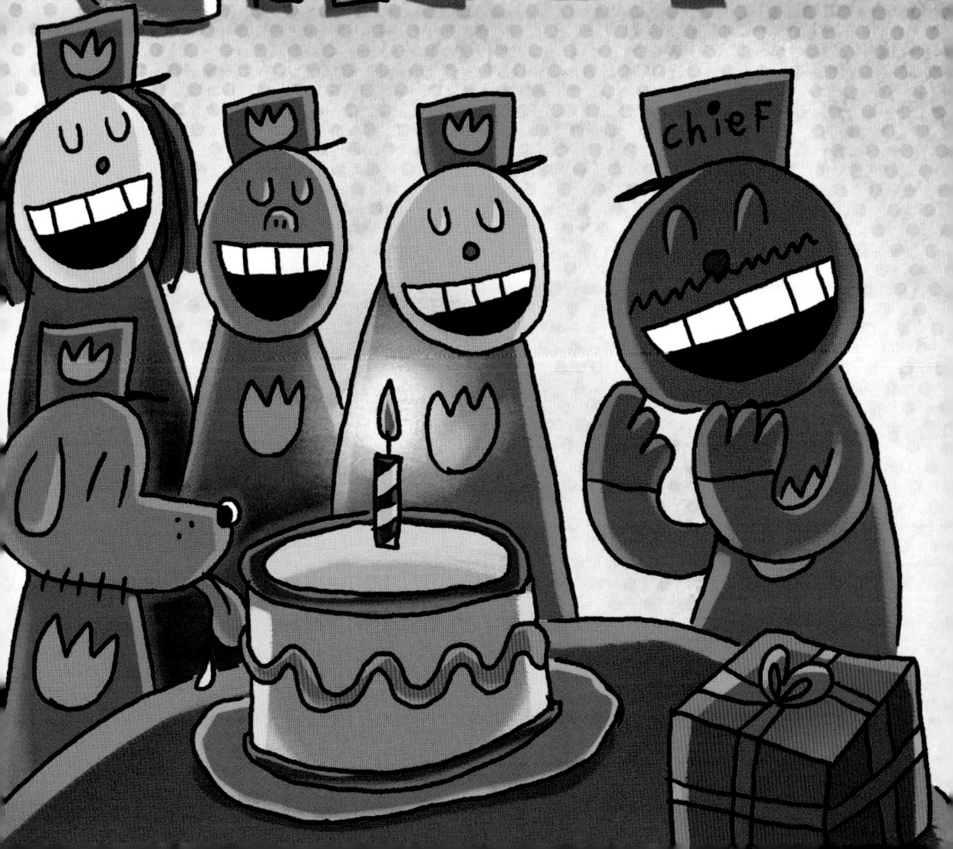
chief

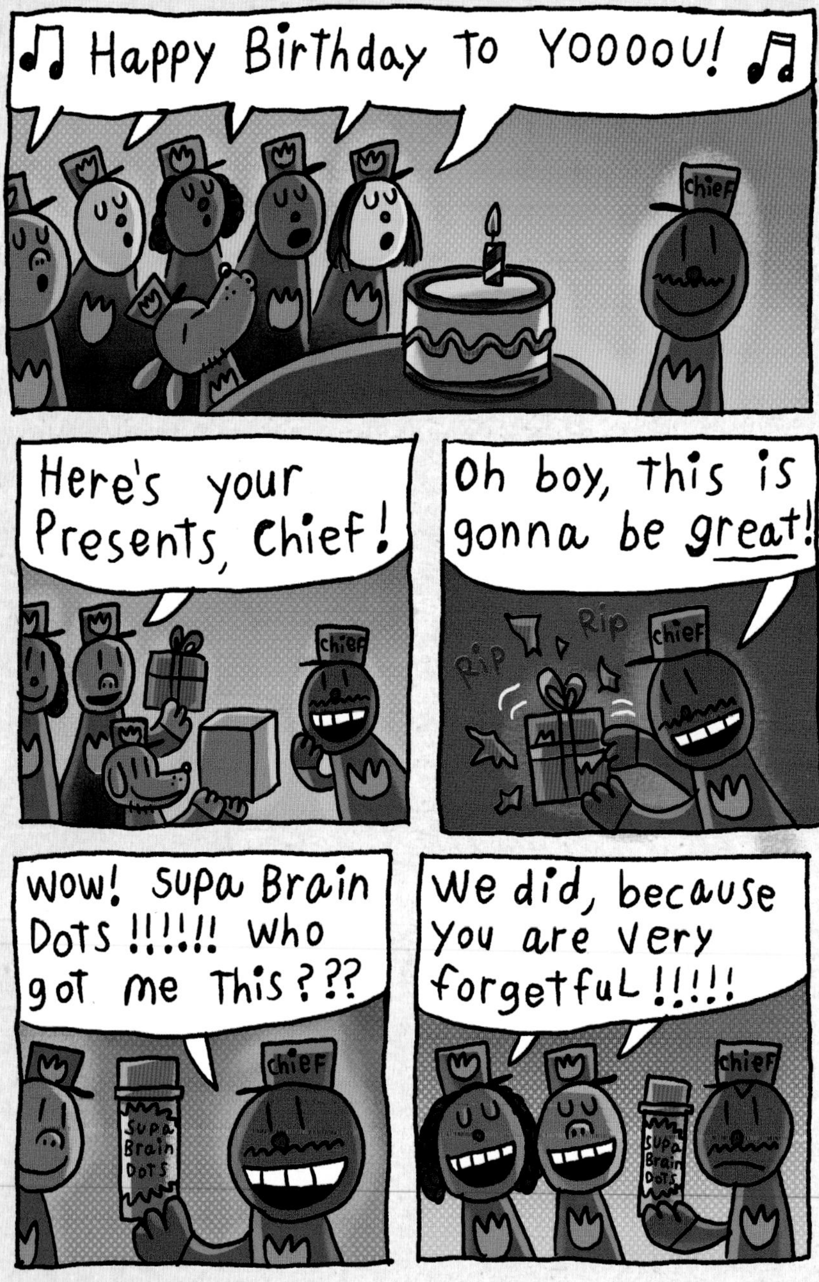

♫ Happy Birthday To YOOOOU! ♫
chief
Here's your Presents, Chief!
chief
Oh boy, this is gonna be great!
Rip
Rip
chief
WOW! SUPA Brain Dots!!!!!! Who got me This???
SUPA Brain DOTS
chief
We did, because you are very forgetful!!!!!
chief
SUPA Brain DOTS

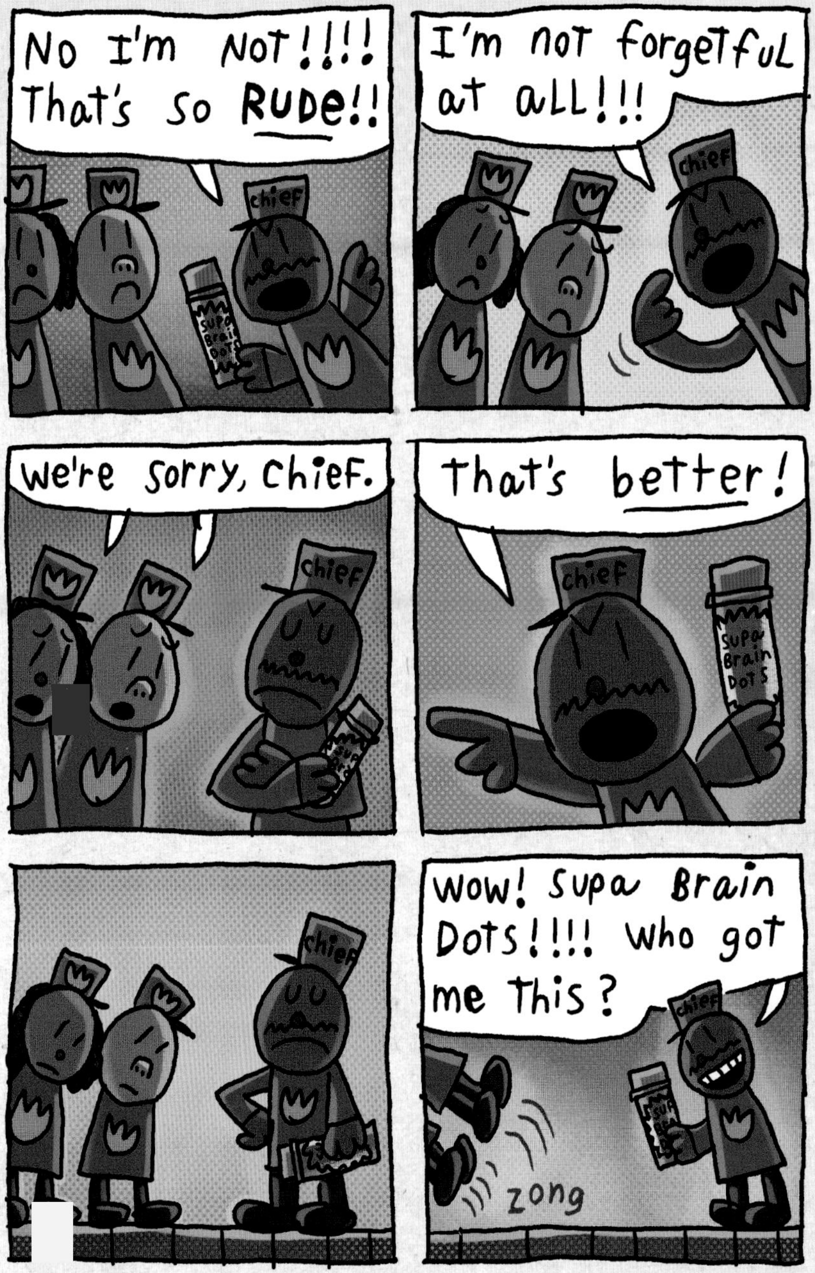
No I'm NOT!!!! That's so RUDE!!
I'm not forgetful at all!!!
We're sorry, Chief.
That's better!
Wow! Supa Brain Dots!!!! Who got me this?
zong

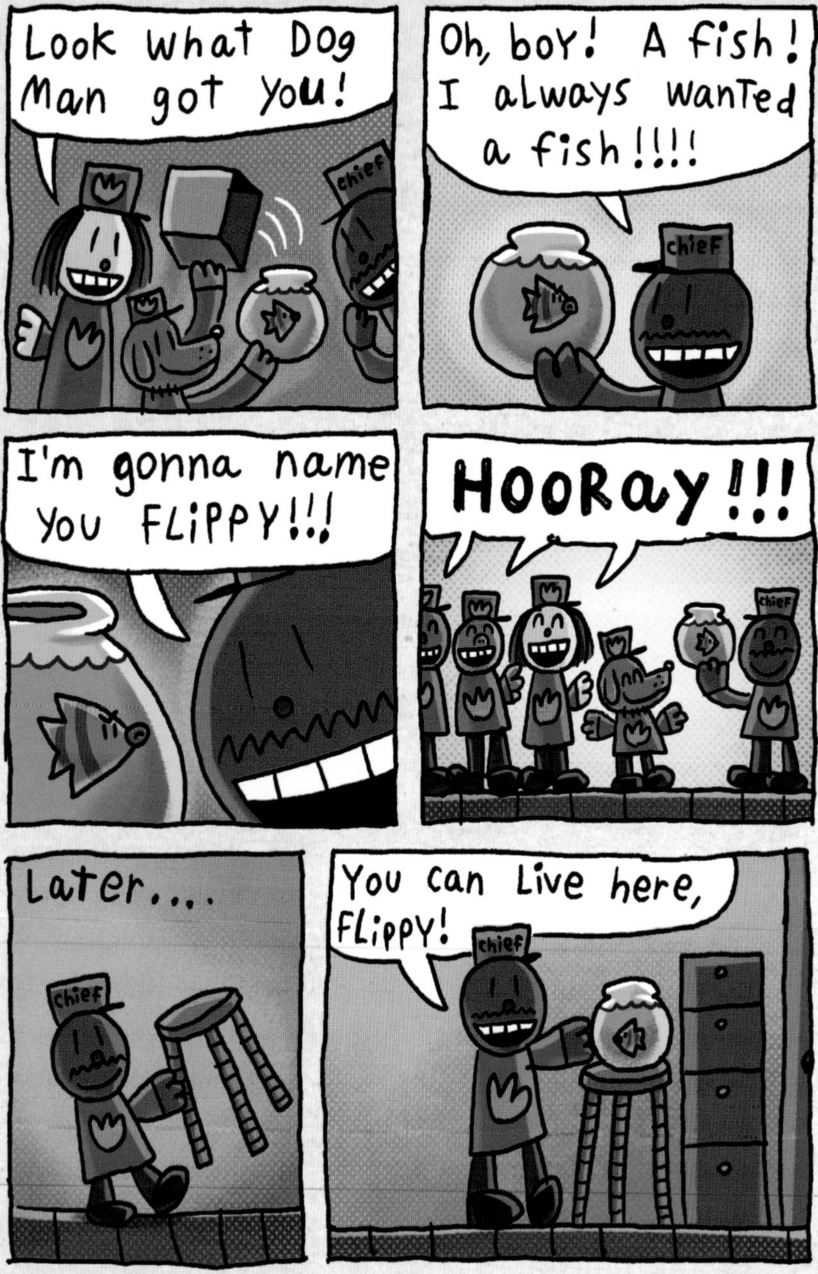
Look what Dog Man got you!
chief
Oh, boy! A fish! I always wanted a fish!!!!
chief
I'm gonna name you FLIPPY!!!
HOORAY!!!
chief
Later....
chief
You can live here, FLIPPY!
chief

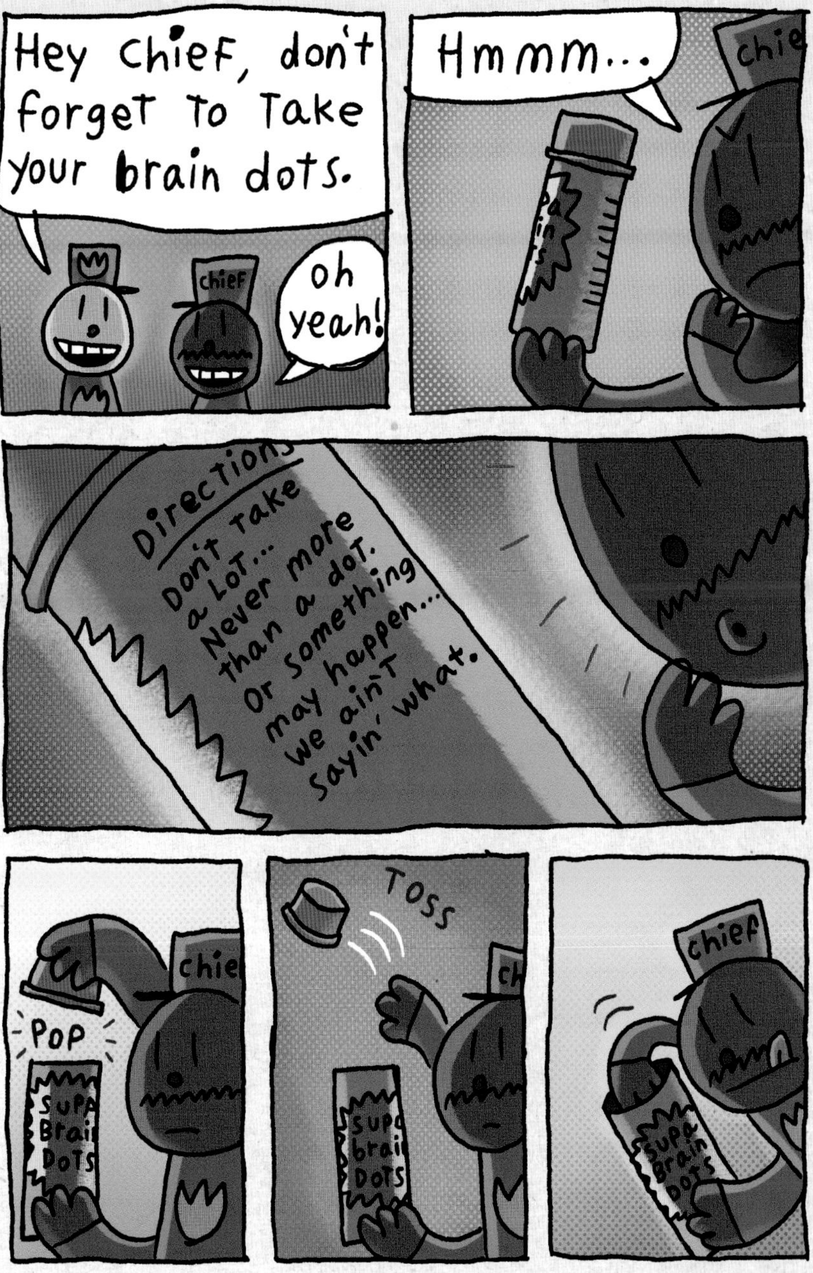
Hey Chief, don't forget to Take your brain dots.
chief
Oh yeah!
Hmmm...
Directions
Don't take a lot... Never more than a dot. Or something may happen... we ain't sayin' what.
POP
TOSS
chief
SUPA Brain DOTS

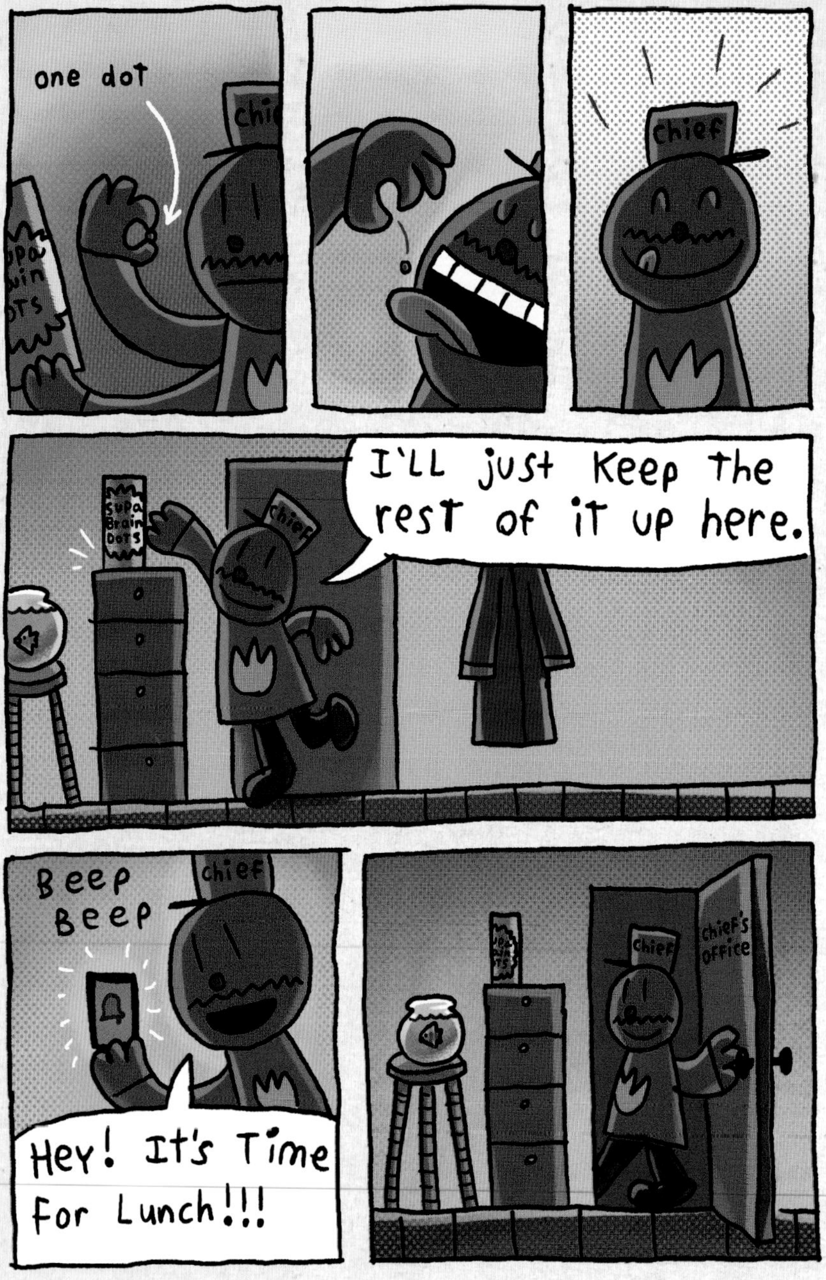
one dot
chief
I'LL just Keep the rest of it up here.
Supa Brain Dots
chief
Beep Beep
chief
Hey! It's Time For Lunch!!!
chief
chief's office

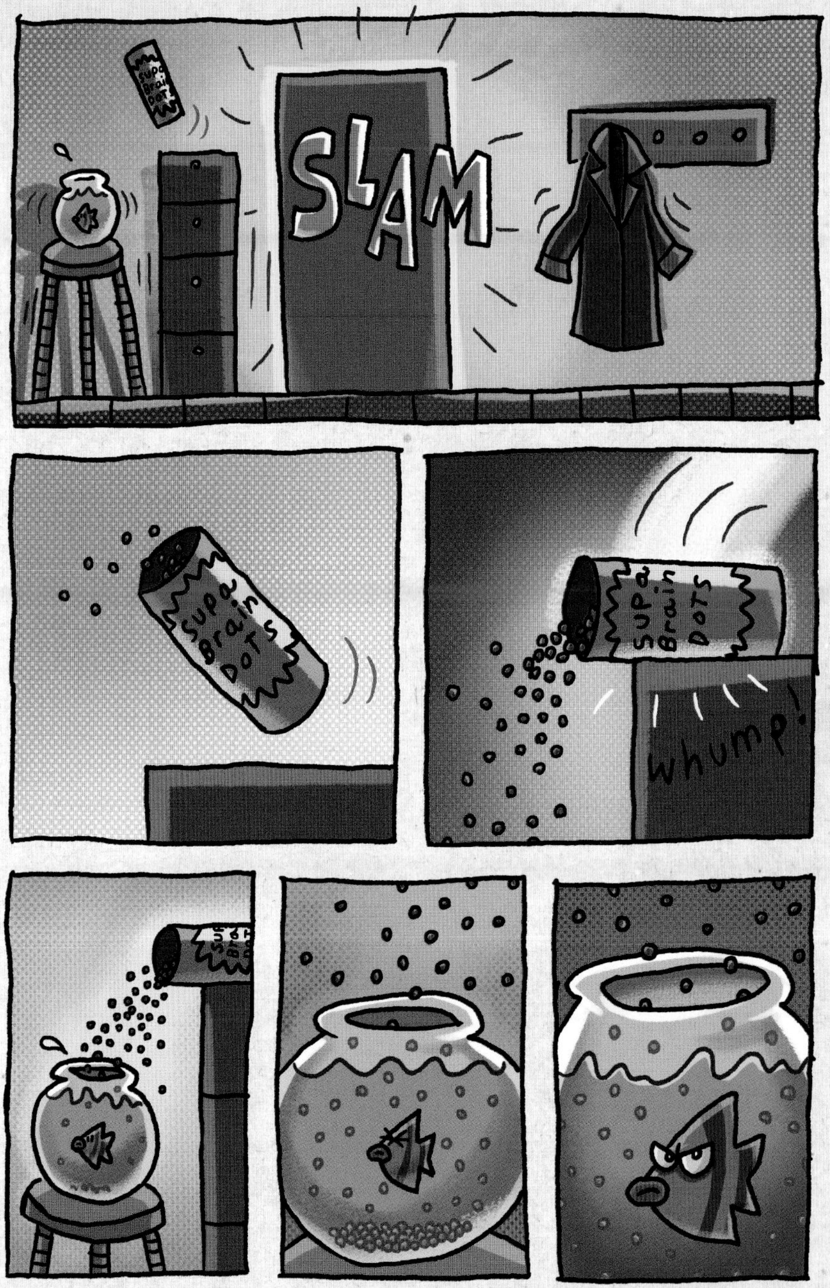
SUPA BRAIN DOTS
SLAM
SUPA BRAIN DOTS
SUPA BRAIN DOTS
WHUMP!

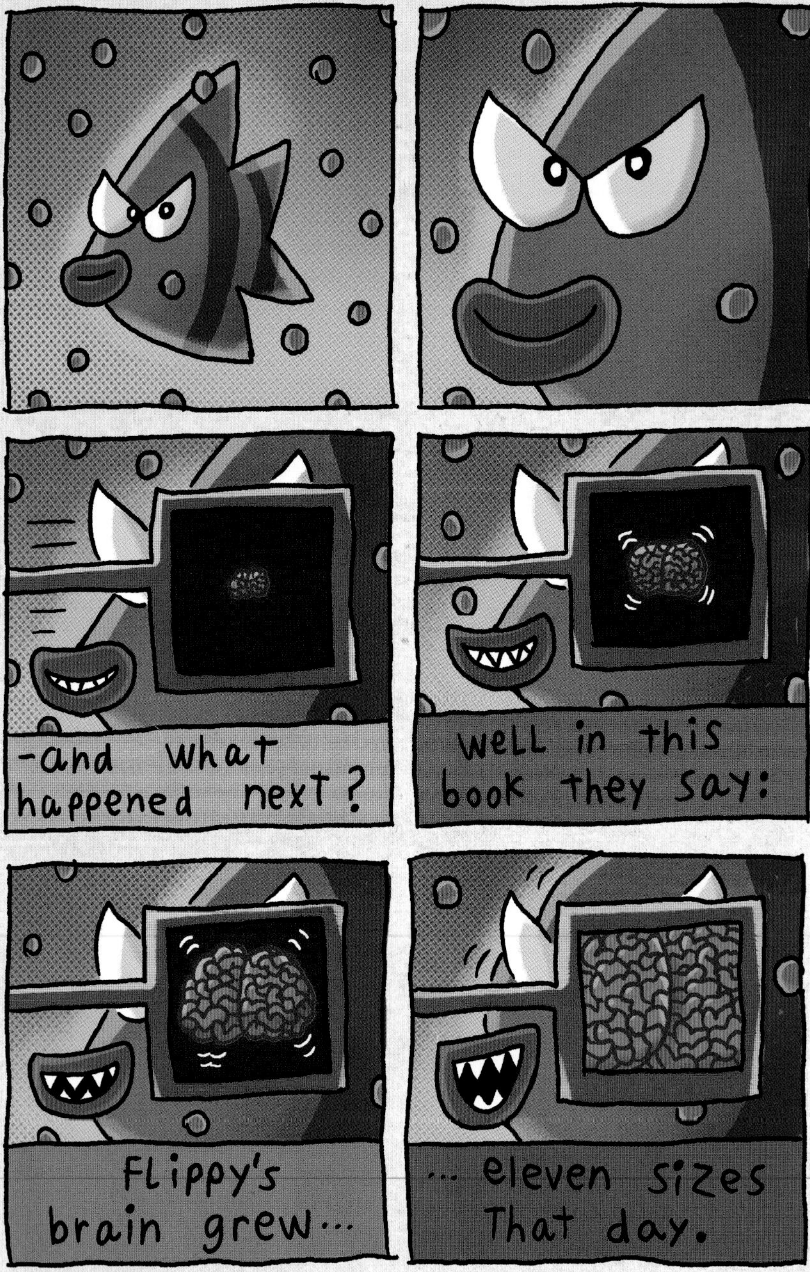
-and what happened next?
well in this book they say:
Flippy's brain grew...
... eleven sizes That day.

Chapter 4
The Big ROBBERY

By George <u>and</u> Harold

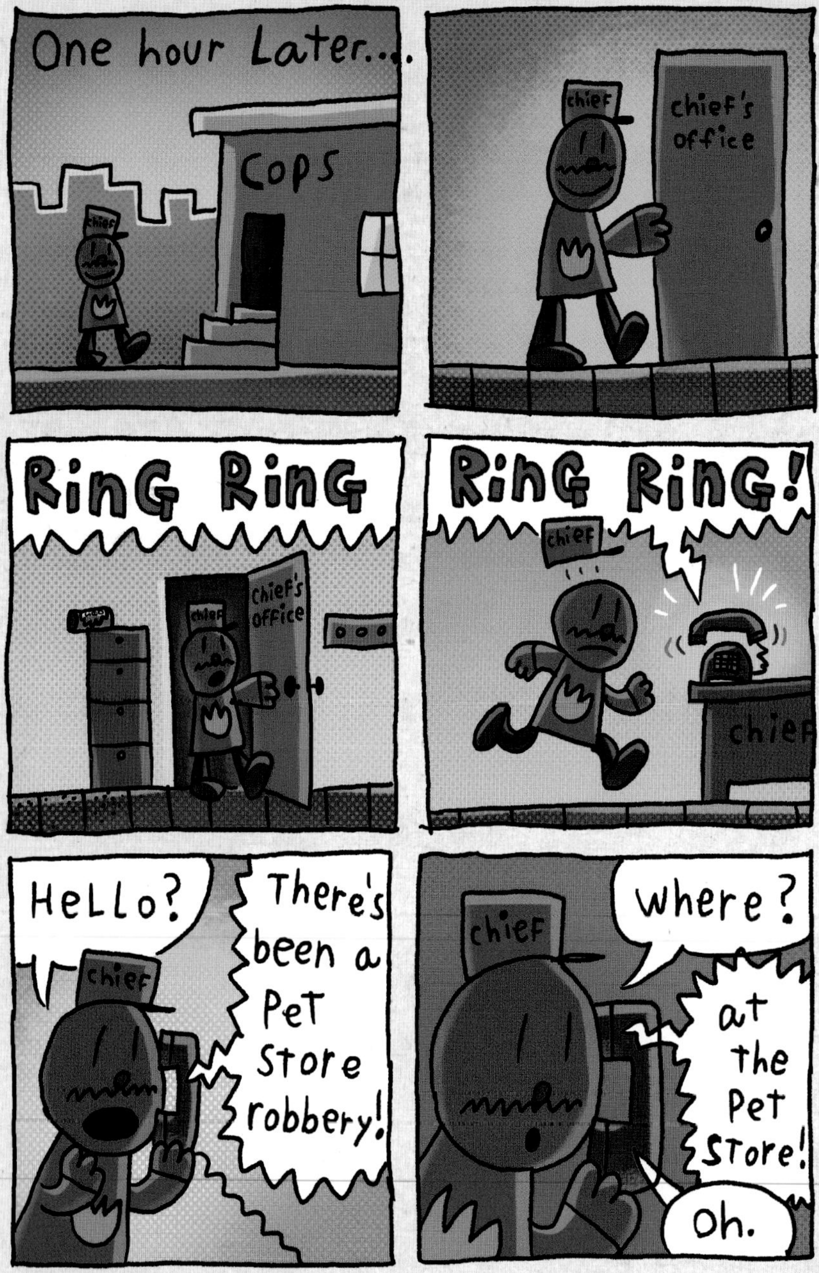
One hour Later....
Cops
chief
chief
chief's office
RinG RinG
chief
chief's office
RinG RinG!
chief
chief
HeLLo?
chief
There's been a Pet Store robbery!
chief
Where?
at the Pet Store!
Oh.

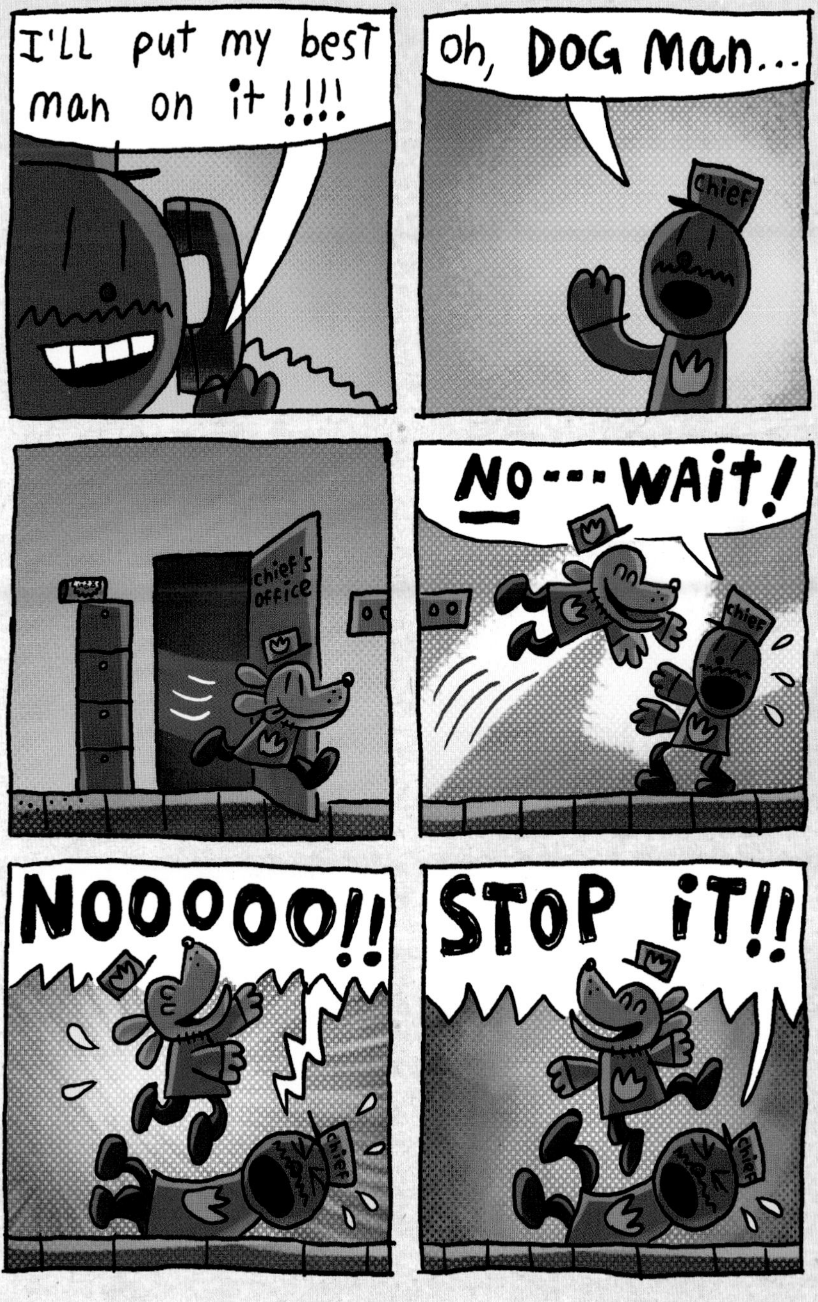
I'LL put my best man on it!!!!
Oh, DOG Man...
chief
chief's office
NO... WAIT!
chief
NOOOOO!!
chief
STOP iT!!
chief

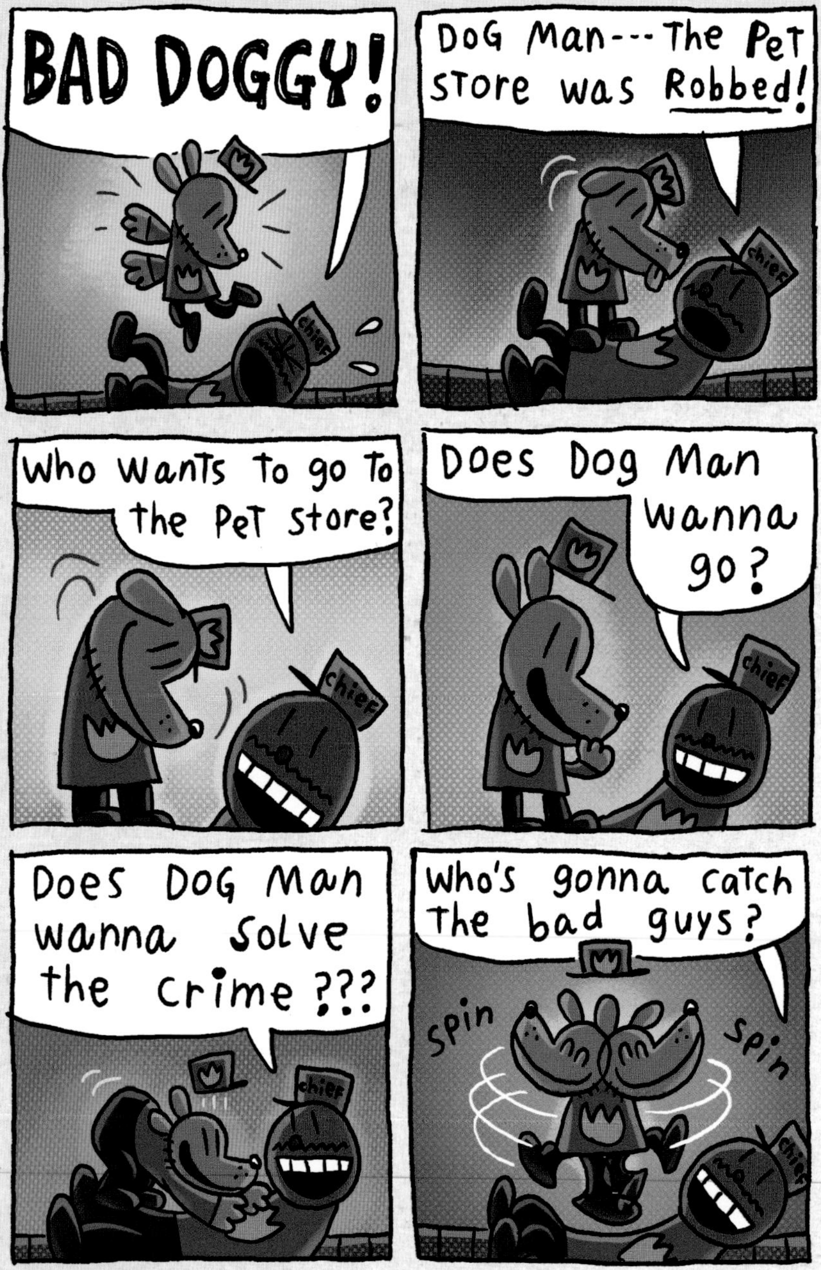
BAD DOGGY!
chief
DOG Man---The PeT STore was Robbed!
chief
Who wanTs To go To the PeT store?
chief
Does Dog Man wanna go?
chief
Does DOG Man wanna Solve the crime???
chief
Who's gonna catch The bad guys?
spin
spin
chief

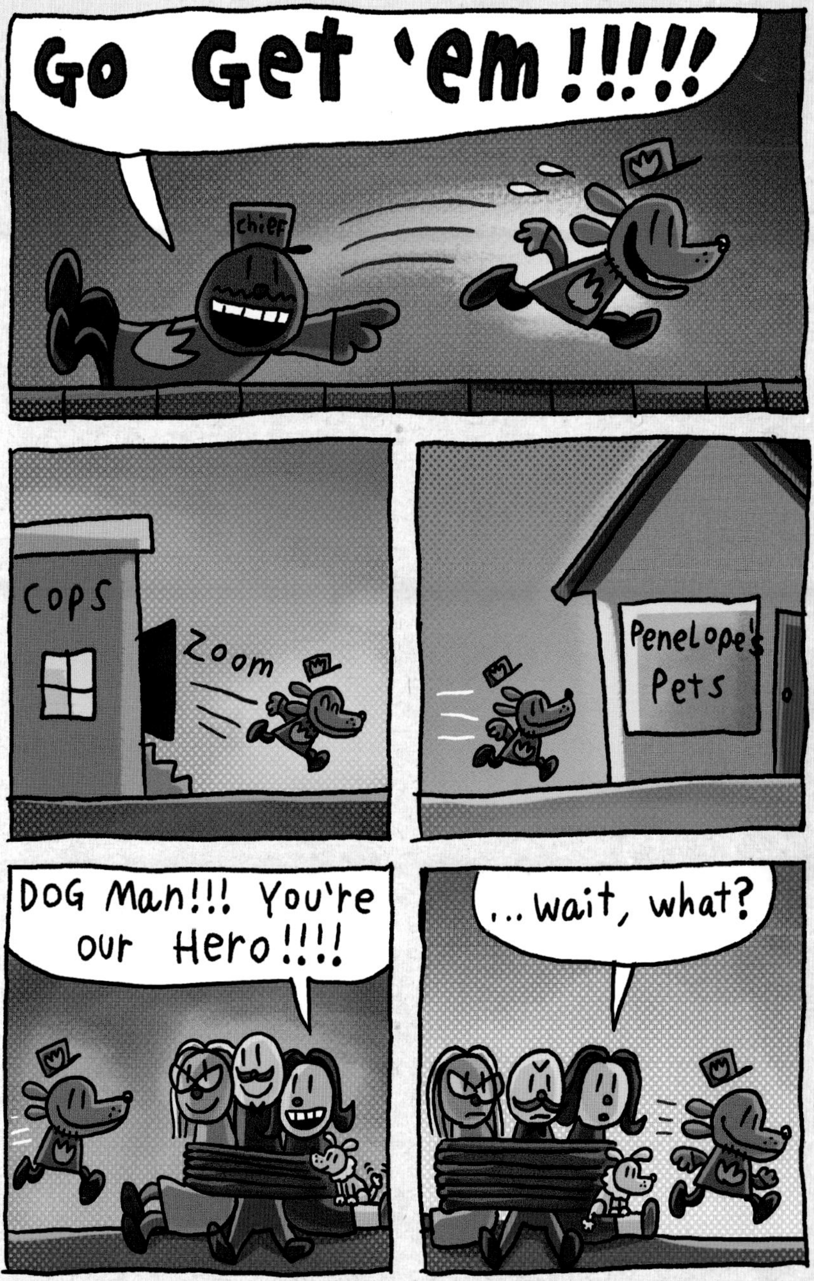

Go Get 'em!!!!!
Chief
Cops
Zoom
Penelope's Pets
DOG Man!!! You're our Hero!!!!
...wait, what?

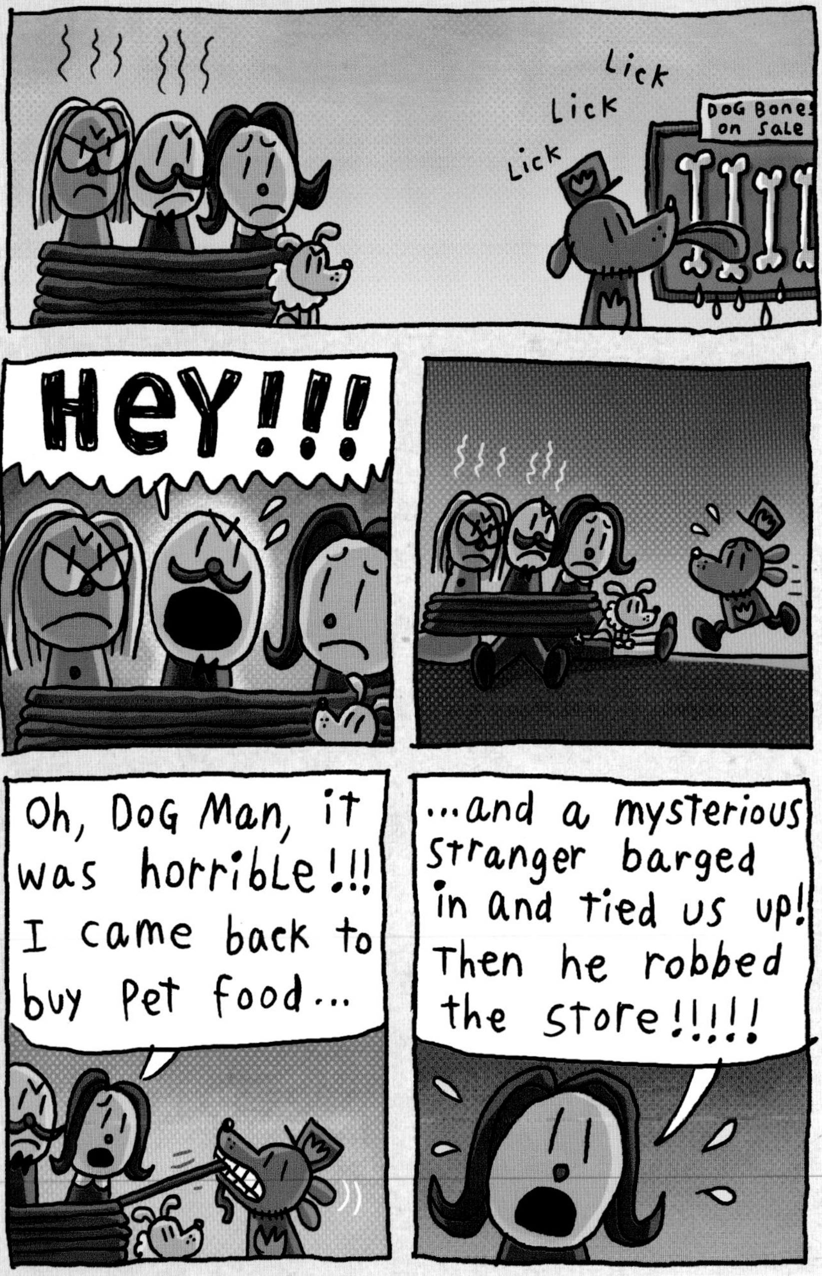
Lick
Lick
Lick
DOG Bones on Sale
HEY!!!
Oh, DOG Man, it was horrible!!! I came back to buy Pet food...
...and a mysterious stranger barged in and tied us up! Then he robbed the store!!!!!

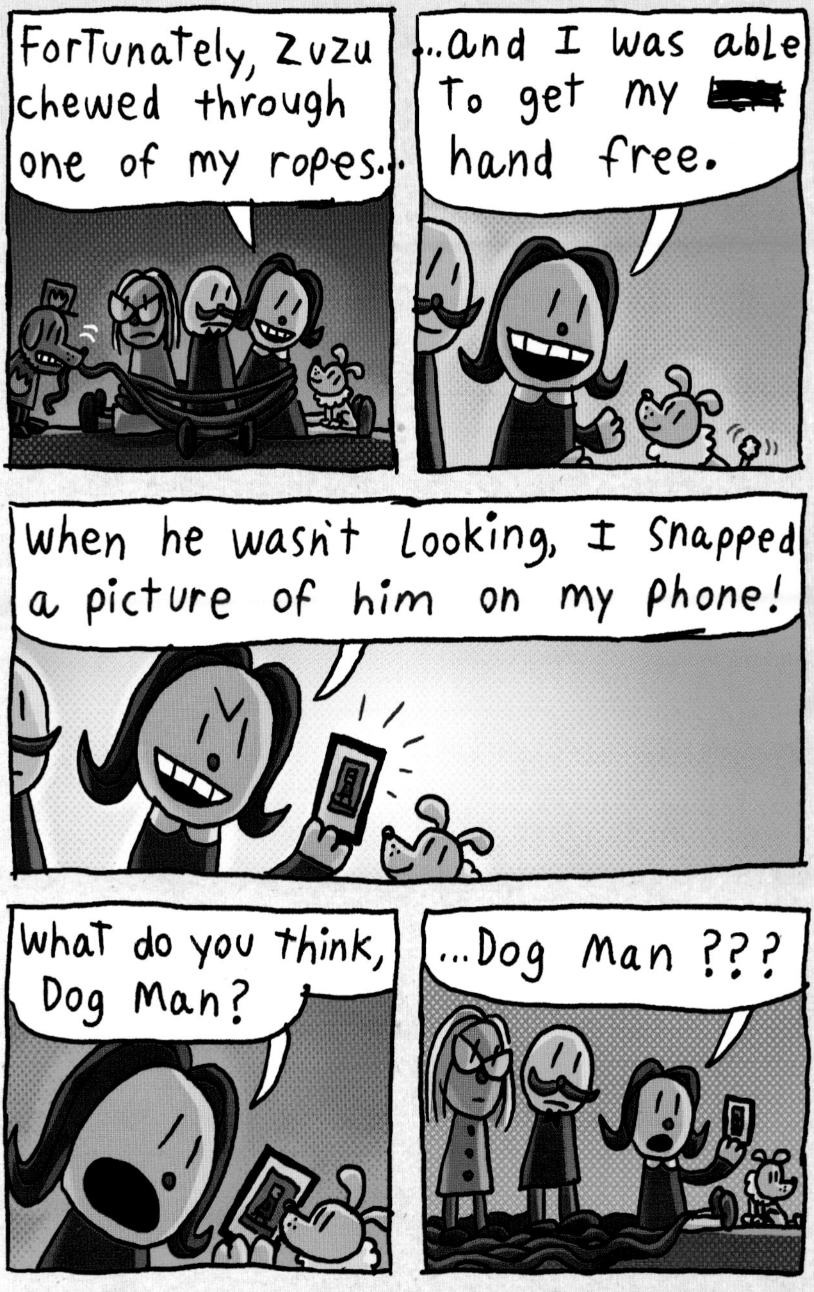
Fortunately, Zuzu chewed through one of my ropes...
...and I was able to get my [redacted] hand free.
When he wasn't looking, I snapped a picture of him on my phone!
What do you think, Dog Man?
...Dog Man???

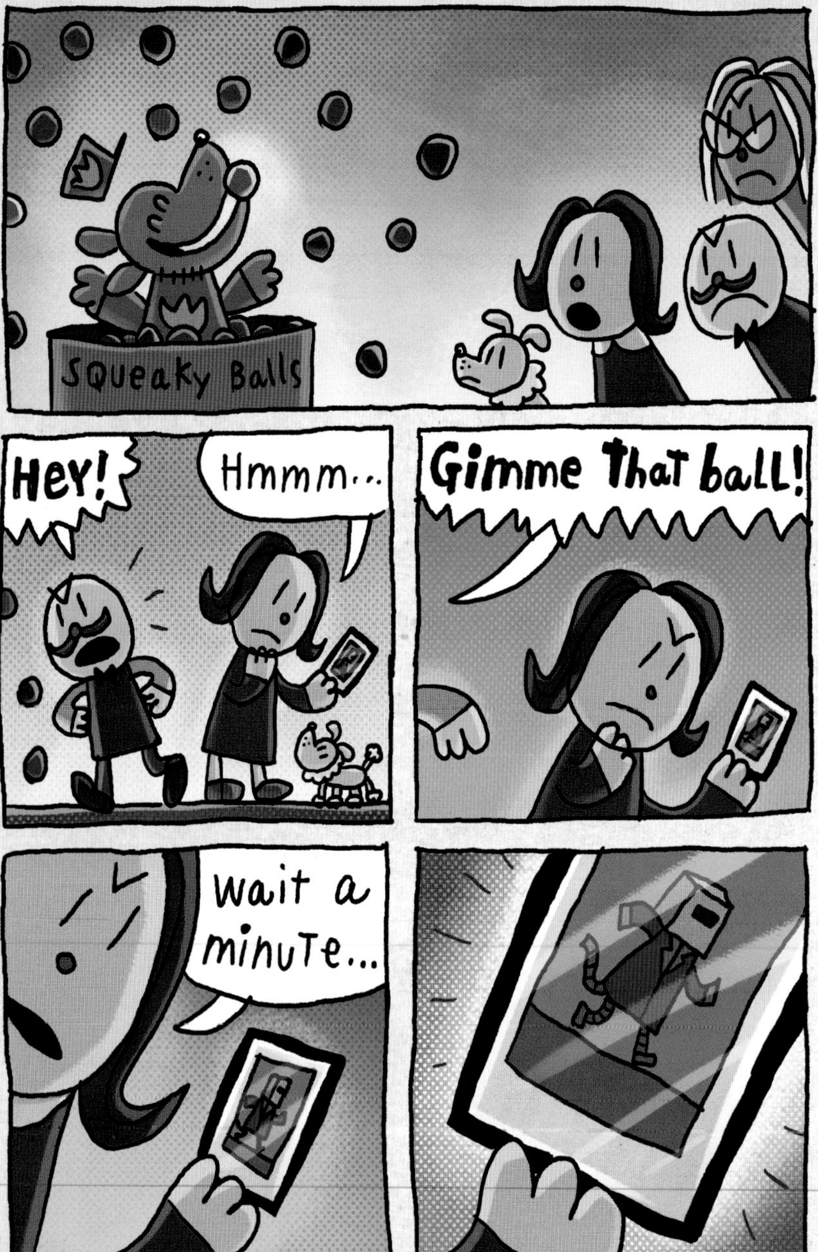
SQUeaky Balls
HEY!
Hmmm...
Gimme That baLL!
wait a minuTe...

Chapter 5
Petey's Big Escape

CAT JAIL

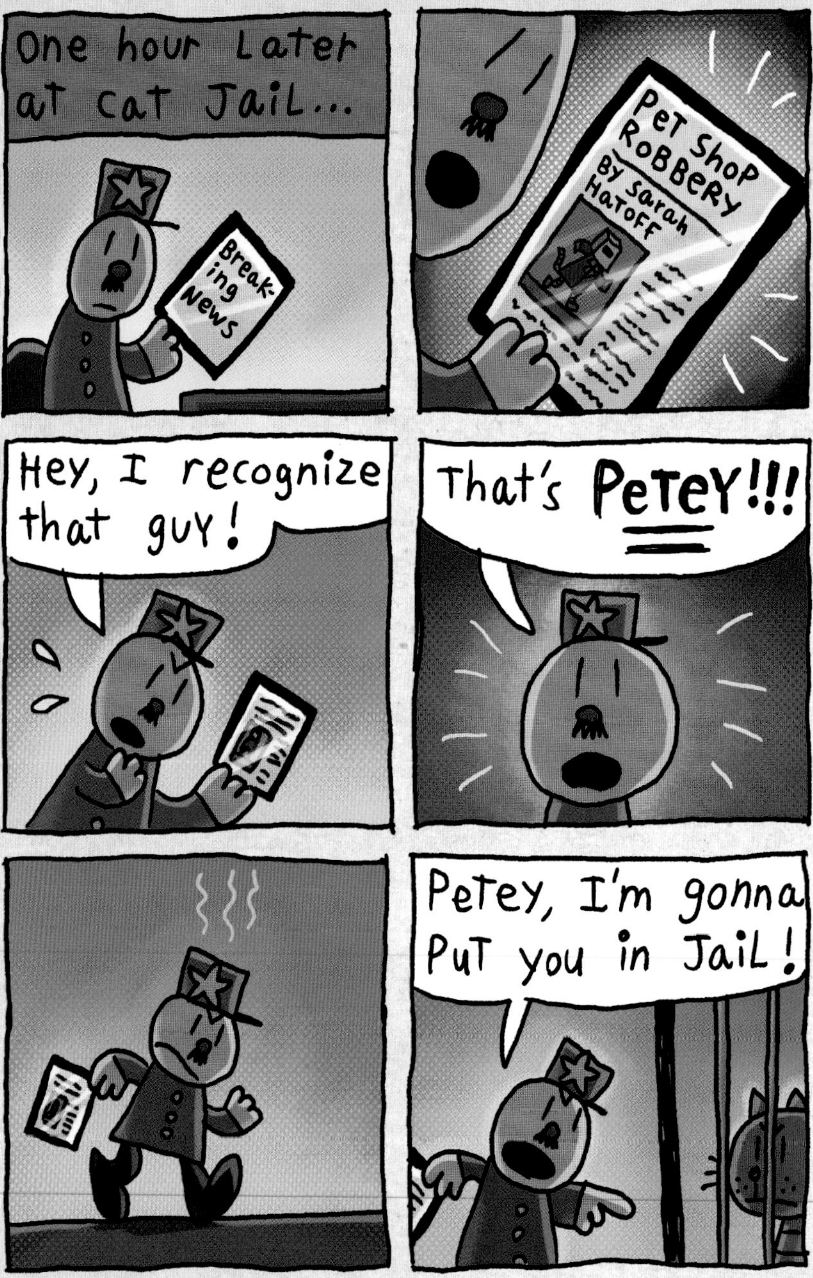
One hour Later at cat Jail...
Breaking News
PeT Shop RoBBeRy
By Sarah HaToFF
Hey, I recognize that guy!
That's PeTeY!!!
PeTey, I'm gonna PuT you in JaiL!

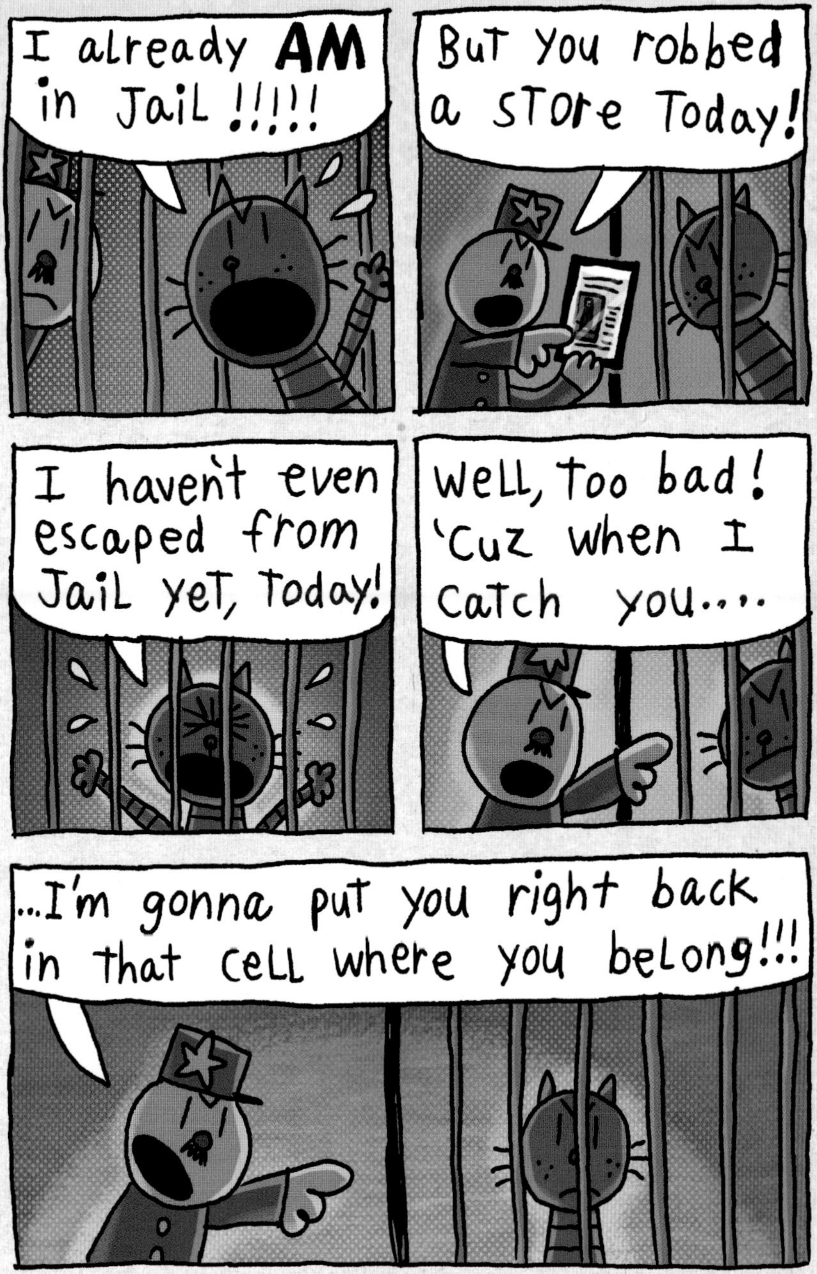
I already AM in JaiL!!!!!
But you robbed a STOre Today!
I haven't even escaped from JaiL yeT, Today!
WeLL, Too bad! 'Cuz when I Catch you....
...I'm gonna put you right back in that ceLL where you beLong!!!

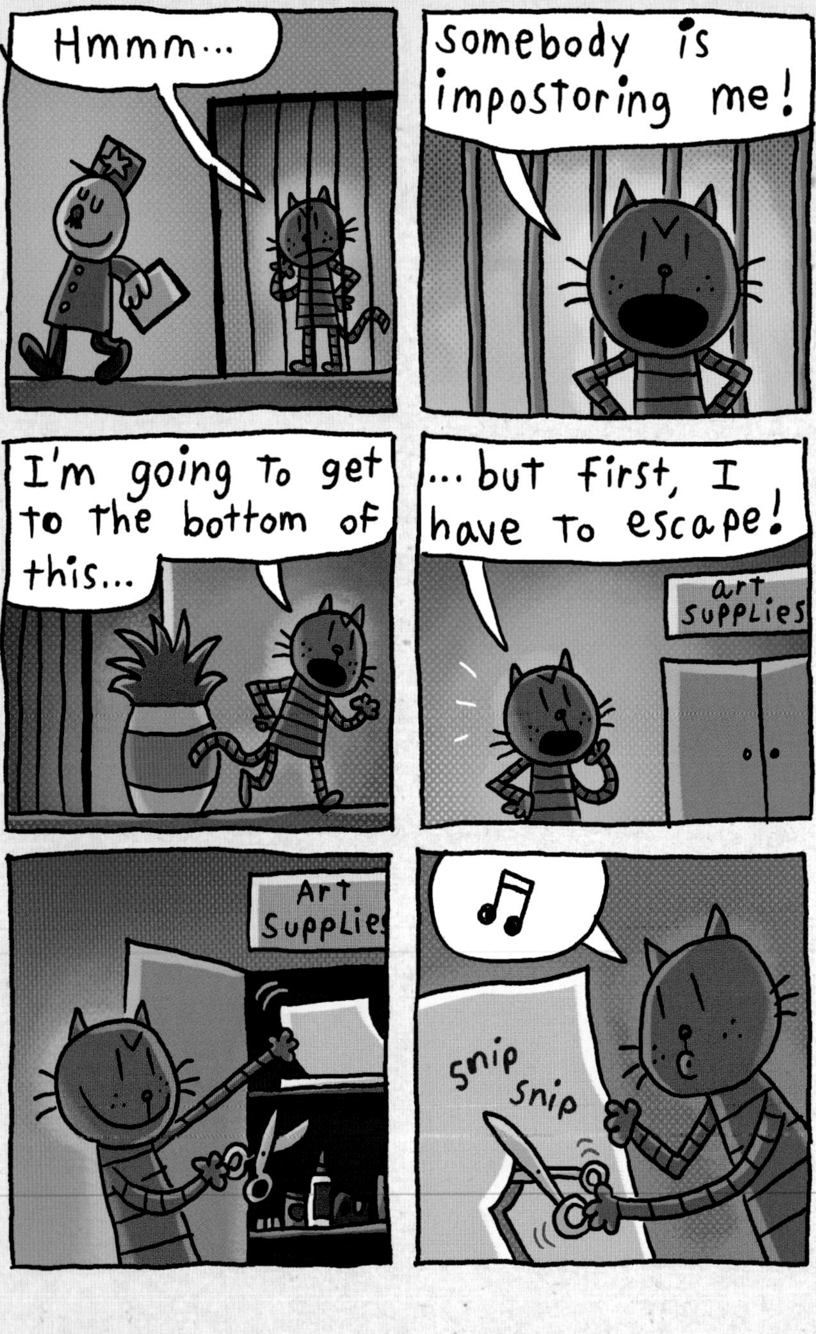
Hmmm...
Somebody is impostoring me!
I'm going to get to the bottom of this...
...but first, I have to escape!
art supplies
Art Supplies
snip snip

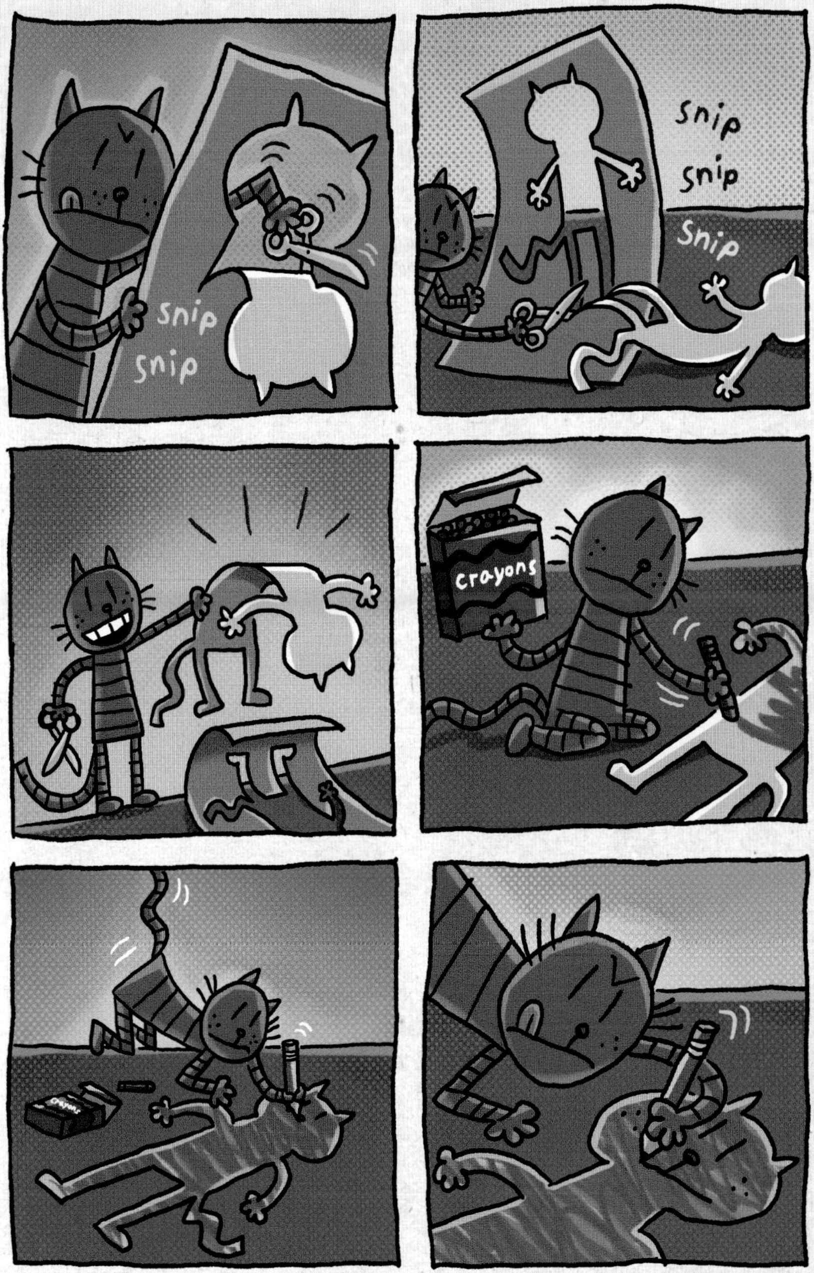
snip
snip
snip
snip
snip
crayons
crayons

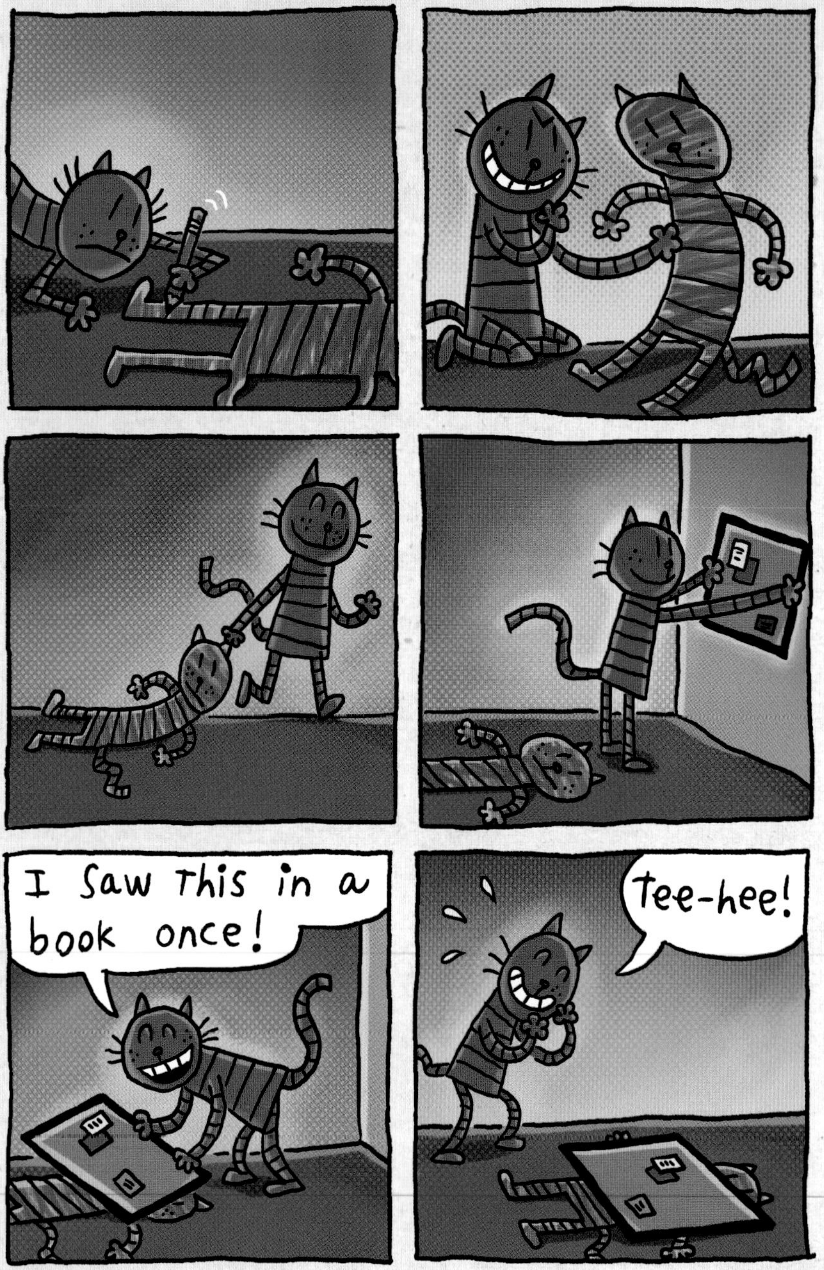
I saw this in a book once!
tee-hee!

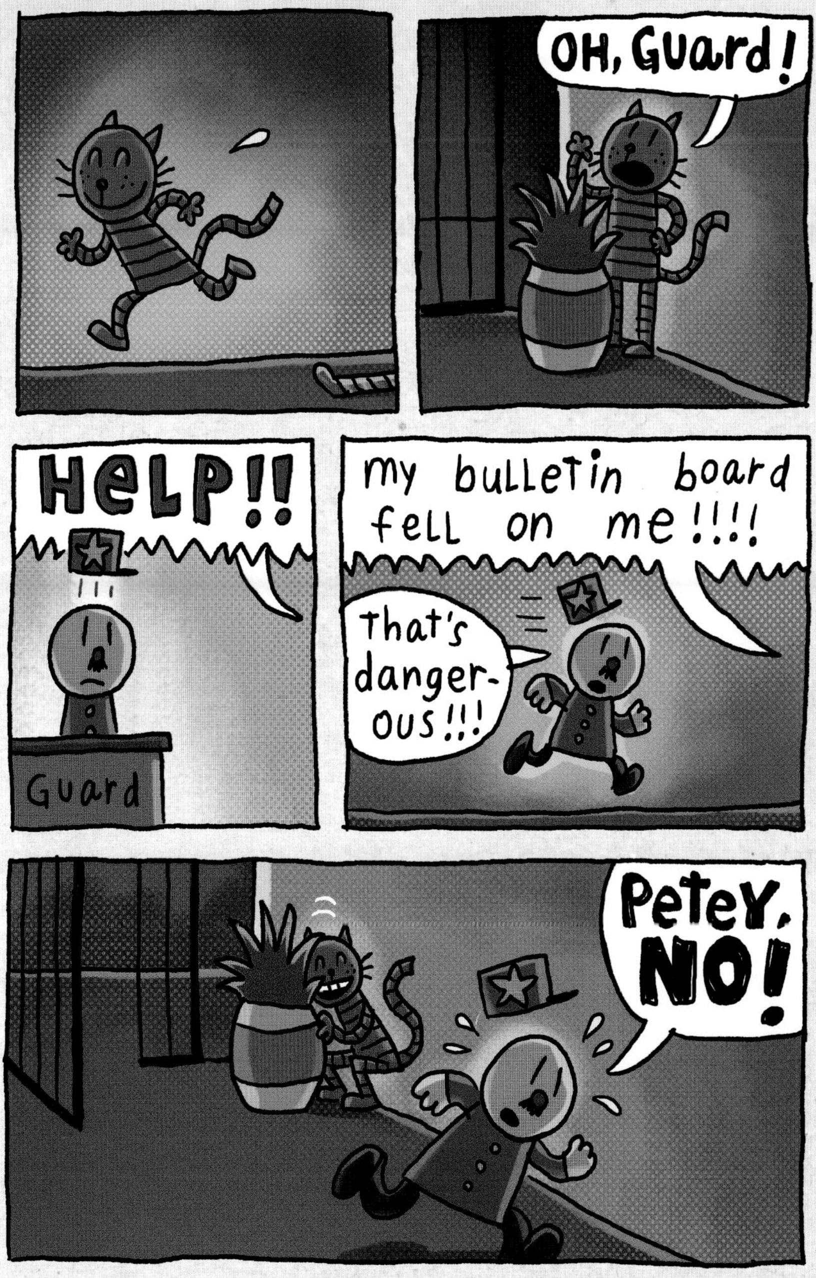

OH, Guard!
HELP!!
my bulletin board fell on me!!!!
That's danger-ous!!!
Guard
Petey, NO!

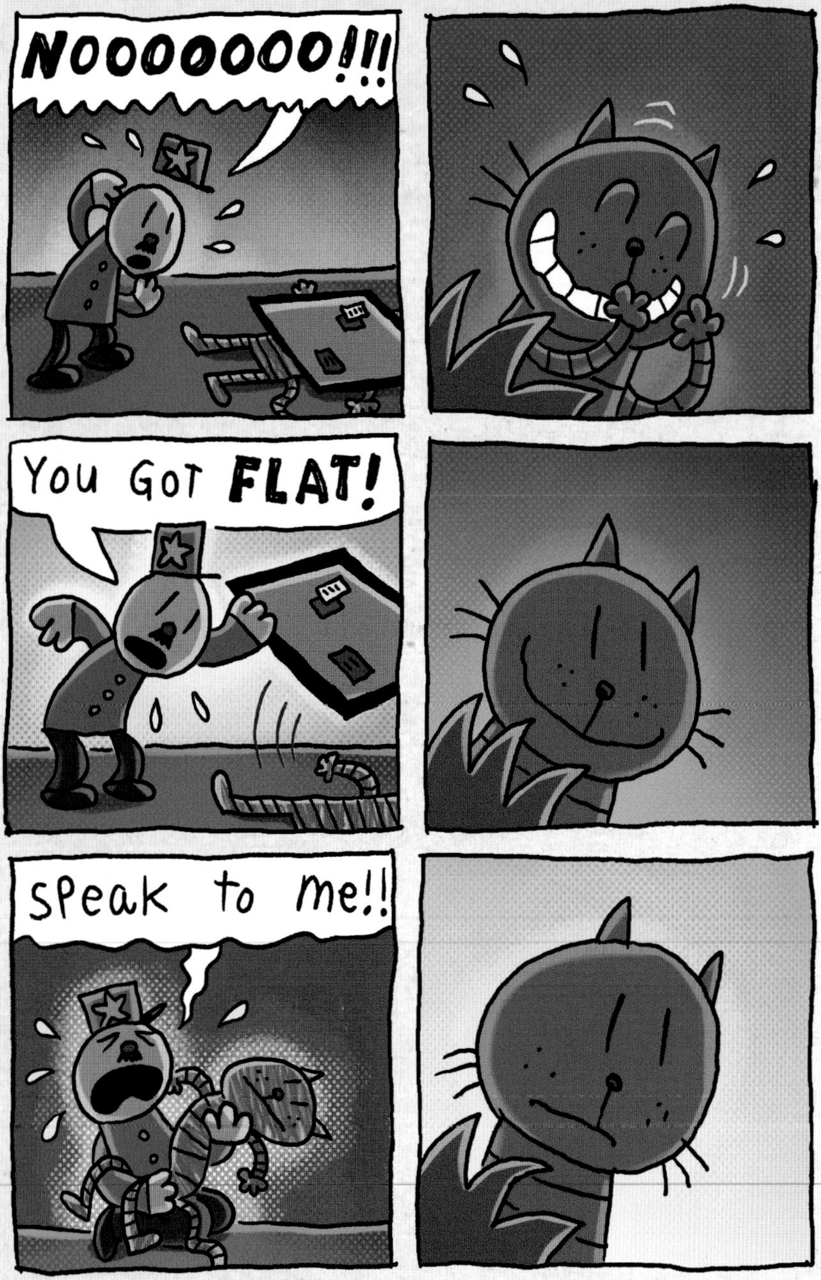
NOOOOOOO!!!
You Got FLAT!
speak to me!!

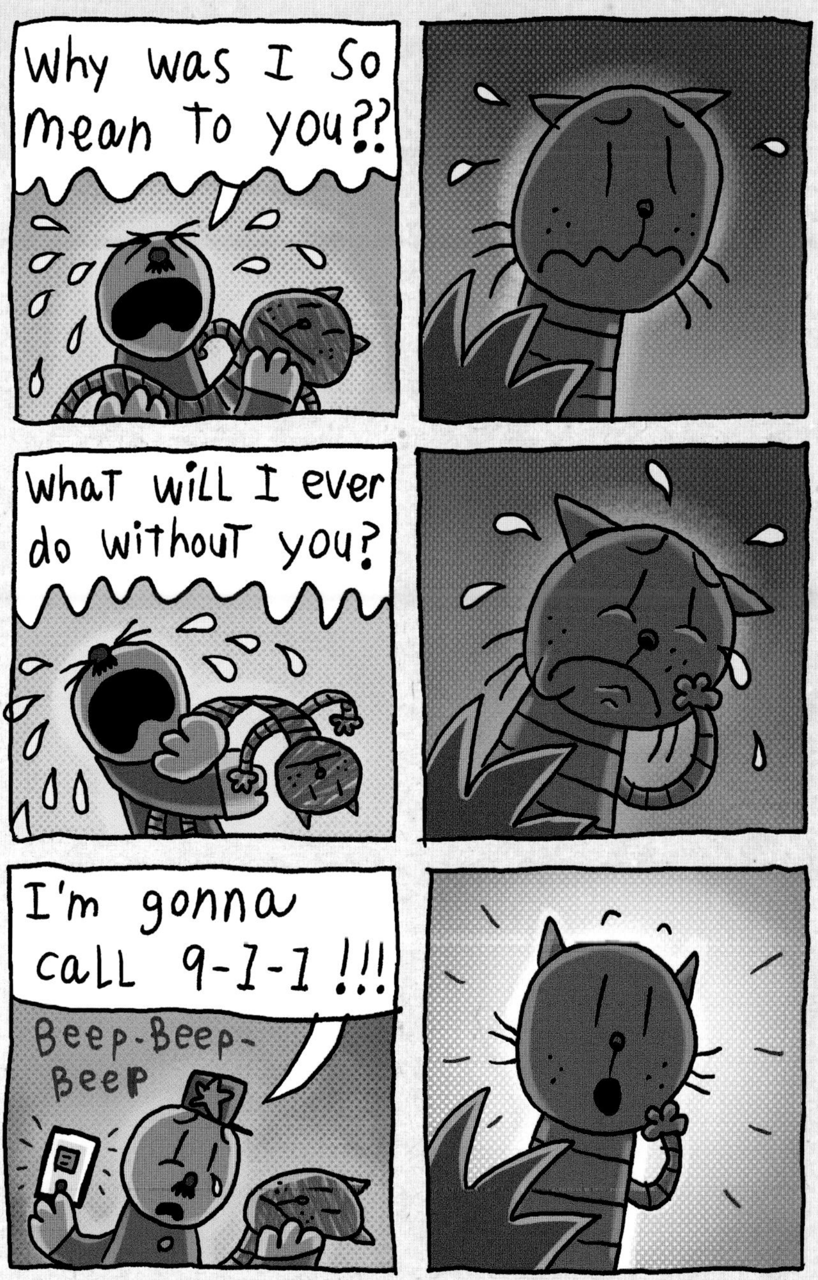
Why was I so mean to you??
What will I ever do without you?
I'm gonna call 9-1-1!!!
Beep-Beep-Beep

DON'T YOU die on me!!! Don't You die on me!!!

Cat Jail

wee-ooo-wee-ooo

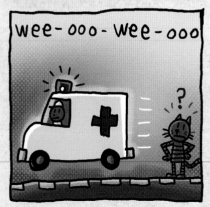

wee-ooo-wee-ooo

Cat Jail

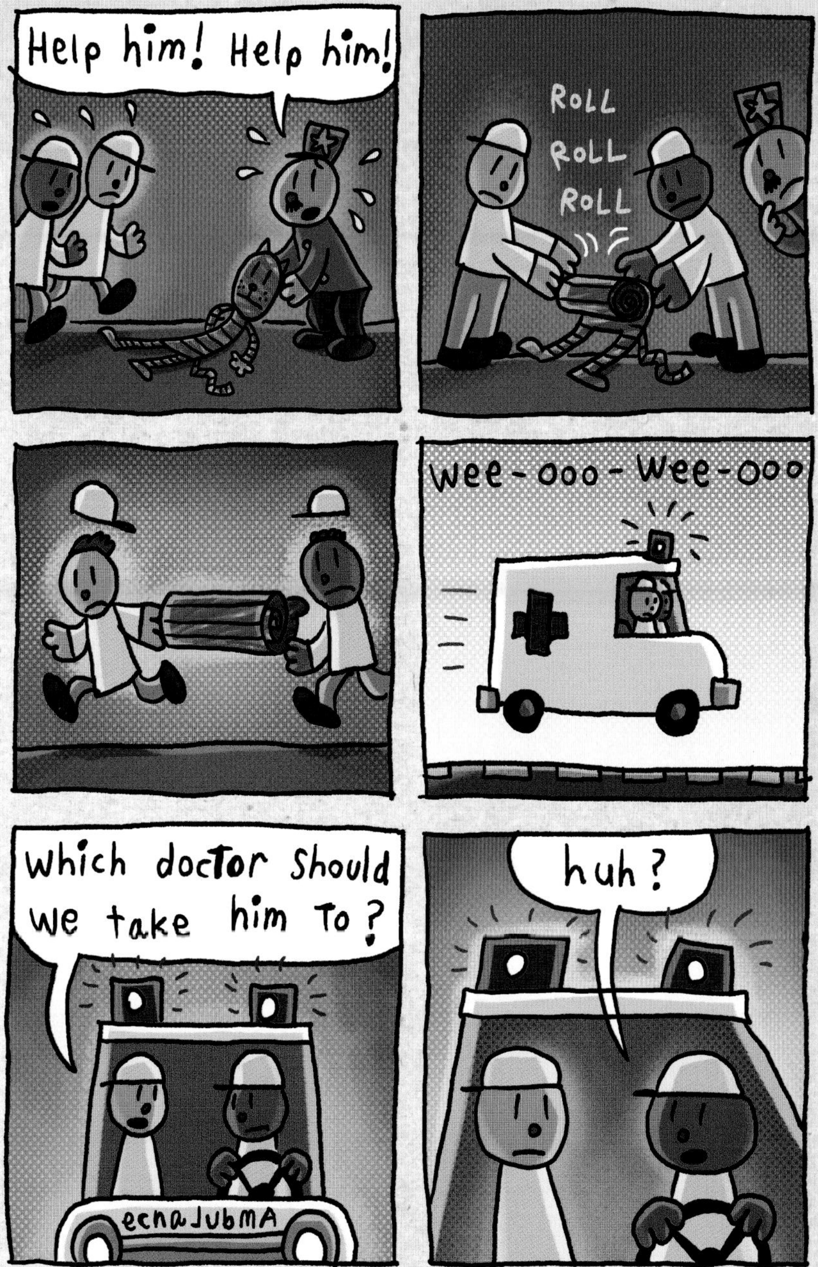
Help him! Help him!
ROLL
ROLL
ROLL
wee-ooo-wee-ooo
Which doctor should we take him to?
ecnaJubmA
huh?

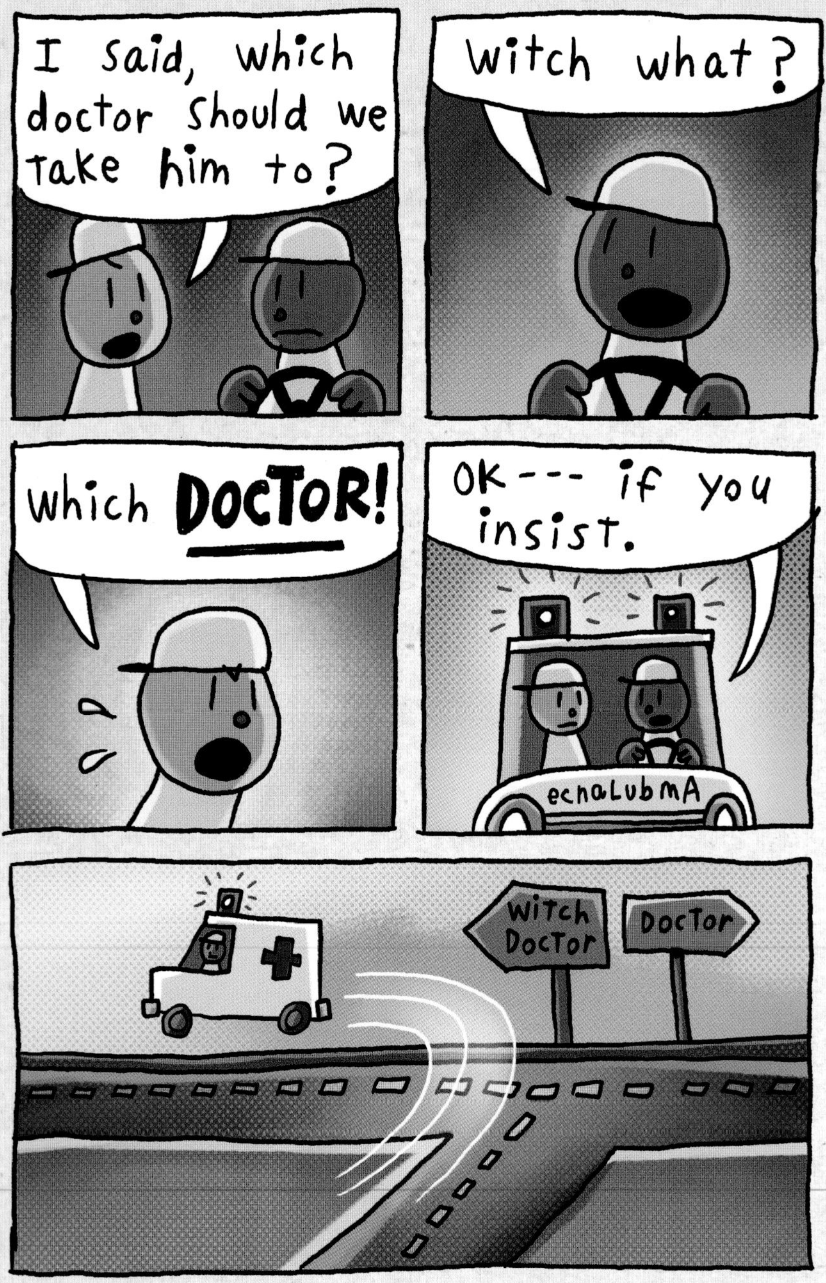
I said, which doctor should we take him to?
Witch what?
which DOCTOR!
OK --- if you insist.
echaLubmA
Witch Doctor
Doctor

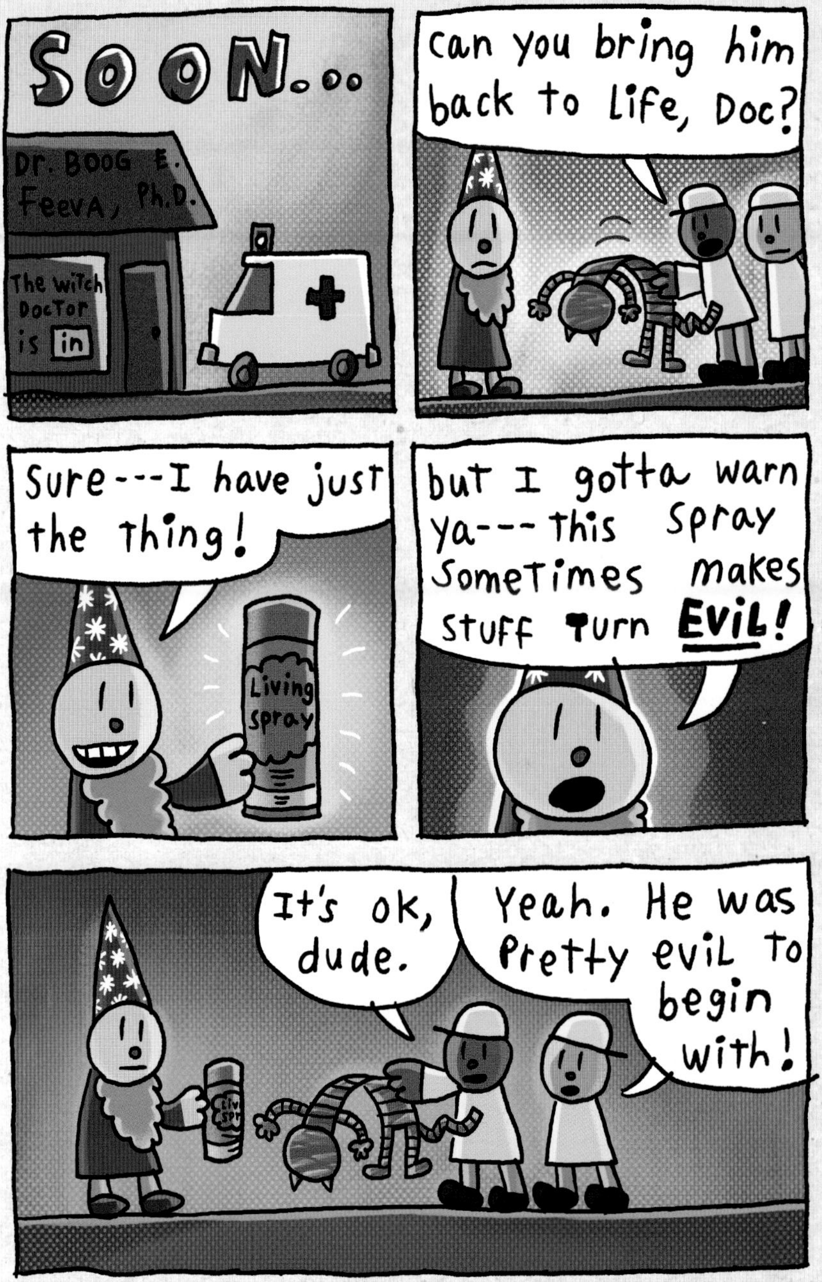
SOON...
Dr. BOOG E. Feeva, Ph.D.
The witch Doctor is in
can you bring him back to Life, Doc?
Sure---I have just the thing!
Living spray
but I gotta warn ya---this spray sometimes makes stuff turn EVIL!
It's ok, dude.
Yeah. He was pretty evil to begin with!

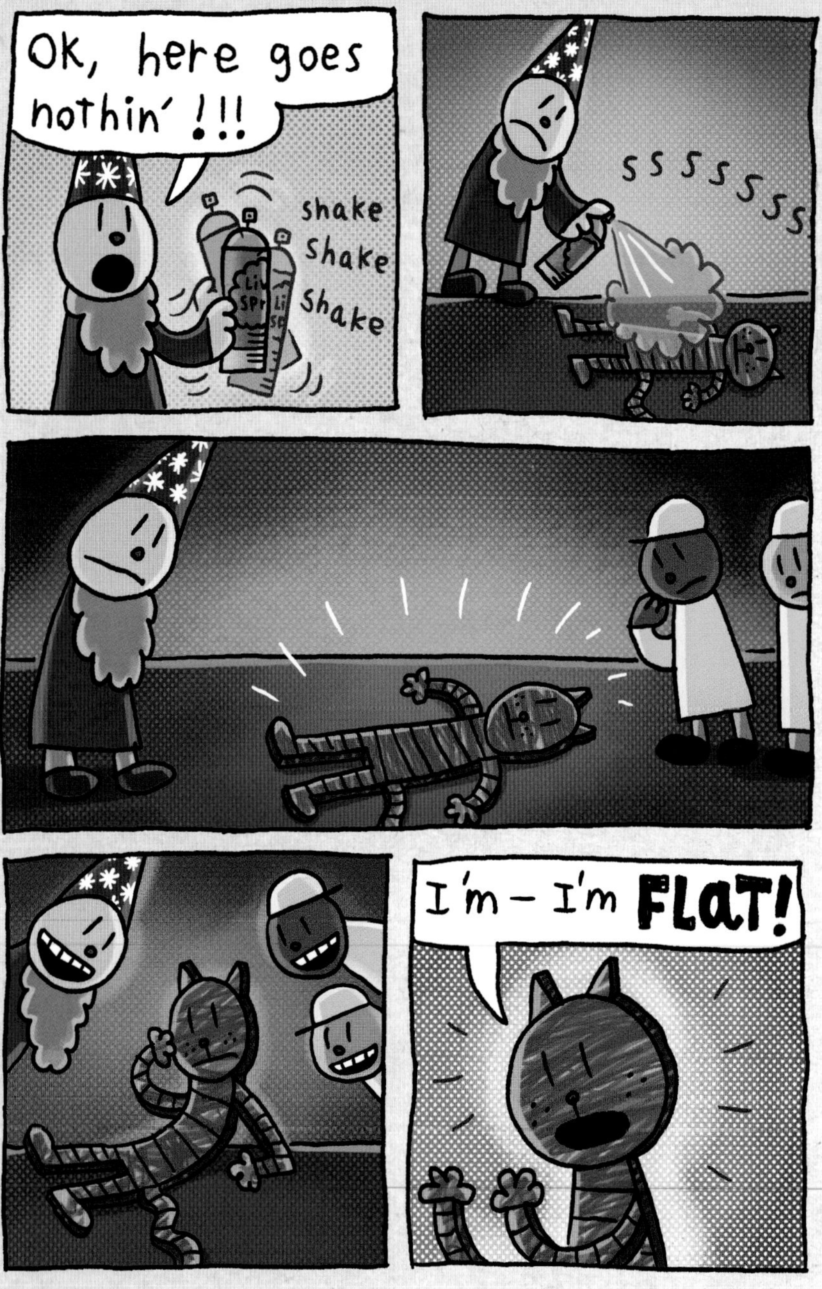
Ok, here goes nothin' !!!
shake
Shake
Shake
SSSSSSSS
I'm – I'm FLAT!

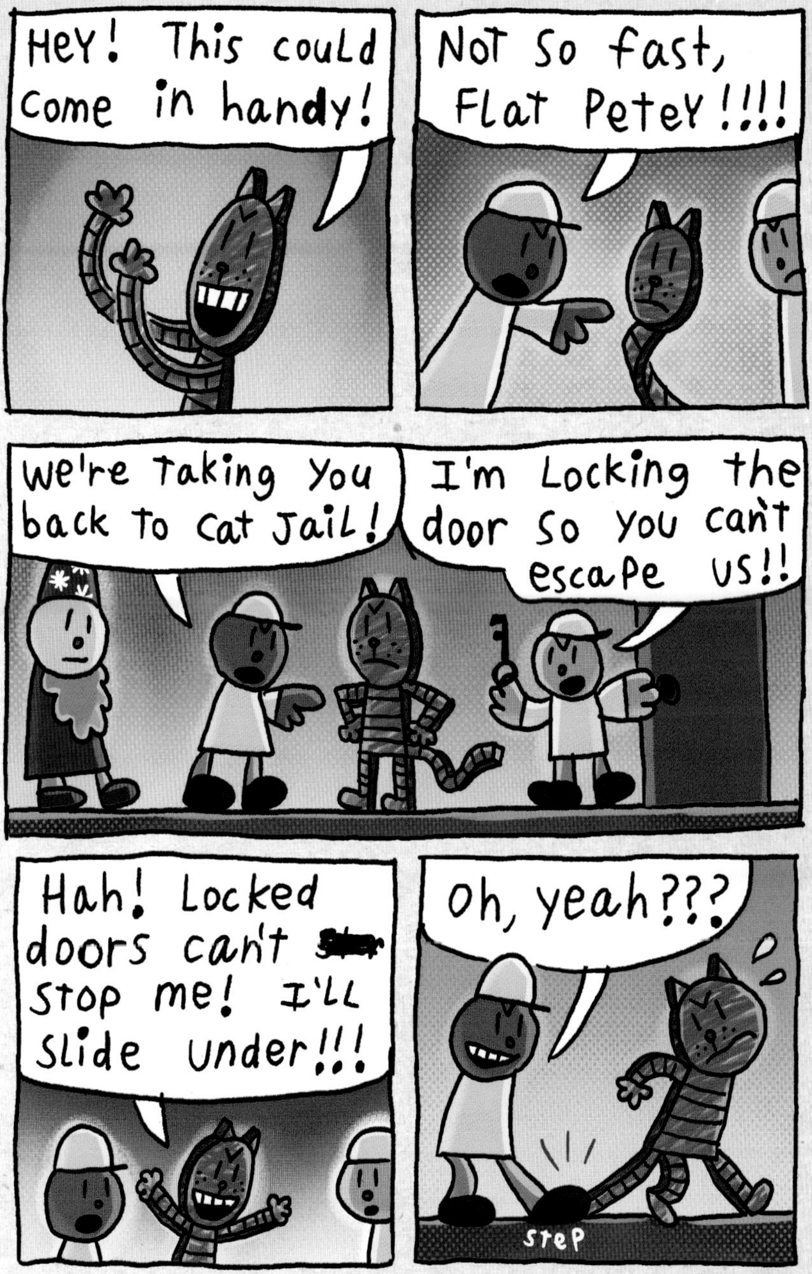
HEY! This could come in handy!
Not so fast, Flat Petey!!!!
We're taking you back to Cat Jail!
I'm locking the door so you can't escape us!!
Hah! Locked doors can't s[redacted] stop me! I'LL slide under!!!
Oh, yeah???
STEP

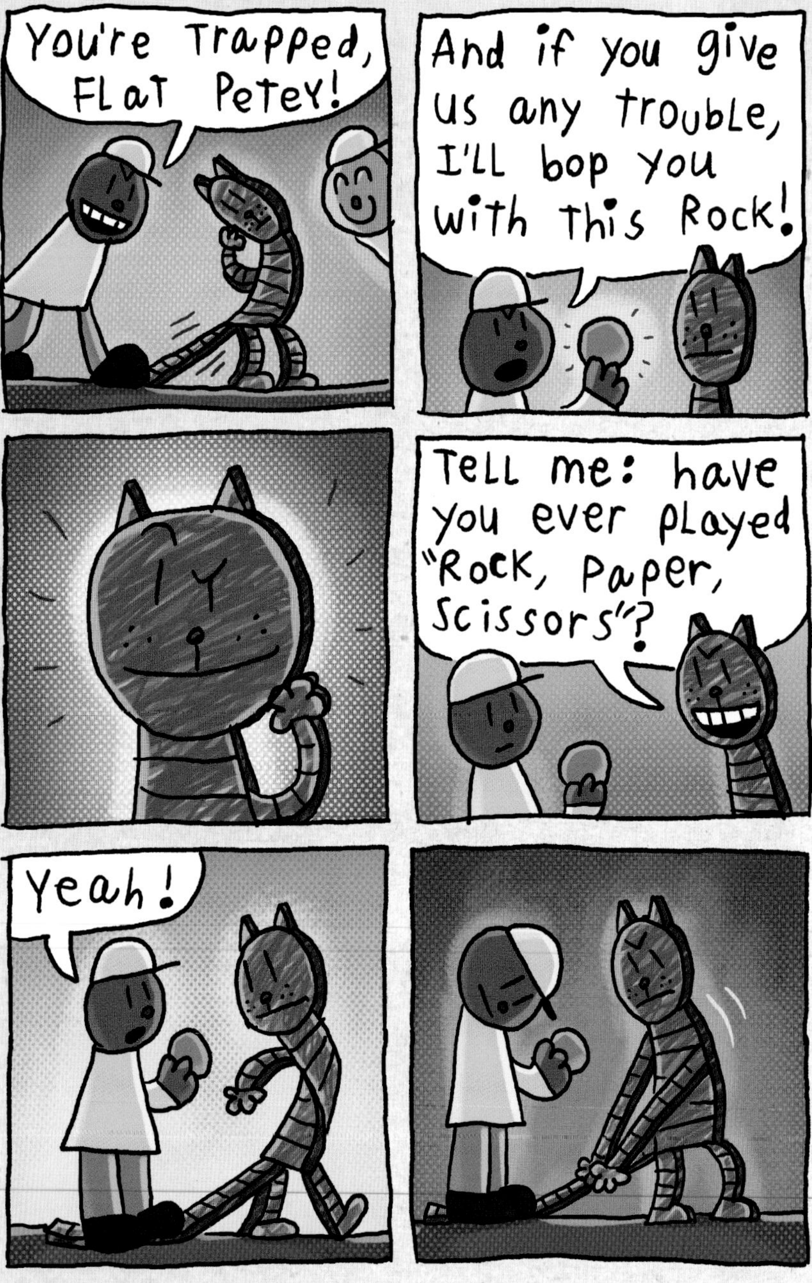
You're Trapped, Flat Petey!
And if you give us any trouble, I'll bop you with this Rock!
Tell me: have you ever played "Rock, Paper, Scissors"?
Yeah!

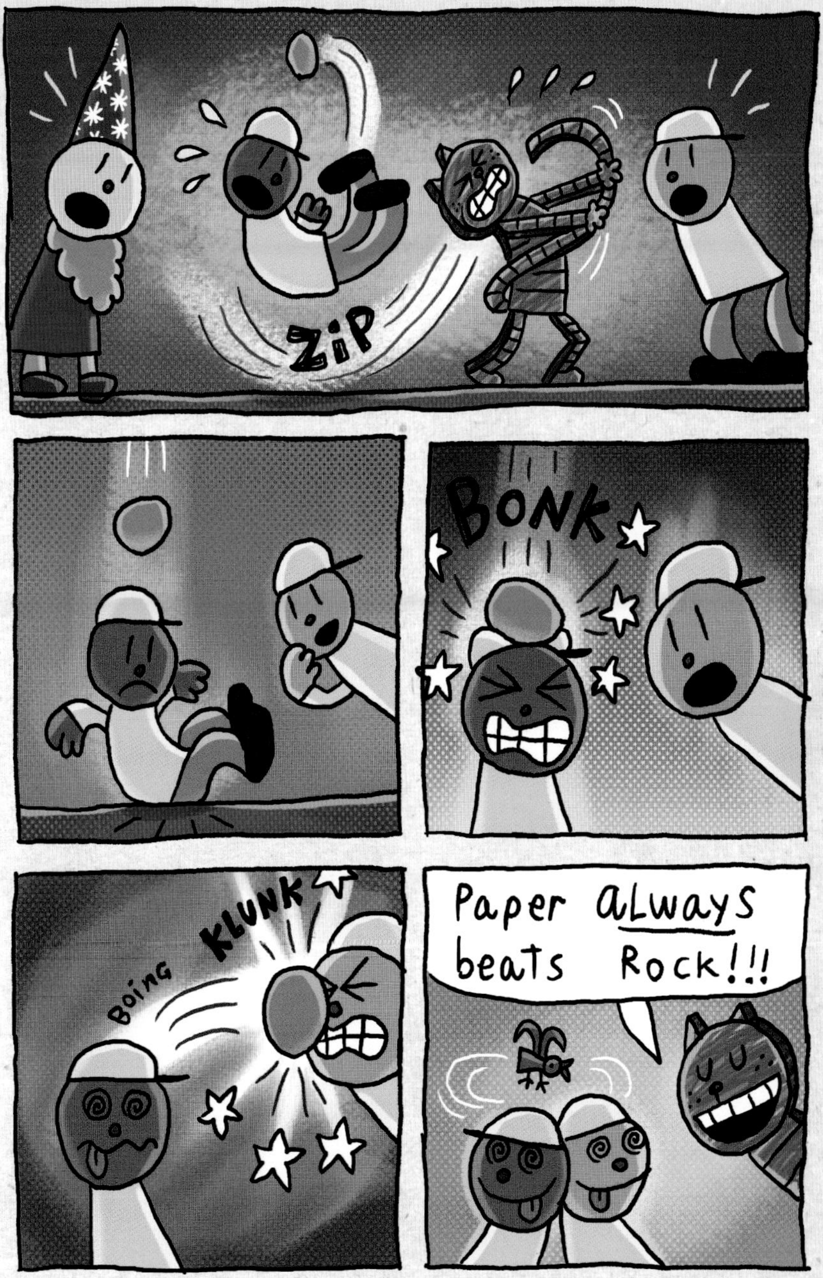
ZiP
BONK
BOING
KLUNK
Paper ALWAYS beats Rock!!!

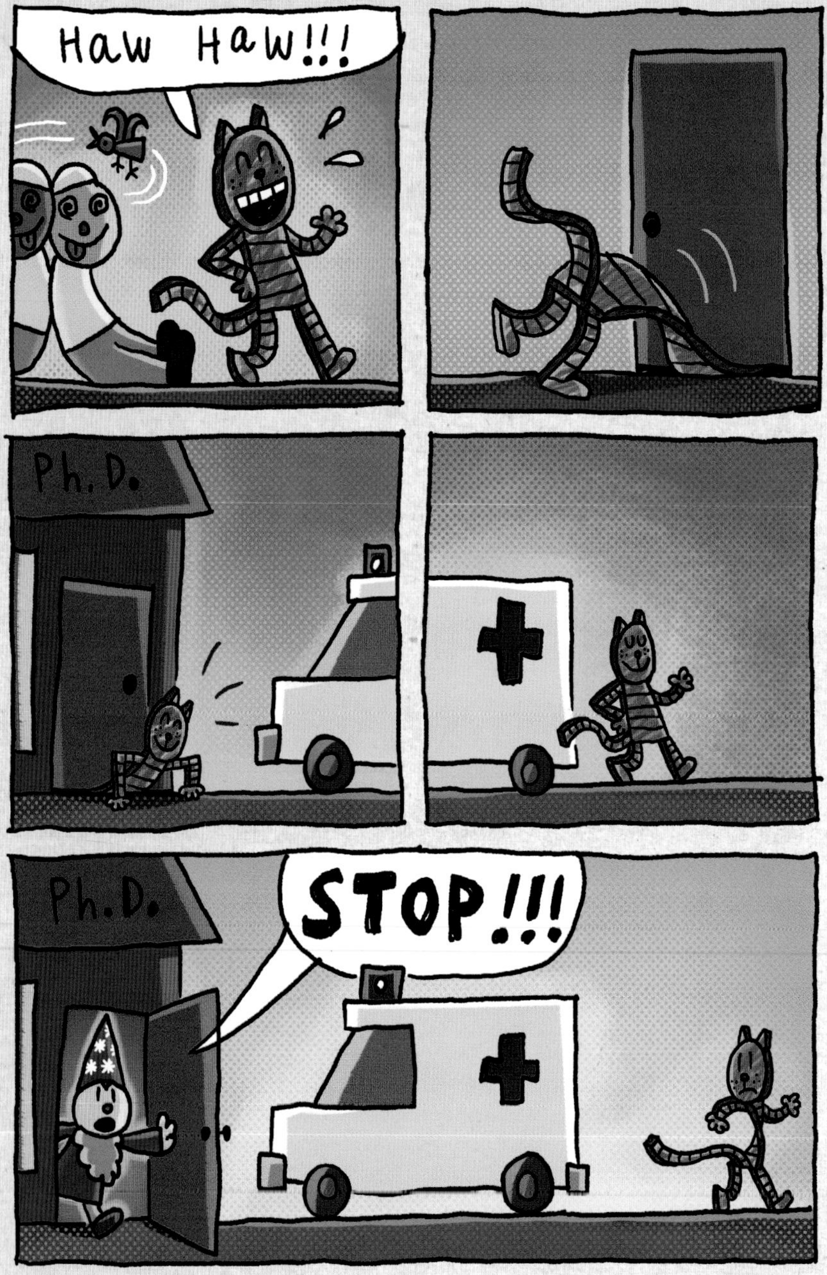
HAW HAW!!!
Ph. D.
Ph. D.
STOP!!!

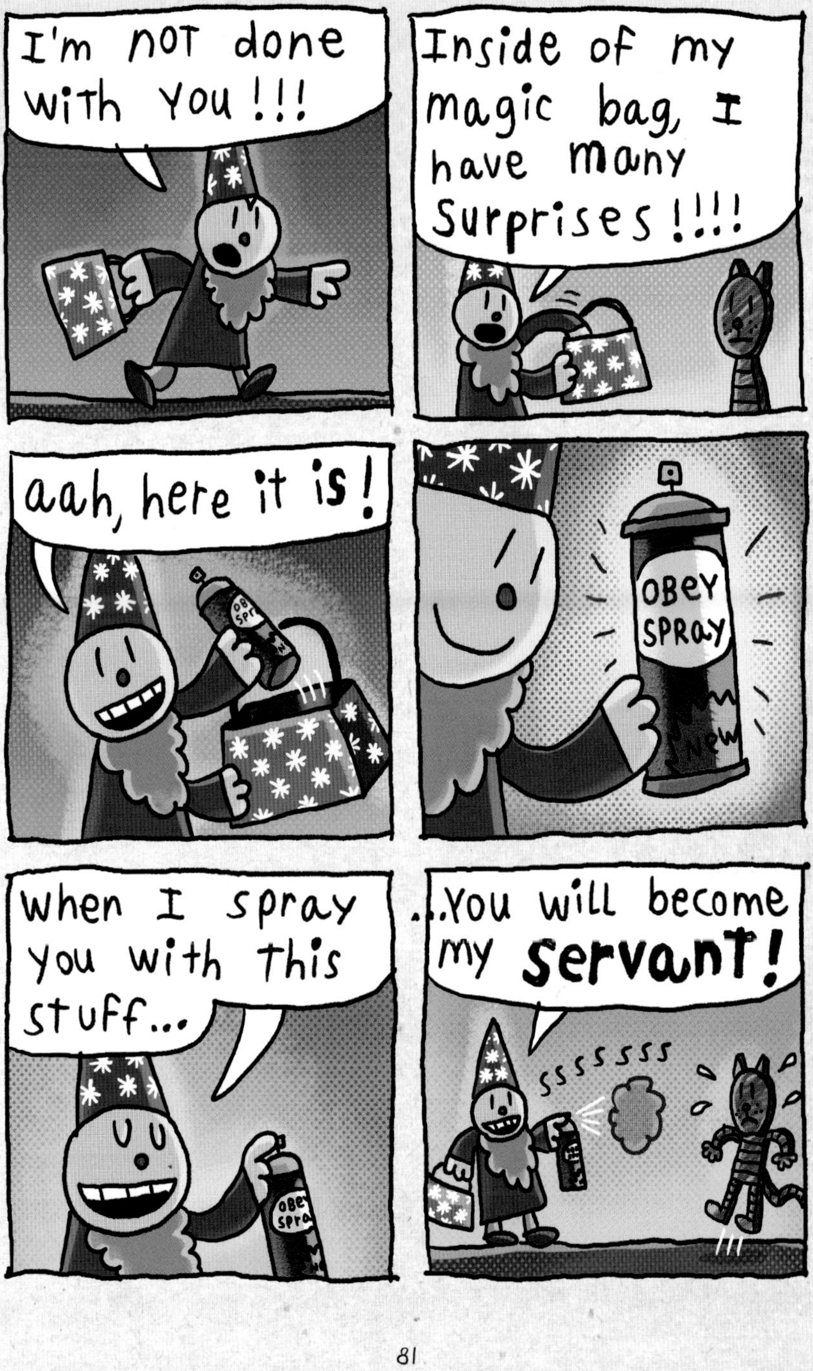
I'm NOT done with You!!!
Inside of my magic bag, I have many Surprises!!!!
aah, here it is!
OBEY SPRAY
NEW
When I spray you with this stuff...
...You will become my servant!
SSSSSSS

The cloud of spray got closer...

...and flat Petey had to act fast!

Quickly, he folded his face...

...into the shape of a fan.

FLIP-O-RAMA

Flip like the wind!

Left hand here.

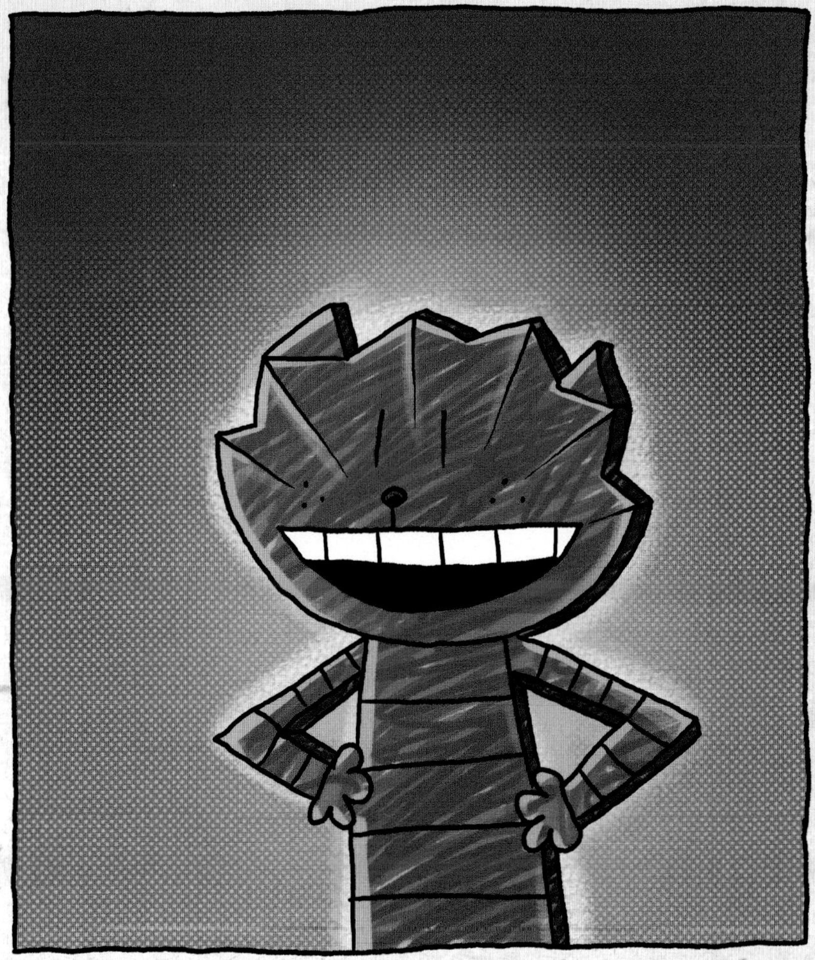

A Fan
with a Plan!

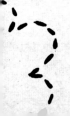

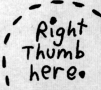

Right Thumb here.

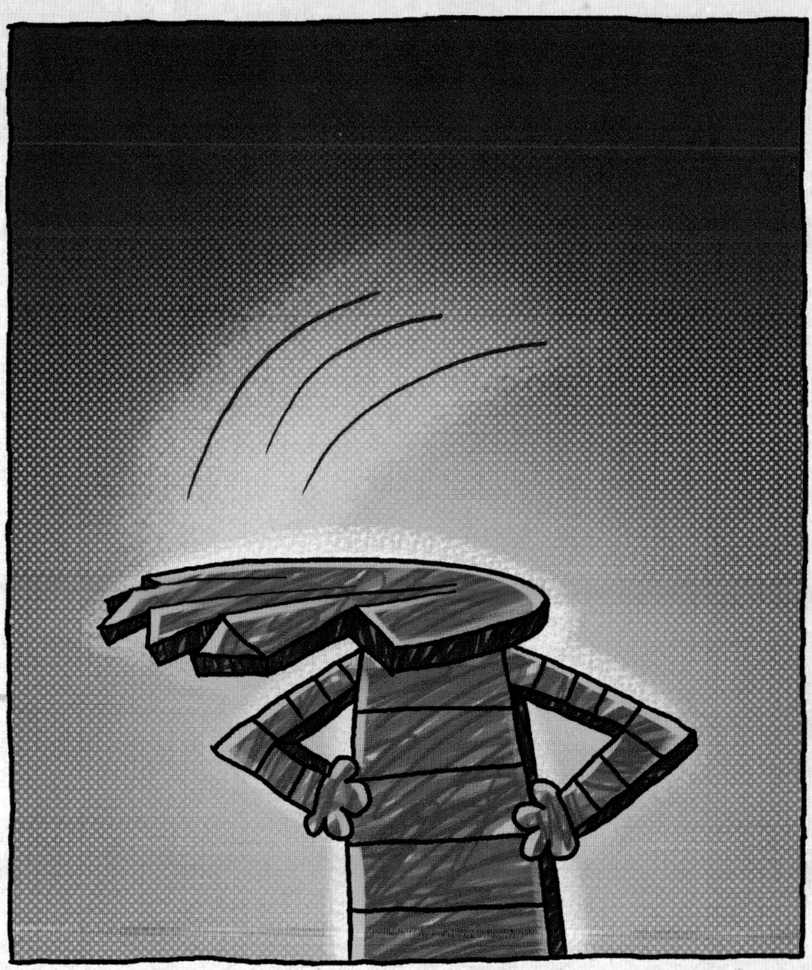

A Fan with a Plan!

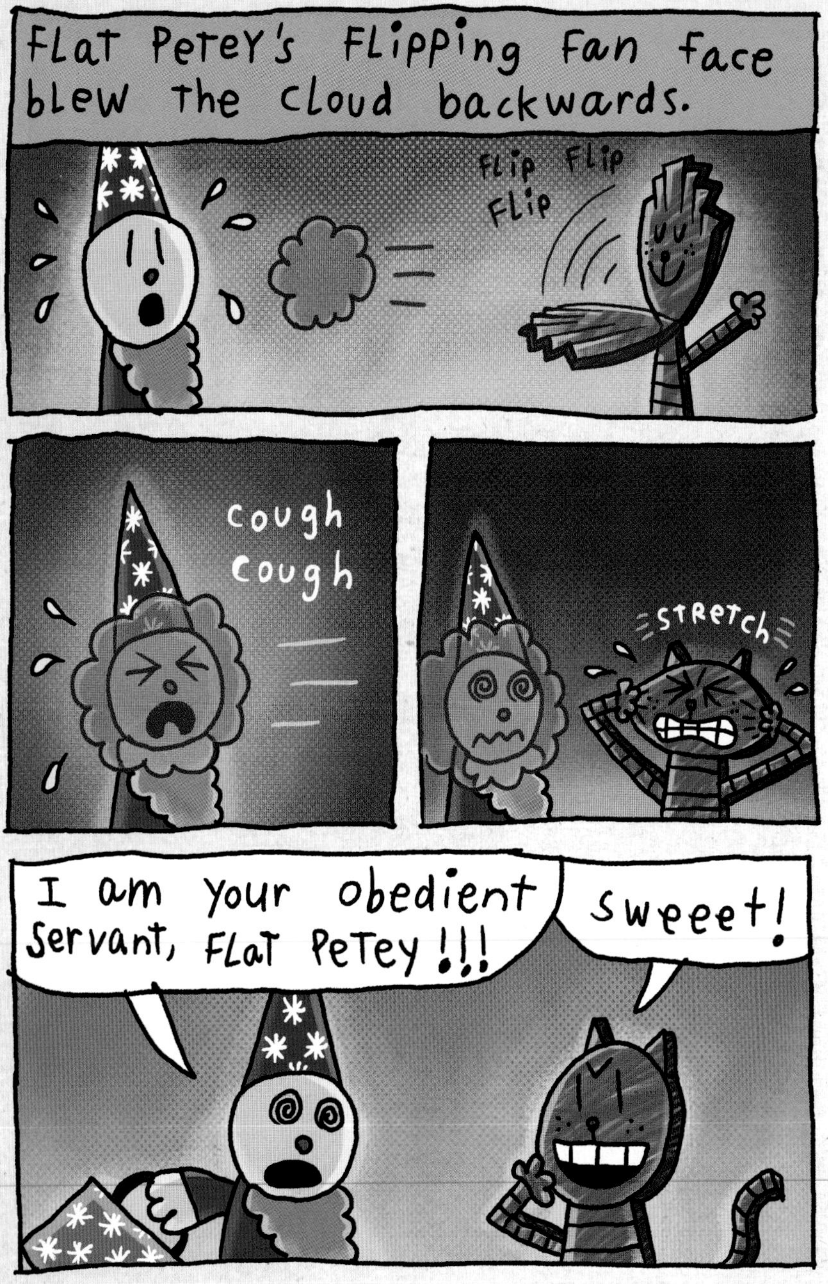
Flat Petey's flipping fan face blew the cloud backwards.
Flip Flip Flip
cough cough
STRETCH
I am your obedient servant, Flat Petey!!!
Sweeet!

Chapter 6

A Buncha STUFF That Happened Next

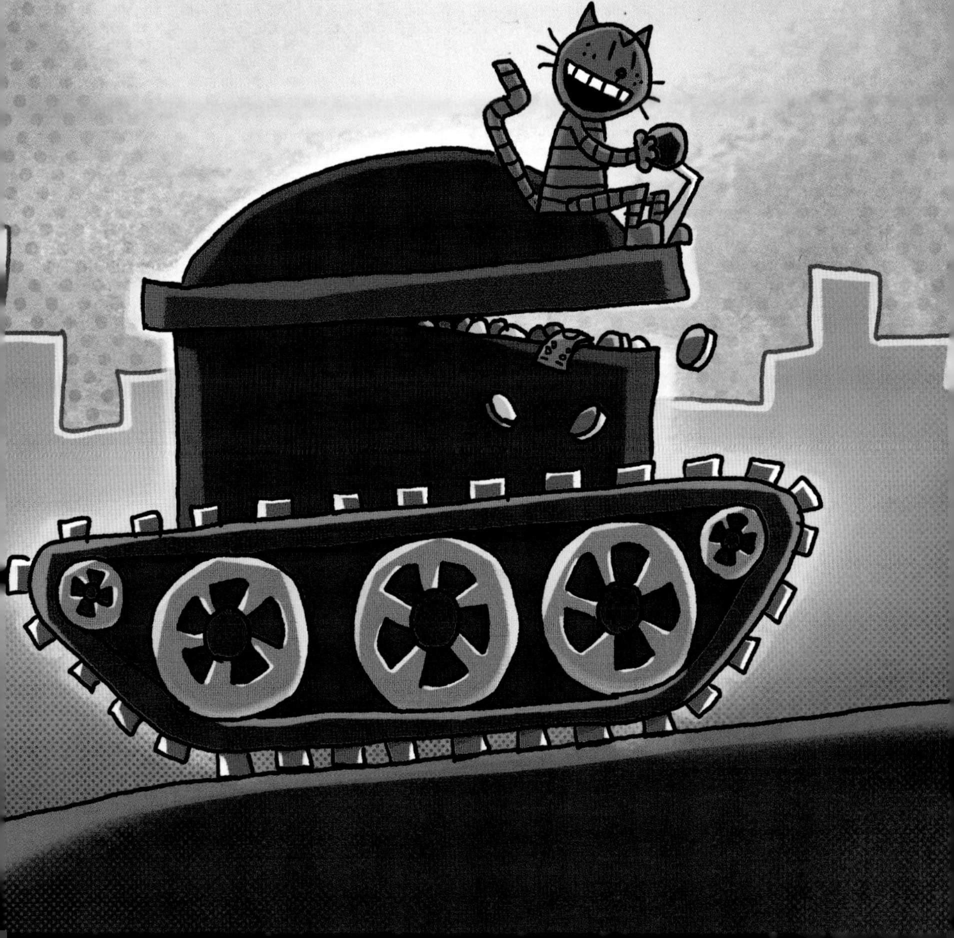

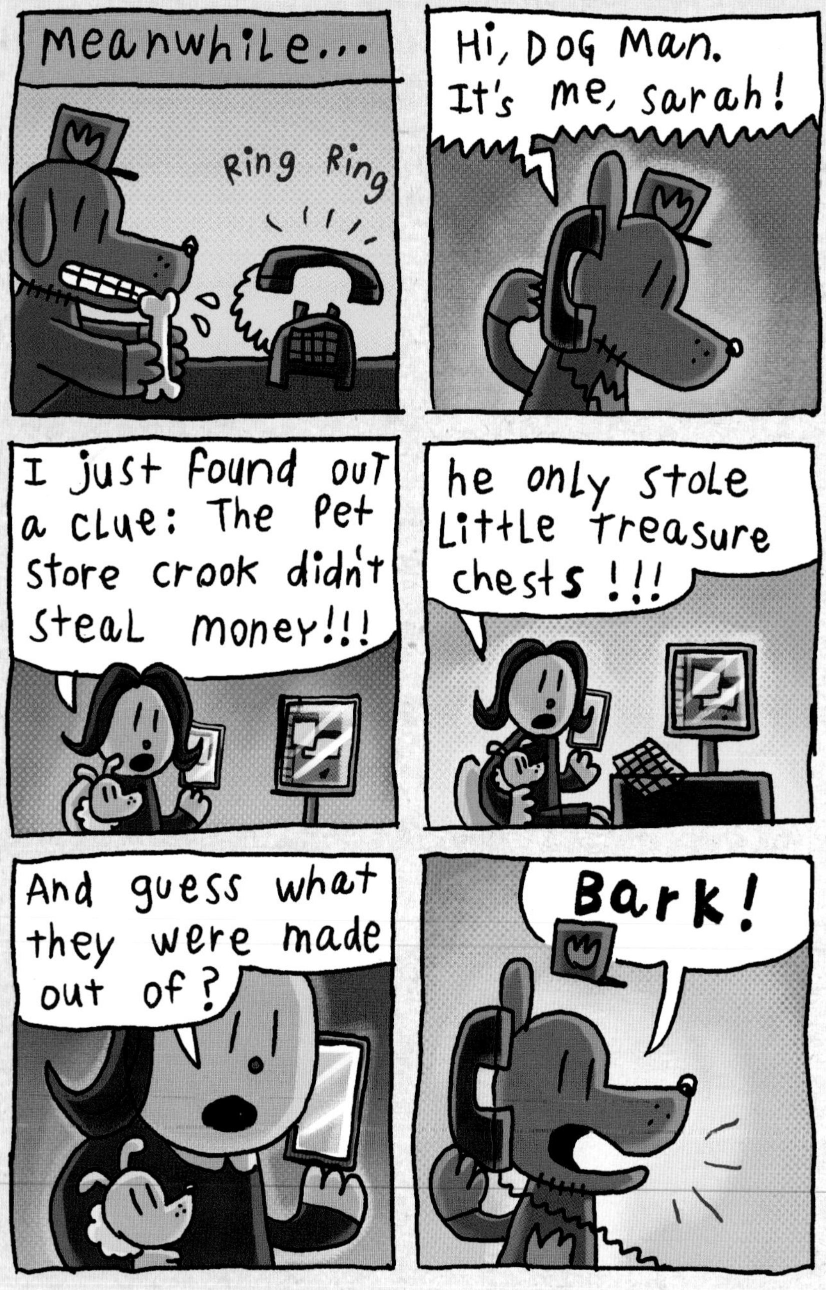
Meanwhile...
Ring Ring
Hi, Dog Man. It's me, Sarah!
I just found out a clue: The pet store crook didn't steal money!!!
He only stole little treasure chests!!!
And guess what they were made out of?
Bark!

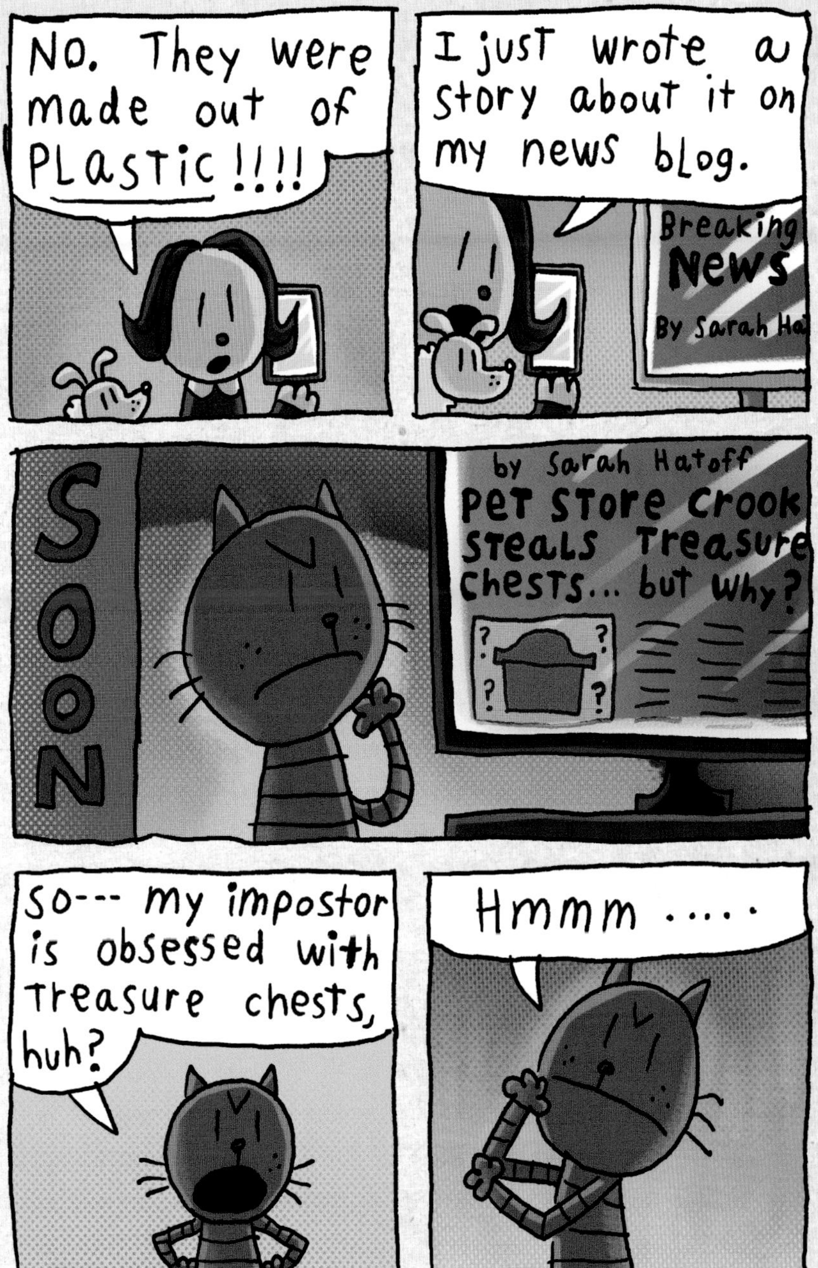
NO. They were made out of PLASTIC!!!!
I just wrote a story about it on my news blog.
Breaking News
By Sarah Ha
SOON
by Sarah Hatoff
PET STORE CROOK STEALS TREASURE CHESTS... but Why?
So--- my impostor is obsessed with Treasure chests, huh?
Hmmm .....

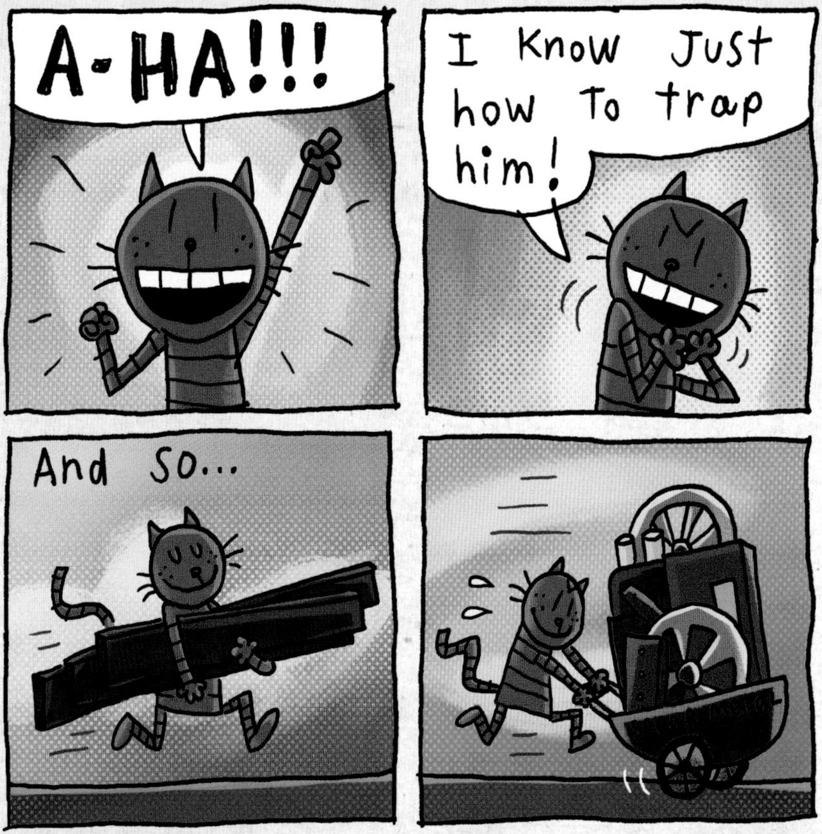
A-HA!!!
I Know Just how To trap him!
And So...

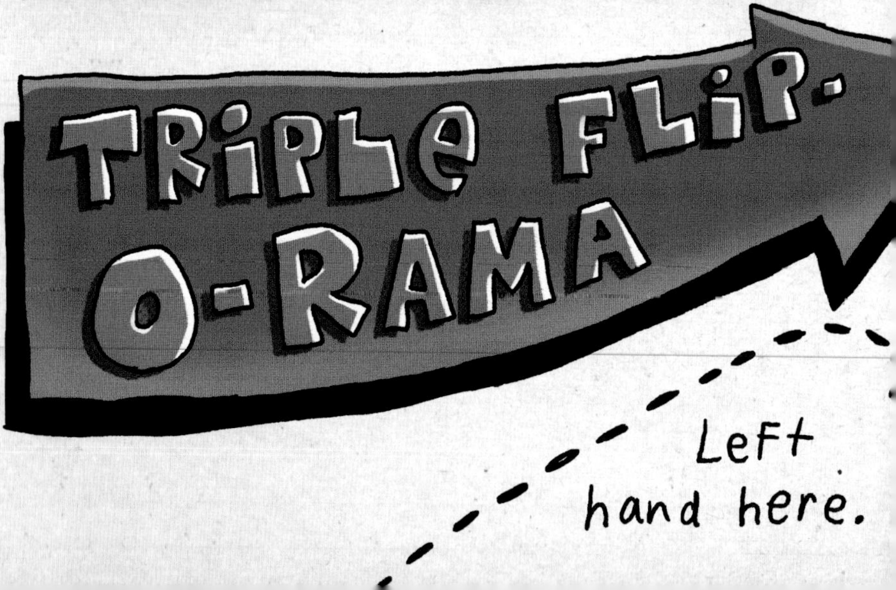
TRIPLE FLIP-O-RAMA

Left hand here.

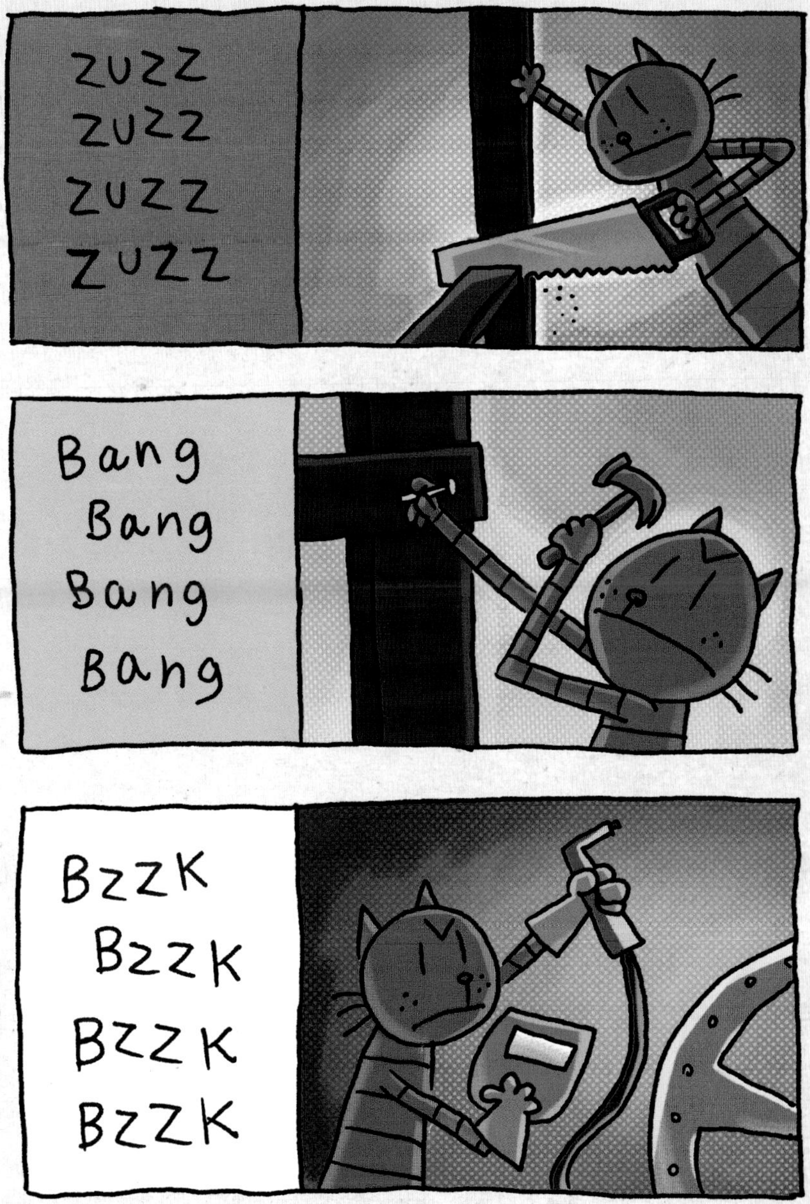
ZUZZ
ZUZZ
ZUZZ
ZUZZ
Bang
Bang
Bang
Bang
BZZK
BZZK
BZZK
BZZK

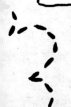

Right Thumb here.

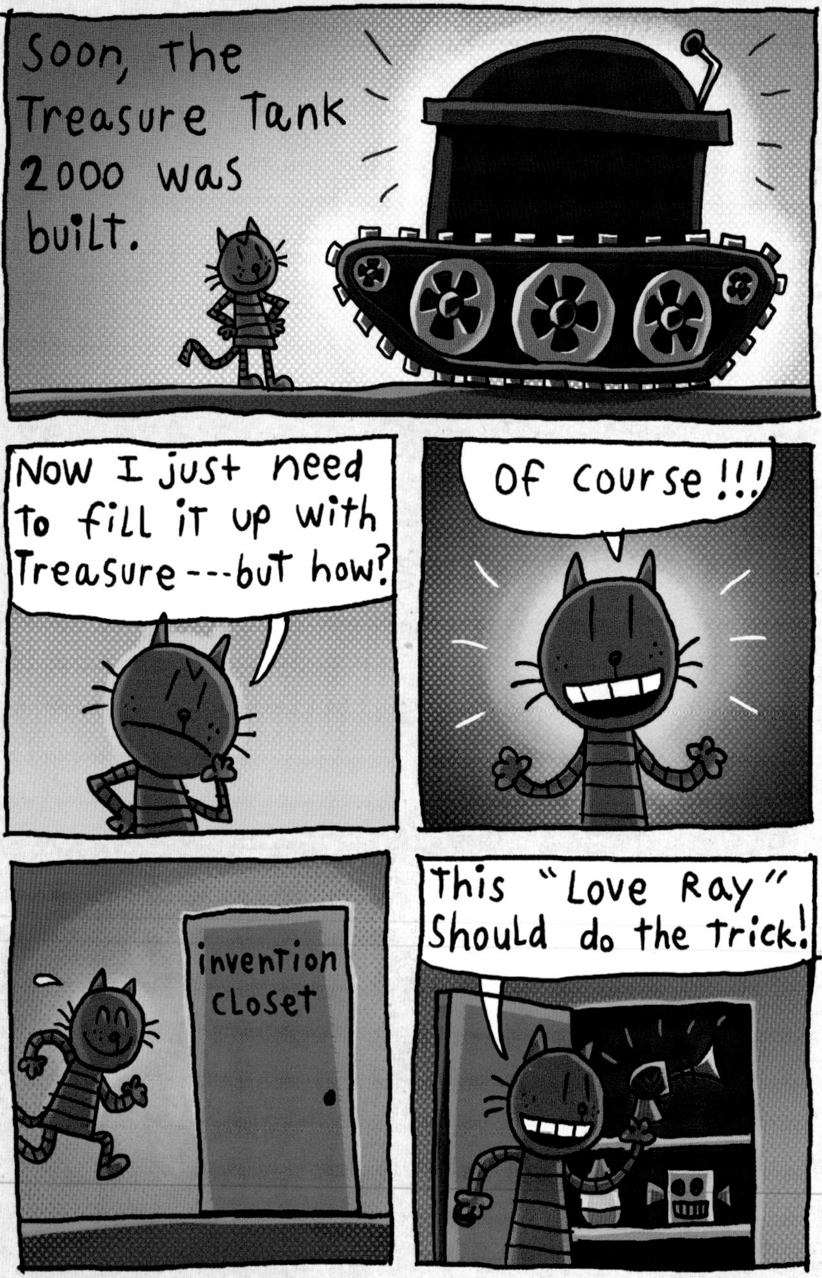
Soon, the Treasure Tank 2000 was built.
Now I just need to fill it up with Treasure---but how?
Of course!!!
invention closet
This "Love Ray" should do the trick!

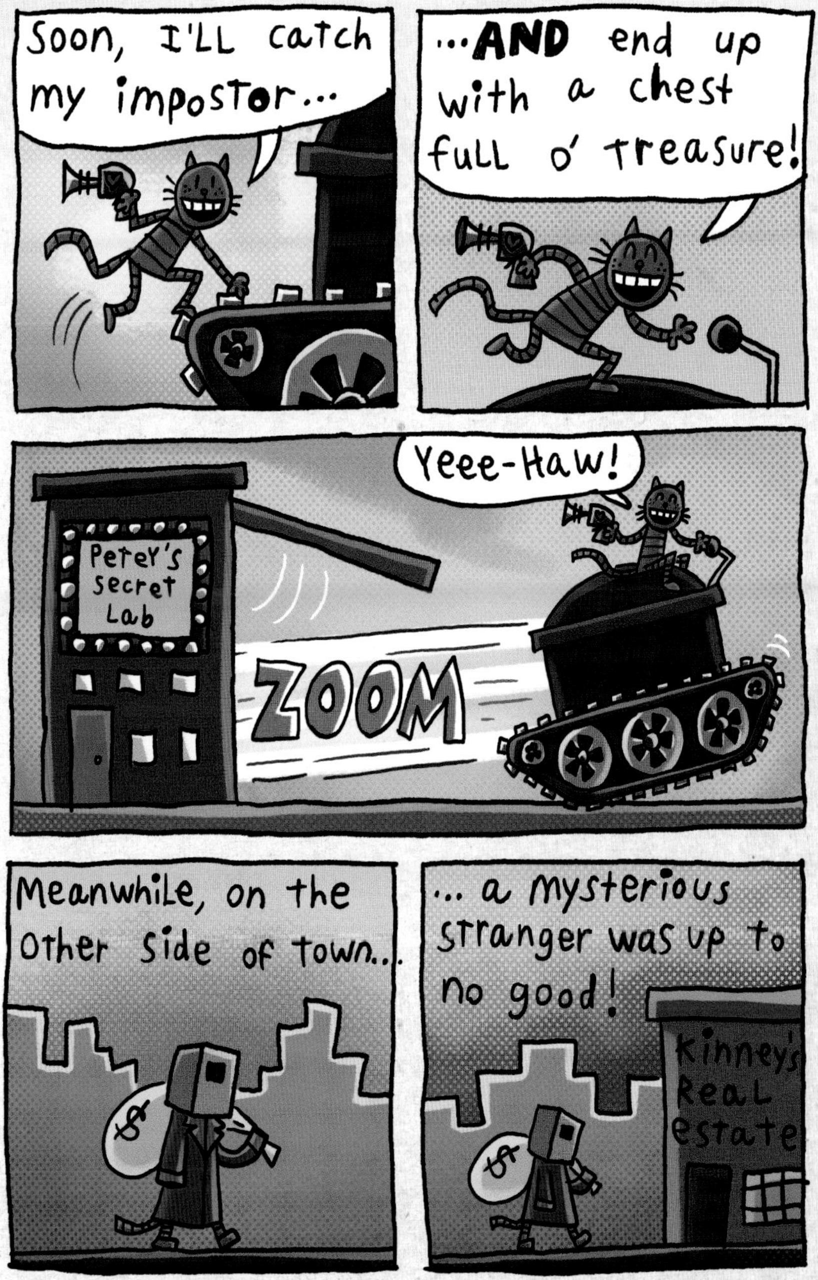
Soon, I'LL catch my impostor...
...AND end up with a chest full o' treasure!
Yeee-Haw!
Peter's Secret Lab
ZOOM
Meanwhile, on the other side of town...
... a mysterious stranger was up to no good!
Kinney's Real estate

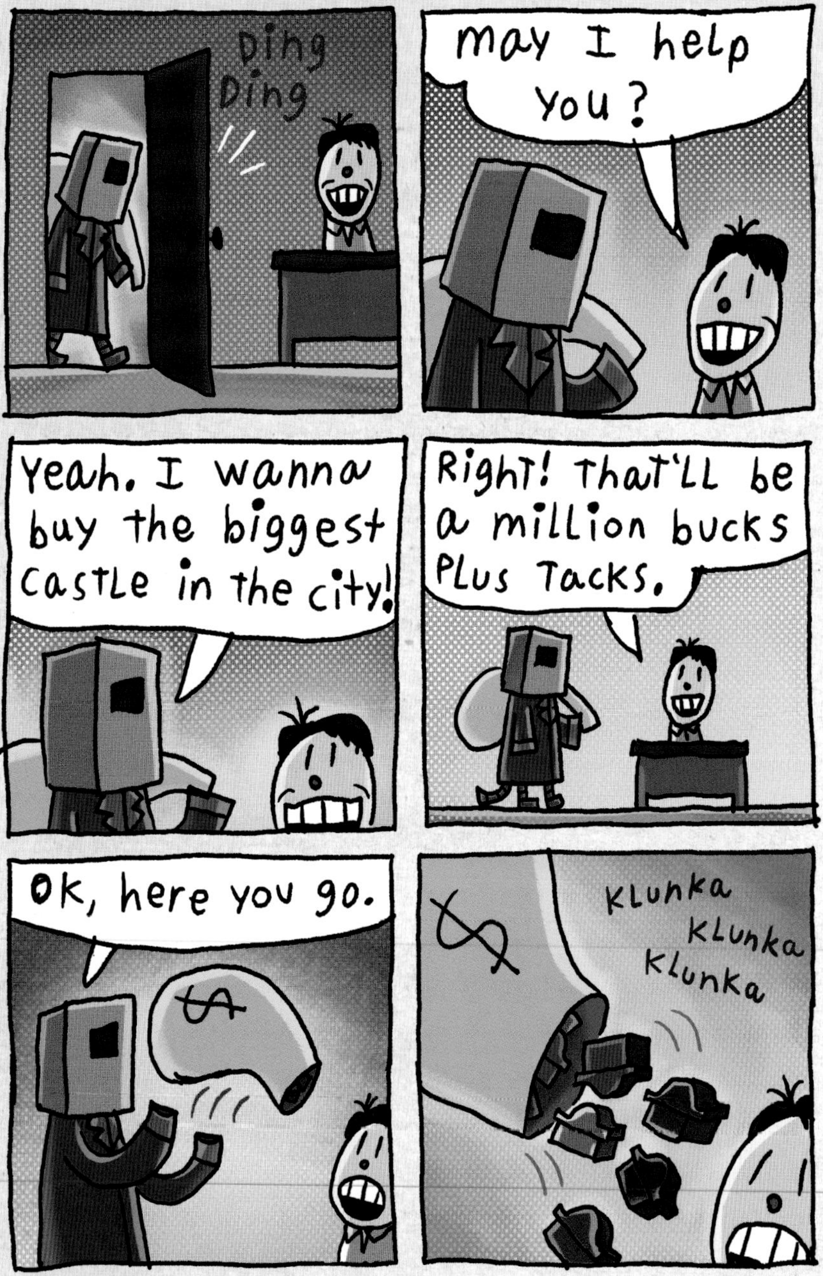
Ding
Ding
May I help you?
Yeah. I wanna buy the biggest castle in the city!
Right! That'll be a million bucks plus tacks.
Ok, here you go.
Klunka
Klunka
Klunka

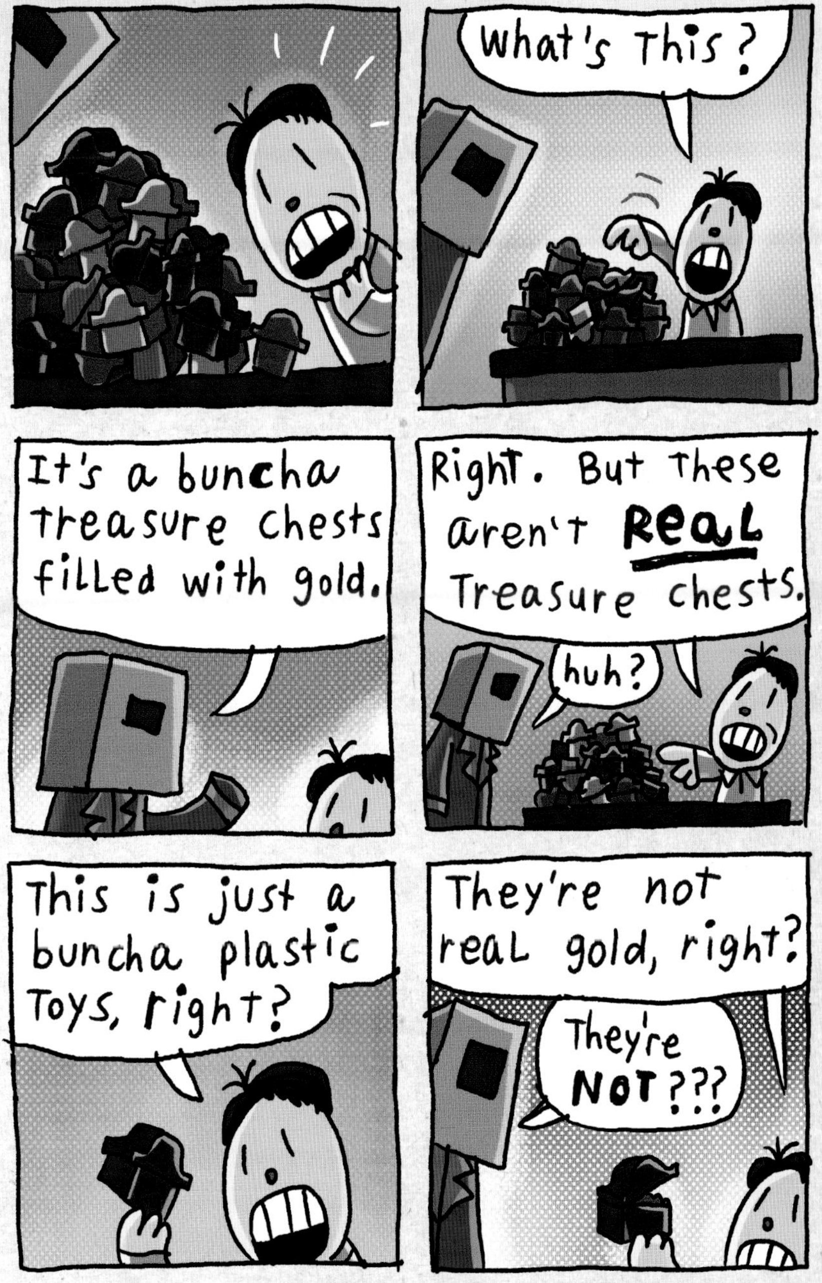
What's This?
It's a buncha treasure chests filled with gold.
Right. But these aren't REAL Treasure chests.
huh?
This is just a buncha plastic Toys, right?
They're not real gold, right?
They're NOT???

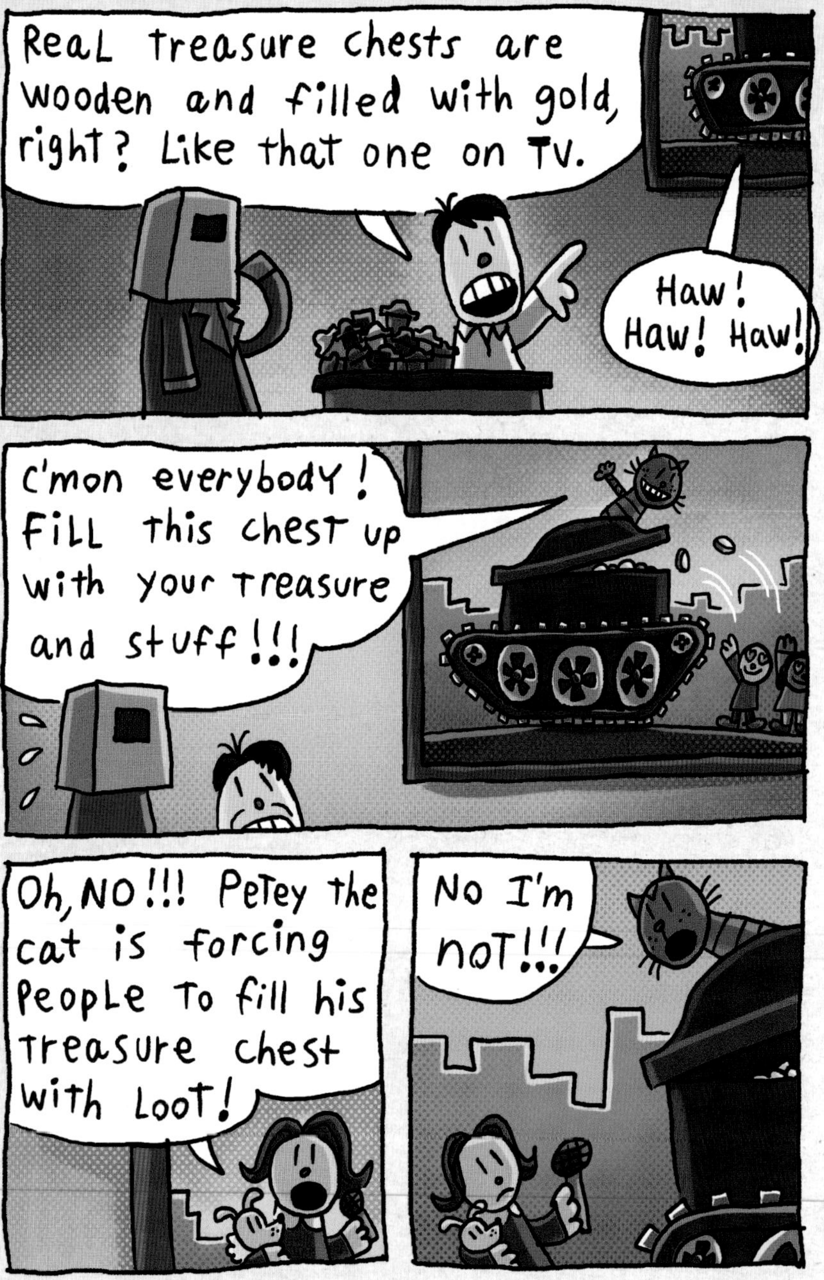
Real treasure chests are wooden and filled with gold, right? Like that one on TV.
Haw! Haw! Haw!
C'mon everybody! Fill this chest up with your treasure and stuff!!!
Oh, NO!!! Petey the cat is forcing people to fill his treasure chest with loot!
No I'm not!!!

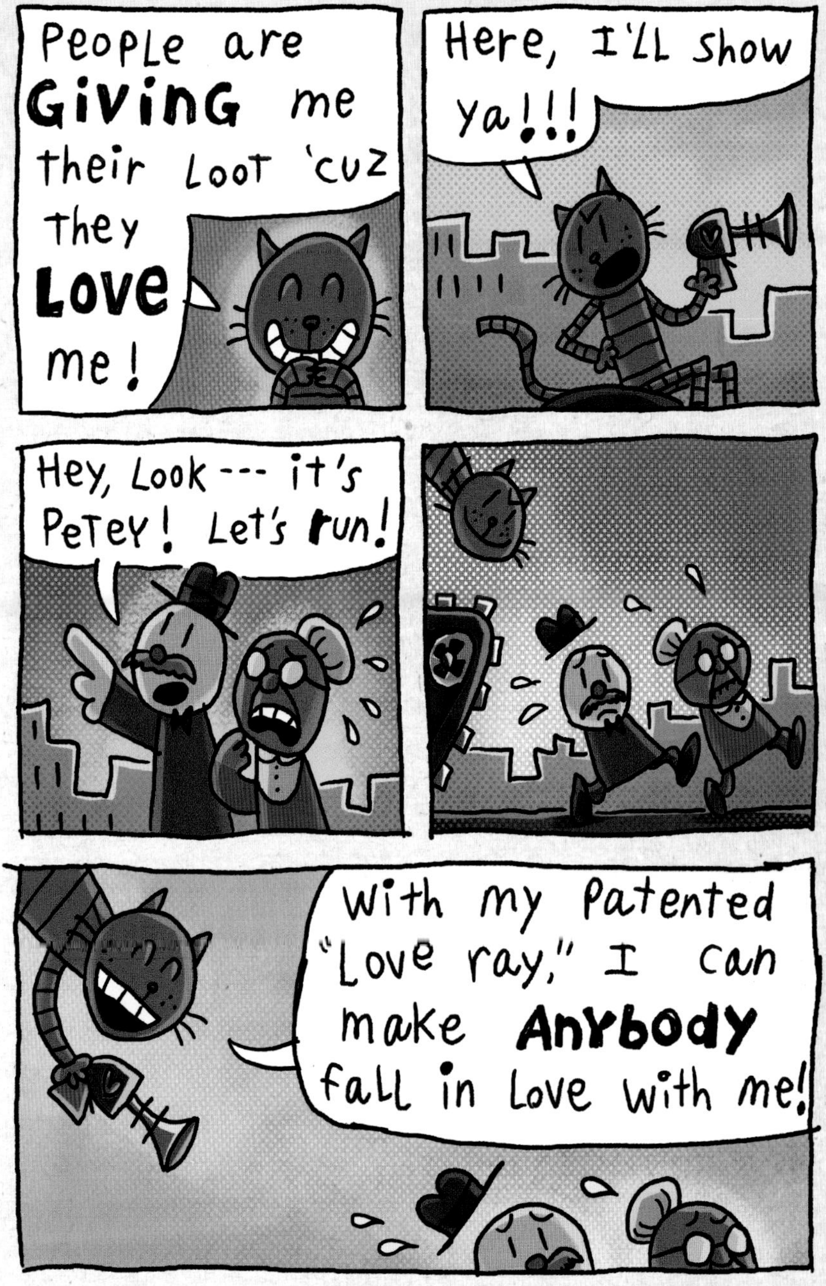
People are GIVING me their Loot 'cuz they LOVE me!
Here, I'LL show ya!!!
Hey, Look --- it's Petey! Let's run!
With my Patented "Love ray," I can make ANYBODY fall in Love with me!

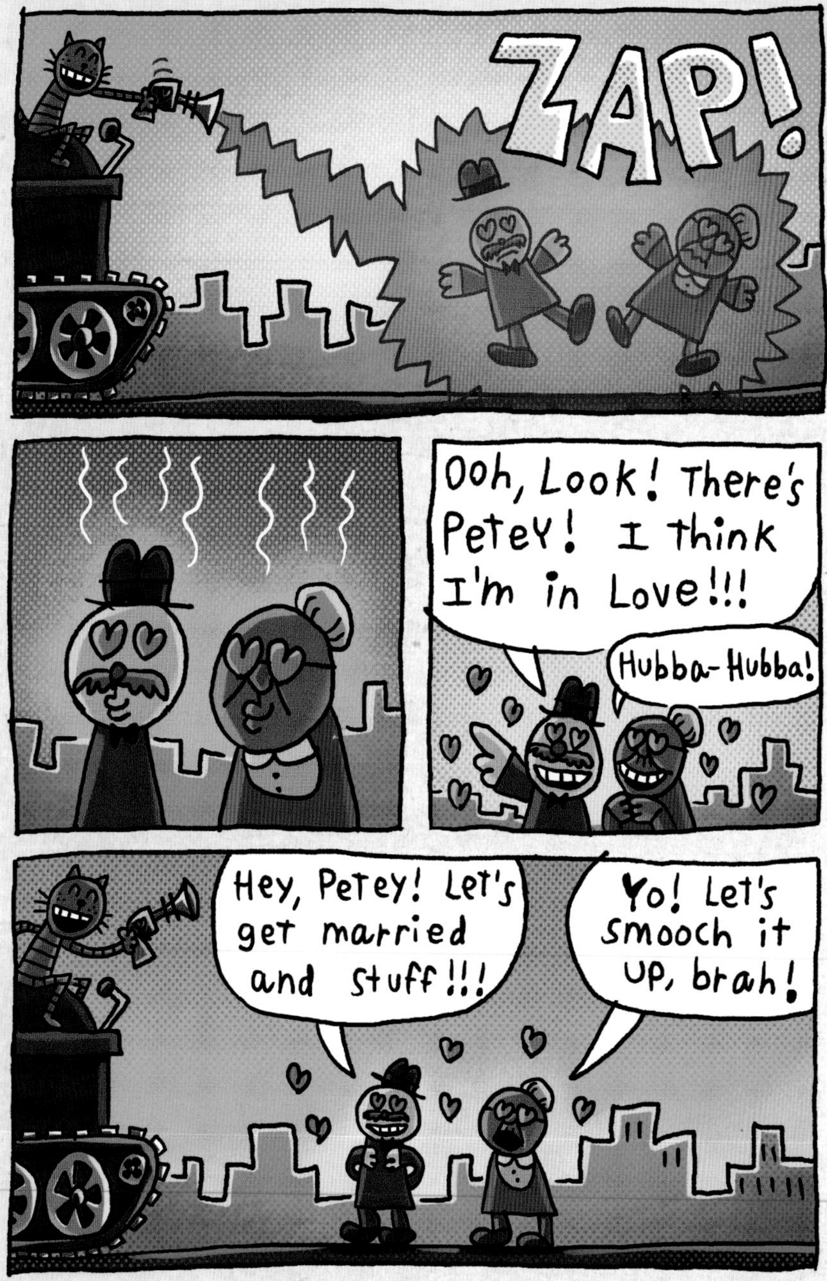
ZAP!
Ooh, Look! There's Petey! I think I'm in Love!!!
Hubba-Hubba!
Hey, Petey! Let's get married and stuff!!!
Yo! Let's smooch it up, brah!

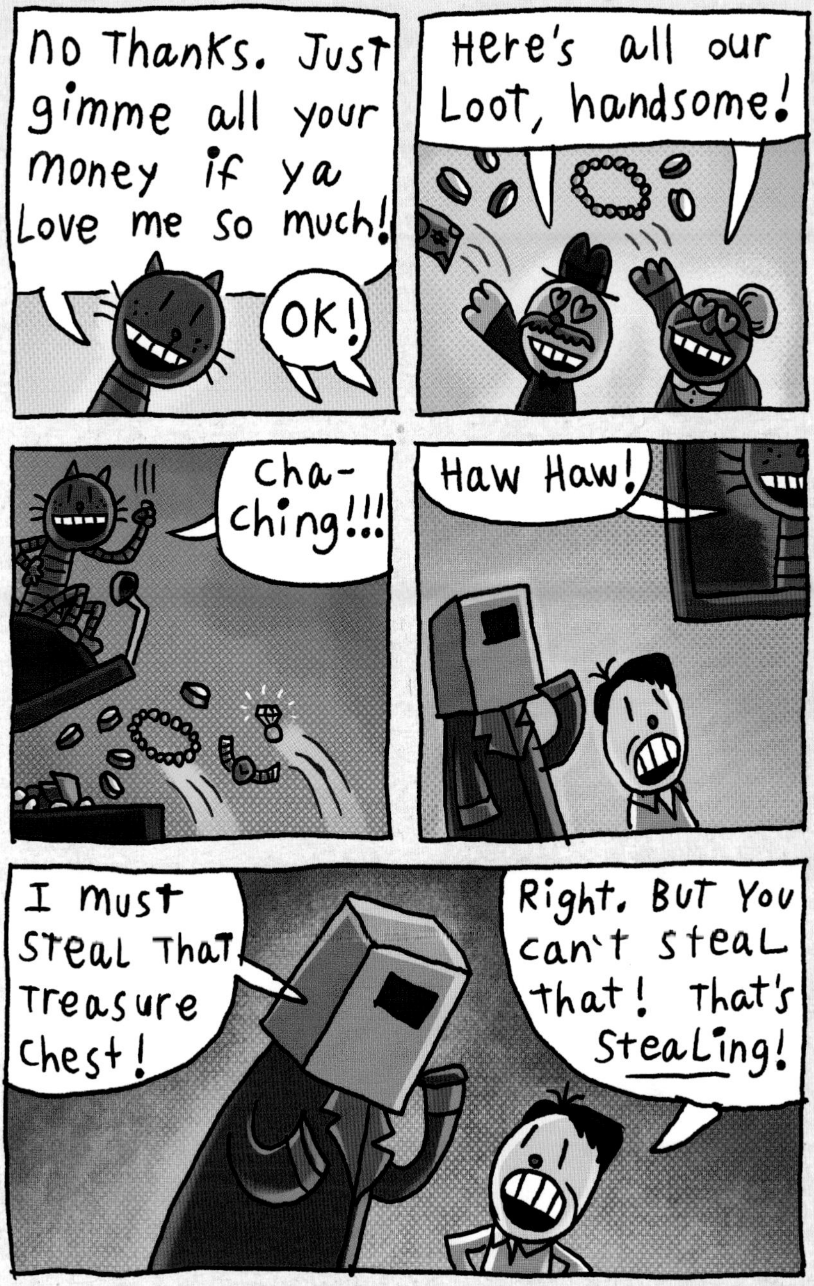
No Thanks. Just gimme all your money if ya Love me so much!
OK!
Here's all our Loot, handsome!
Cha-ching!!!
Haw Haw!
I must steal that treasure chest!
Right. But you can't steal that! That's stealing!

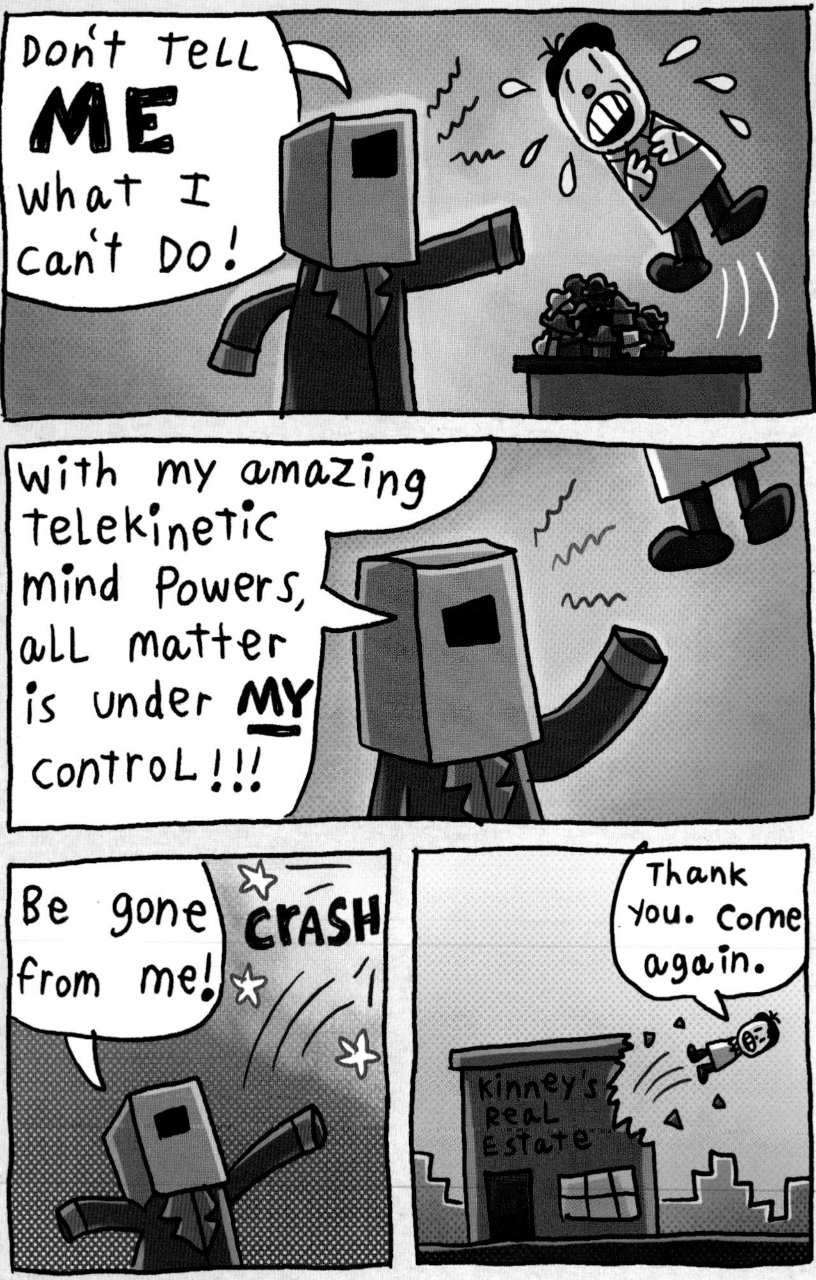
Don't TeLL
ME
what I
can't Do!
with my amazing
teLekinetic
mind Powers,
aLL matter
is under MY
controL!!!
Be gone
from me!
CRASH
Thank
You. Come
again.
Kinney's
ReaL
Estate

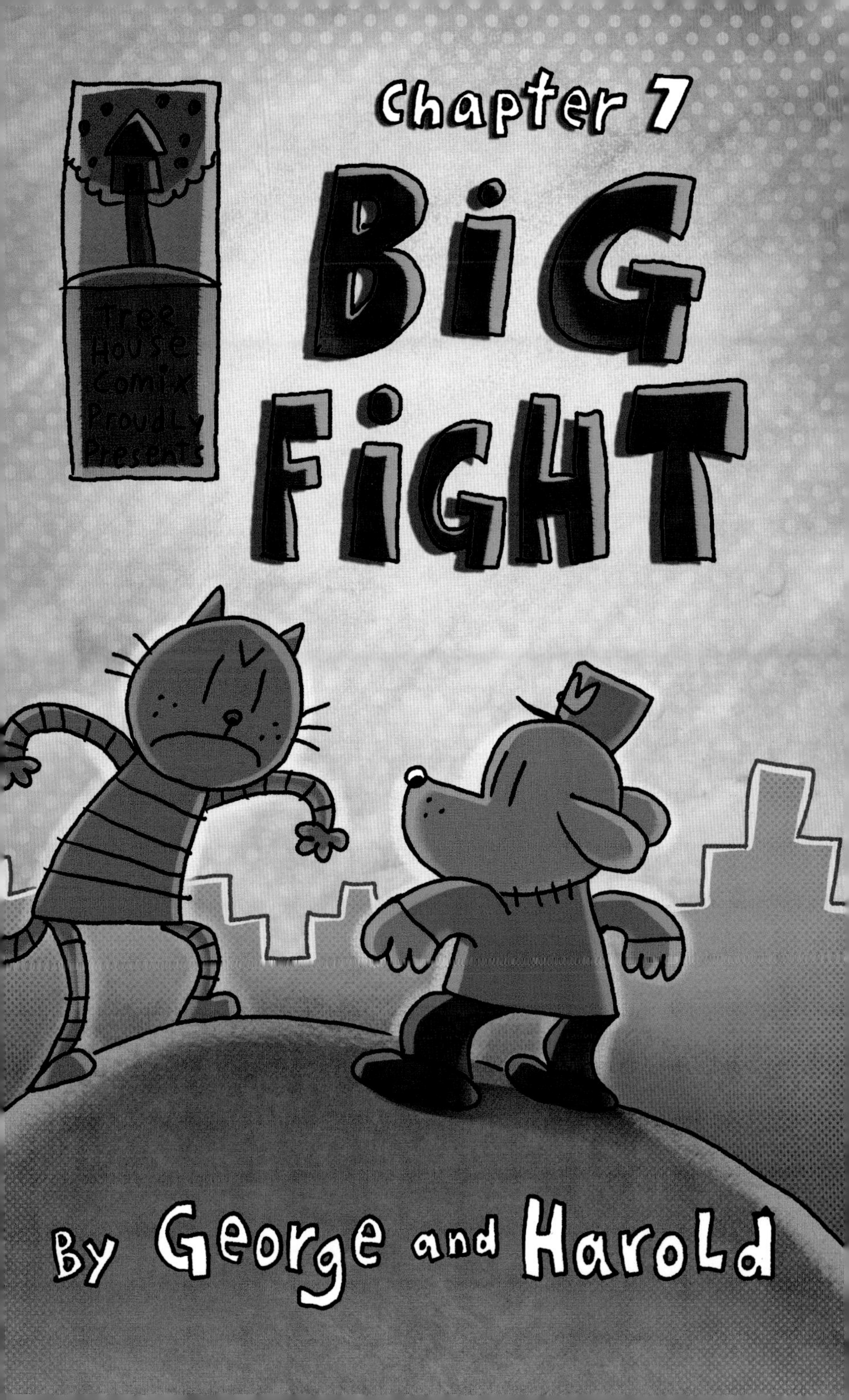
Tree House Comix Proudly Presents
Chapter 7
BiG FiGHT
By George and Harold

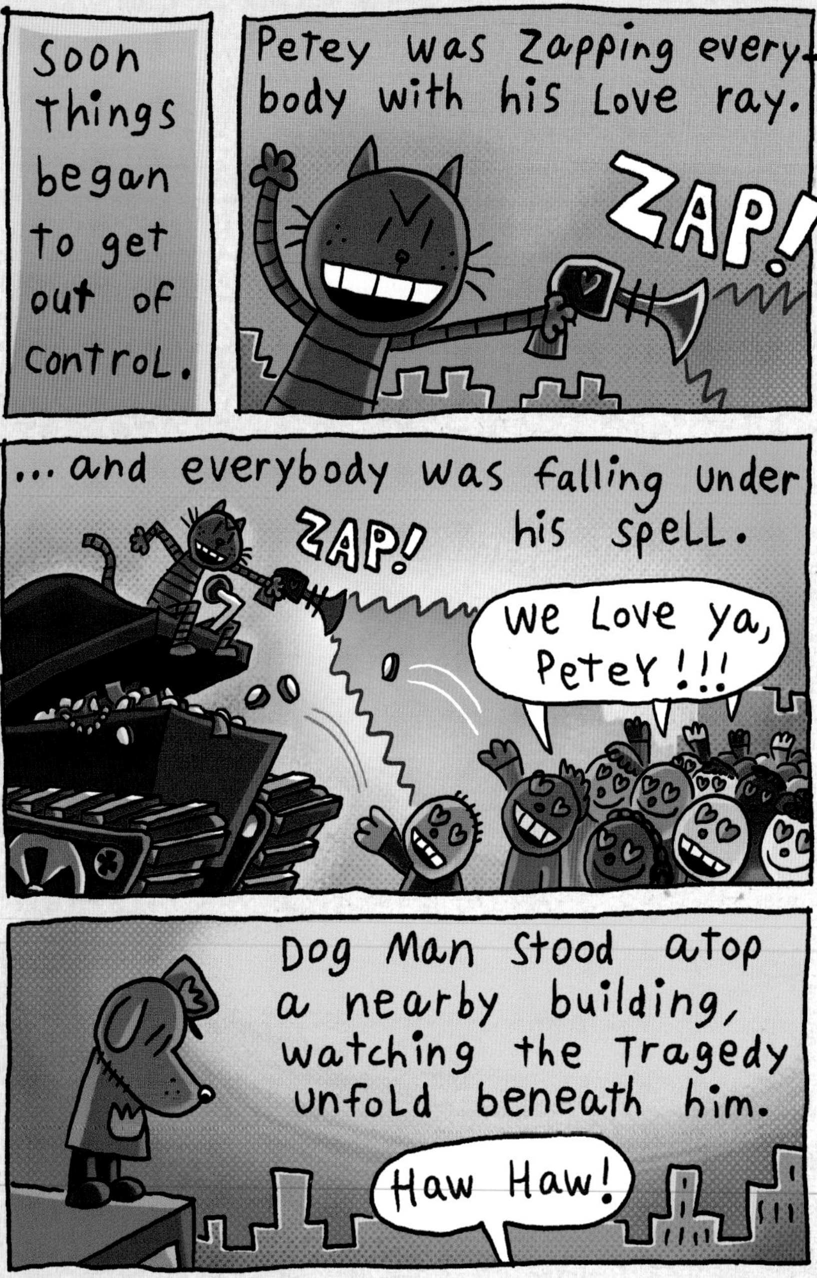
Soon things began to get out of control.
Petey was zapping every-body with his love ray.
ZAP!
...and everybody was falling under his spell.
ZAP!
We love ya, Petey!!!
Dog Man stood atop a nearby building, watching the tragedy unfold beneath him.
Haw Haw!

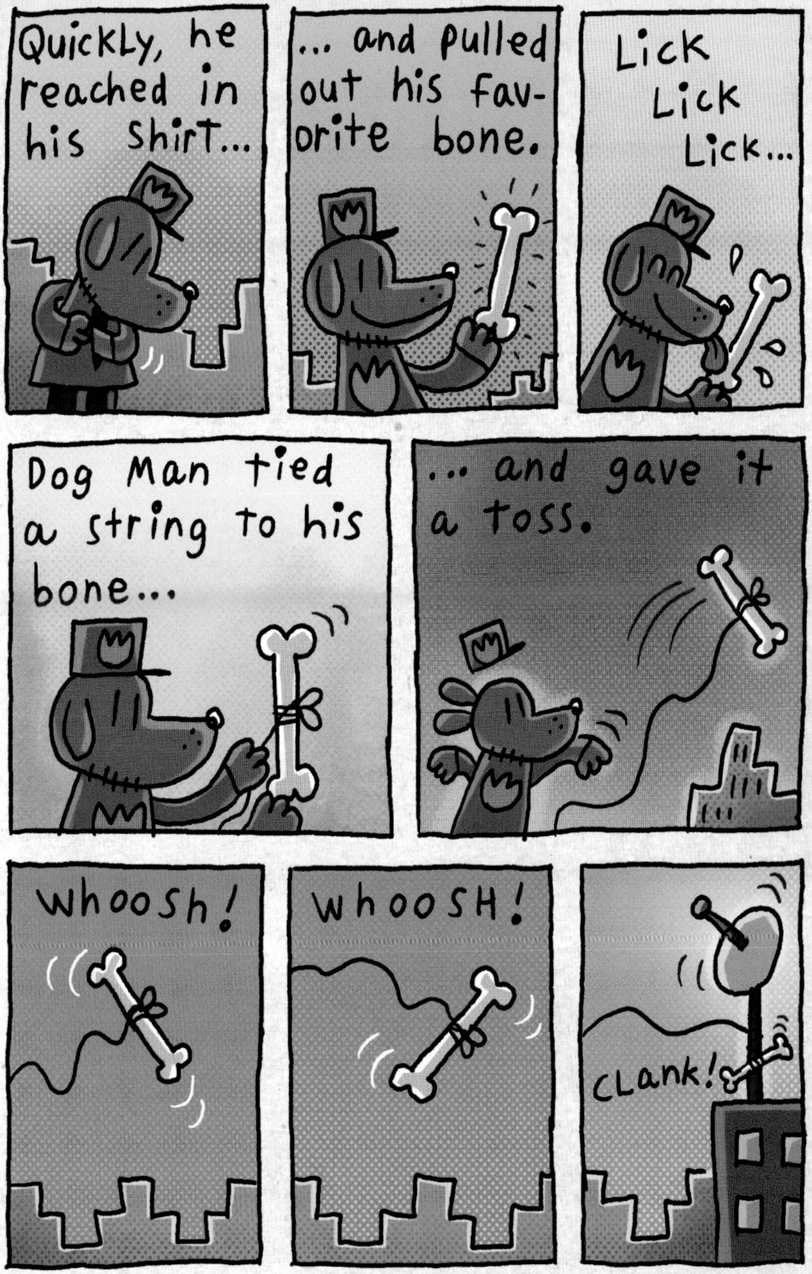
Quickly, he reached in his Shirt...
... and pulled out his favorite bone.
Lick Lick Lick...
Dog Man tied a string to his bone...
... and gave it a toss.
whoosh!
whooSH!
cLank!

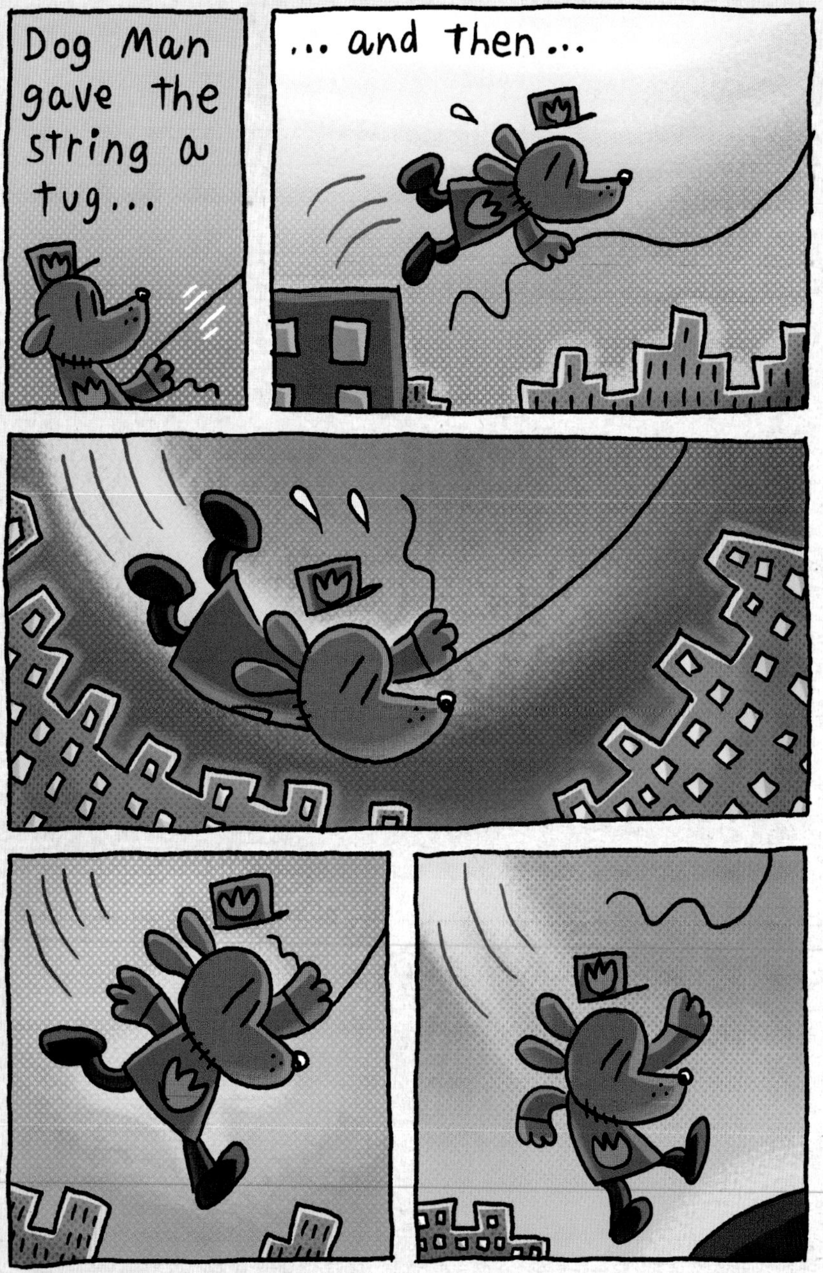
Dog Man gave the string a tug...
... and then...

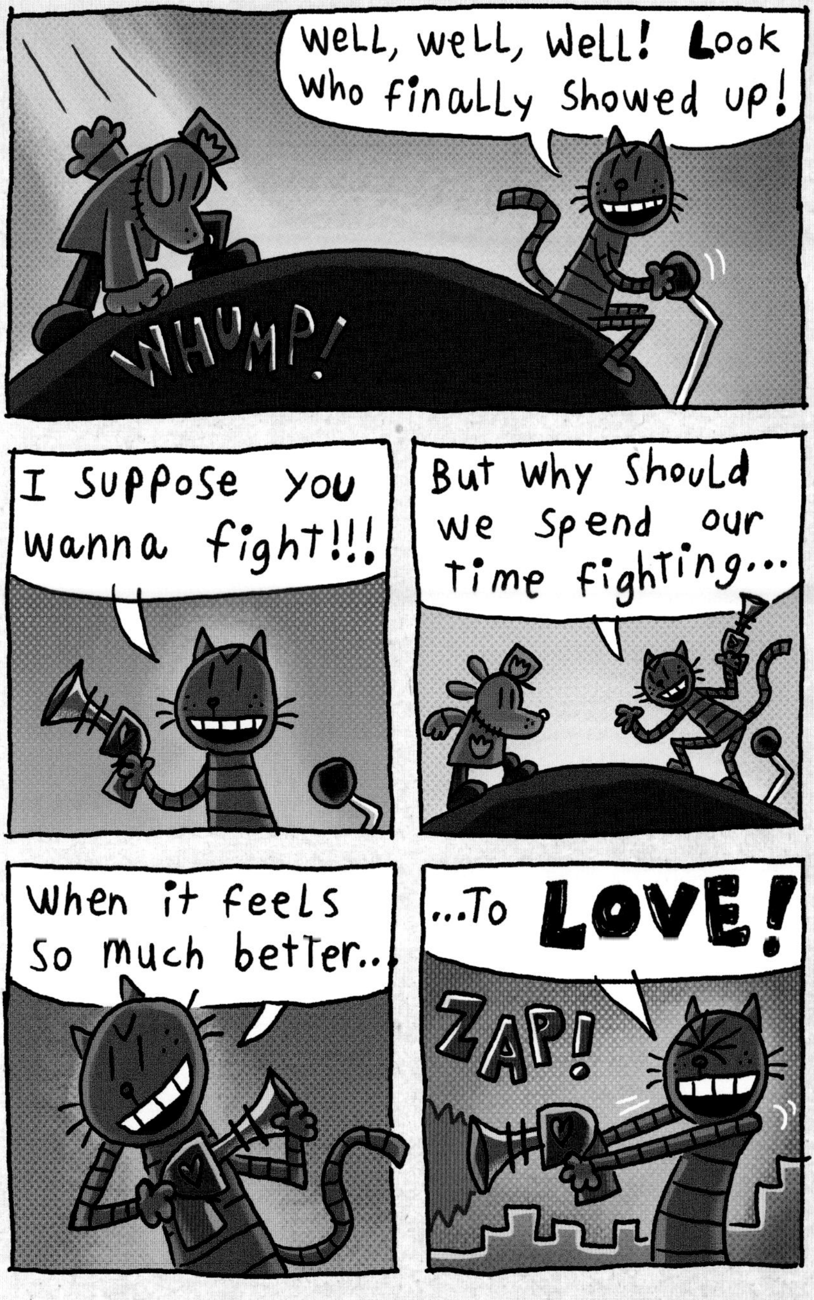
WELL, WELL, WELL! LOOK WHO FINALLY SHOWED UP!
WHUMP!
I SUPPOSE YOU WANNA FIGHT!!!
BUT WHY SHOULD WE SPEND OUR TIME FIGHTING...
WHEN IT FEELS SO MUCH BETTER...
...TO LOVE!
ZAP!

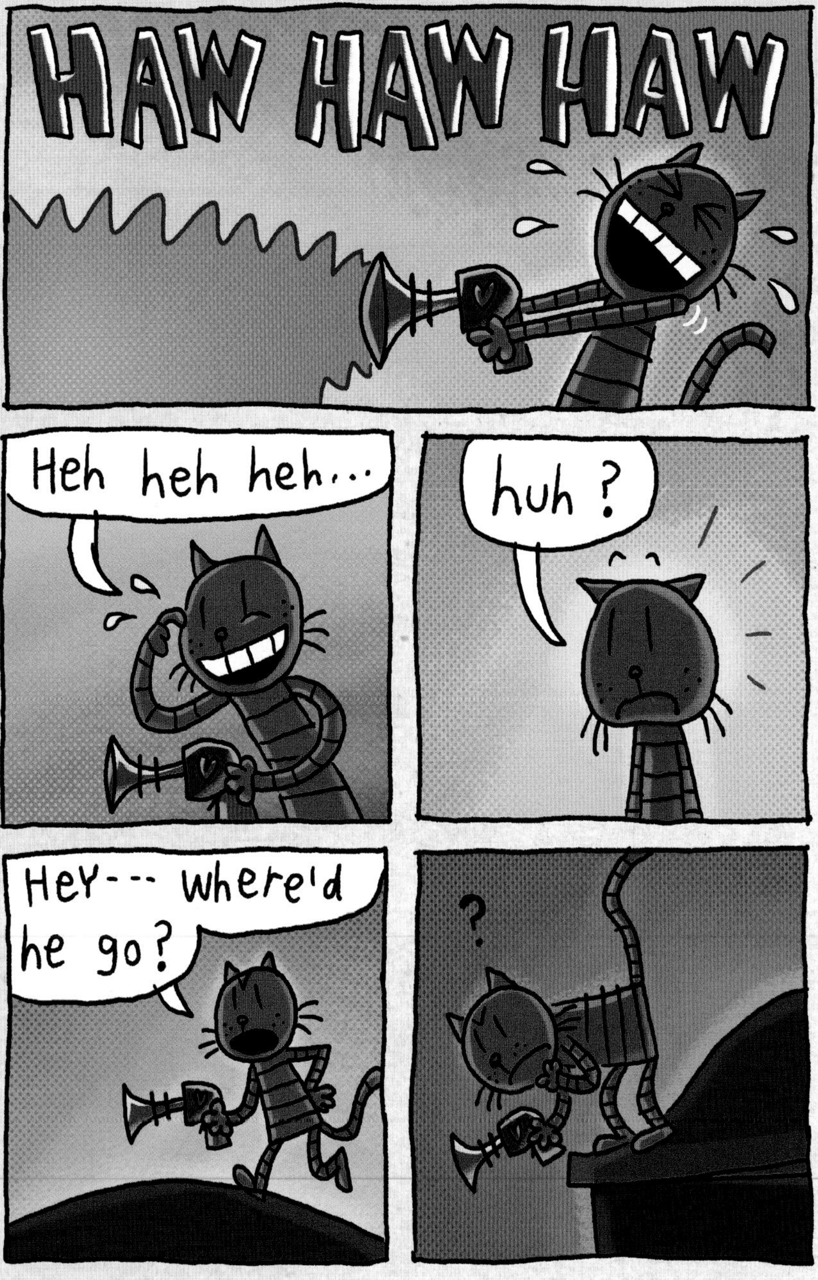
HAW HAW HAW
Heh heh heh...
huh ?
Hey--- where'd he go?
?

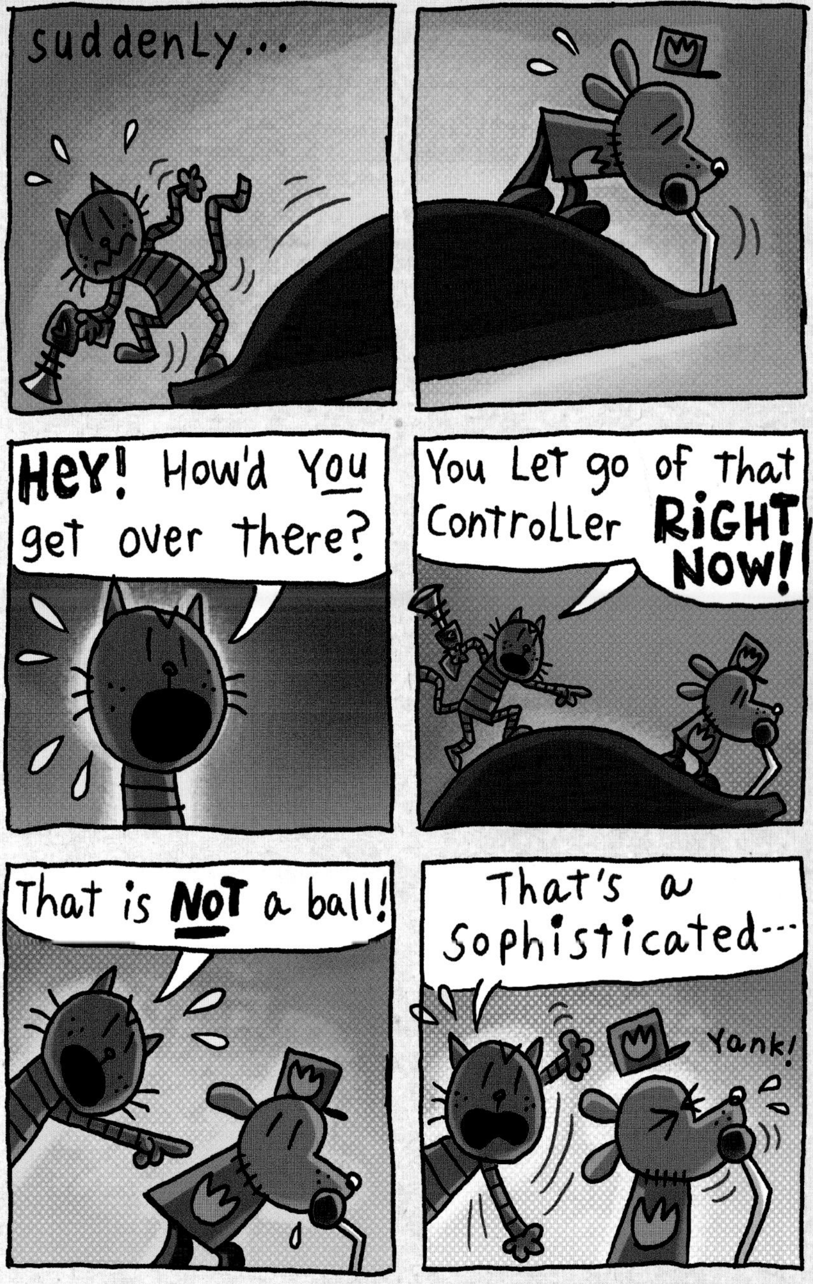
suddenLy...
HEY! How'd You get over there?
You Let go of that Controller RIGHT NOW!
That is NOT a ball!
That's a Sophisticated...
Yank!

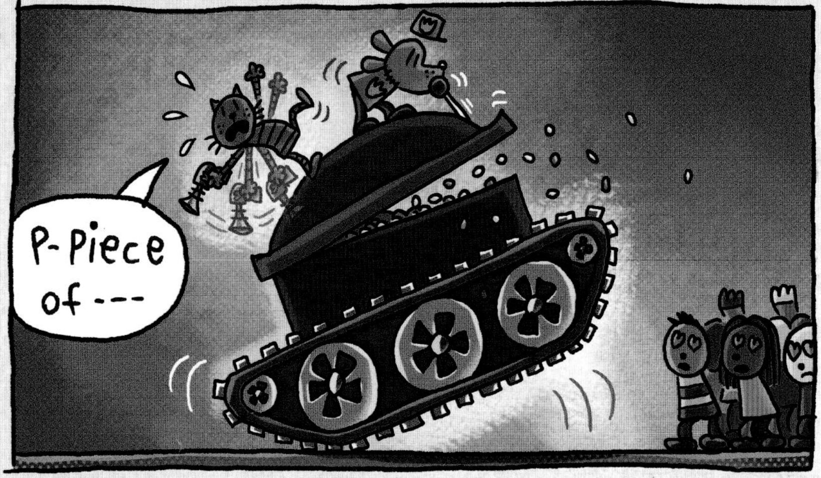
P-Piece of ---

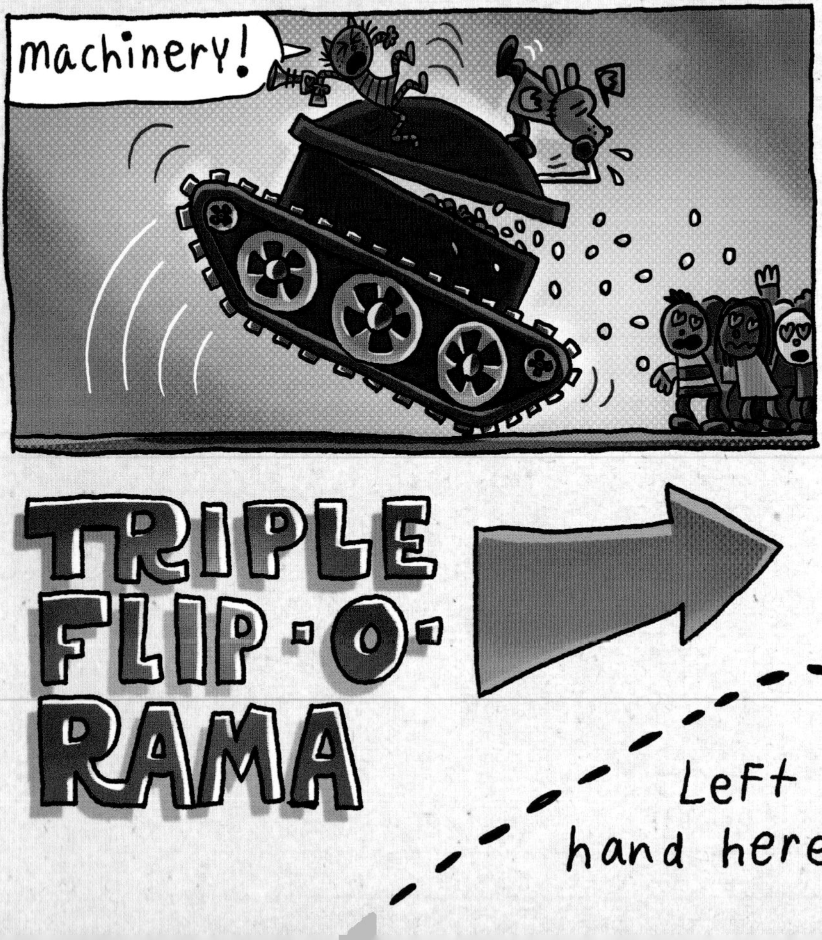
machinery!

TRIPLE FLIP-O-RAMA

Left hand here.

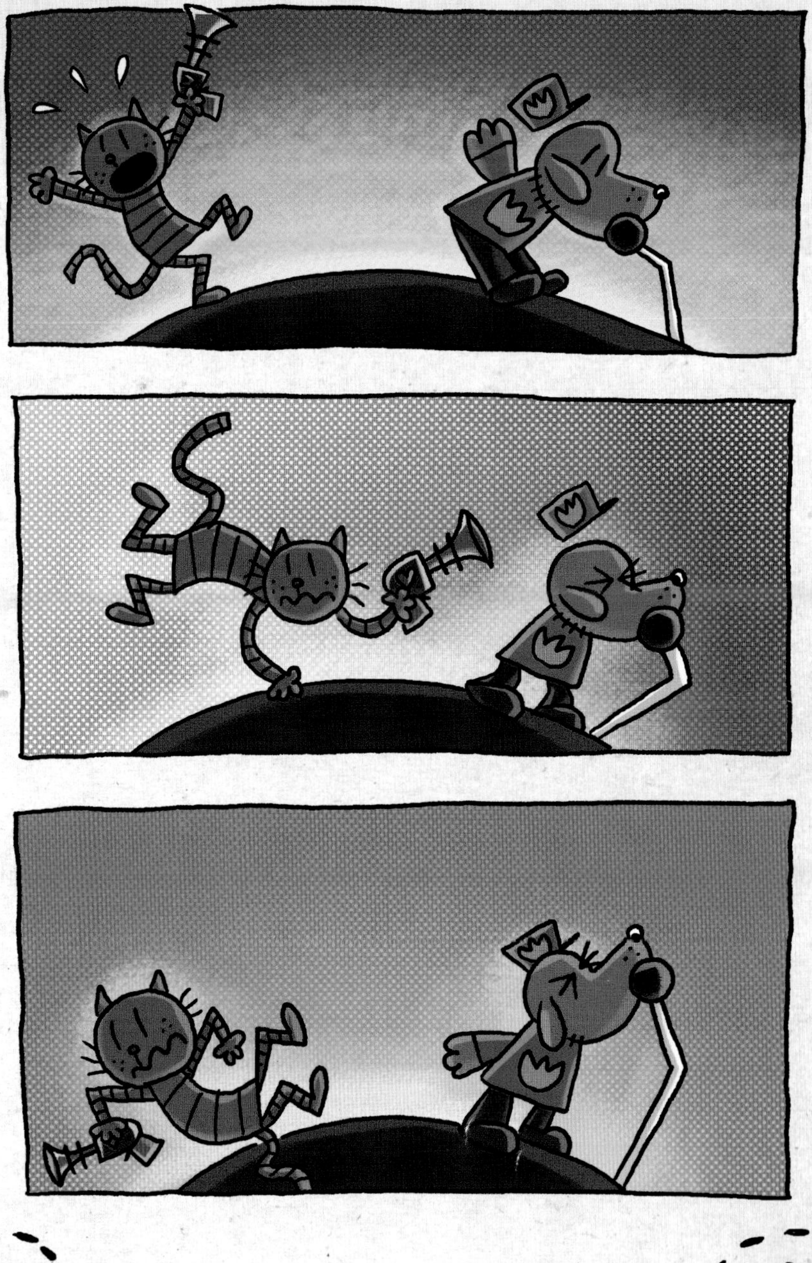

Right Thumb here.

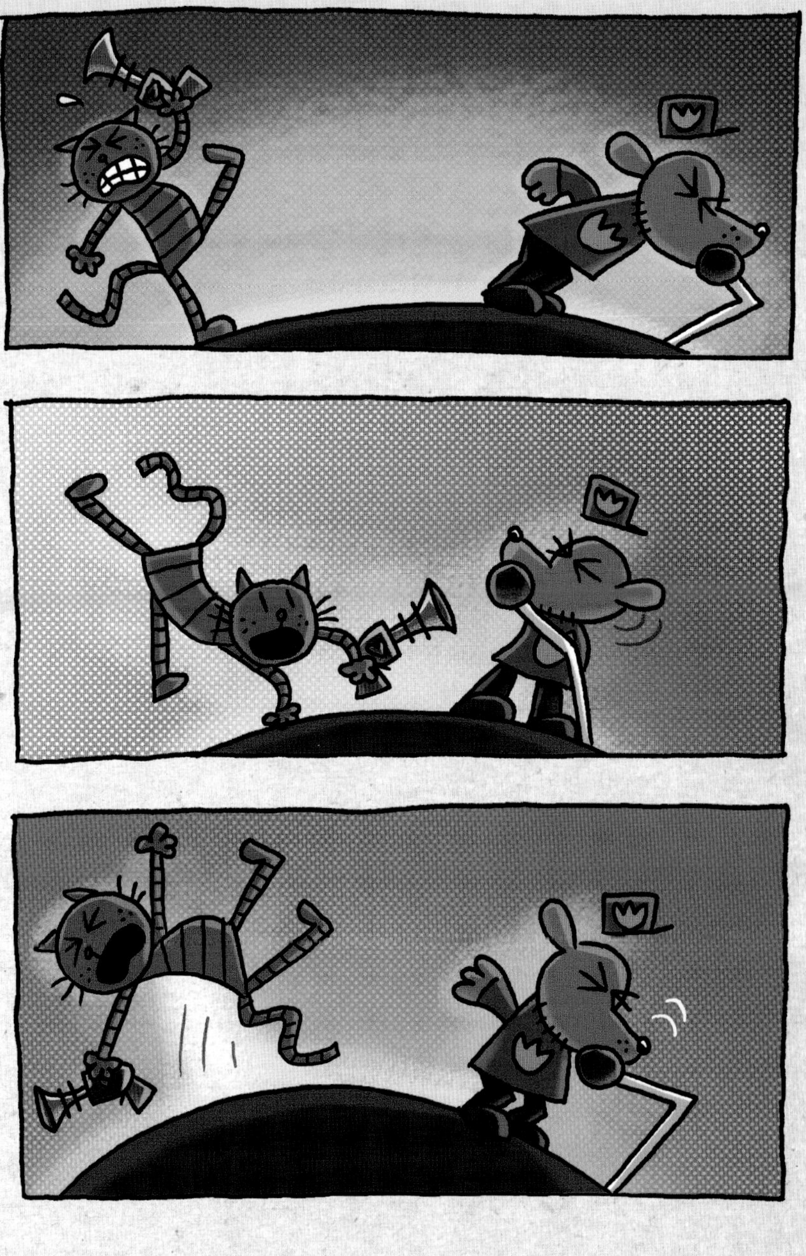

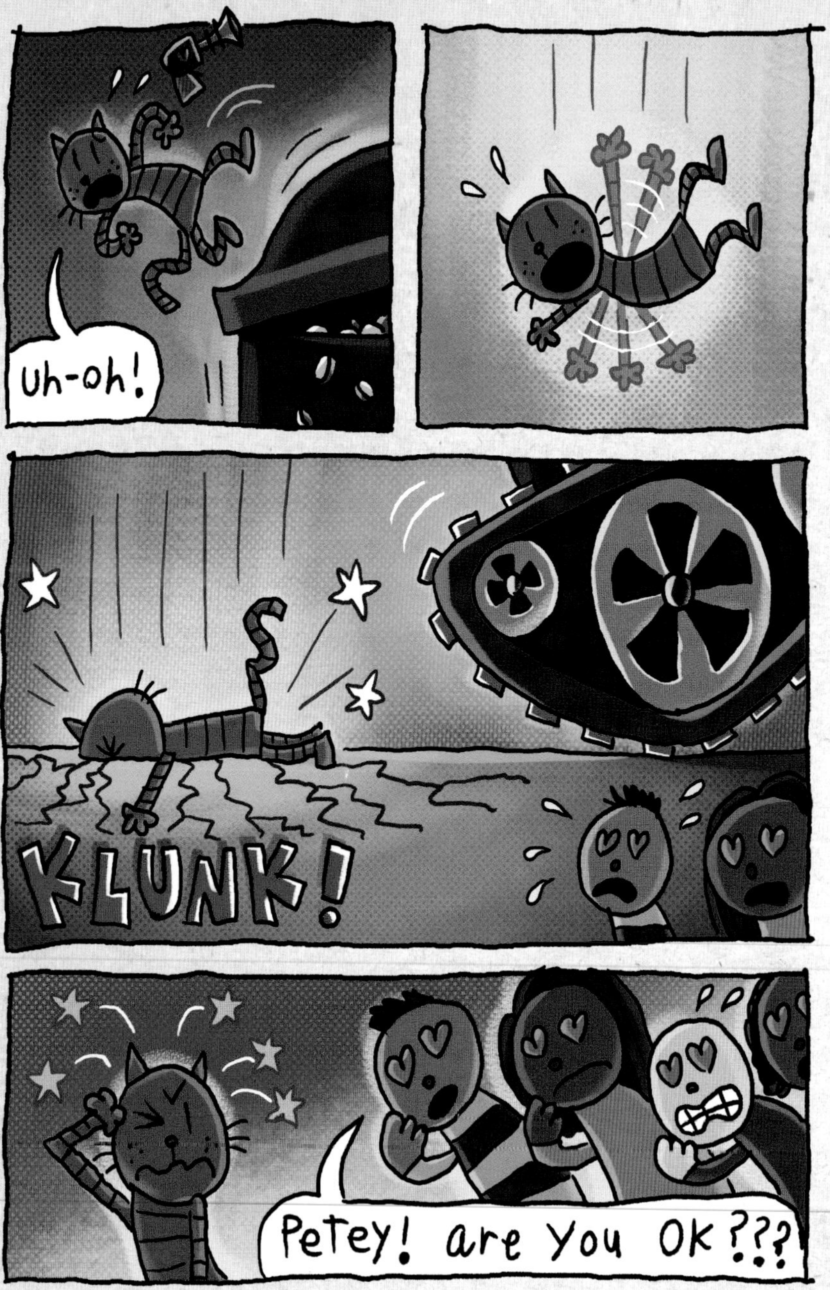
Uh-oh!
KLUNK!
Petey! are You OK???

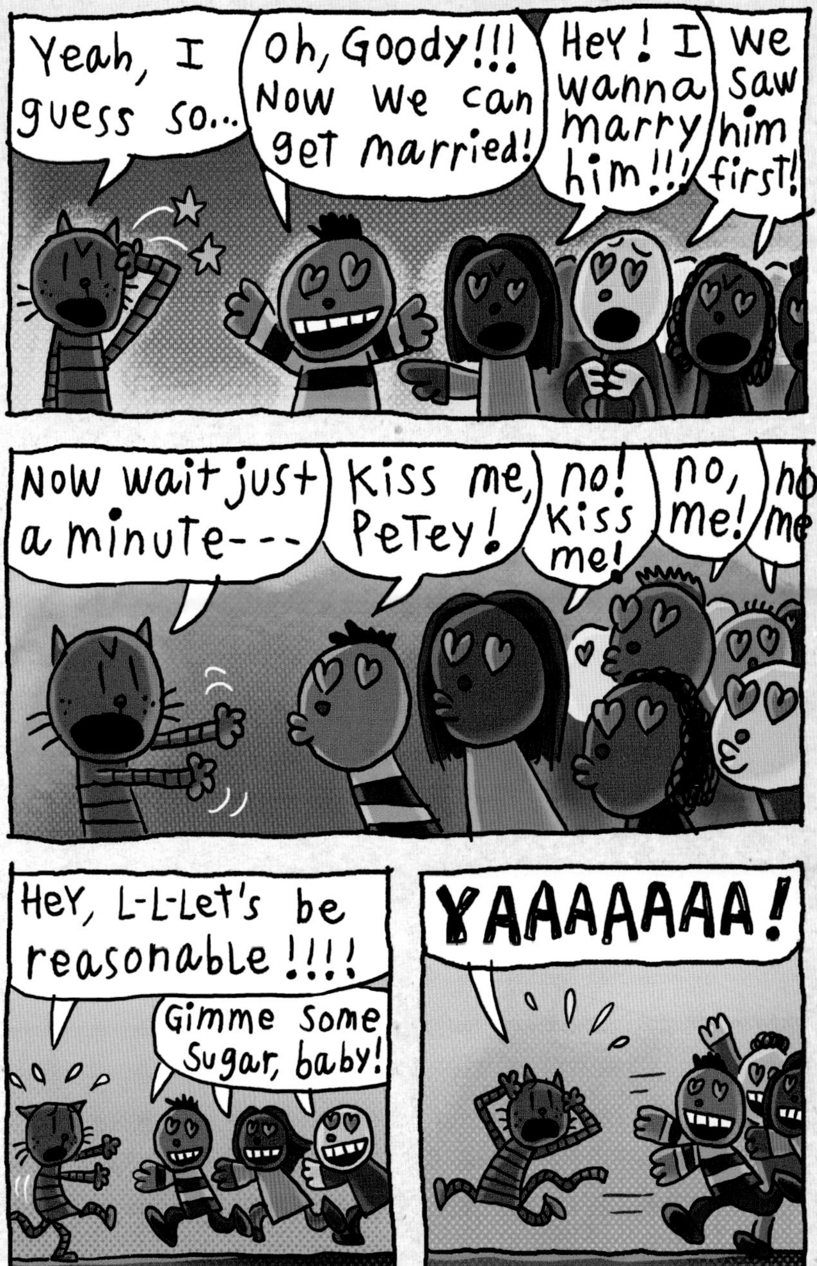
Yeah, I guess so...
Oh, Goody!!! Now we can get married!
Hey! I wanna marry him!!!
We saw him first!
Now wait just a minute---
Kiss me, Petey!
no! Kiss me!
no, me!
no me
Hey, L-L-Let's be reasonable!!!!
Gimme some sugar, baby!
YAAAAAAA!

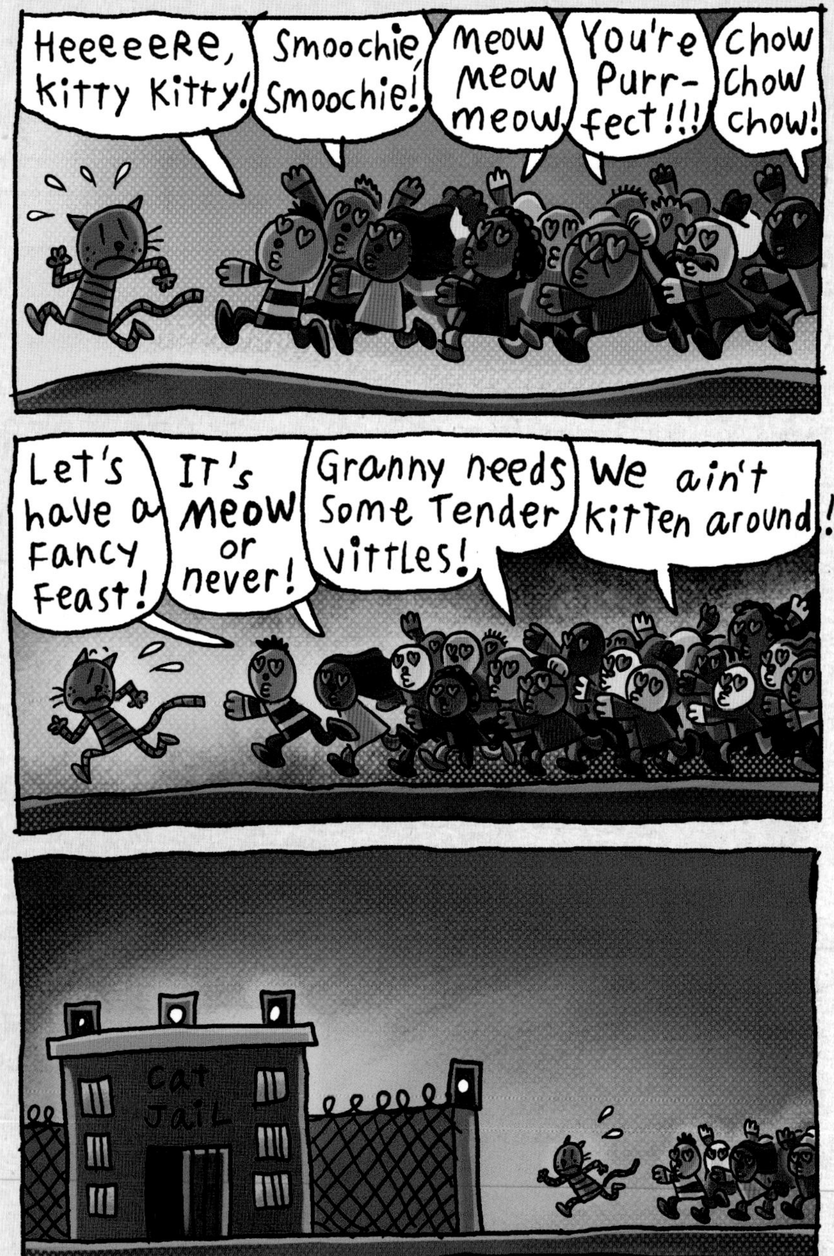
Heeeeere, kitty kitty!
Smoochie, Smoochie!
Meow meow meow
You're purr-fect!!!
Chow chow chow!
Let's have a Fancy Feast!
It's MEOW or never!
Granny needs some Tender Vittles!
We ain't kitten around!
Cat Jail

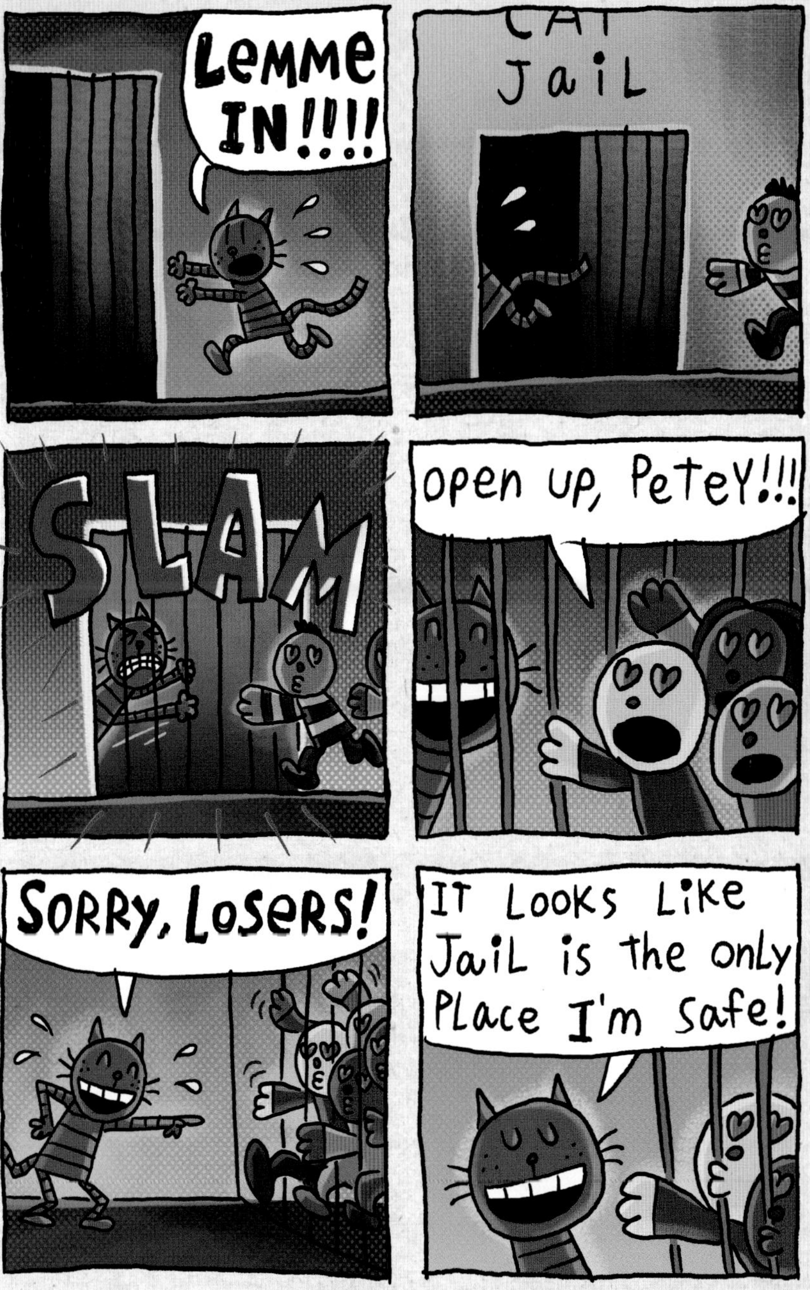
LEMME IN!!!!
CAT JAIL
SLAM
OPEN UP, PETEY!!!
SORRY, LOSERS!
IT LOOKS LIKE JAIL IS THE ONLY PLACE I'M SAFE!

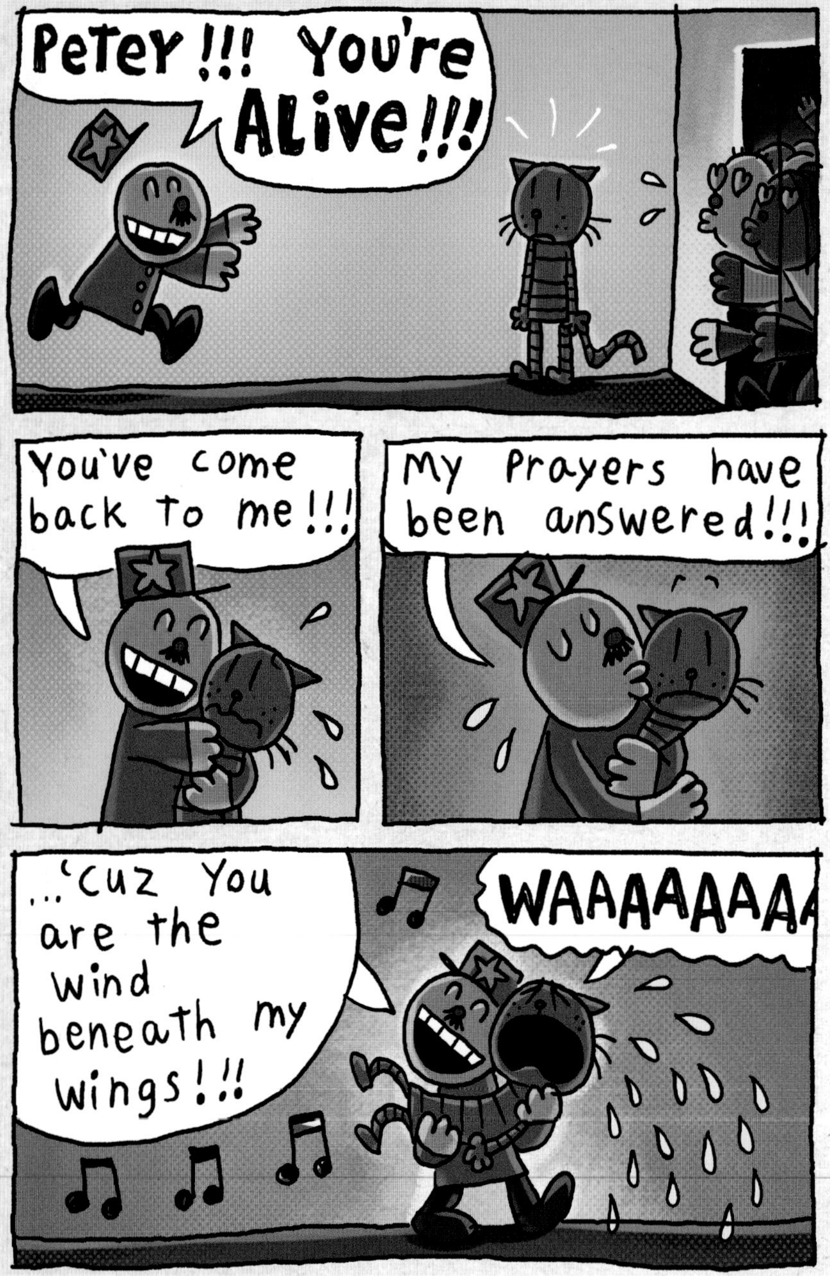
PETEY!!! You're ALIVE!!!
You've come back to me!!!
My Prayers have been answered!!!
...'cuz You are the wind beneath my wings!!!
WAAAAAAA

Chapter 8

FLAT CAT FEVER

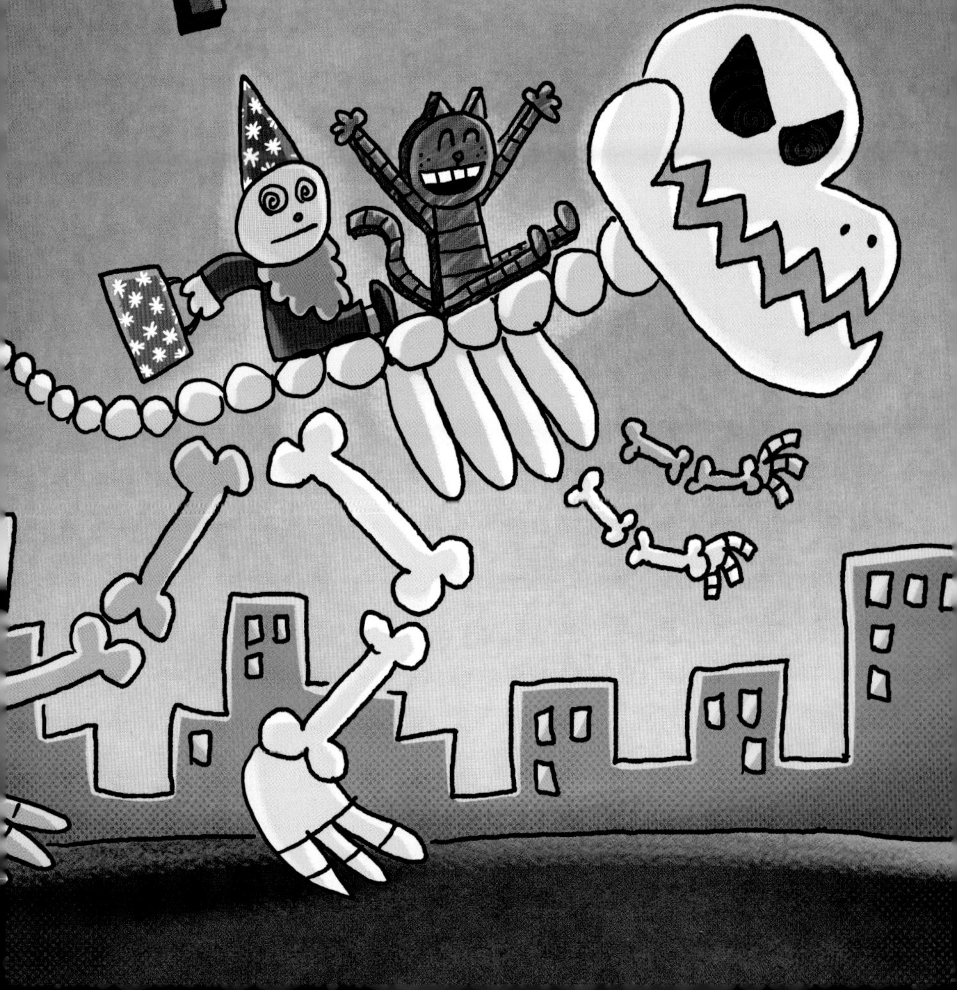

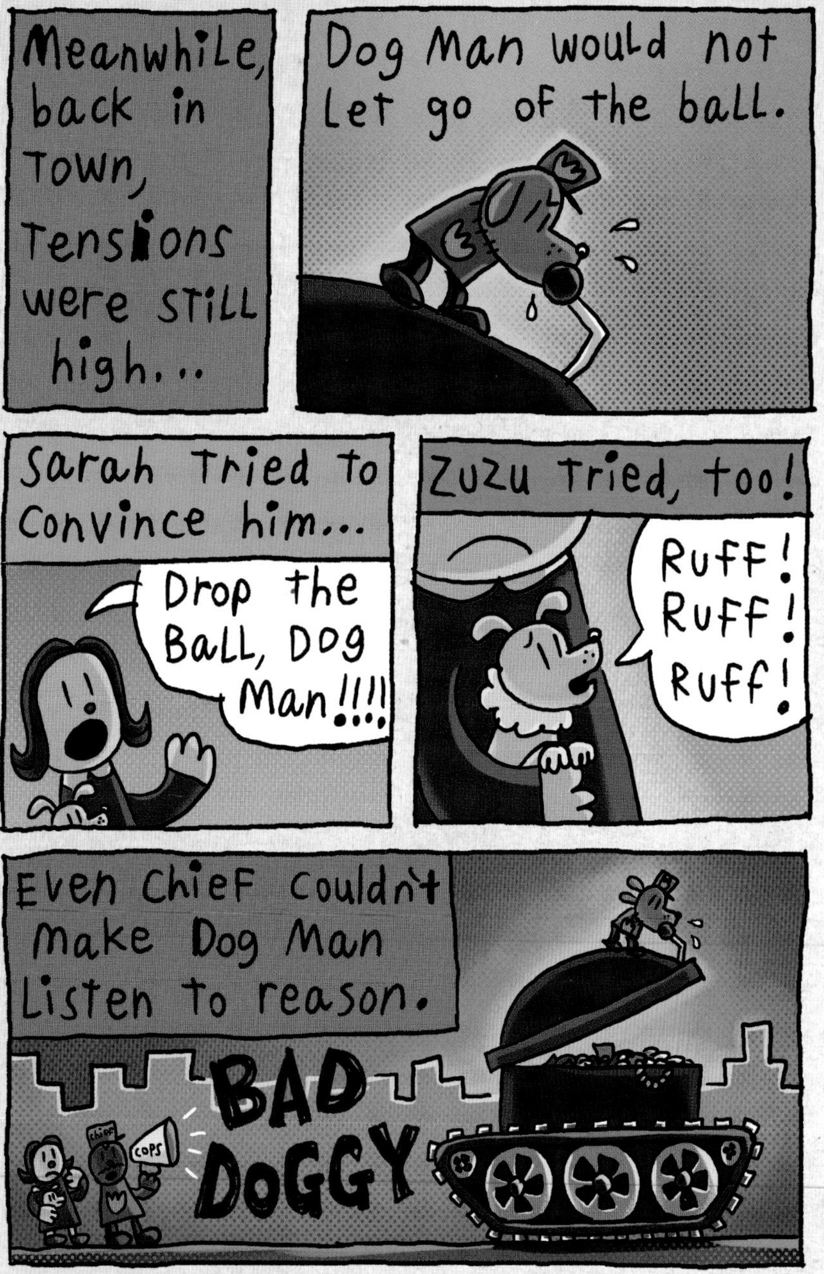
Meanwhile, back in Town, Tensions were STILL high...
Dog Man would not Let go of the ball.
Sarah Tried to Convince him...
Drop the BaLL, Dog Man!!!!
Zuzu Tried, too!
Ruff! Ruff! Ruff!
Even Chief Couldn't make Dog Man Listen to reason.
Chief
COPS
BAD DOGGY

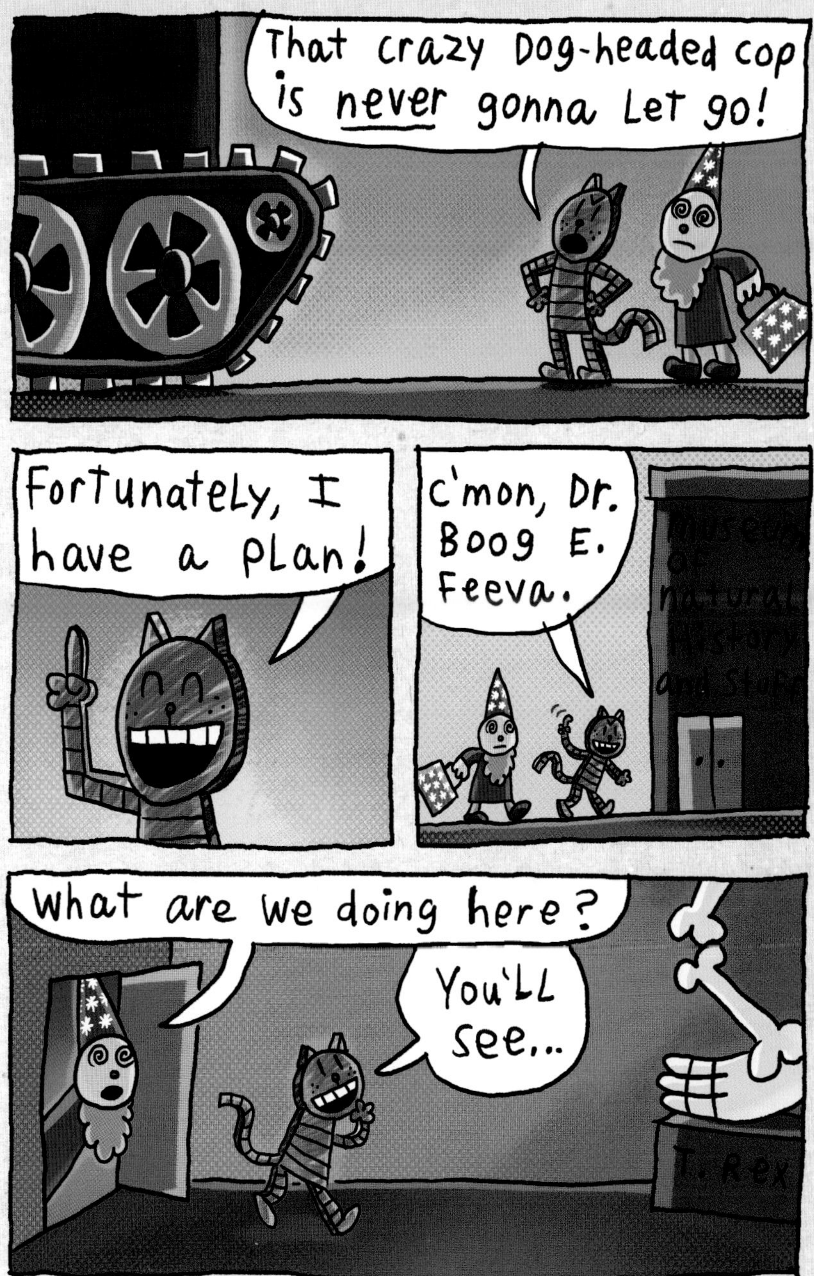
That crazy Dog-headed cop is never gonna Let go!
FortunateLy, I have a pLan!
c'mon, Dr. Boog E. Feeva.
What are we doing here?
You'LL see...
T. Rex

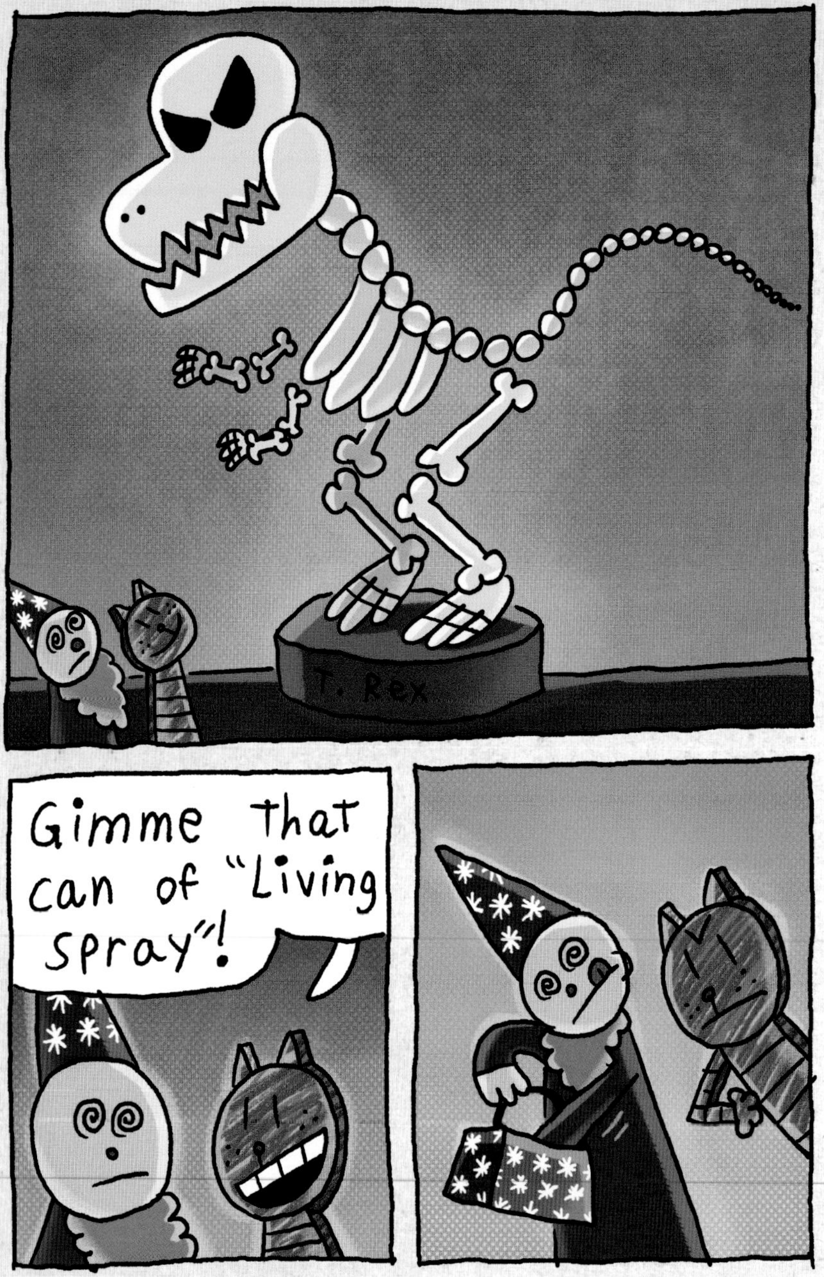
T. Rex
Gimme that can of "Living spray"!

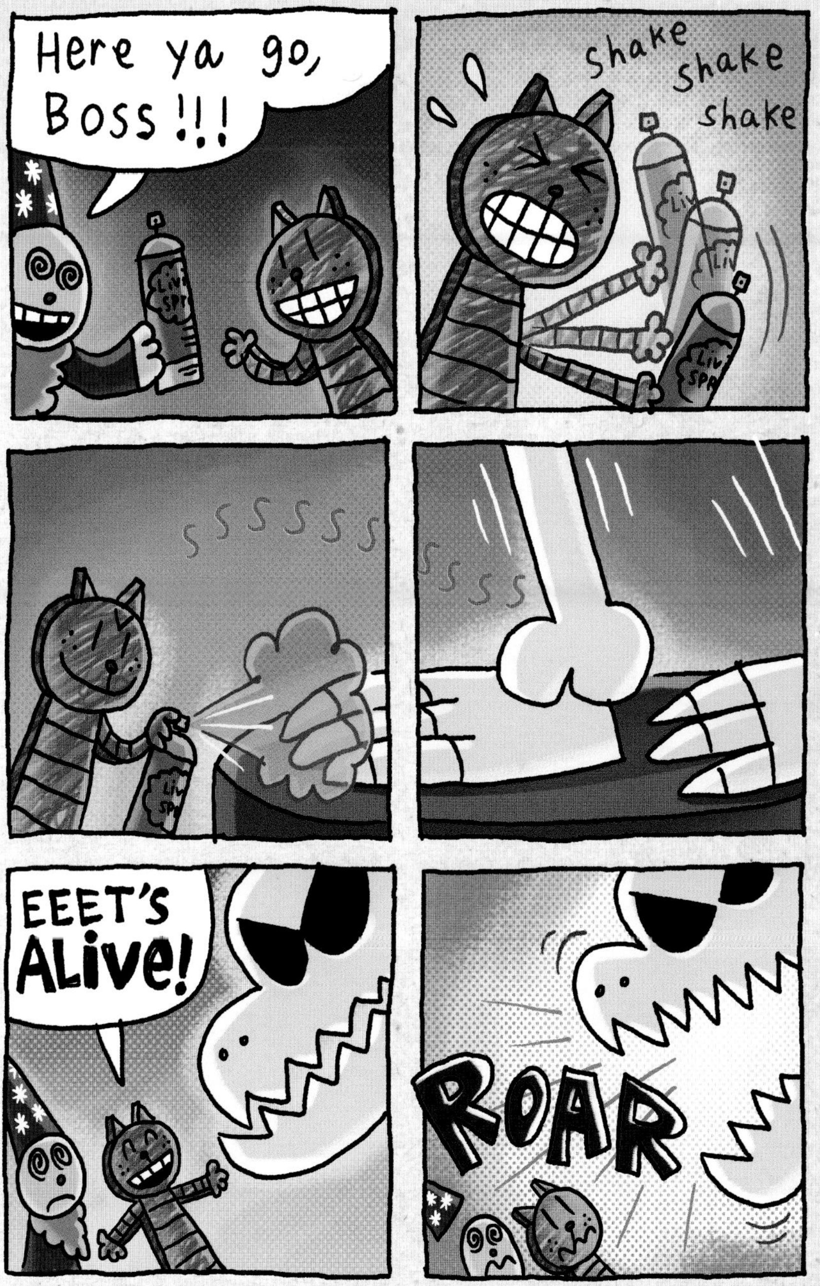
Here ya go, Boss!!!
shake shake shake
SSSSSS
SSSS
EEET'S ALive!
ROAR

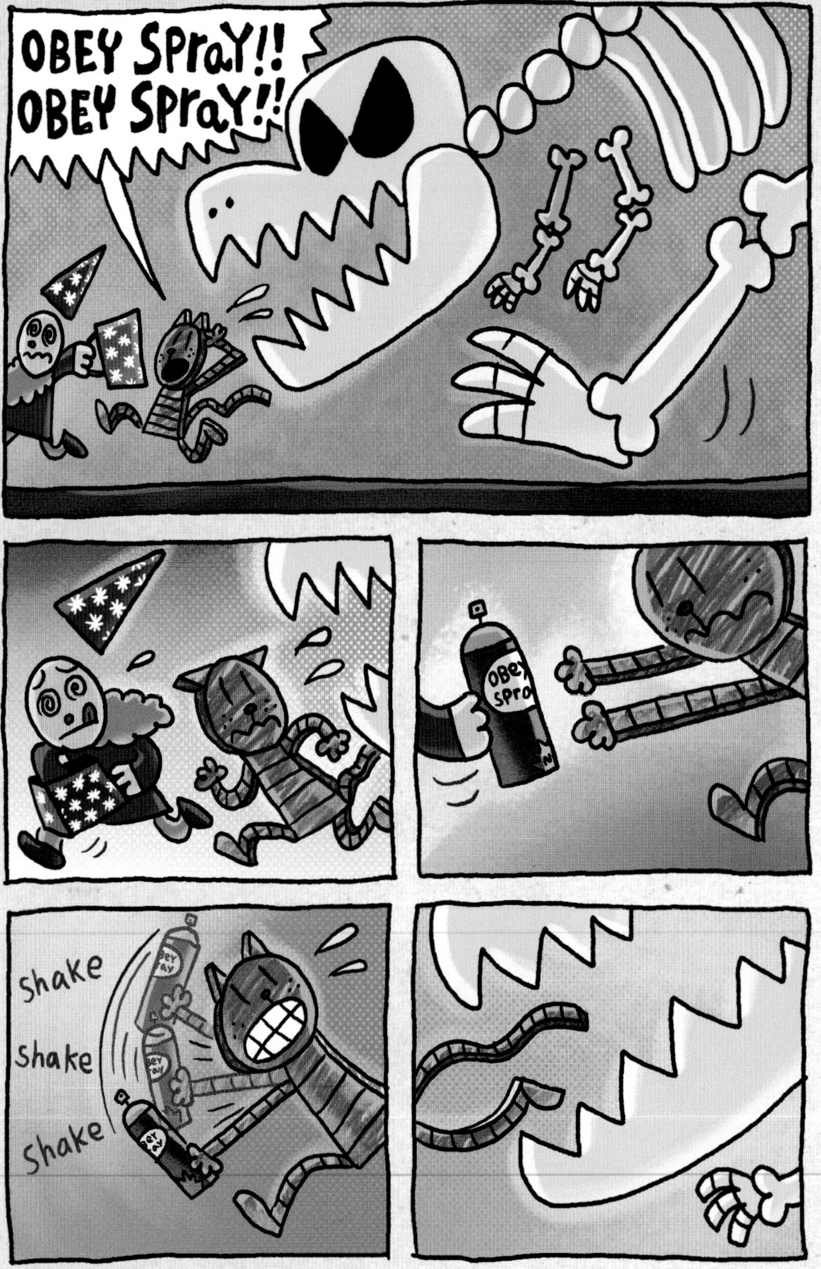
OBEY SPRAY!! OBEY SPRAY!!
OBEY SPRA
Shake
Shake
Shake

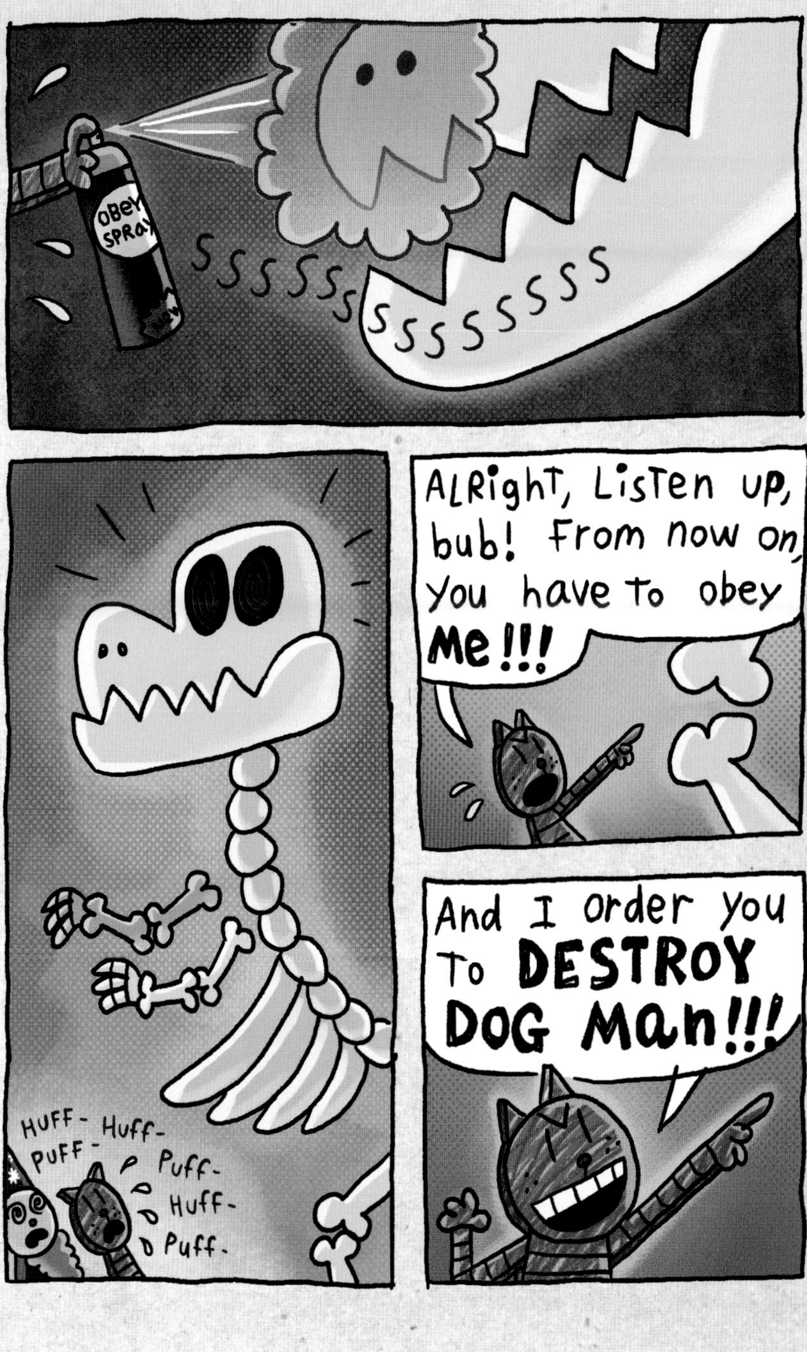
OBEY SPRAY
SSSSSSSSSSSSSSSSS
ALRight, LisTen up, bub! From now on, You have To obey Me!!!
HUFF- PUFF-
Huff- Puff- Huff- Puff-
And I order you To DESTROY DOG Man!!!

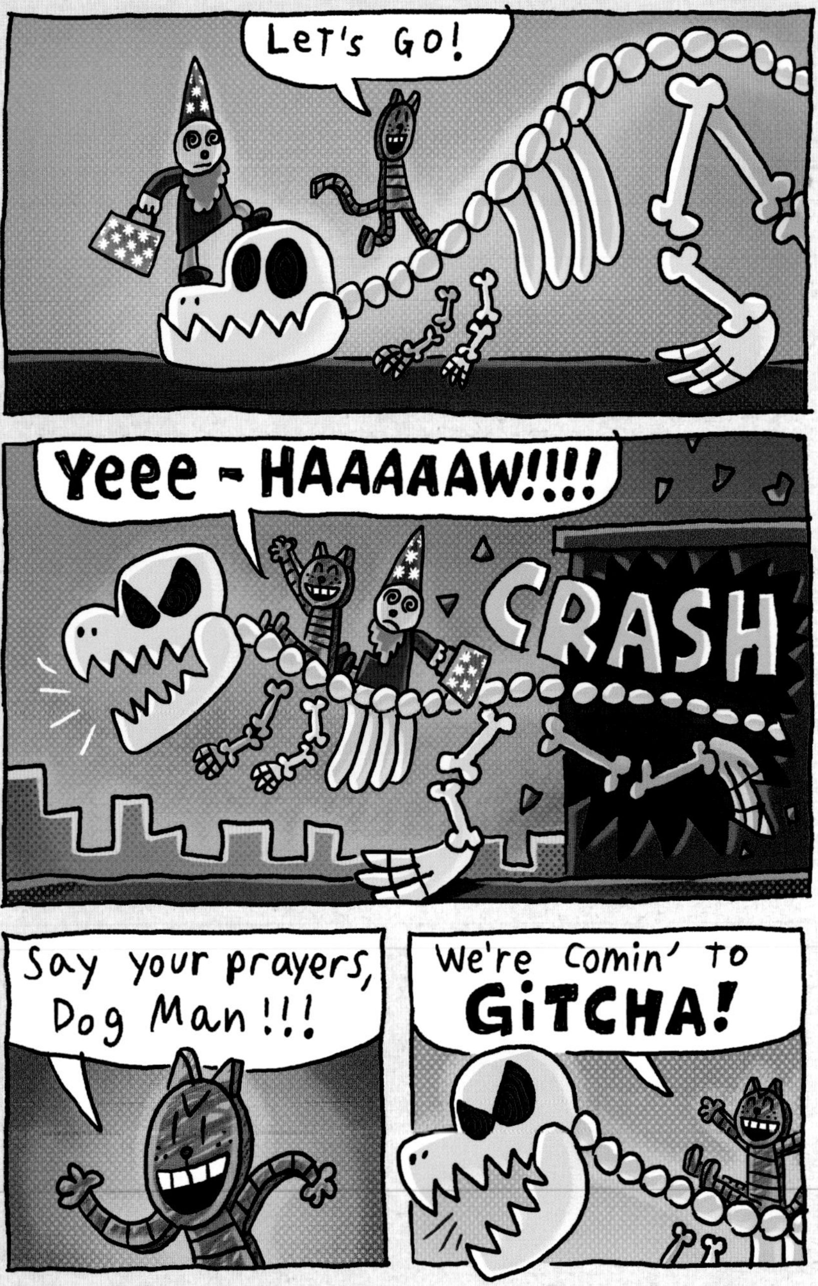
Let's GO!
Yeee - HAAAAAW!!!!
CRASH
Say your prayers, Dog Man!!!
We're Comin' to GiTCHA!

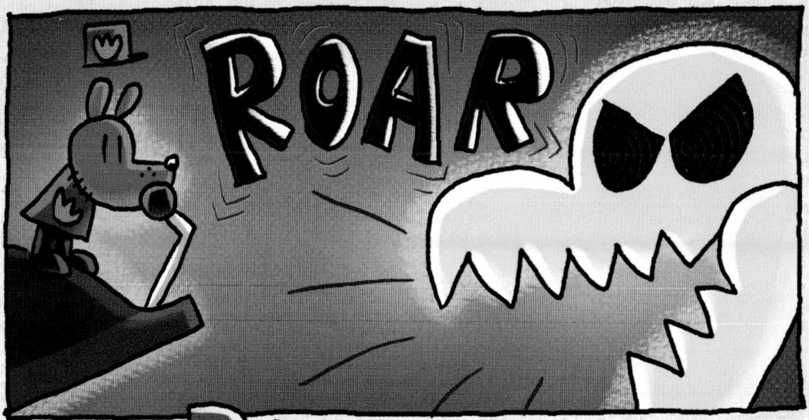
ROAR

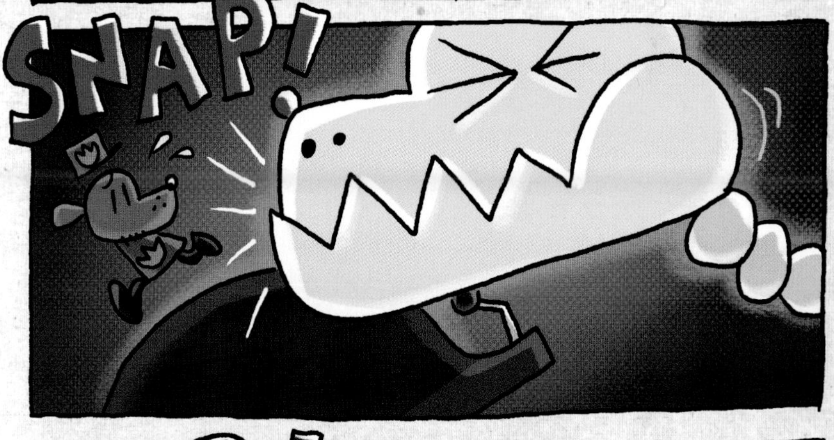
SNAP!

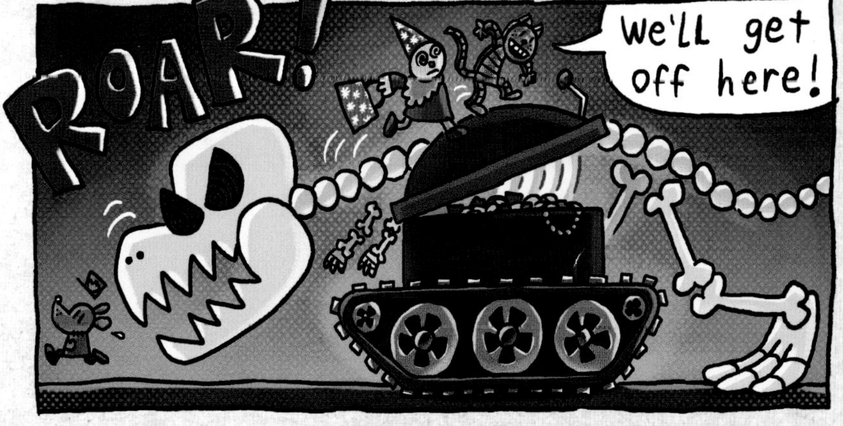
ROAR!
We'LL get off here!

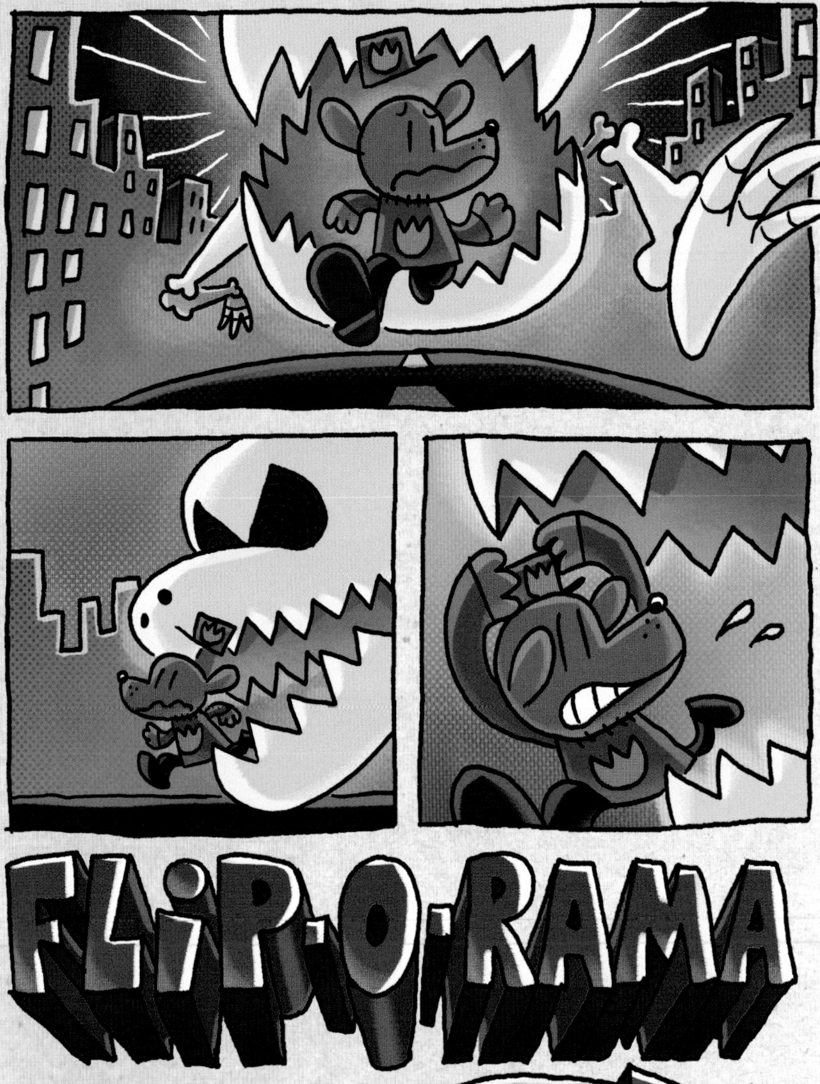

FLIP-O-RAMA

Cheesy Animation Technology...

Left hand here.

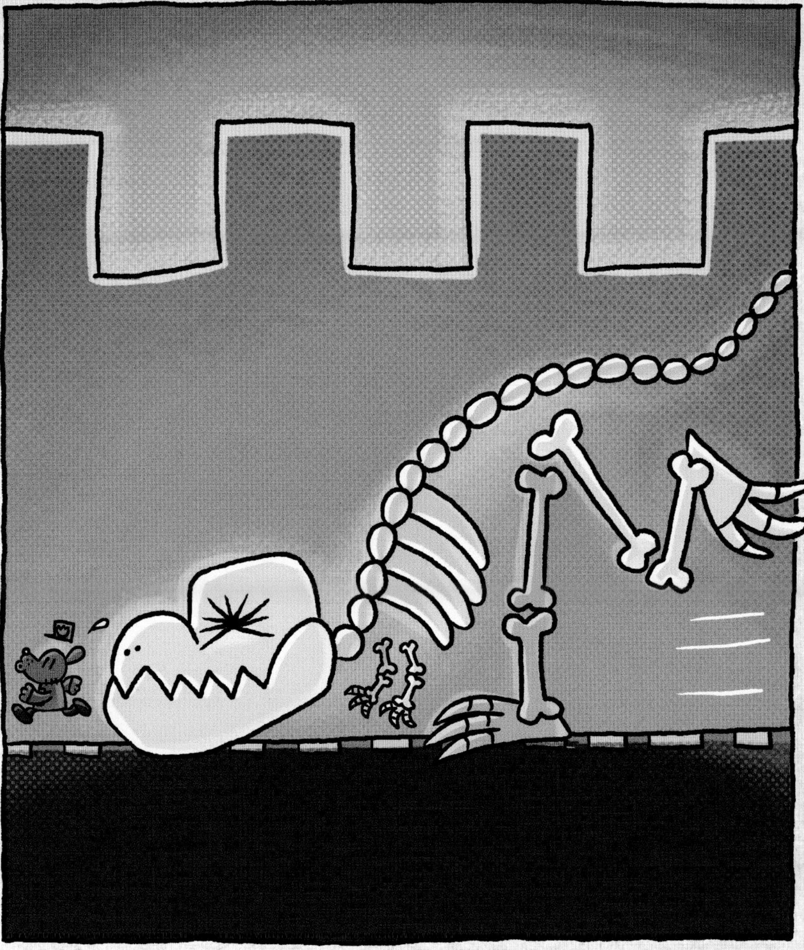

Jurassic Bark

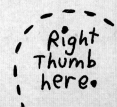

Right Thumb here.

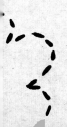

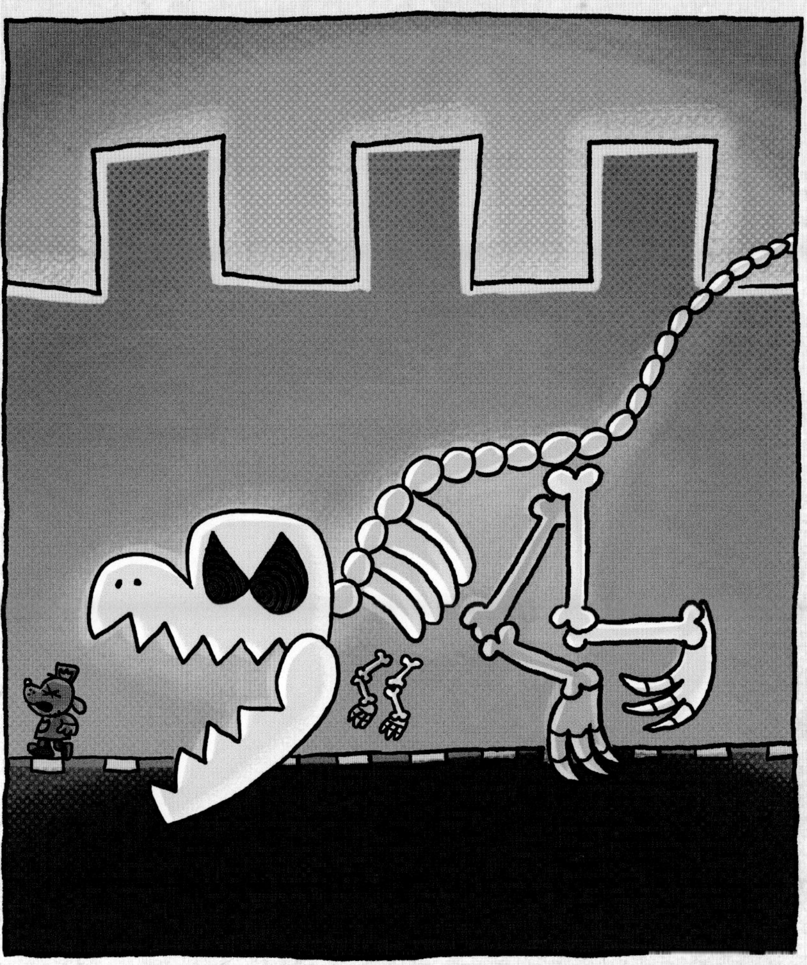

Jurassic Bark

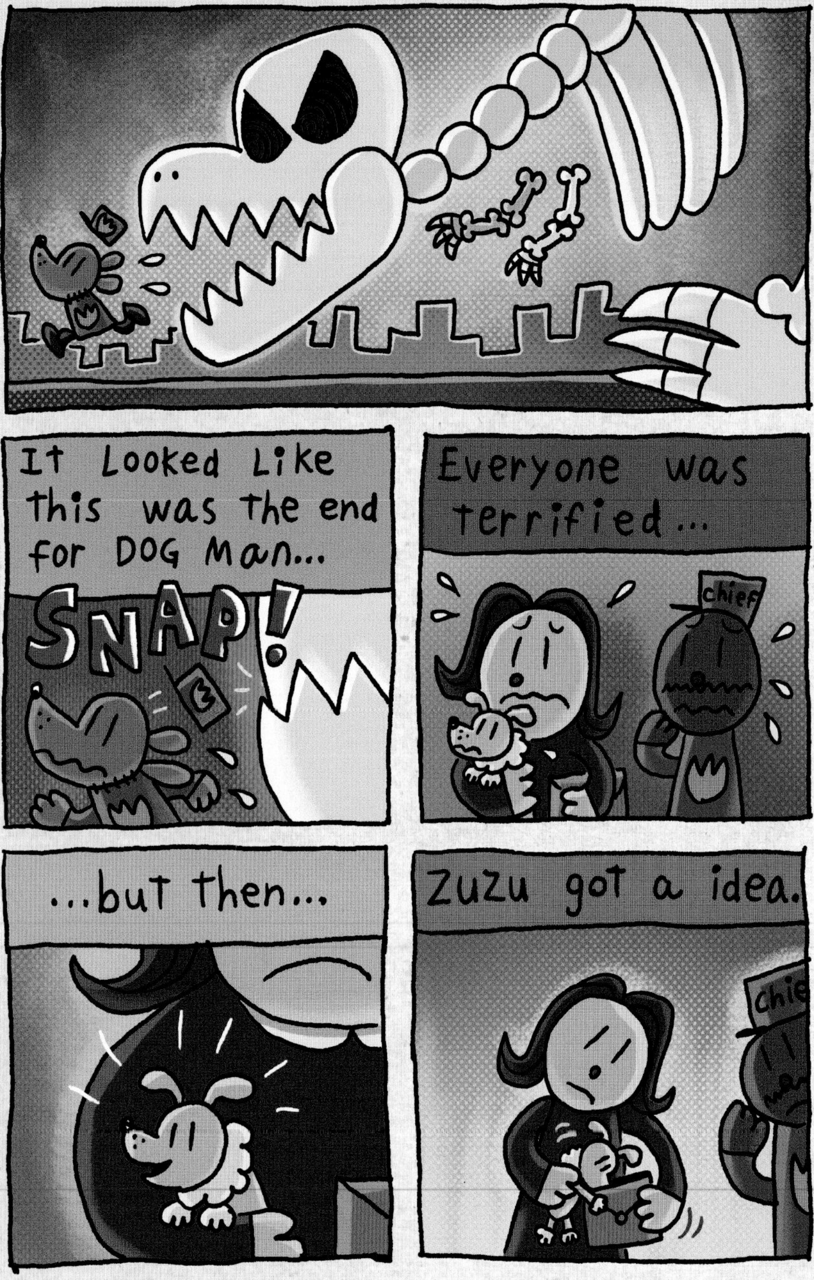

It Looked Like this was the end for DOG Man...
SNAP!
Everyone was terrified...
chief
...but then...
Zuzu got a idea.
chie

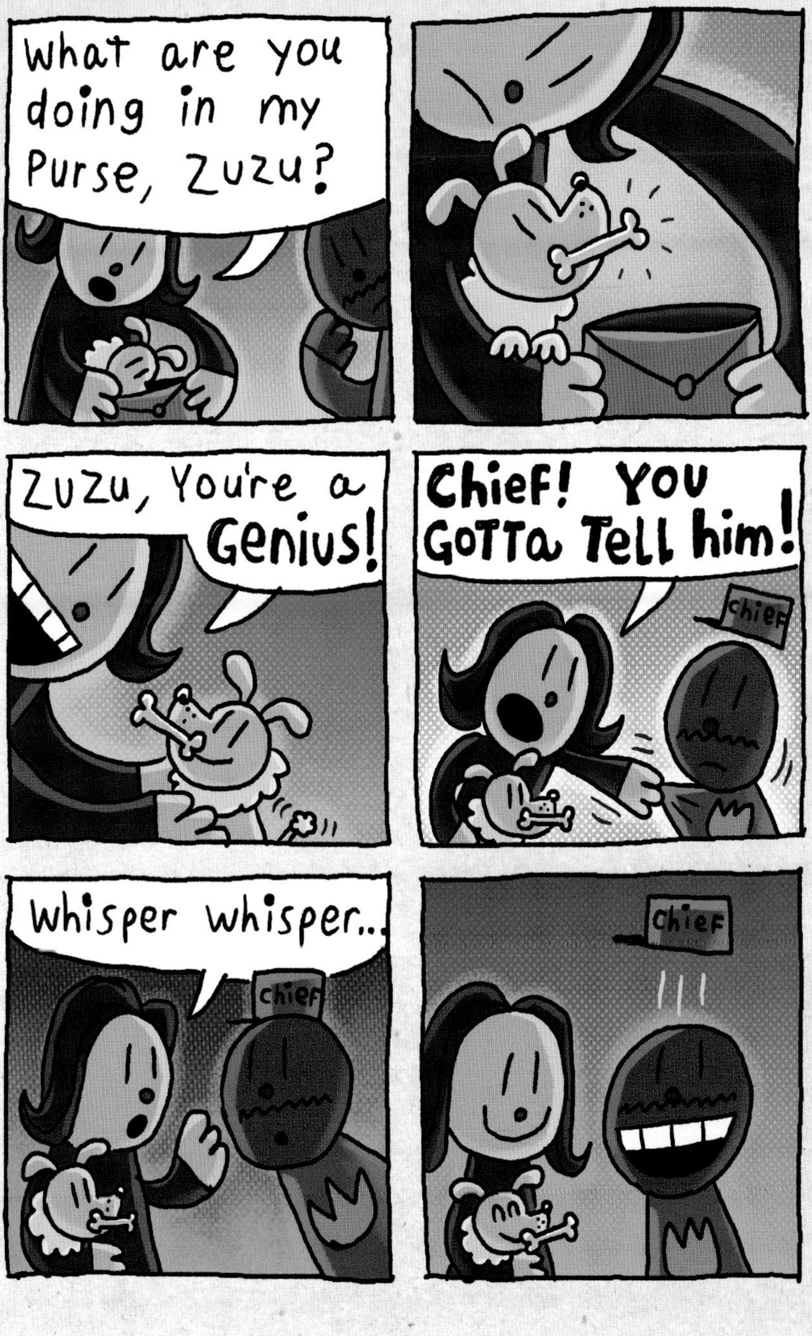
What are you doing in my Purse, Zuzu?
Zuzu, You're a Genius!
Chief! You GoTTa Tell him!
chief
Whisper whisper...
chief
chief

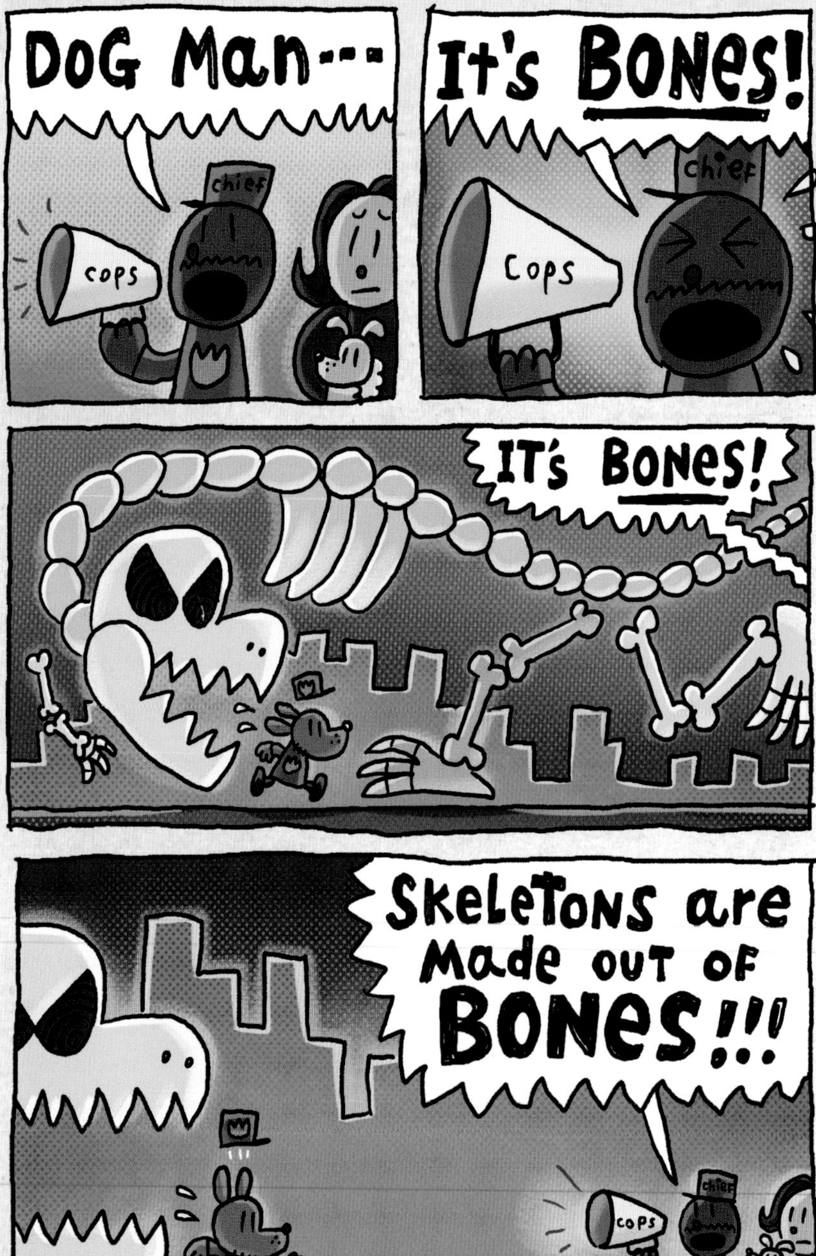
DOG Man...
It's BONES!
cops
chief
cops
chief
IT's BONES!
SkeLeTONS are Made OUT OF BONES!!!
cops
chief

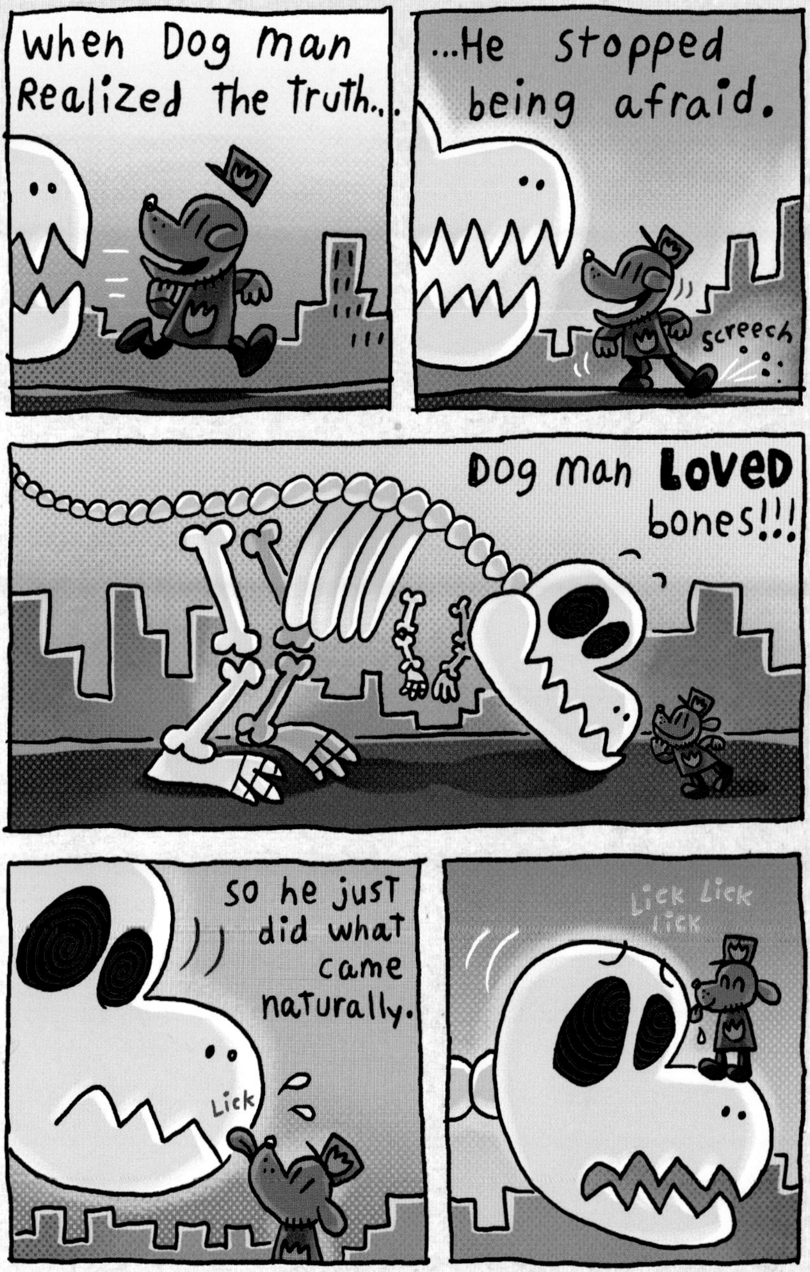
When Dog Man Realized the Truth...
...He stopped being afraid.
screech
Dog Man LOVED bones!!!
So he just did what came naturally.
Lick
Lick Lick Lick

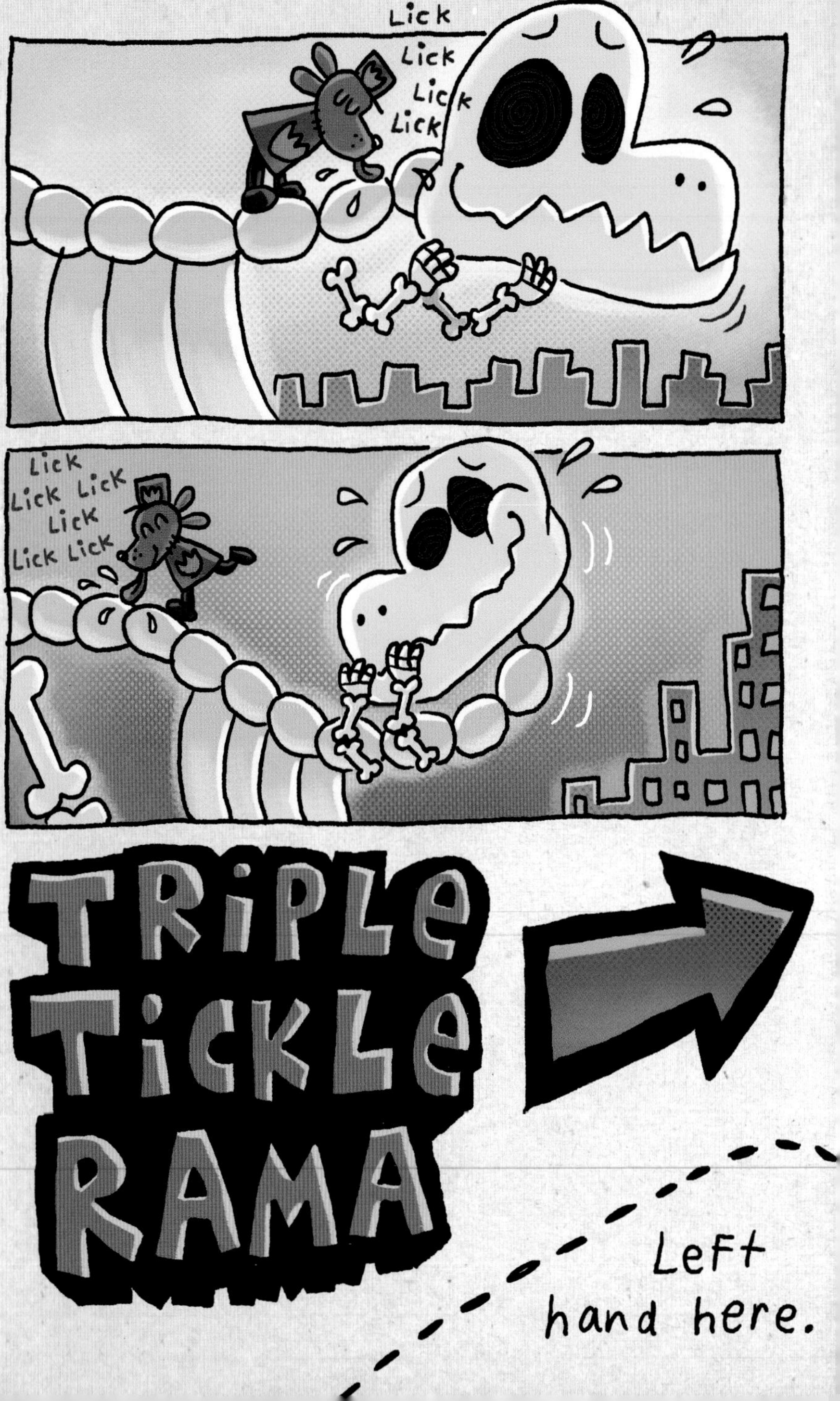
Lick
Lick
Lick
Lick
Lick
Lick Lick
Lick
Lick Lick
TRIPLE TICKLE RAMA
Left hand here.

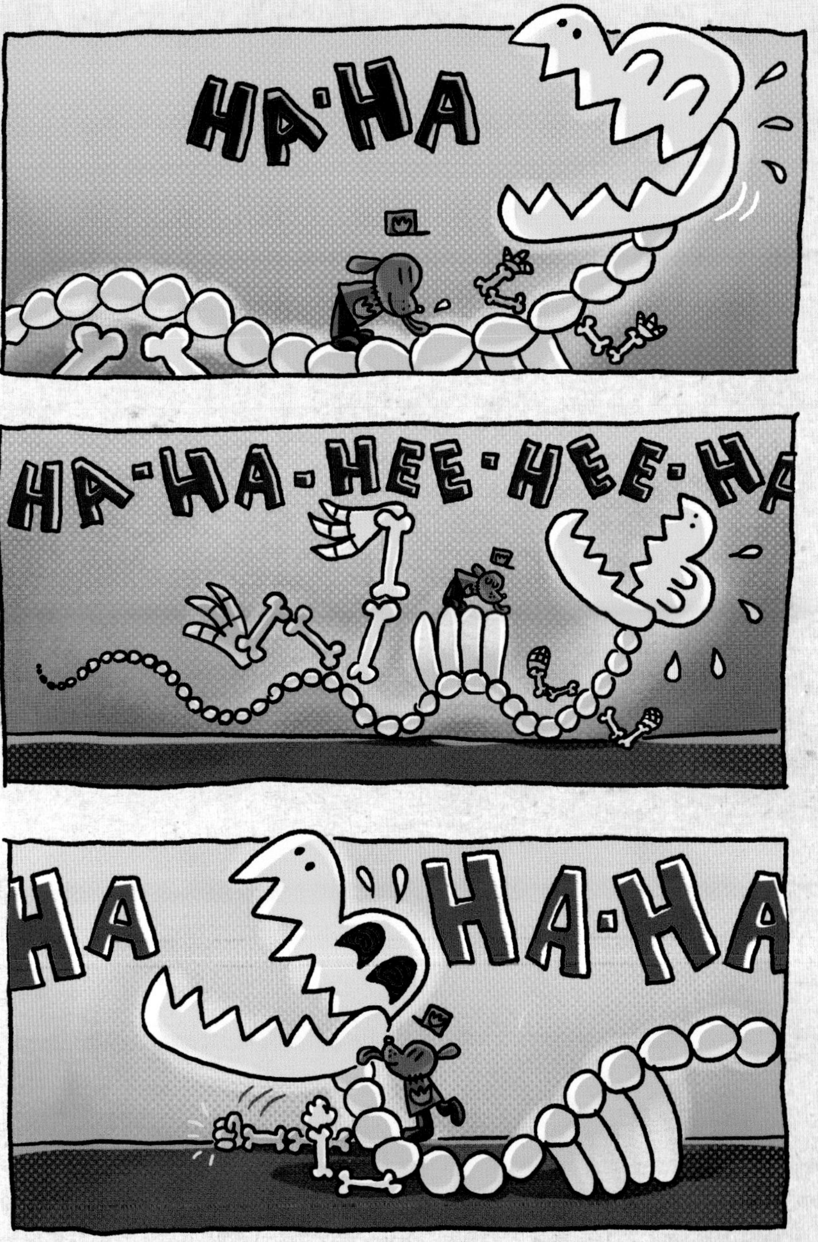
HA-HA
HA-HA-HEE-HEE-H
HA
HA-HA

Right Thumb here.

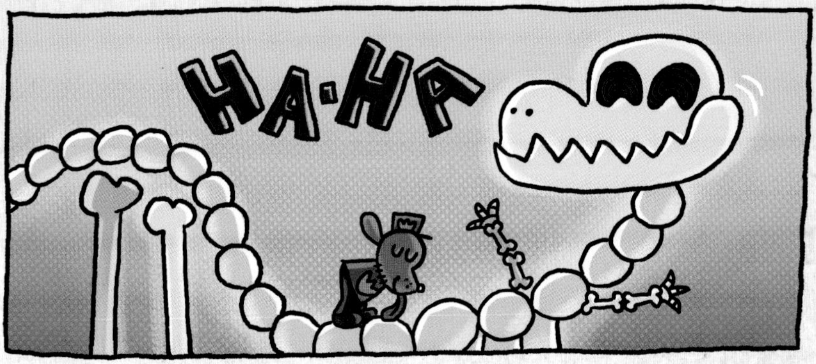
HA-HA

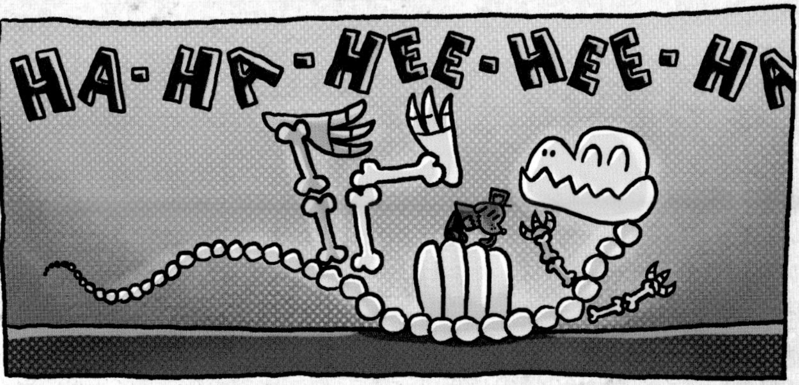
HA-HA-HEE-HEE-HA

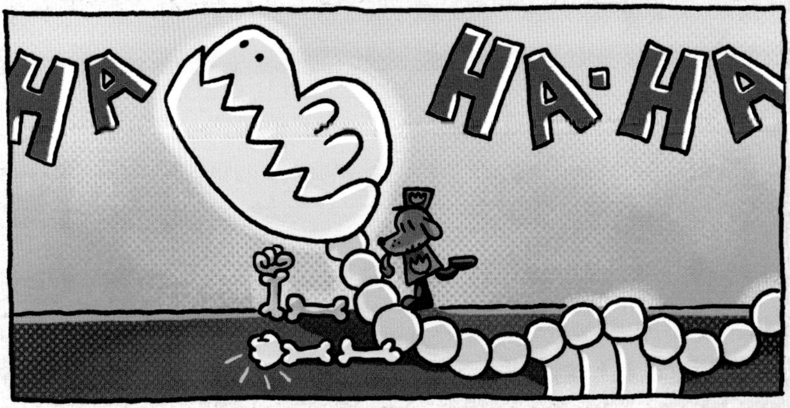
HA
HA-HA

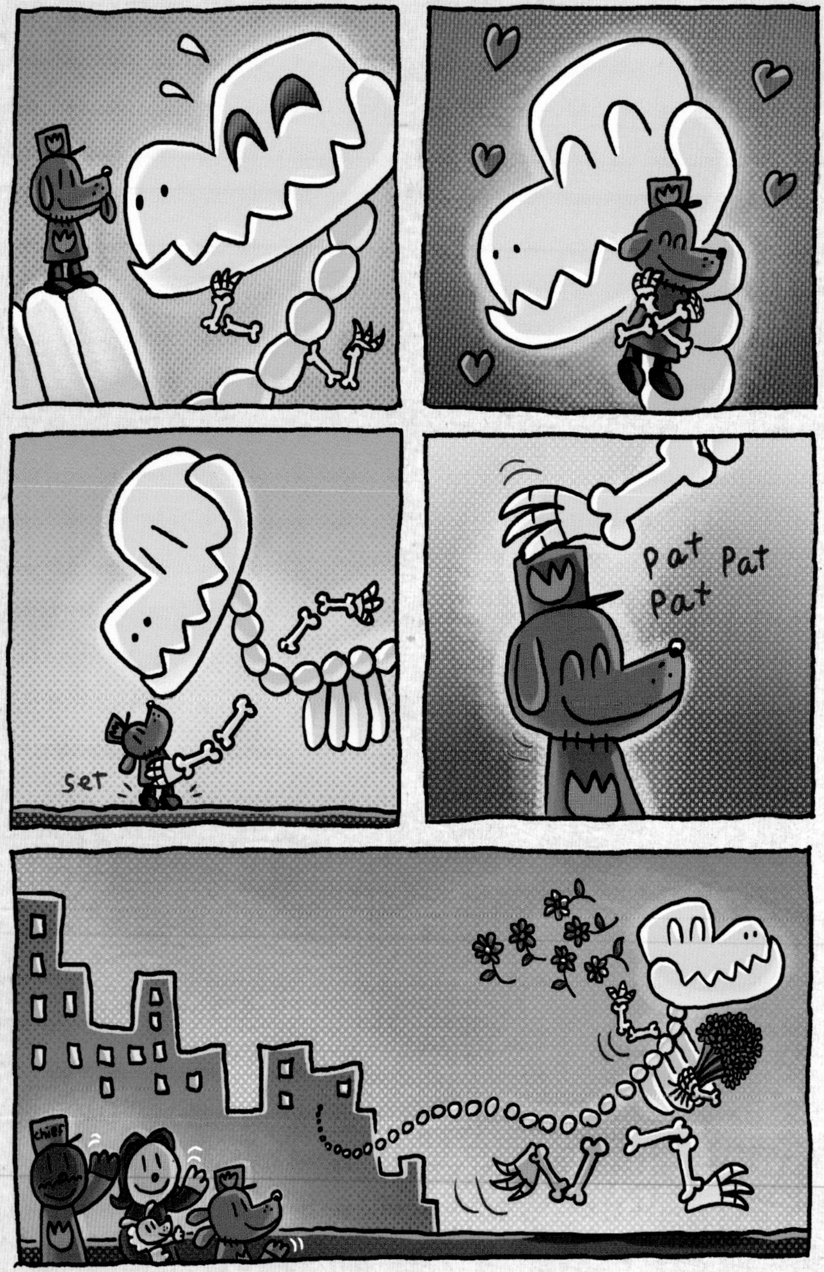
set
Pat Pat
Pat
chief

HEY!!!
OBEY Spray
New
OBEY Spra
may
effects

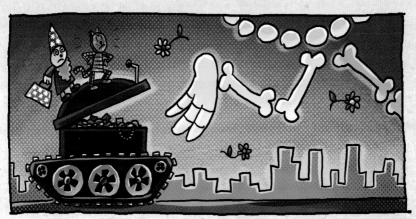

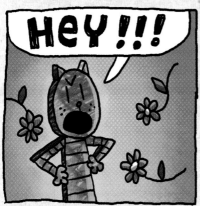

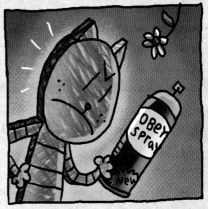

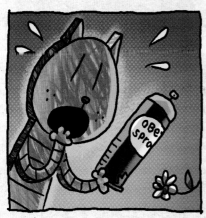

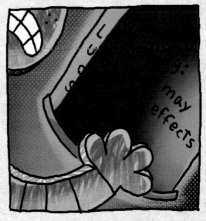

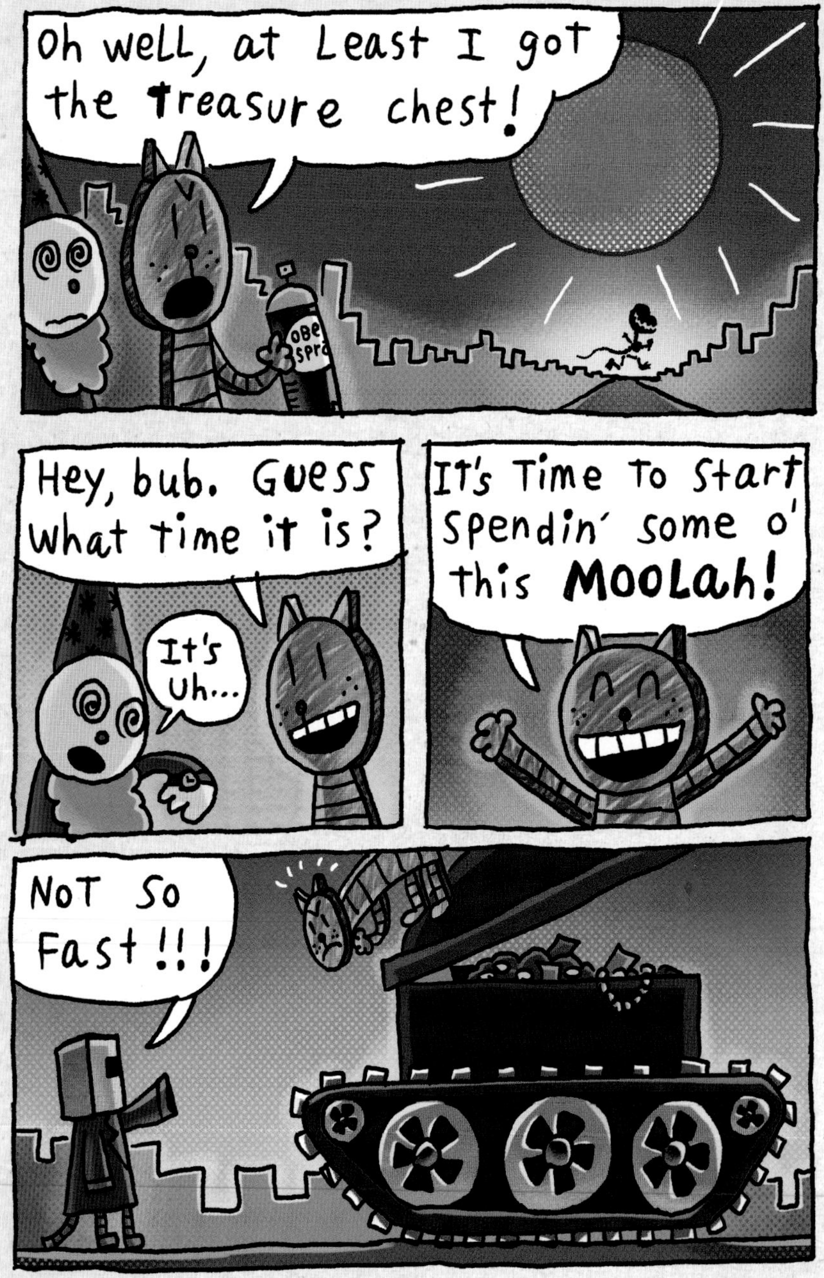
Oh WELL, at Least I got the Treasure chest!
OBEY SPRA
Hey, bub. Guess what time it is?
It's Uh...
IT's Time To Start Spendin' some o' this MOOLah!
NoT So Fast!!!

Chapter 9
The Mysterious Stranger Returns

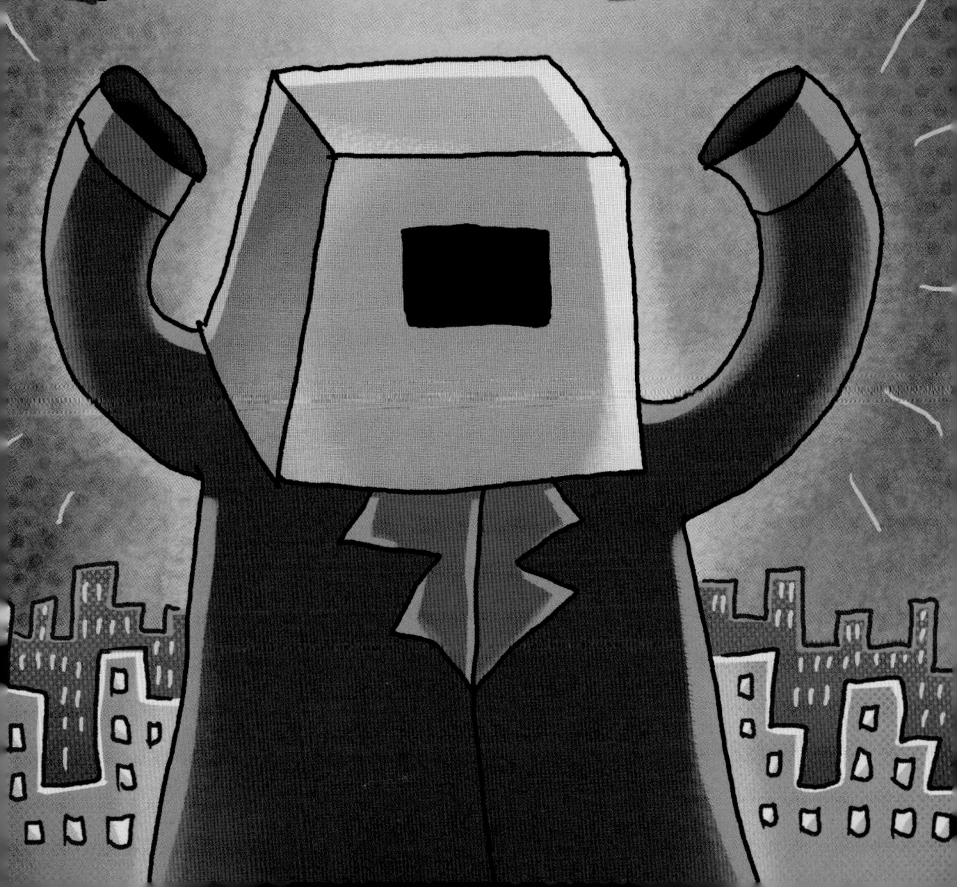

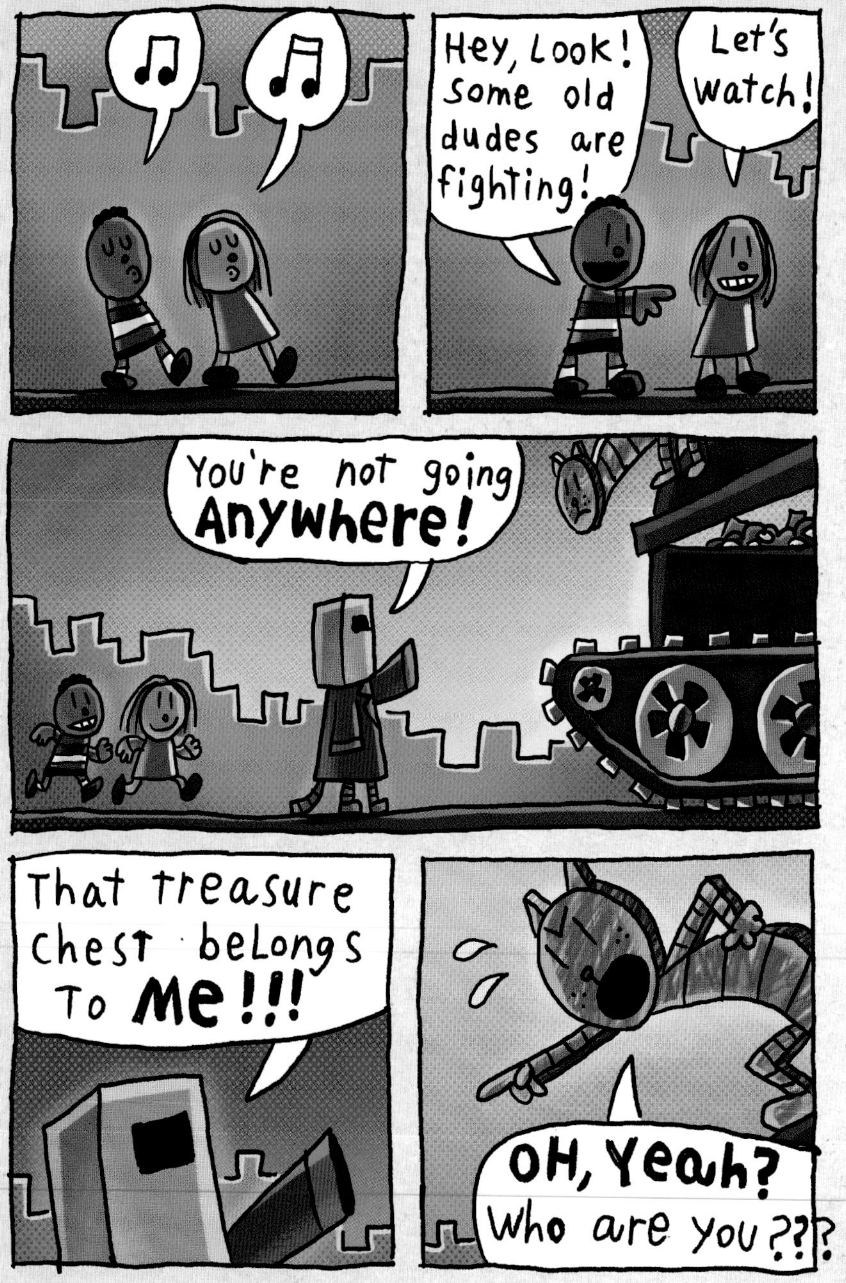
Hey, Look! Some old dudes are fighting!
Let's watch!
You're not going Anywhere!
That treasure chest belongs To Me!!!
OH, Yeah? Who are you???

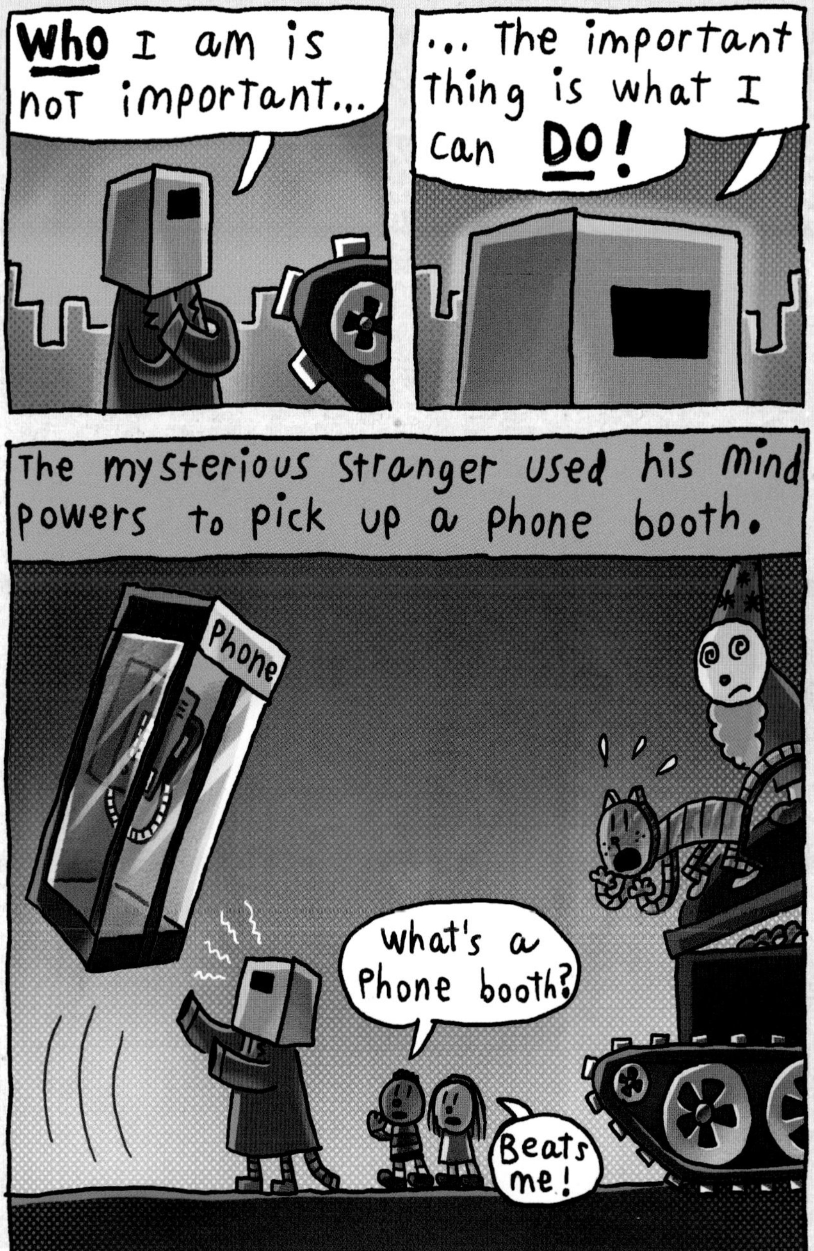
WHO I am is not important...
... The important thing is what I can DO!
The mysterious stranger used his mind powers to pick up a phone booth.
Phone
What's a Phone booth?
Beats me!

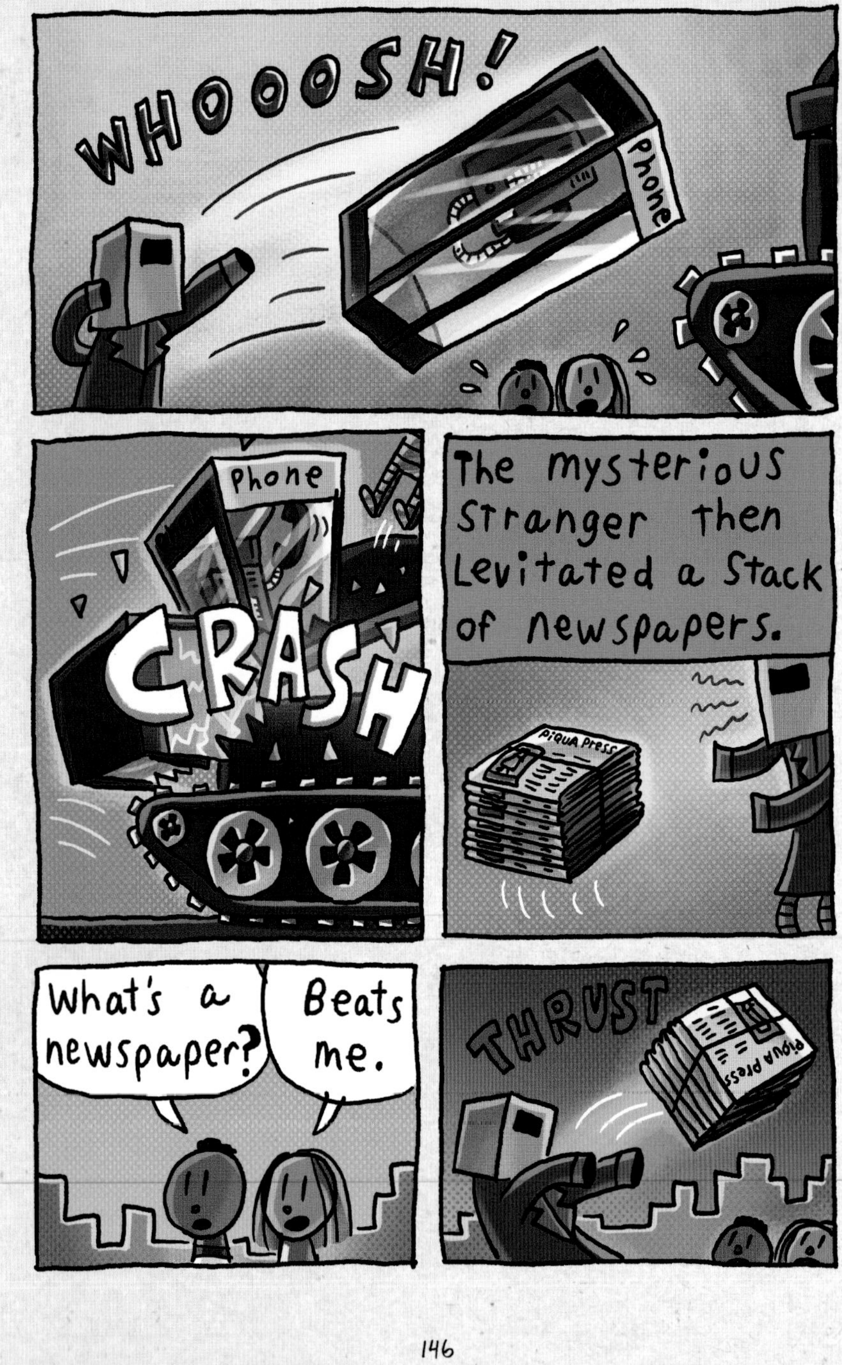
WHOOOSH!
Phone
Phone
CRASH
The mysterious Stranger then Levitated a Stack of newspapers.
Piqua Press
What's a newspaper?
Beats me.
THRUST
Piqua Press

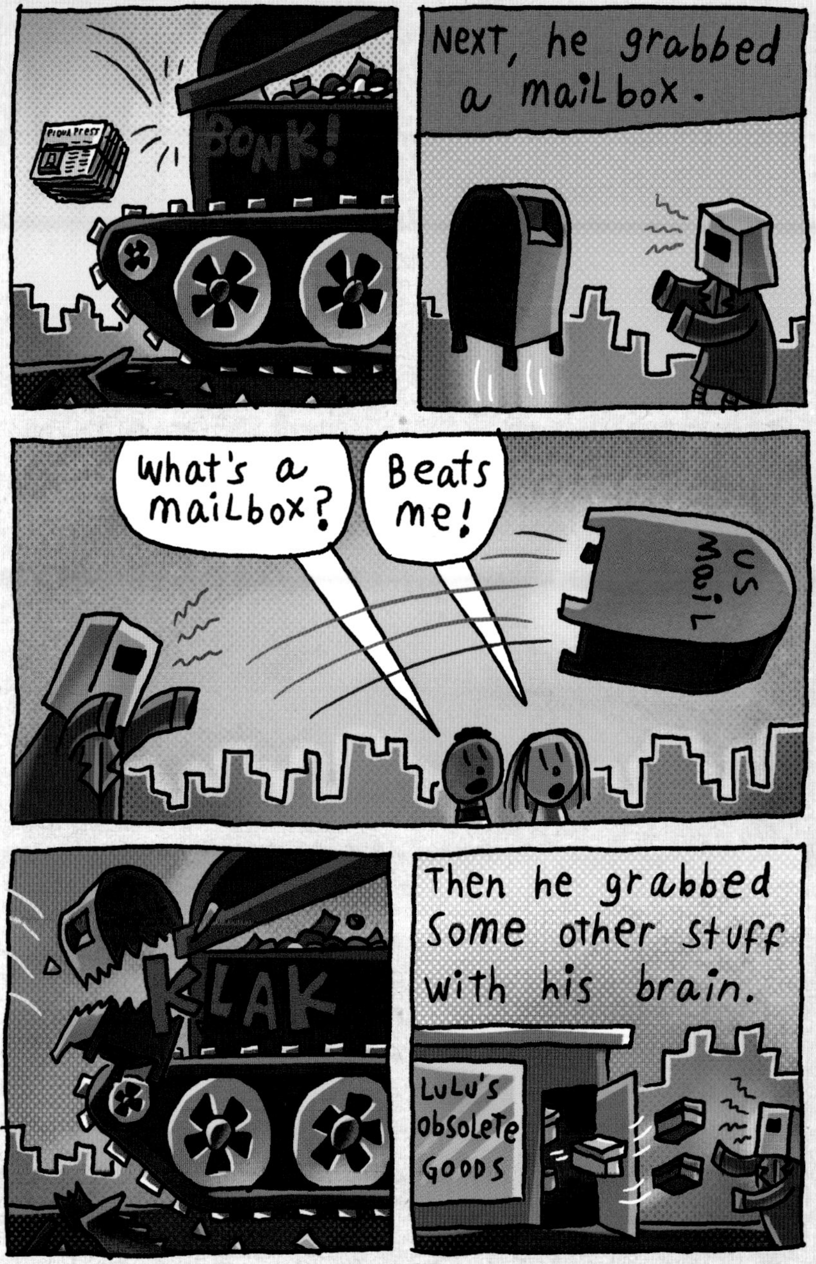
PIQUA PRESS
BONK!
NEXT, he grabbed a mailbox.
What's a mailbox?
Beats me!
US Mail
KLAK
Then he grabbed some other stuff with his brain.
LuLu's obsolete goods

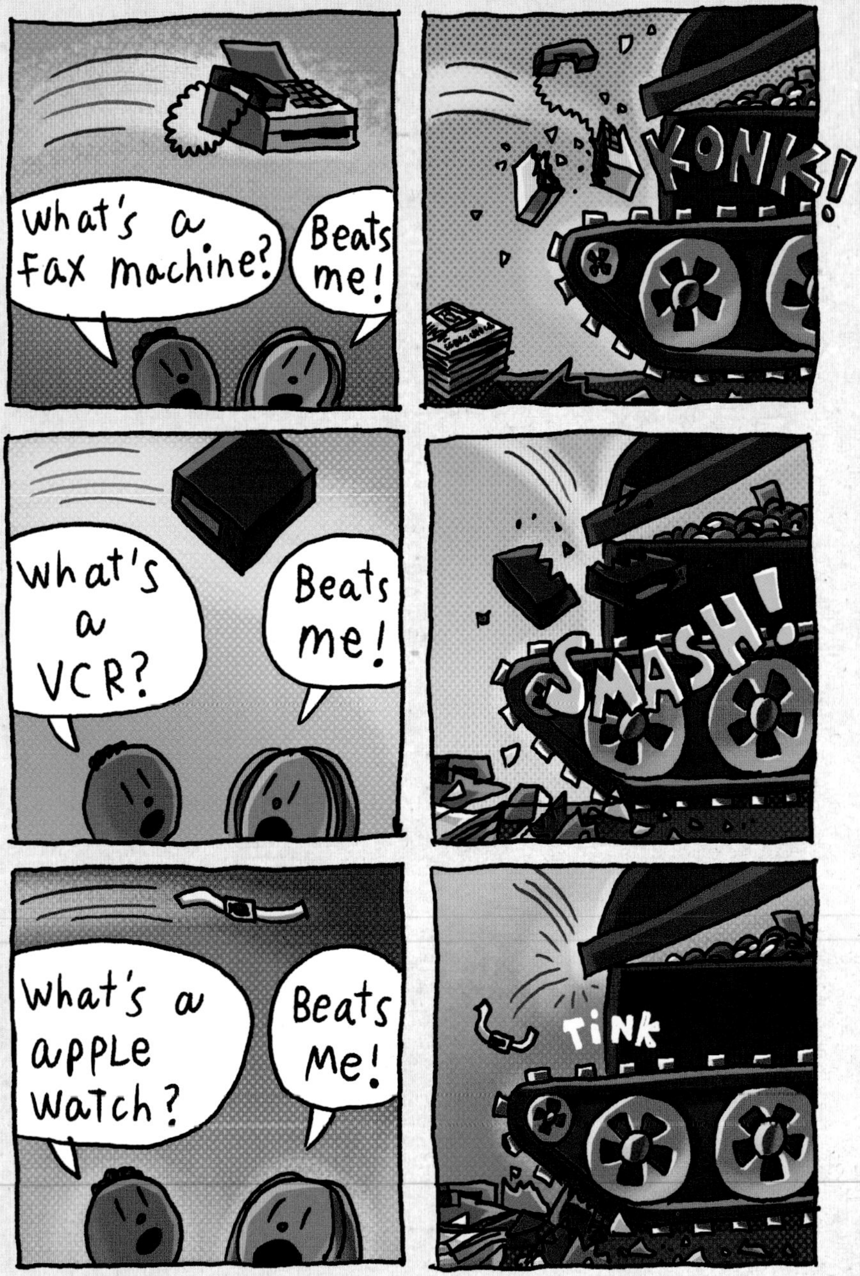
What's a fax machine?
Beats me!
KONK!
What's a VCR?
Beats me!
SMASH!
What's a apple watch?
Beats me!
TINK

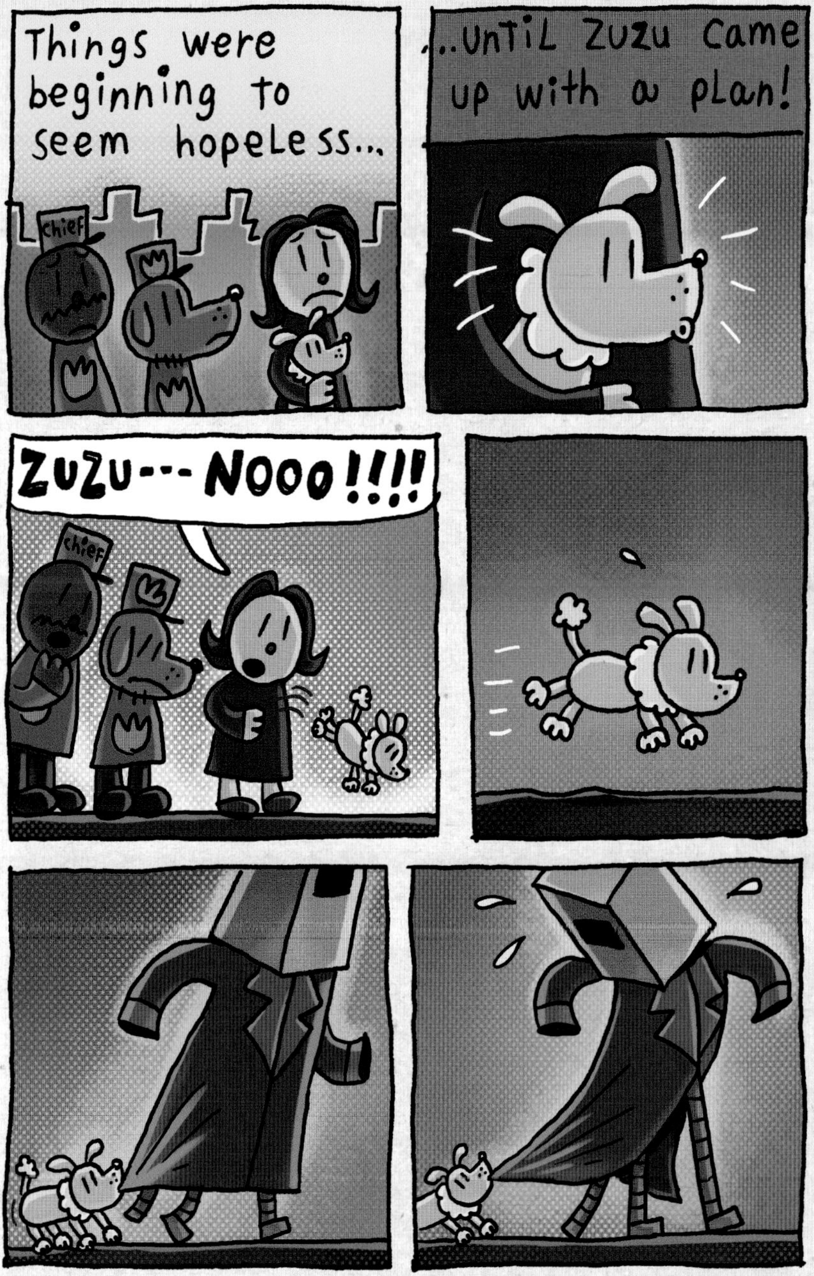
Things were beginning to seem hopeless...
chief
...UNTIL ZUZU Came up with a pLan!
ZUZU---NOOO!!!!
chief

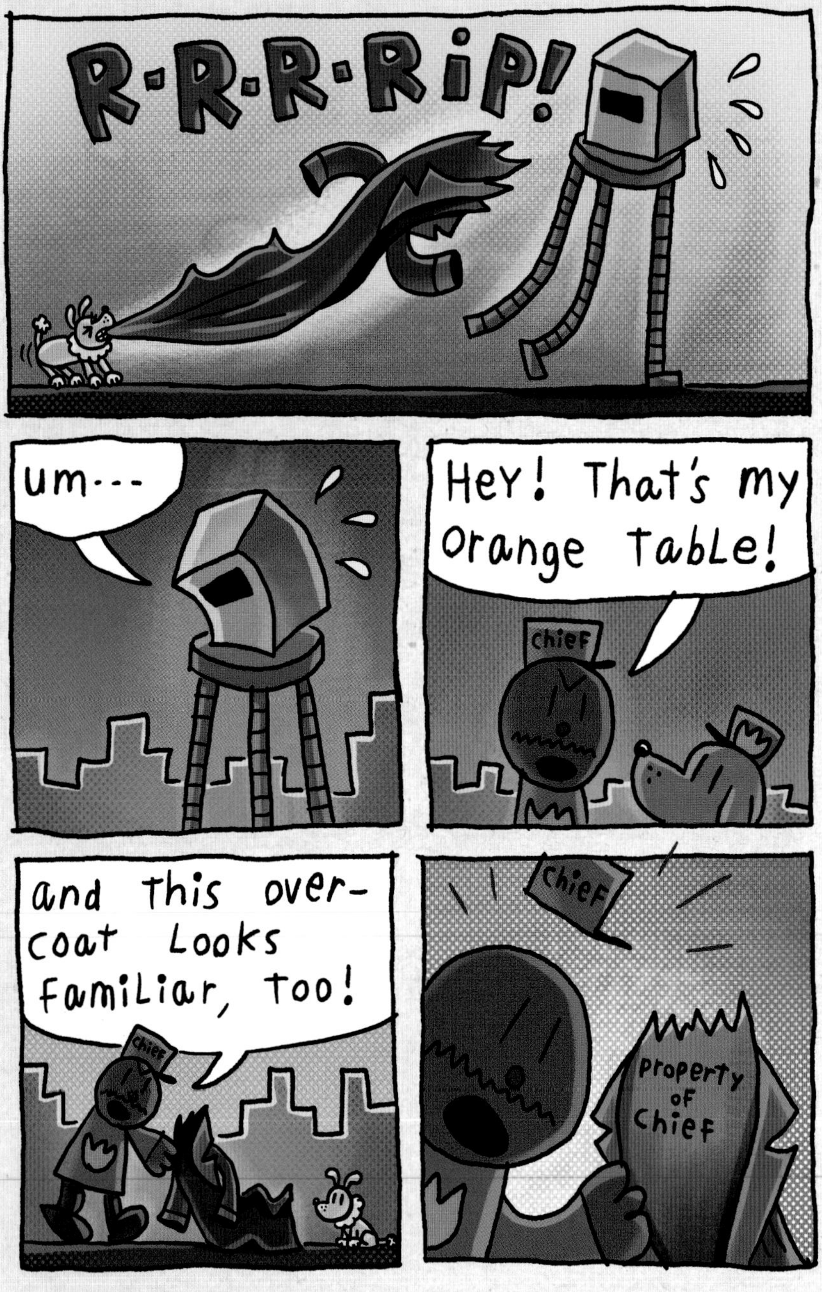
R-R-R-RIP!
um...
Hey! That's my Orange Table!
CHIEF
and this over-coat Looks familiar, too!
CHIEF
CHIEF
Property of Chief

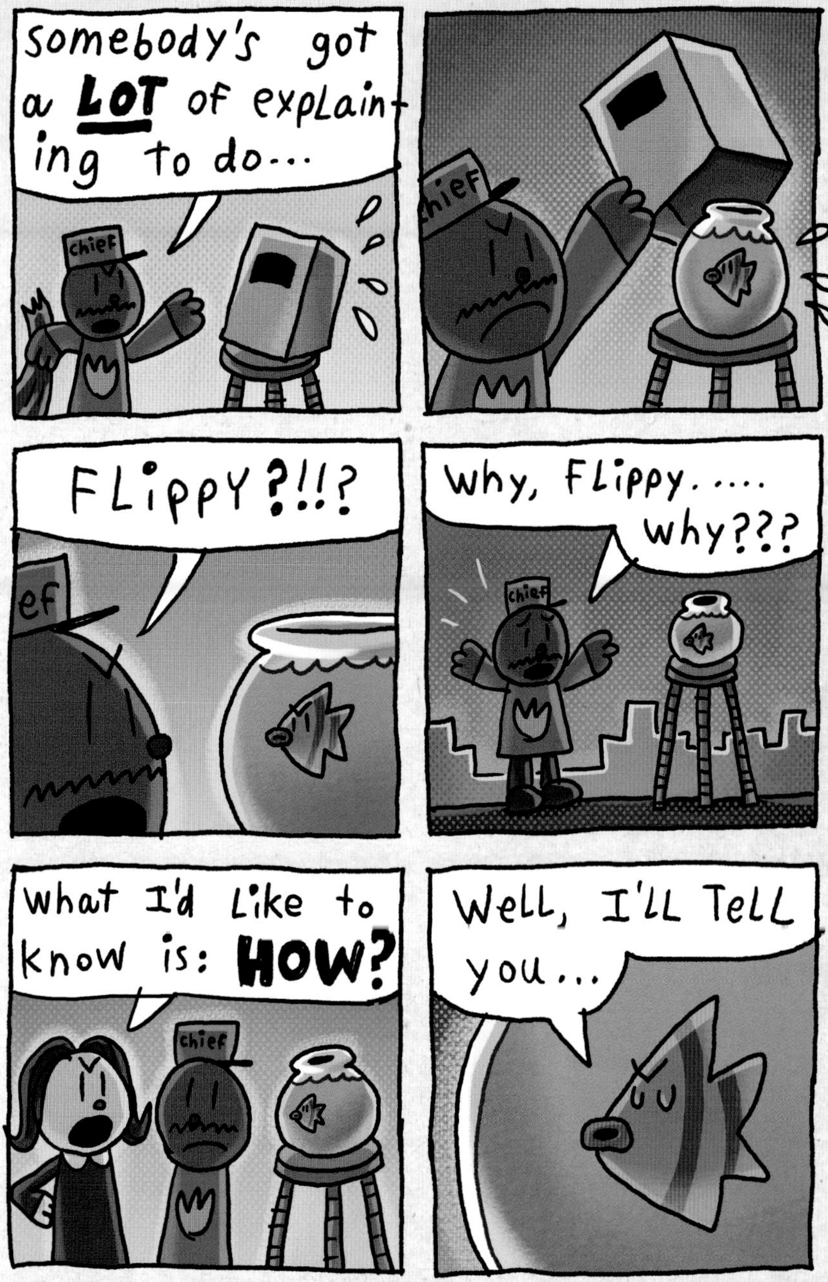
somebody's got a LOT of explaining to do...
chief
chief
FLIPPY?!!?
ef
Why, FLIPPY.....
why???
chief
What I'd like to know is: HOW?
chief
Well, I'LL TeLL you...

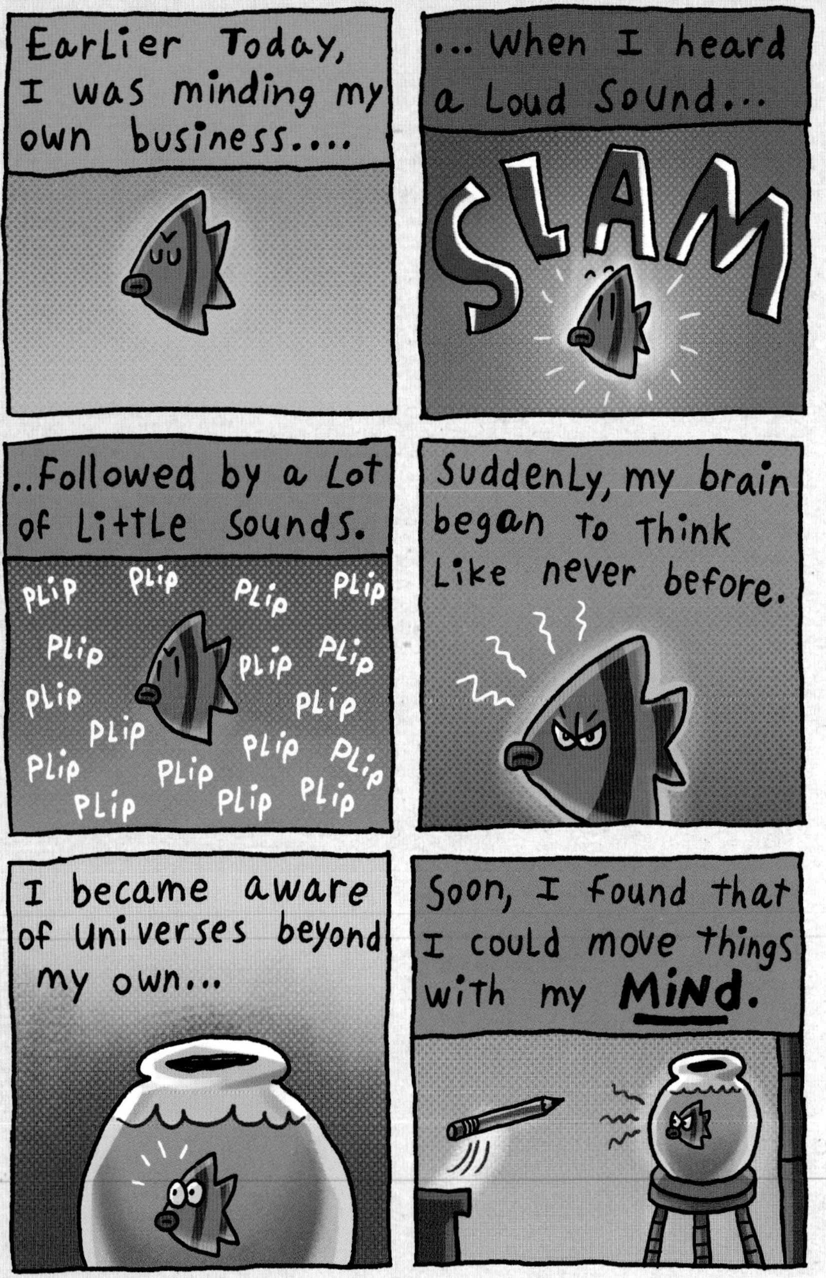
Earlier Today, I was minding my own business....
... When I heard a Loud Sound...
SLAM
...Followed by a Lot of Little Sounds.
PLIP PLIP PLIP PLIP PLIP PLIP PLIP PLIP PLIP PLIP PLIP PLIP PLIP PLIP PLIP PLIP PLIP
Suddenly, my brain began to Think Like never before.
I became aware of Universes beyond my own...
Soon, I found that I could move things with my MIND.

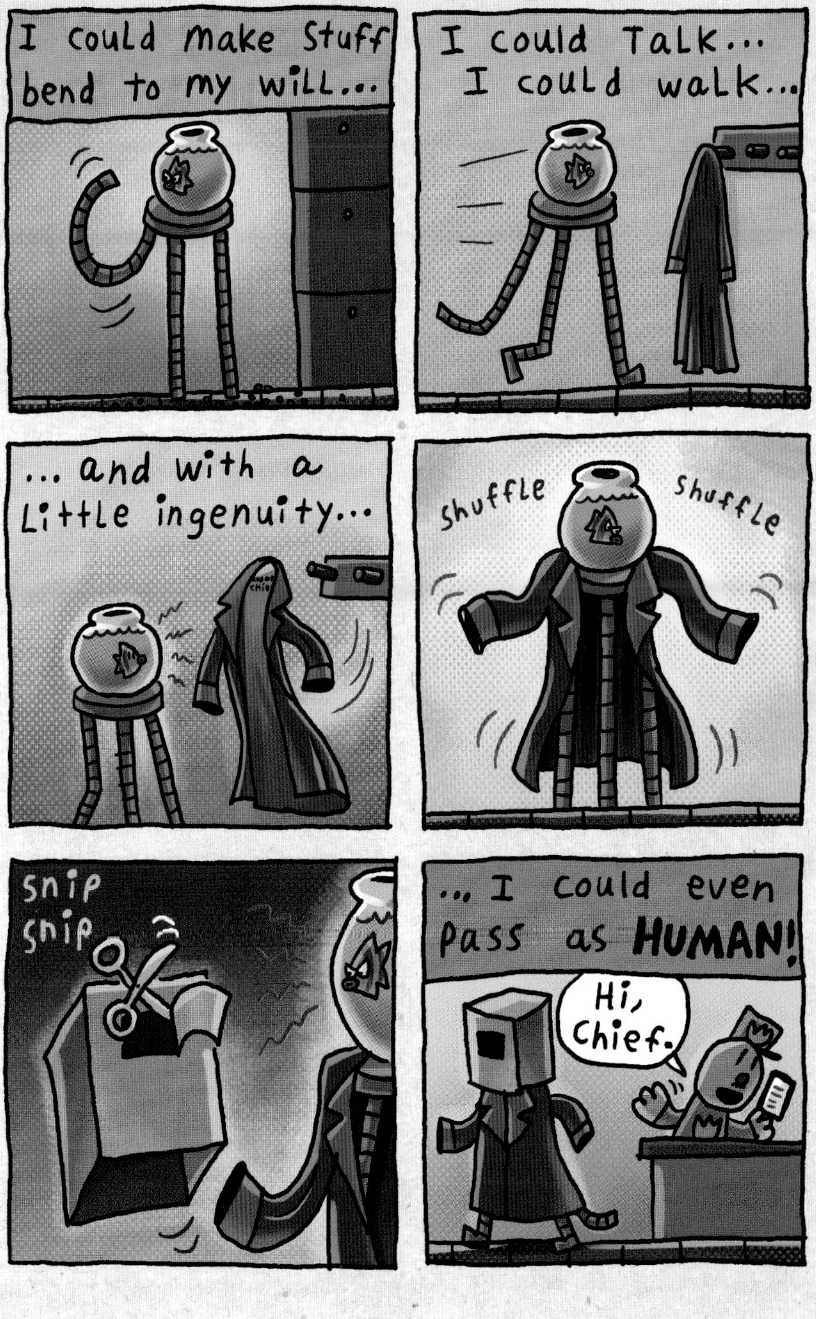
I could make Stuff bend to my will...
I could Talk... I could walk...
... and with a Little ingenuity...
shuffle
shuffle
snip snip
... I could even Pass as HUMAN!
Hi, Chief.

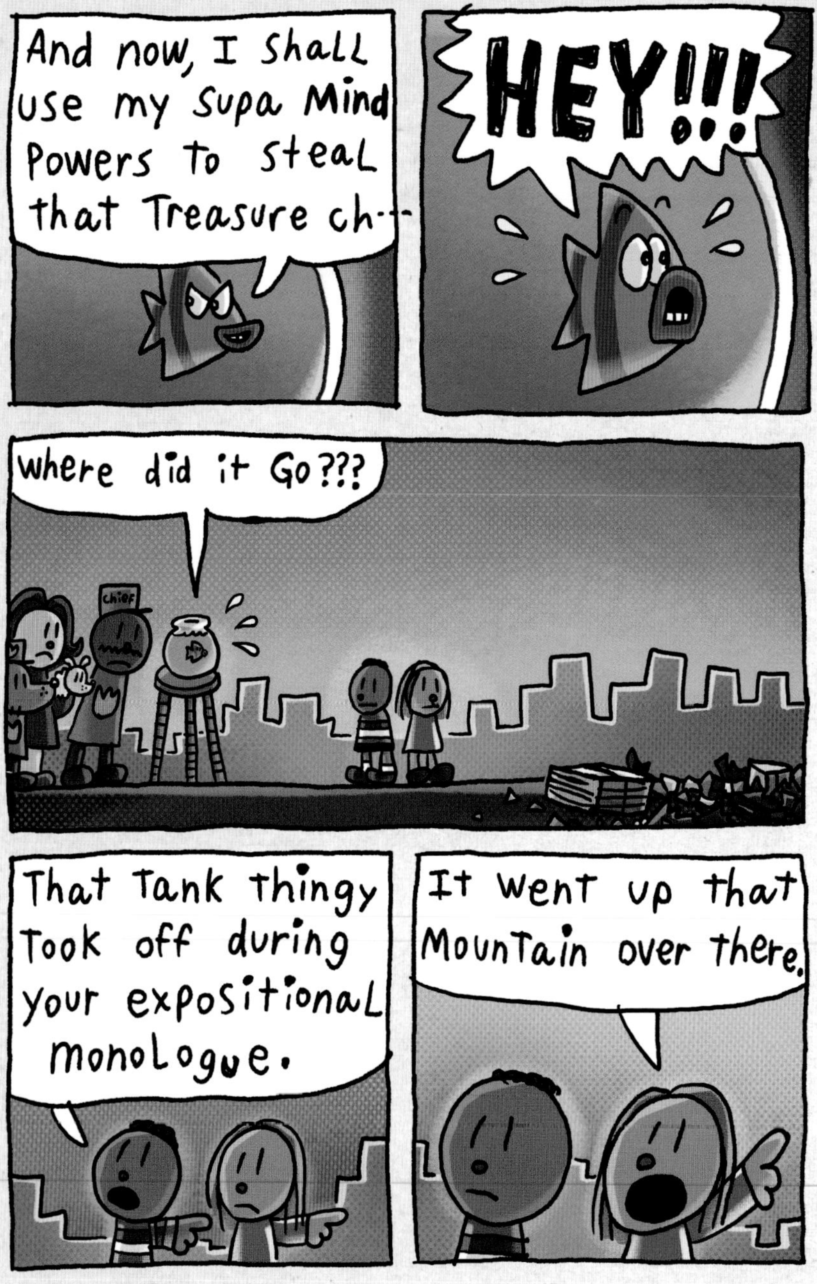
And now, I shall use my Supa Mind Powers to steal that Treasure ch···
HEY!!!
where did it Go???
chief
That Tank thingy Took off during your expositional monologue.
It went up that Mountain over there.

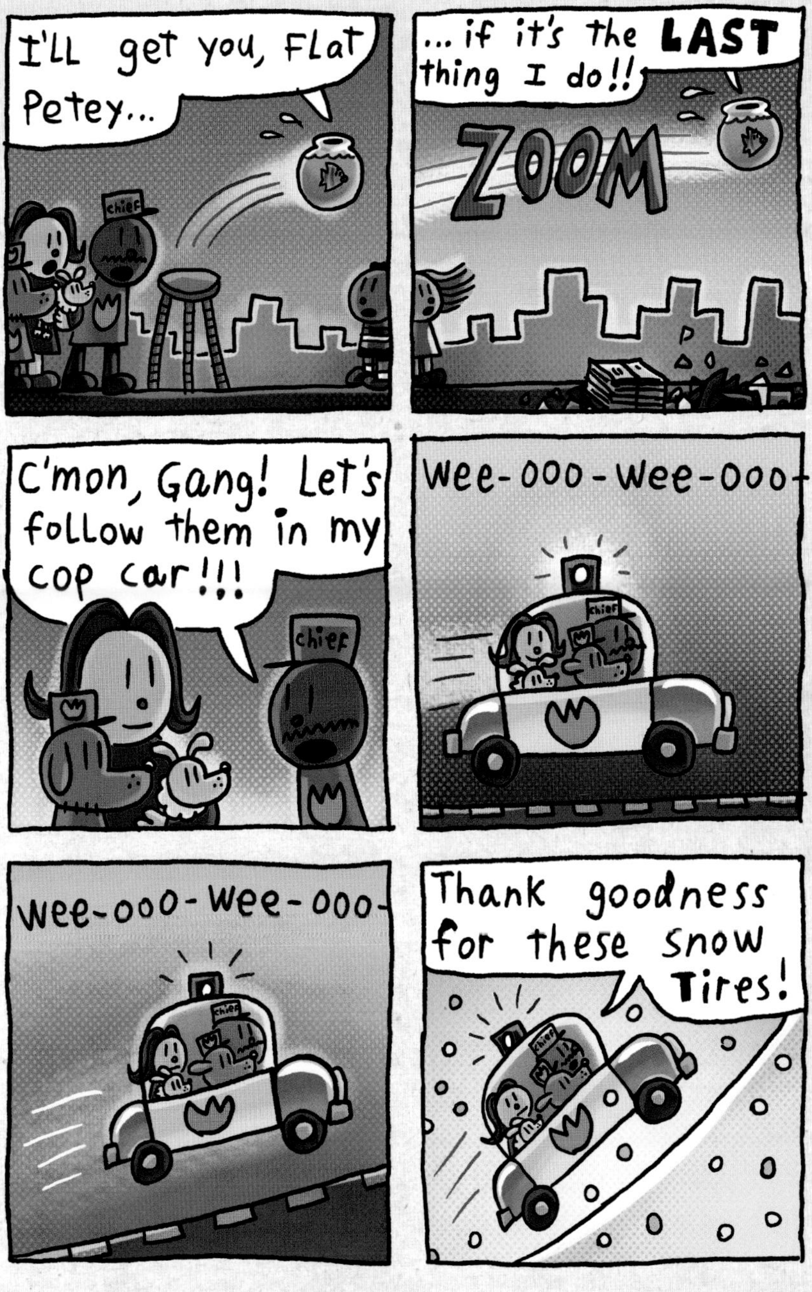
I'LL get you, Flat Petey...
...if it's the LAST thing I do!!
ZOOM
chief
C'mon, Gang! Let's follow them in my cop car!!!
chief
Wee-ooo-wee-ooo-
Wee-ooo-wee-ooo-
Thank goodness for these snow Tires!

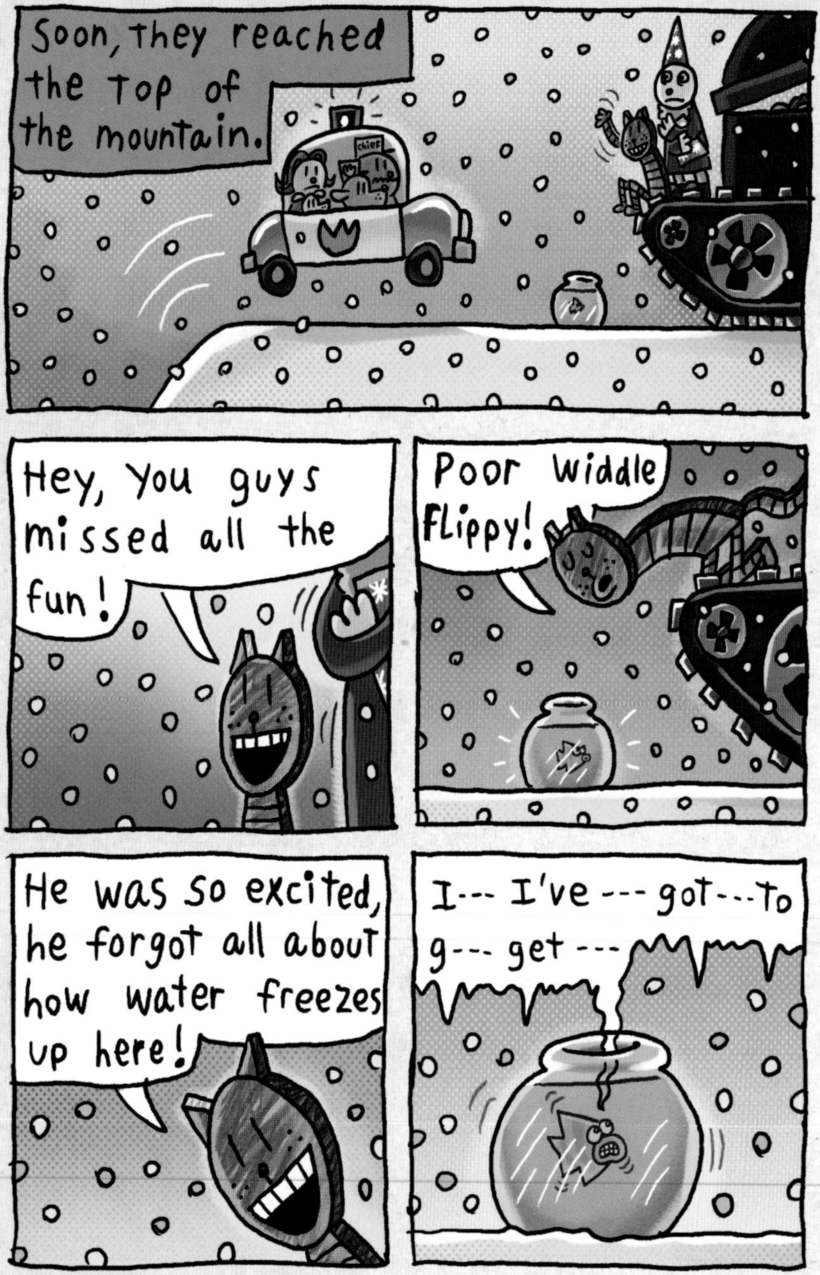
Soon, they reached the top of the mountain.
chief
Hey, you guys missed all the fun!
Poor widdle Flippy!
He was so excited, he forgot all about how water freezes up here!
I--- I've --- got---to g--- get ---

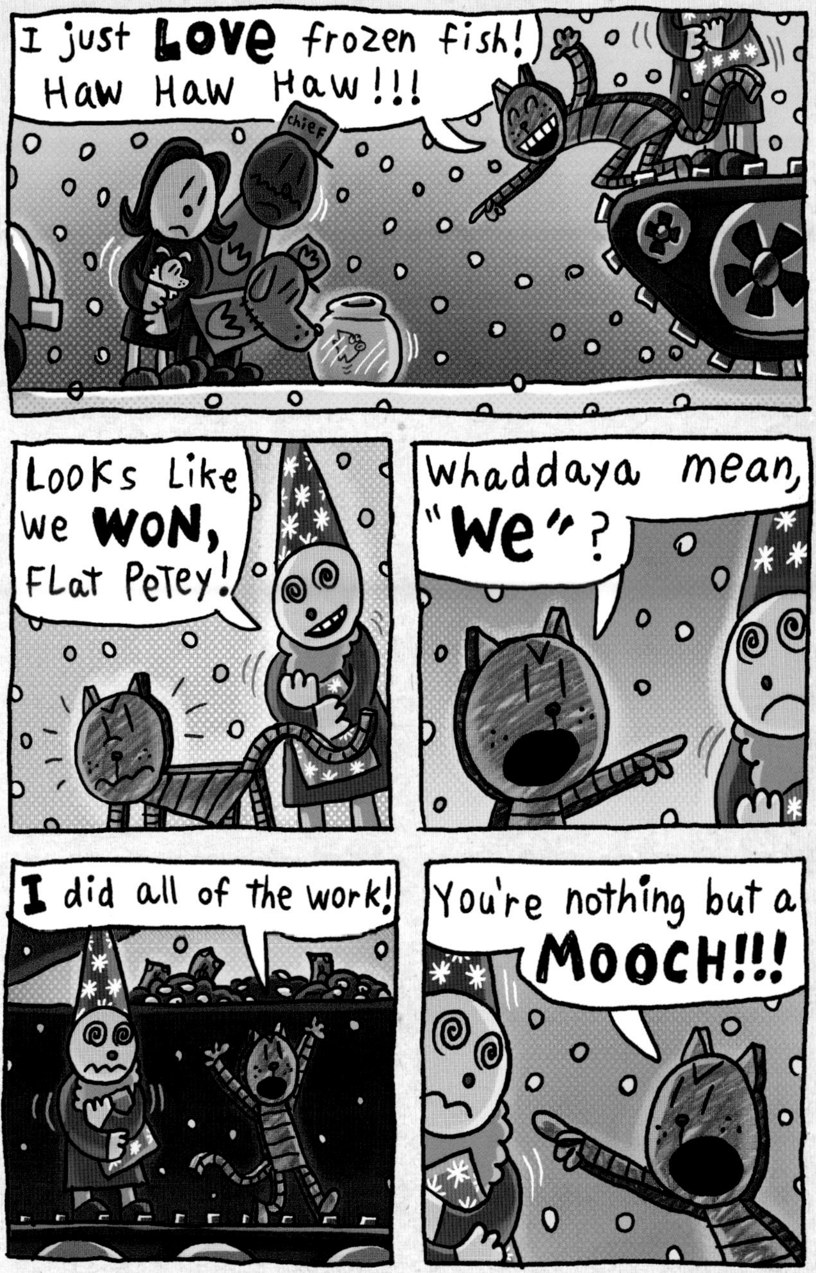
I just LOVE frozen fish! Haw Haw Haw!!!
CHIEF
Looks Like we WON, FLat Petey!
Whaddaya mean, "We"?
I did all of the work!
You're nothing but a MOOCH!!!

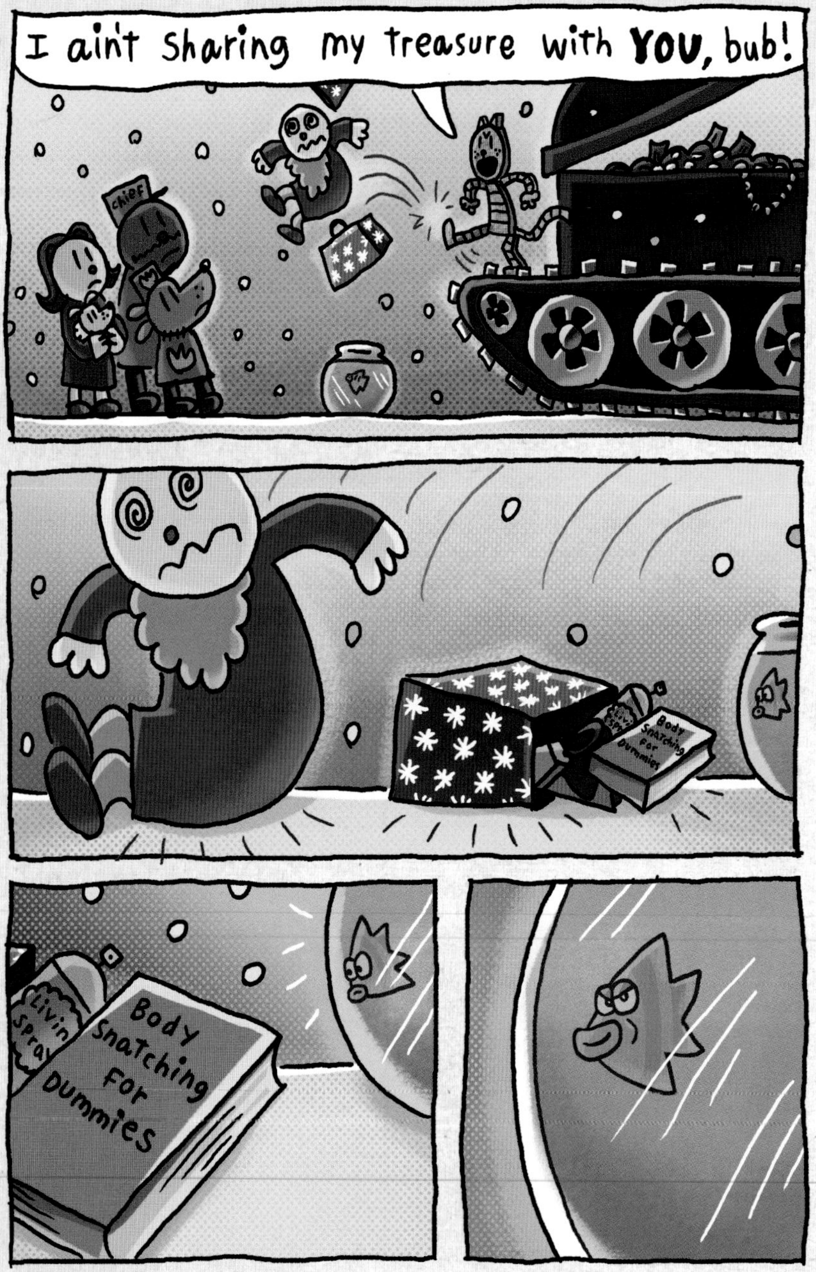
I ain't sharing my treasure with **YOU**, bub!
CHIEF
Body Snatching for Dummies
Body Snatching for Dummies

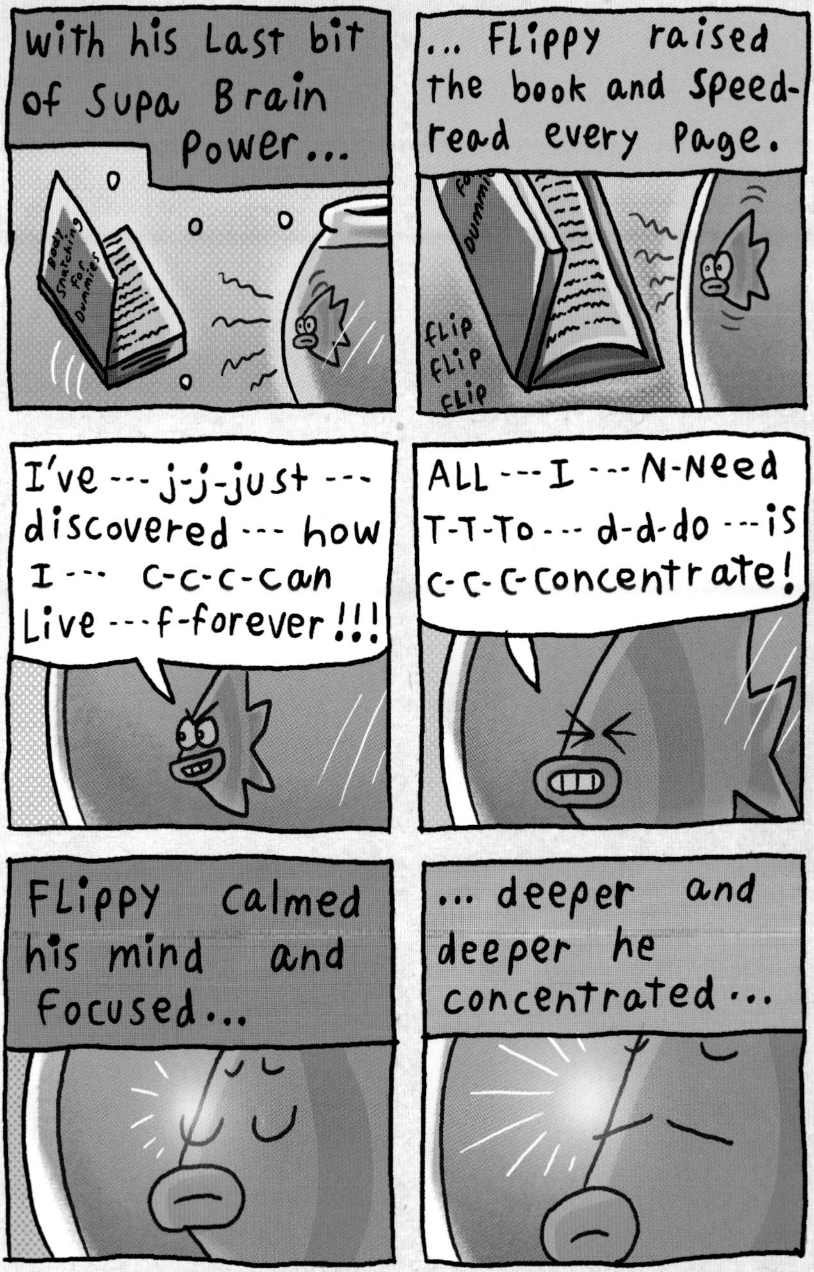
With his Last bit of Supa Brain Power...
Body Snatching for Dummies
... Flippy raised the book and speed-read every page.
FLIP FLIP FLIP
I've --- j-j-just --- discovered --- how I --- c-c-c-can Live --- f-forever!!!
ALL --- I --- N-Need T-T-To --- d-d-do --- is c-c-c-concentrate!
Flippy calmed his mind and focused...
... deeper and deeper he concentrated...

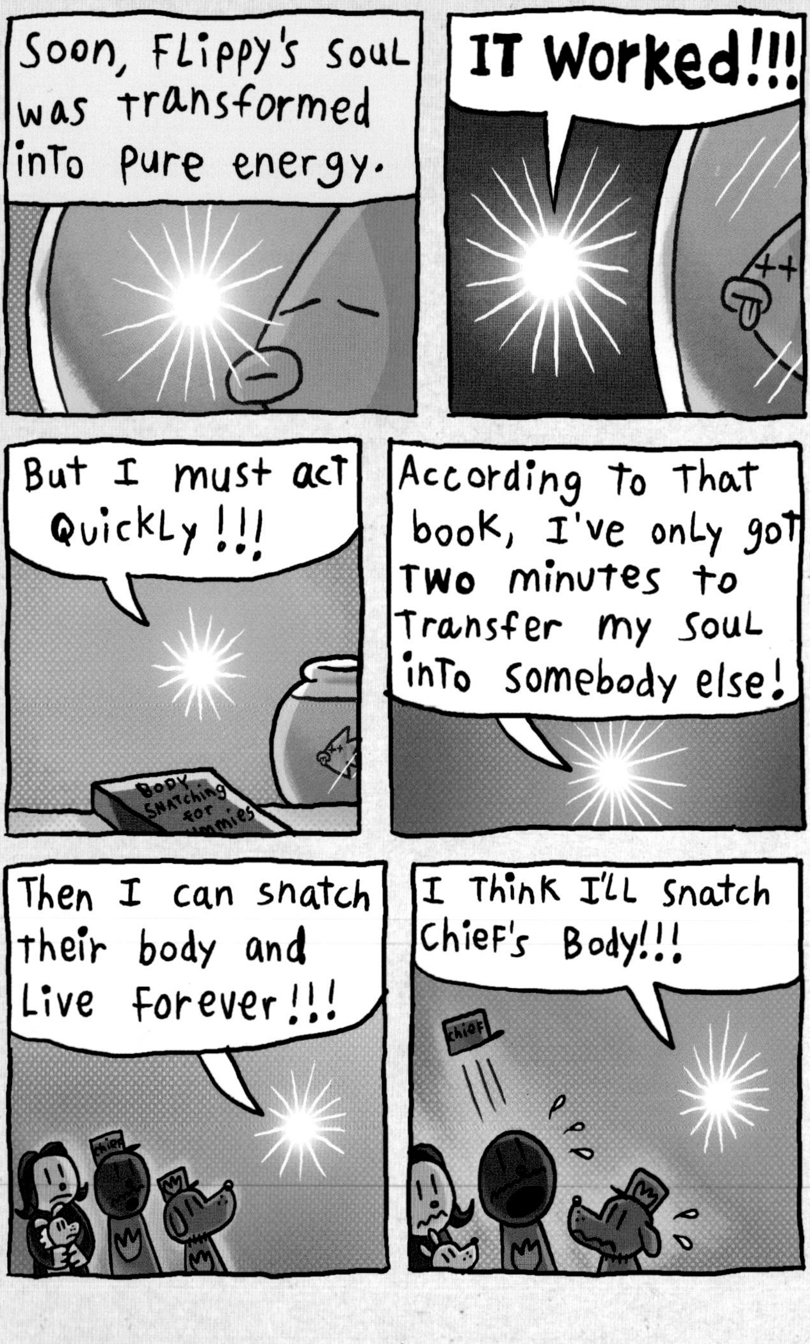
Soon, Flippy's soul was transformed into pure energy.
IT Worked!!!
But I must act quickly!!!
According to that book, I've only got two minutes to transfer my soul into somebody else!
BODY SNATCHING FOR
Then I can snatch their body and live forever!!!
I think I'll snatch Chief's body!!!
CHIEF

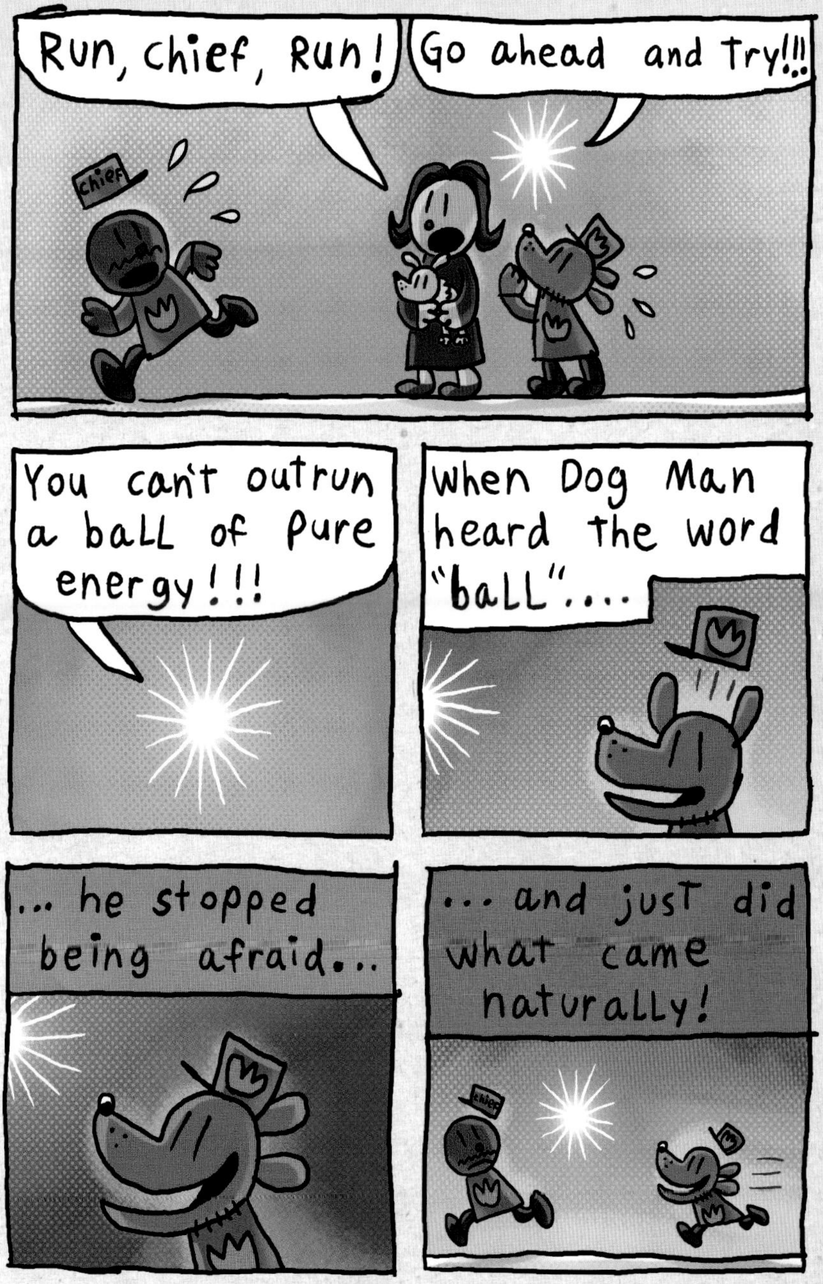
Run, chief, Run!
Go ahead and Try!!!
chief
You can't outrun a baLL of Pure energy!!!
When Dog Man heard the word "baLL"...
... he stopped being afraid...
... and just did what came naturaLLy!

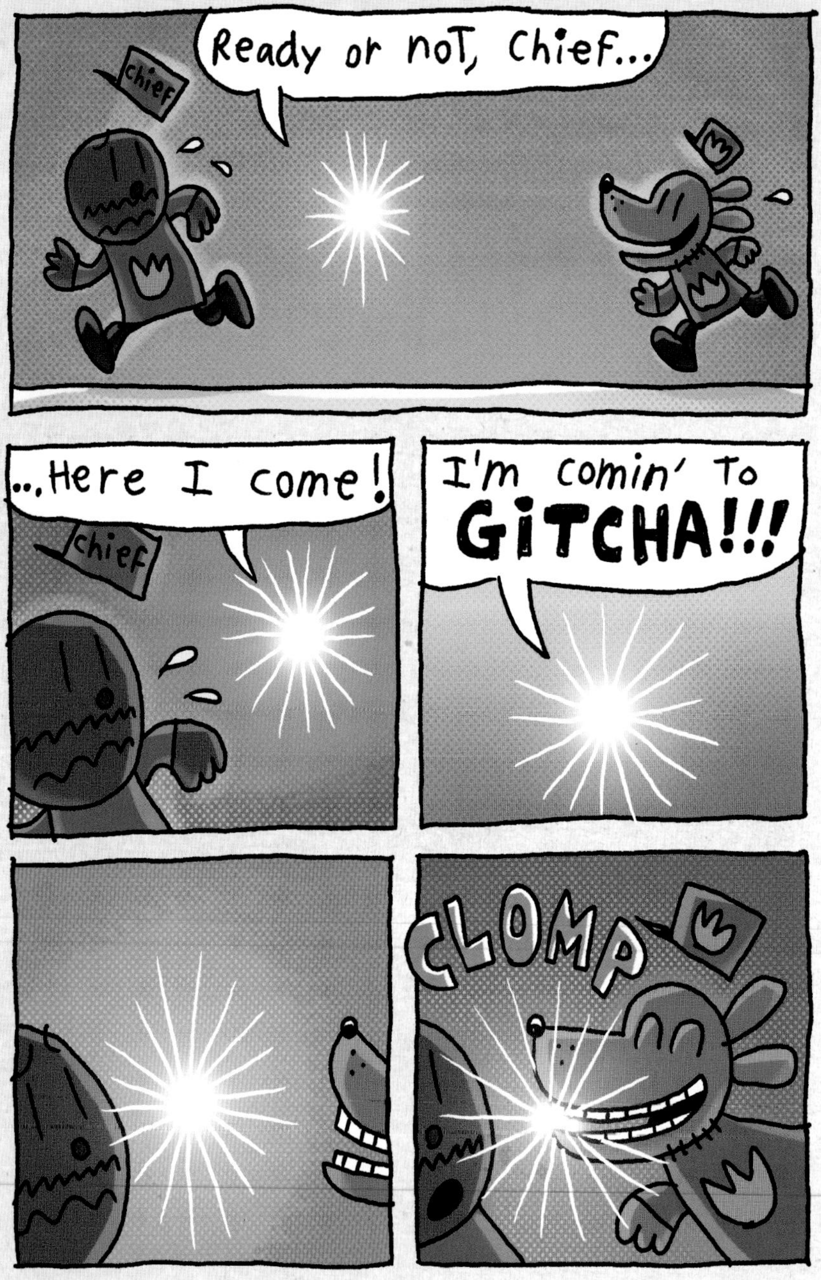
Ready or not, Chief...
chief
...Here I come!
chief
I'm comin' to
GITCHA!!!
CLOMP

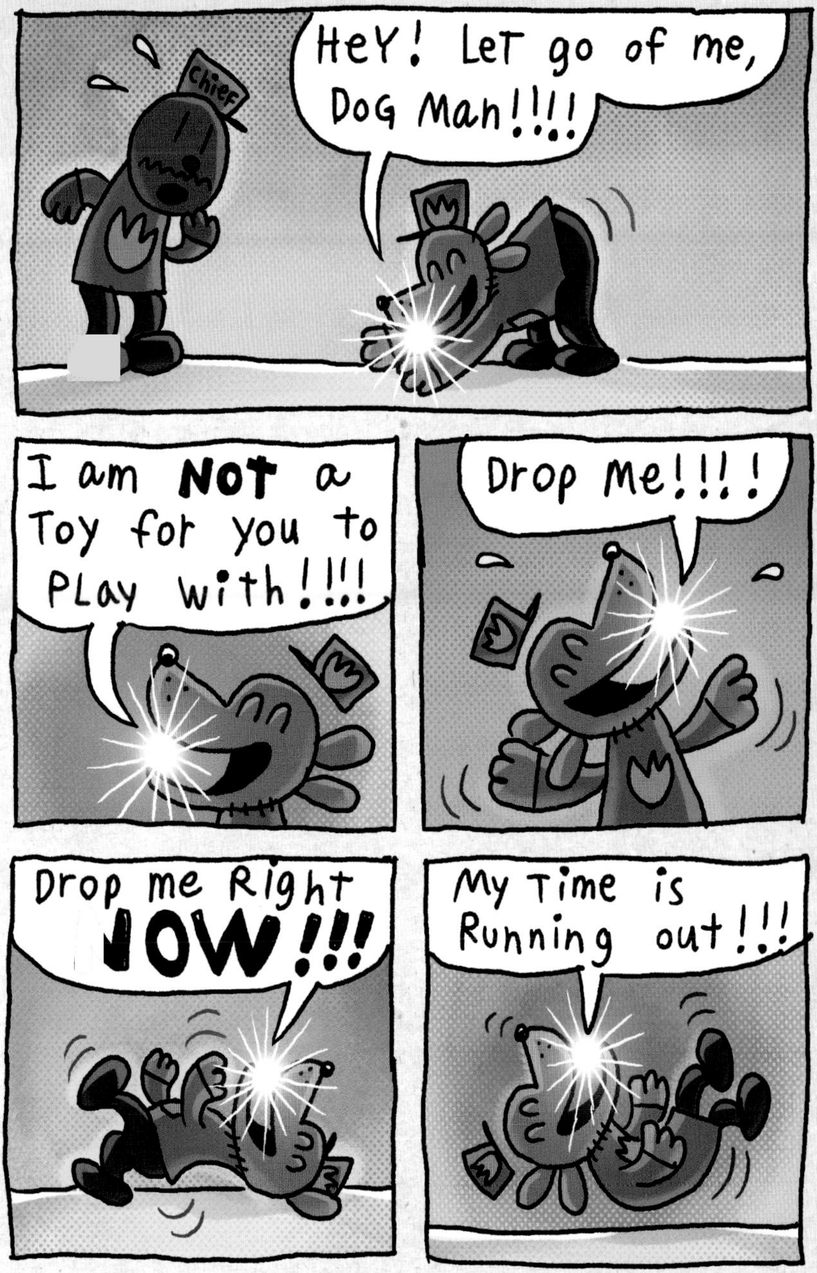
HeY! LeT go of me, DoG Man!!!!
I am NOT a Toy for you to PLay with!!!!
Drop Me!!!!
Drop me Right NOW!!!
My Time is Running out!!!

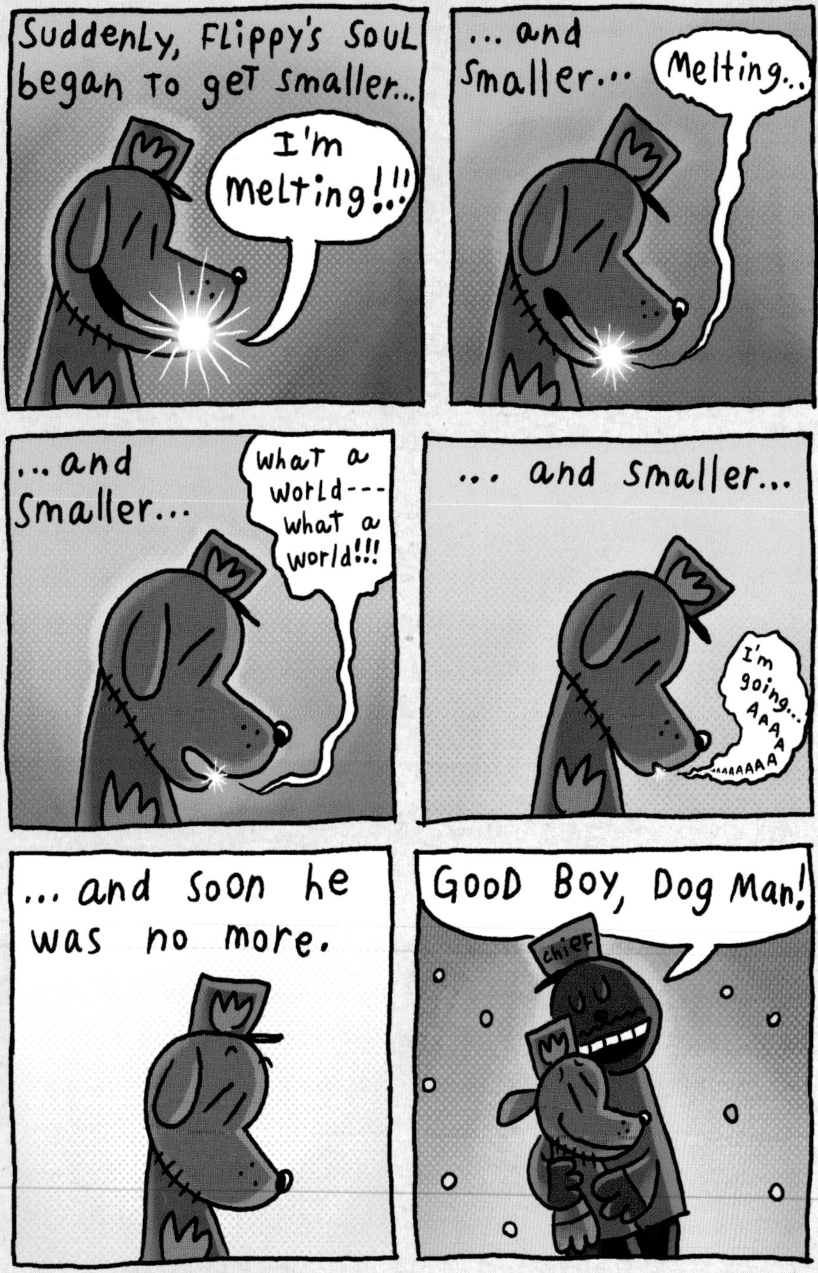
Suddenly, Flippy's soul began to get smaller...
I'm melting!!!
... and smaller...
Melting...
... and smaller...
What a world--- what a world!!!
... and smaller...
I'm going... AAAAAAAAAA
... and soon he was no more.
Good boy, Dog Man!
Chief

CHAPTER 10

An Ice ENDING

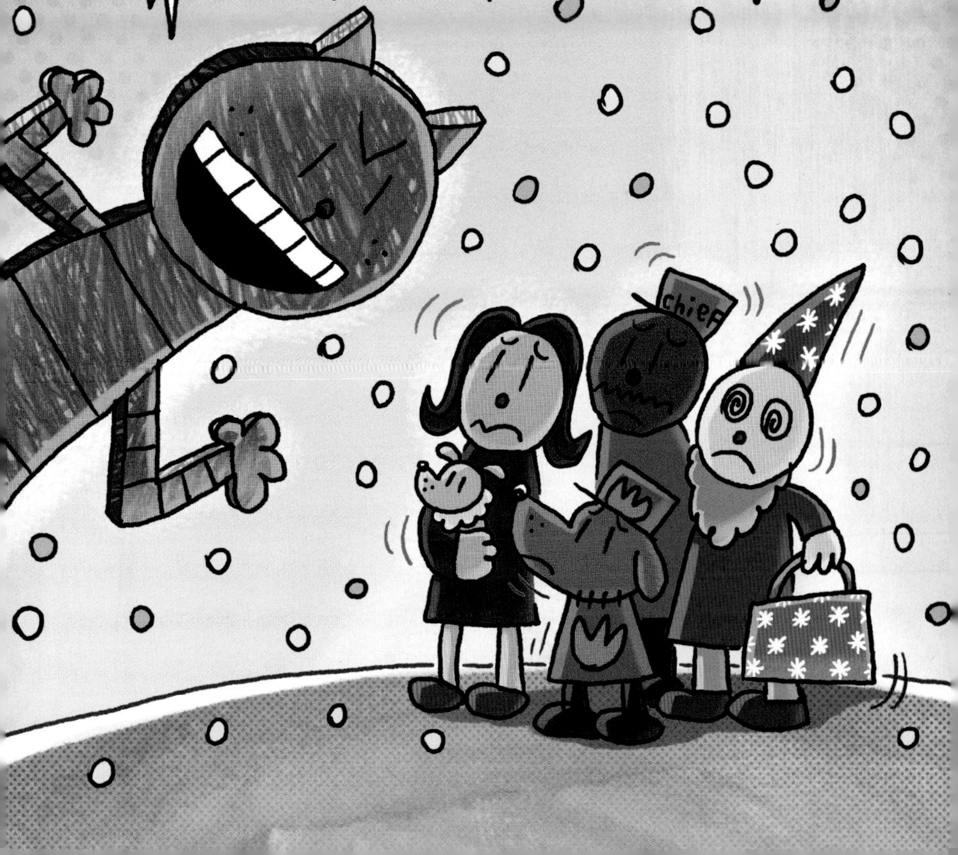

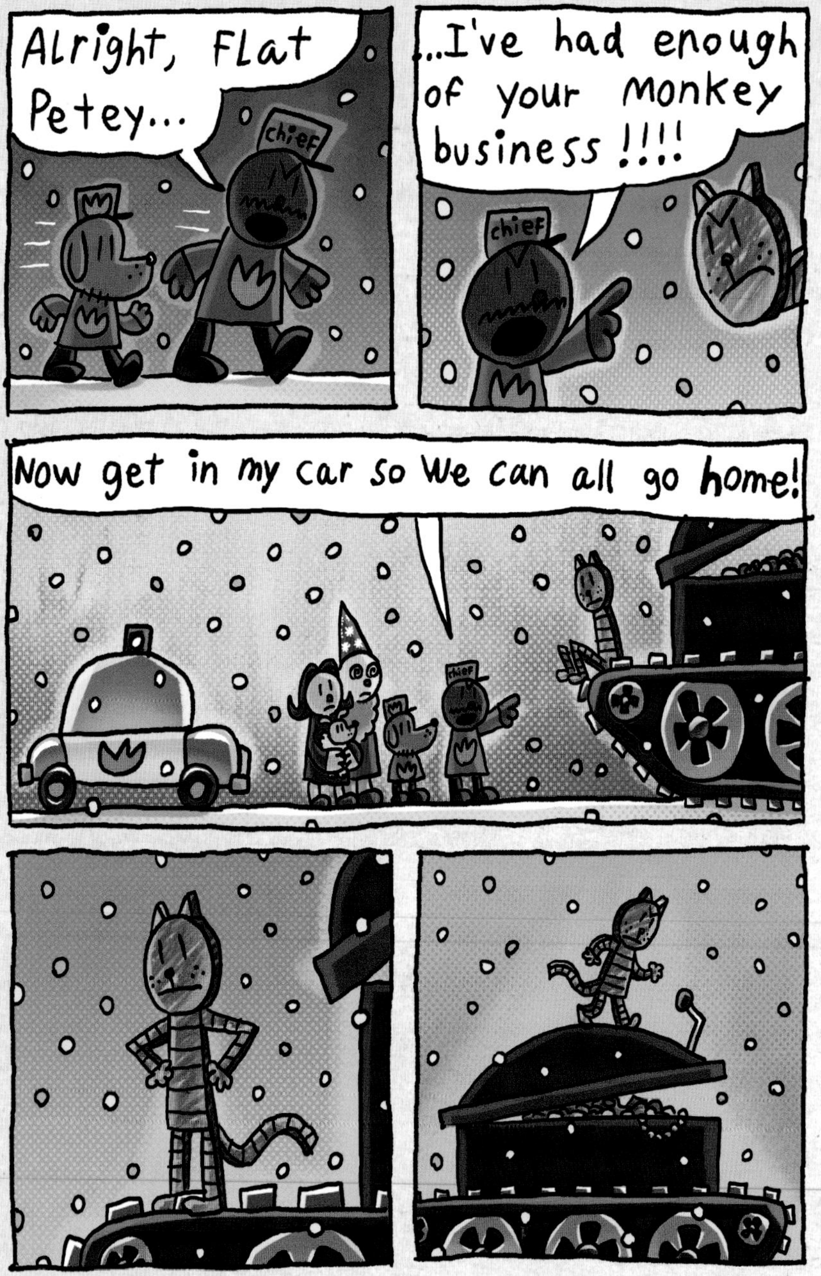
Alright, Flat Petey...
chief
...I've had enough of your monkey business!!!!
chief
Now get in my car so we can all go home!
chief

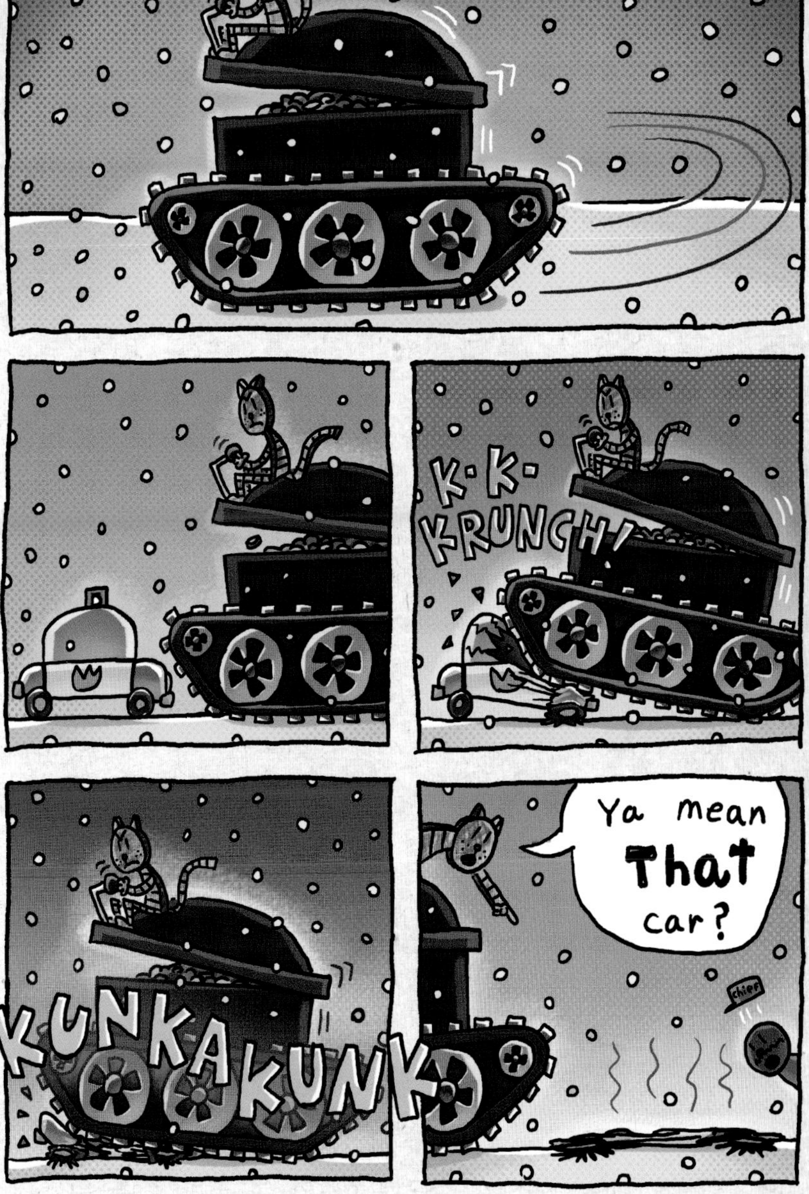
K-K-KRUNCH!
KUNKAKUNK
Ya mean That car?
chief

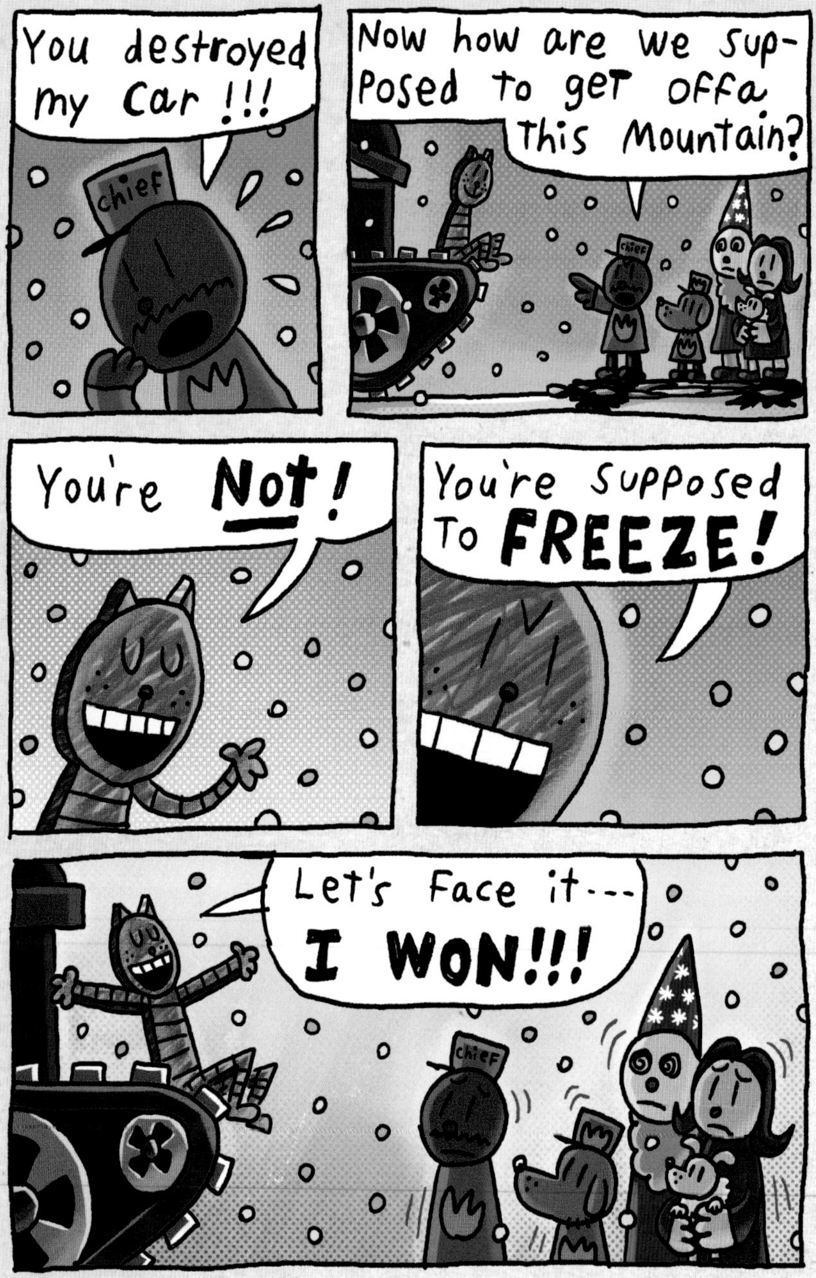
You destroyed my Car !!!
Now how are we sup-posed to get offa this Mountain?
You're Not!
You're supposed To FREEZE!
Let's Face it---
I WON!!!

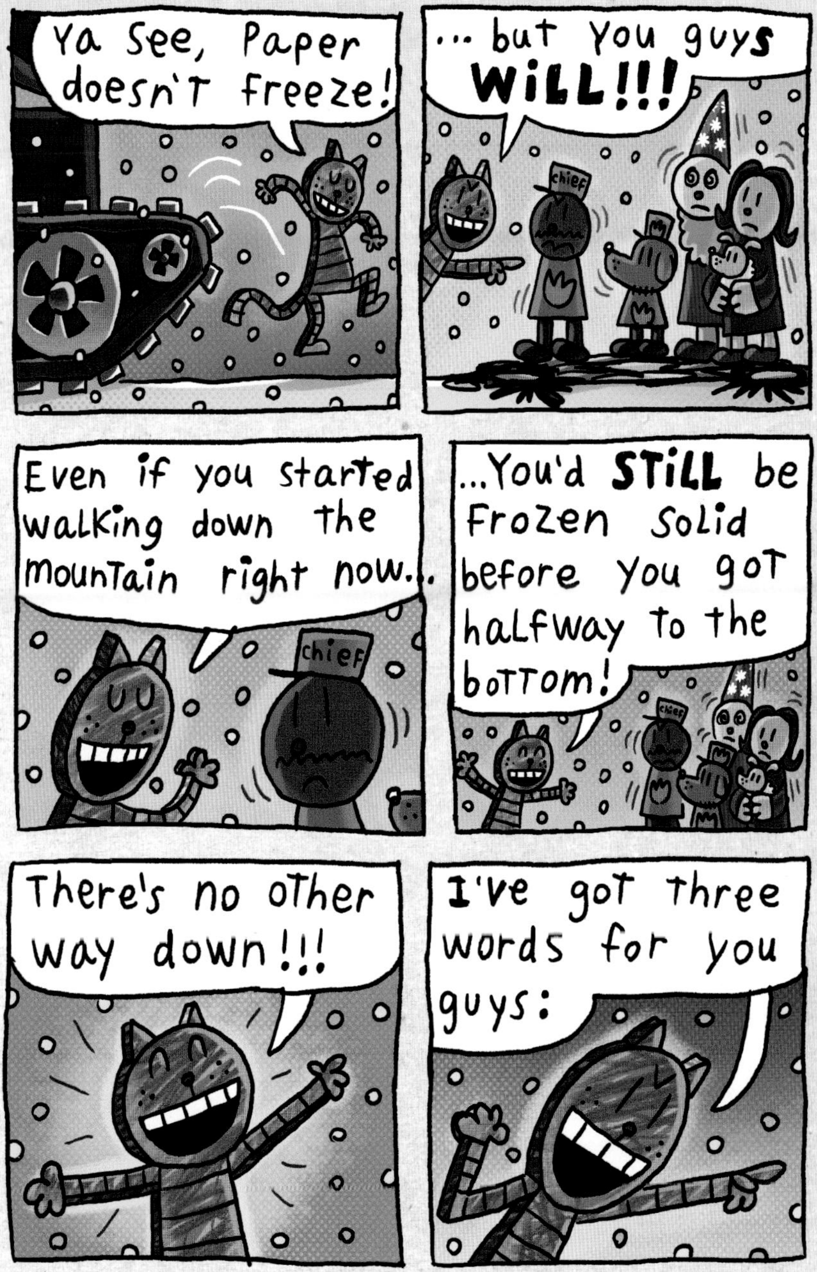
Ya See, Paper doesn't freeze!
... but you guys WILL!!!
Even if you started walking down the mountain right now...
...You'd STILL be Frozen Solid before you got halfway to the bottom!
There's no other way down!!!
I've got three words for you guys:

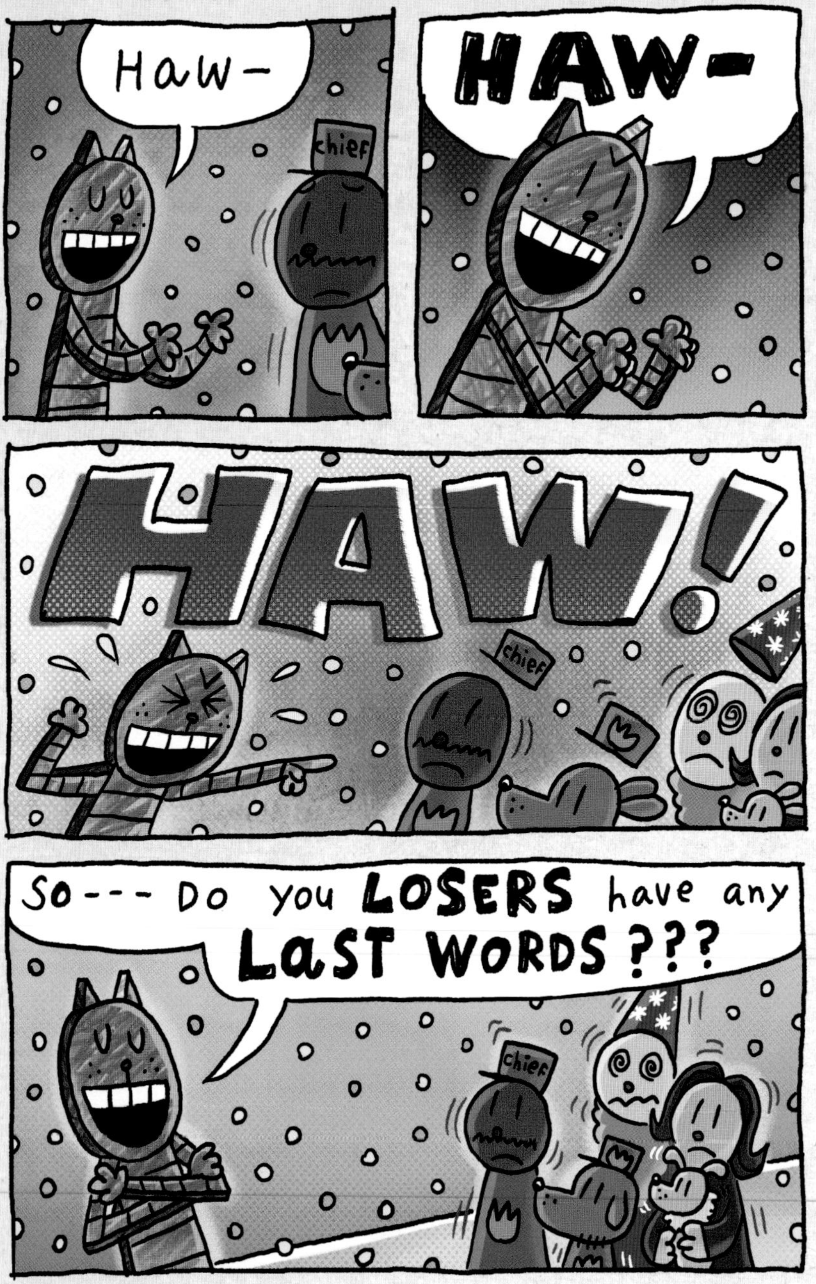
Haw-
chief
HAW-
HAW!
chief
So--- Do you LOSERS have any LAST WORDS???
chief

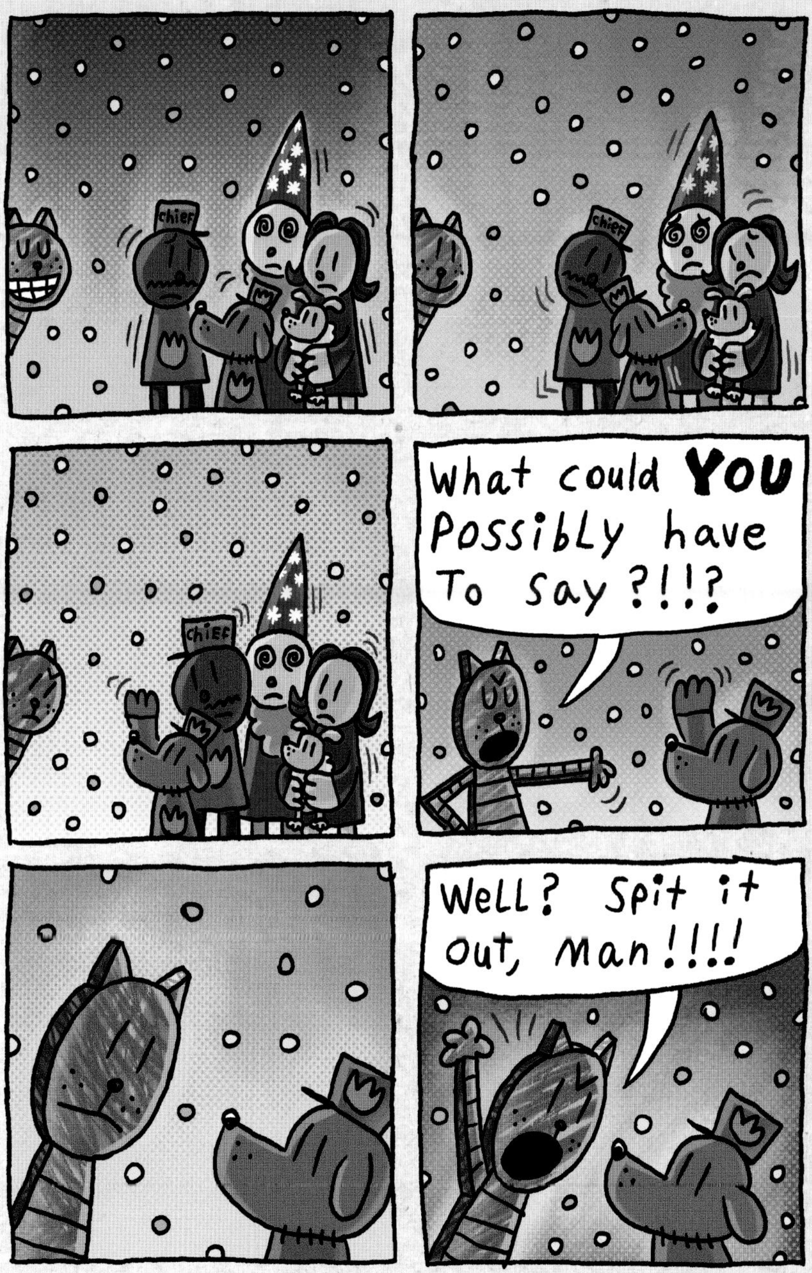
What could YOU Possibly have To say?!!?
Well? Spit it out, man!!!!

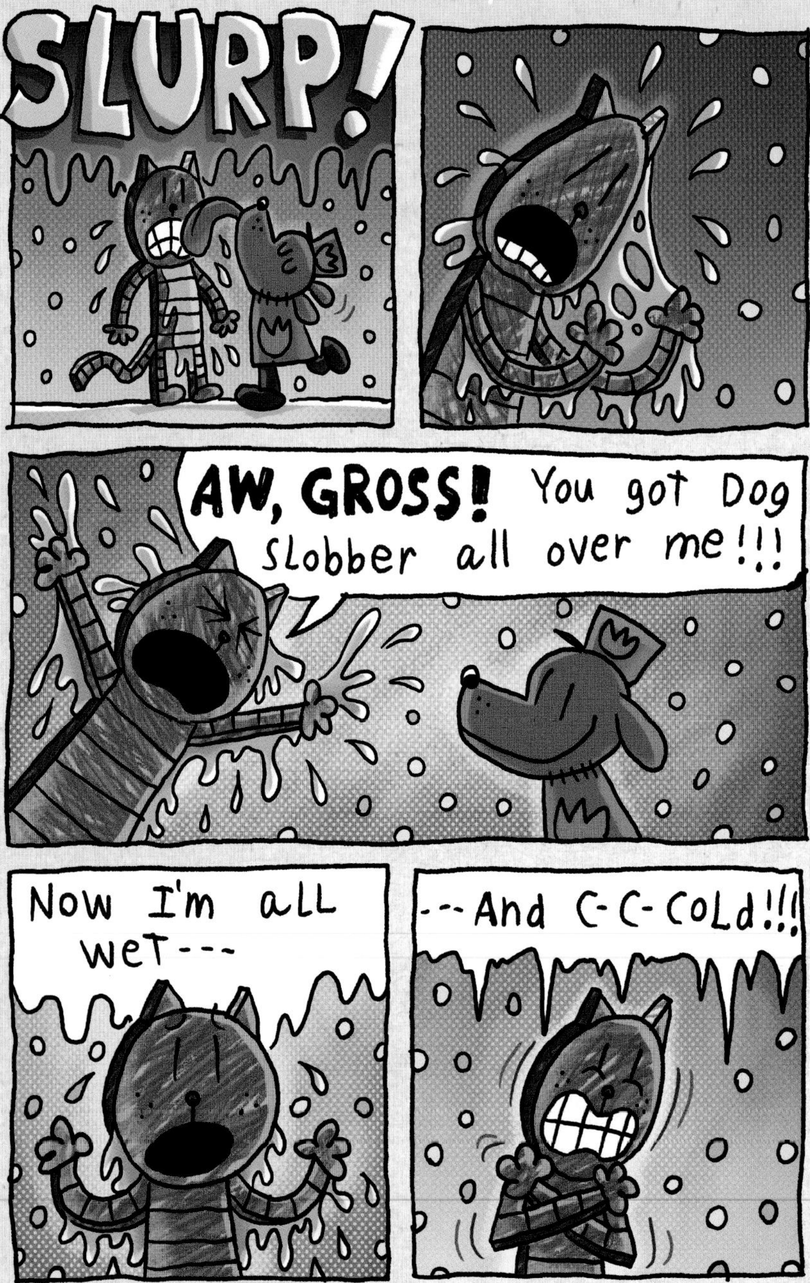
SLURP!
AW, GROSS! You got Dog slobber all over me!!!
Now I'm all wet---
---And C-C-COLd!!!

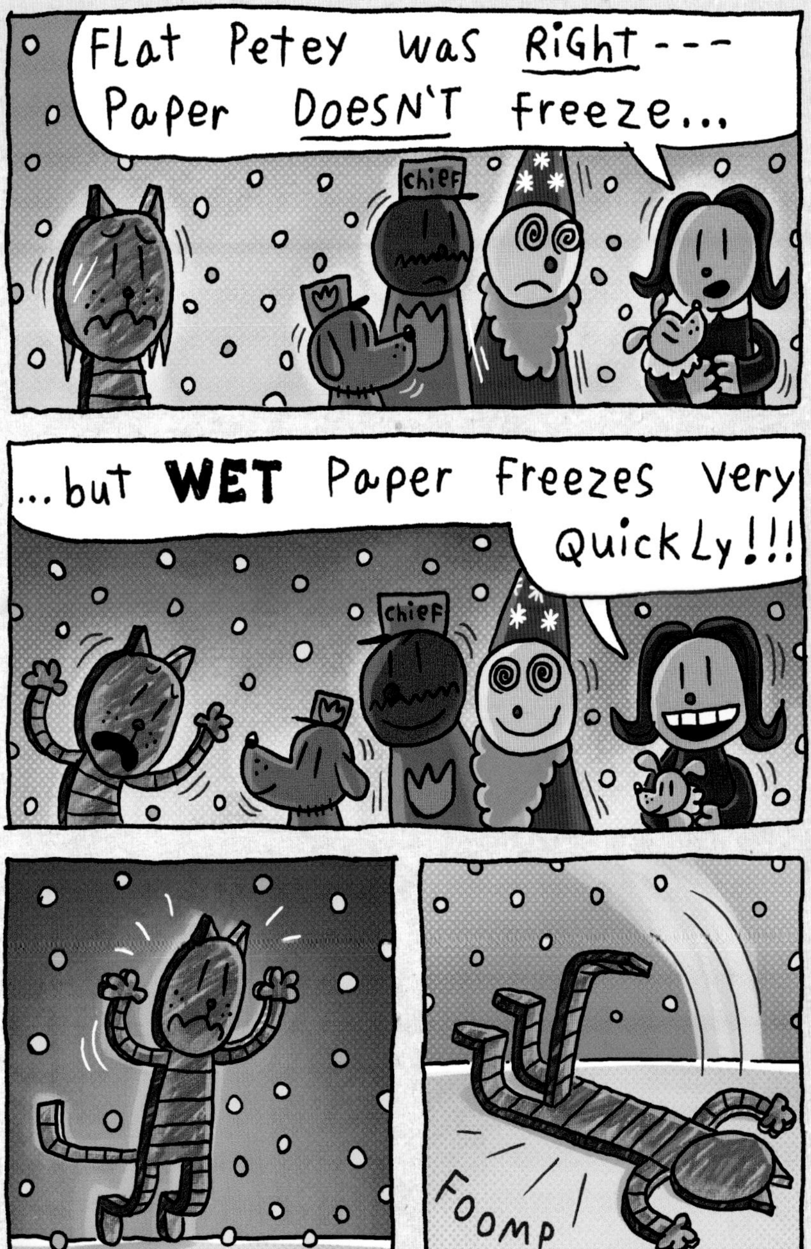
Flat Petey was RiGht---
Paper DOESN'T freeze...
chief
...but WET Paper Freezes very QuickLy!!!
chief
FOOMP

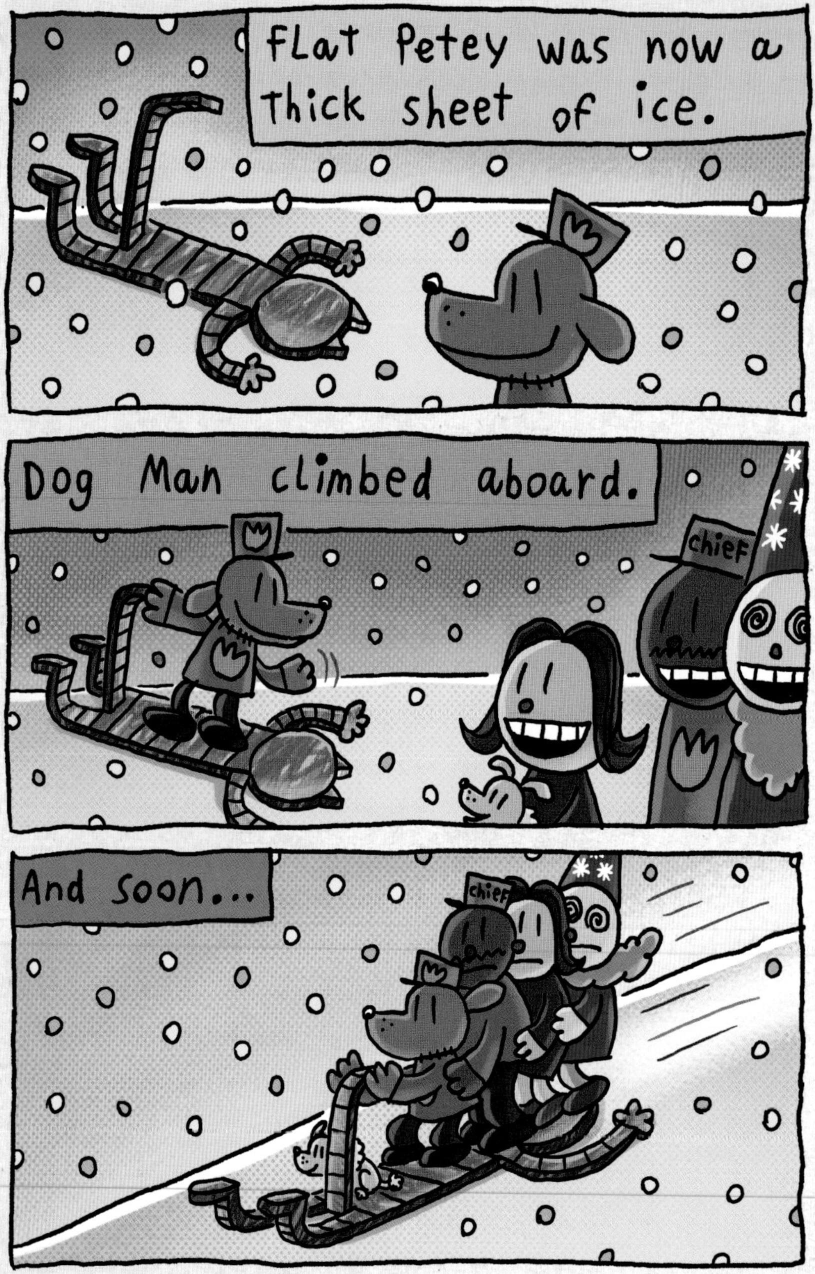
Flat Petey was now a thick sheet of ice.
Dog Man climbed aboard.
chief
And soon...
chief

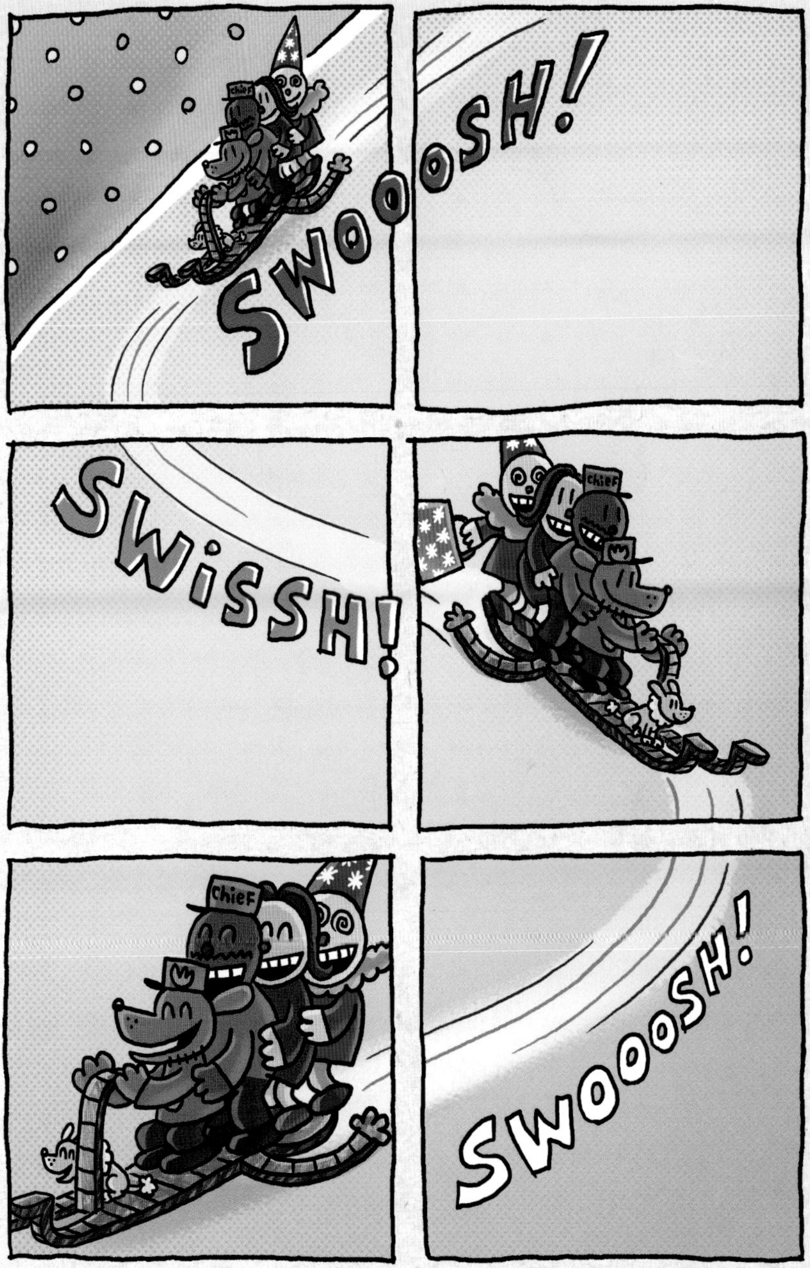
Chief
SWOOOSH!
SWiSSH!
Chief
Chief
SWOOOSH!

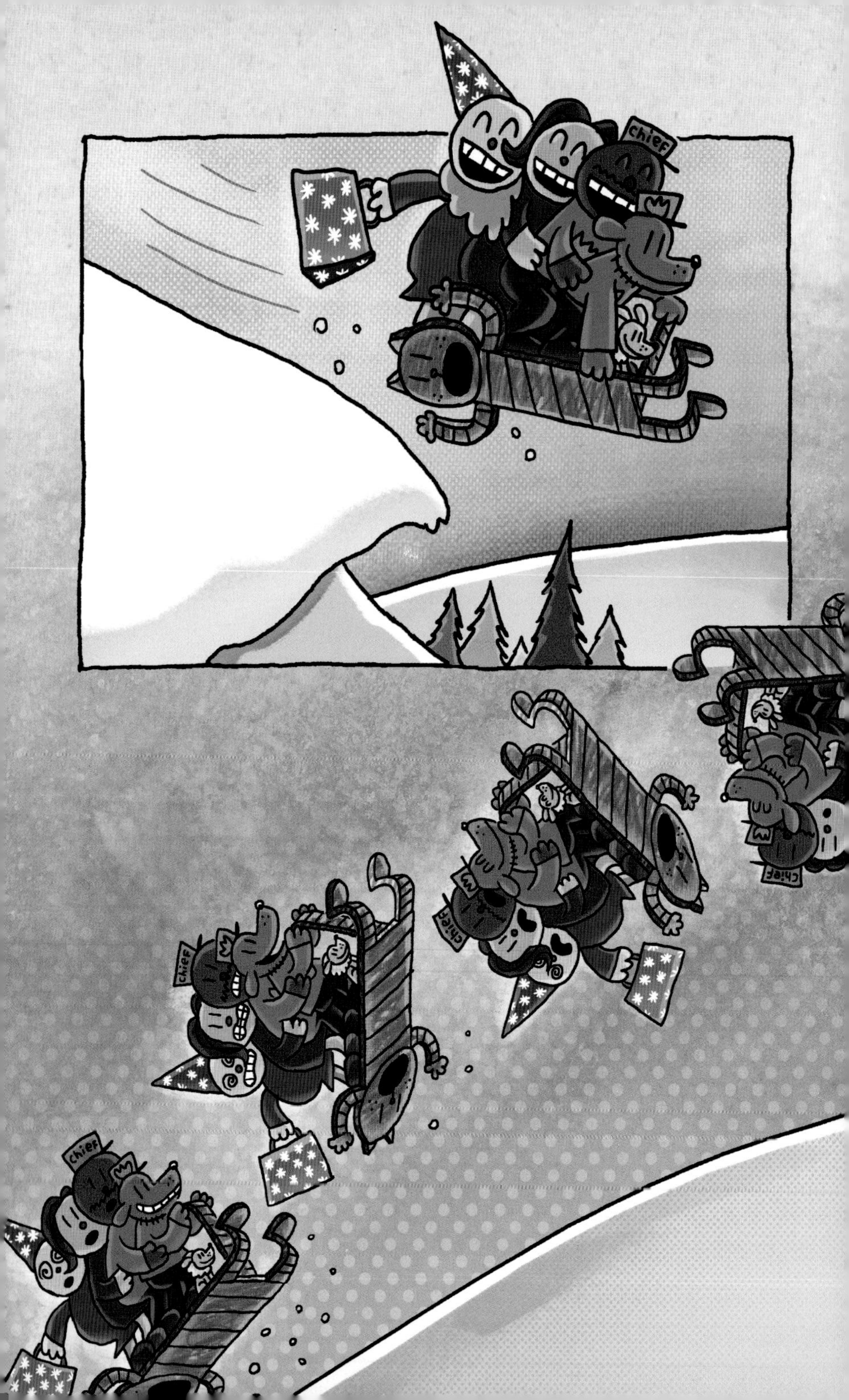
chief
chief
chief
chief

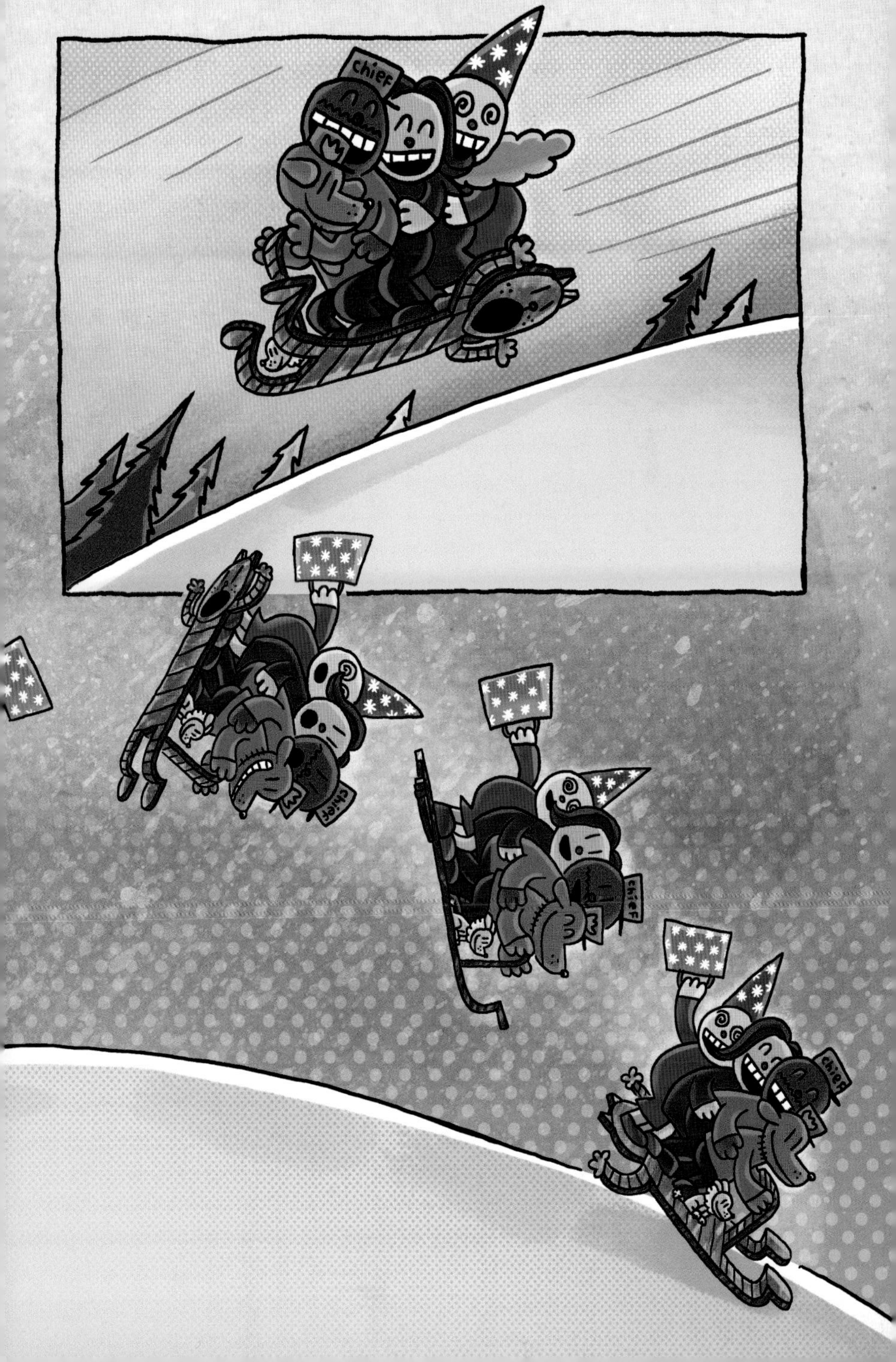
chief
chief
chief
chief

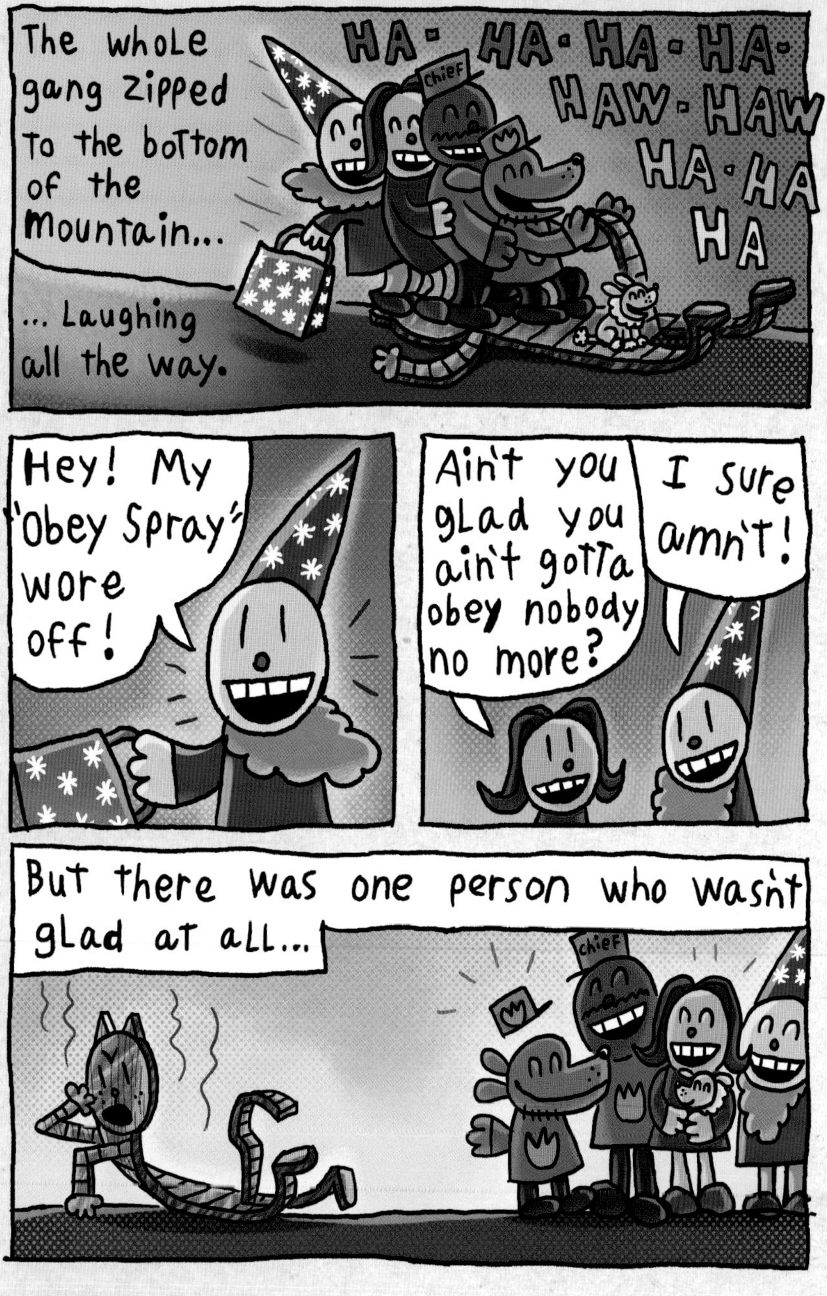
The whole gang zipped to the bottom of the mountain...
... Laughing all the way.
HA-HA-HA-HA-HAW-HAW HA-HA HA
Chief
Hey! My "Obey Spray" wore off!
Ain't you glad you ain't gotta obey nobody no more?
I sure amn't!
But there was one person who wasn't glad at all...
Chief

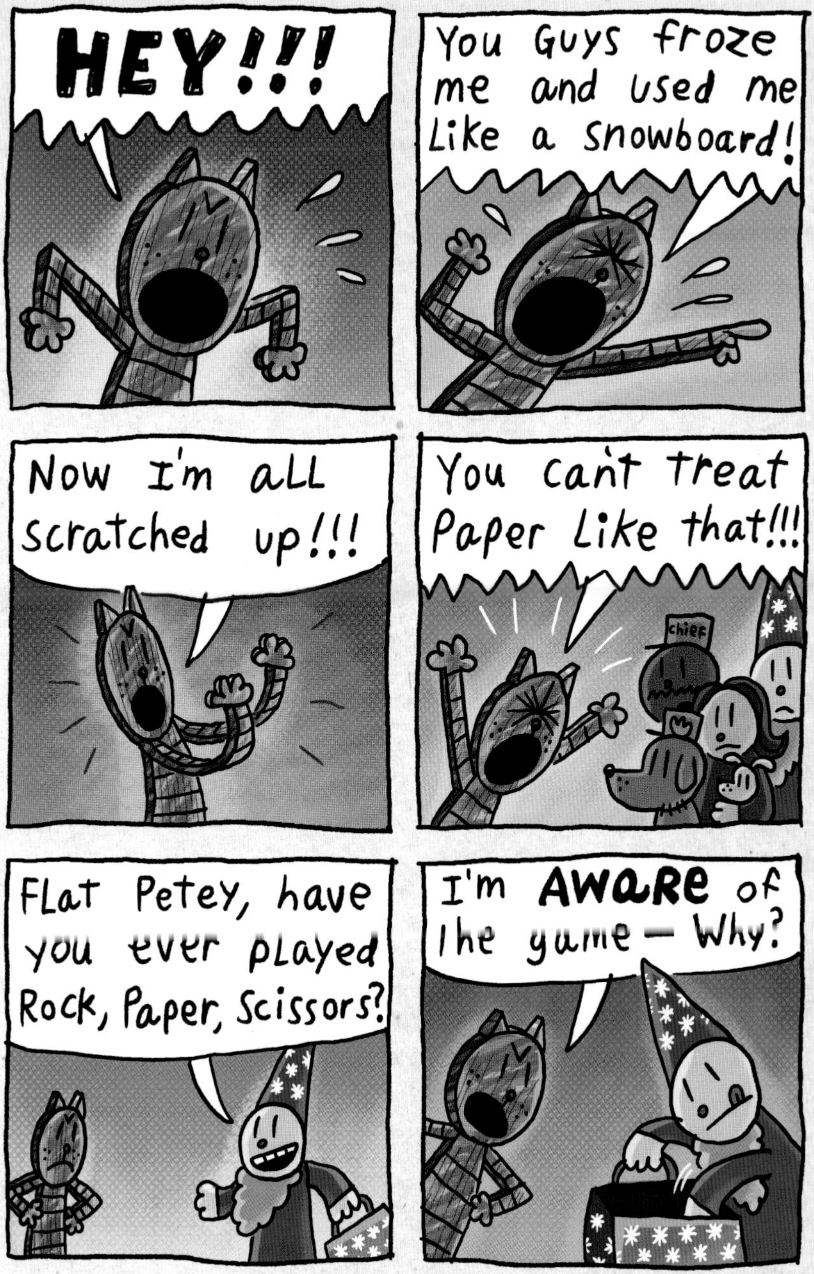
HEY!!!
You Guys froze me and used me Like a snowboard!
Now I'm aLL scratched up!!!
You can't treat Paper Like that!!!
chief
Flat Petey, have you ever pLayed Rock, Paper, Scissors?
I'm AWARE of the game— Why?

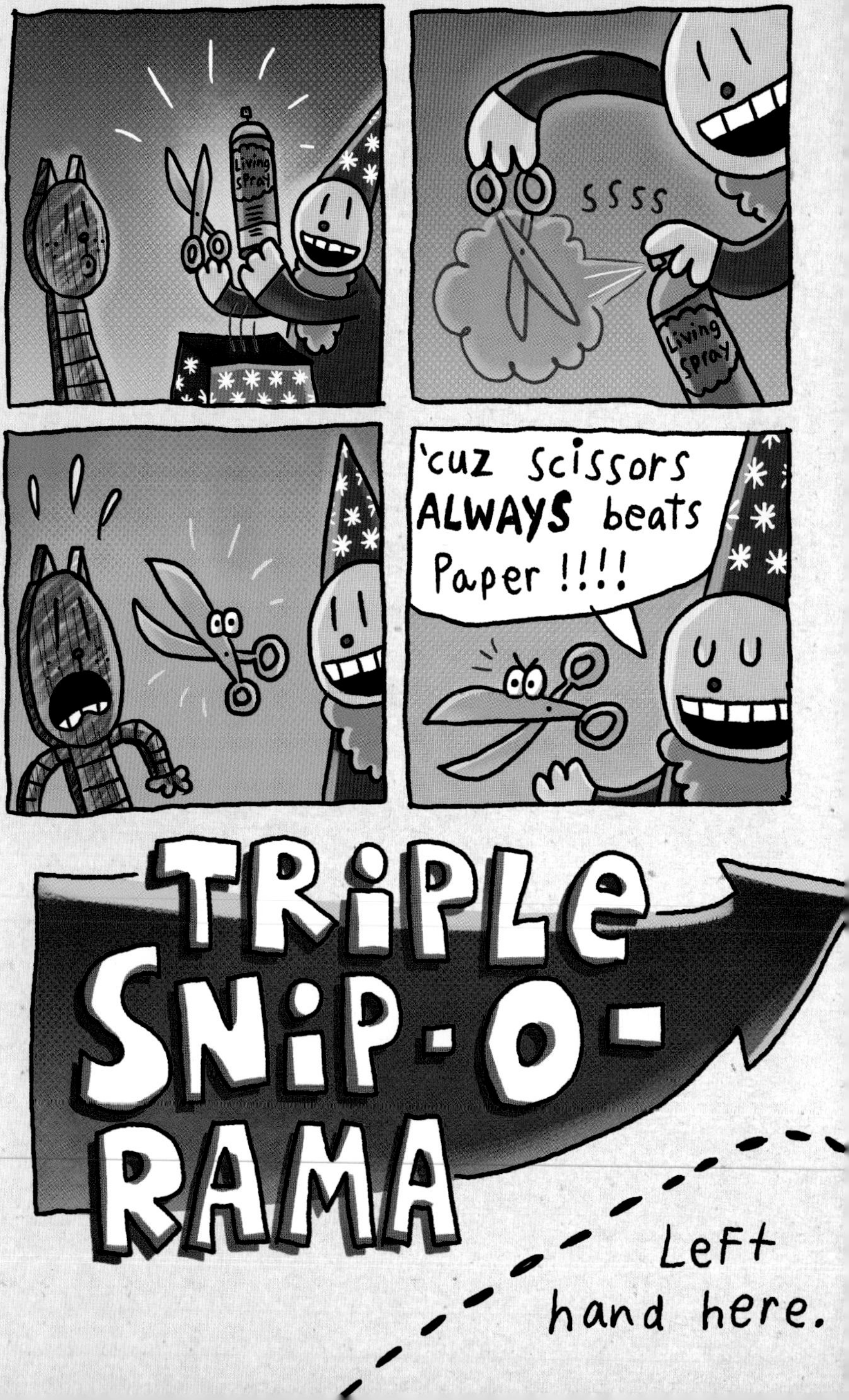
Living Spray
ssss
Living Spray
'cuz scissors ALWAYS beats Paper !!!!
TRIPLE SNIP-O-RAMA
Left hand here.

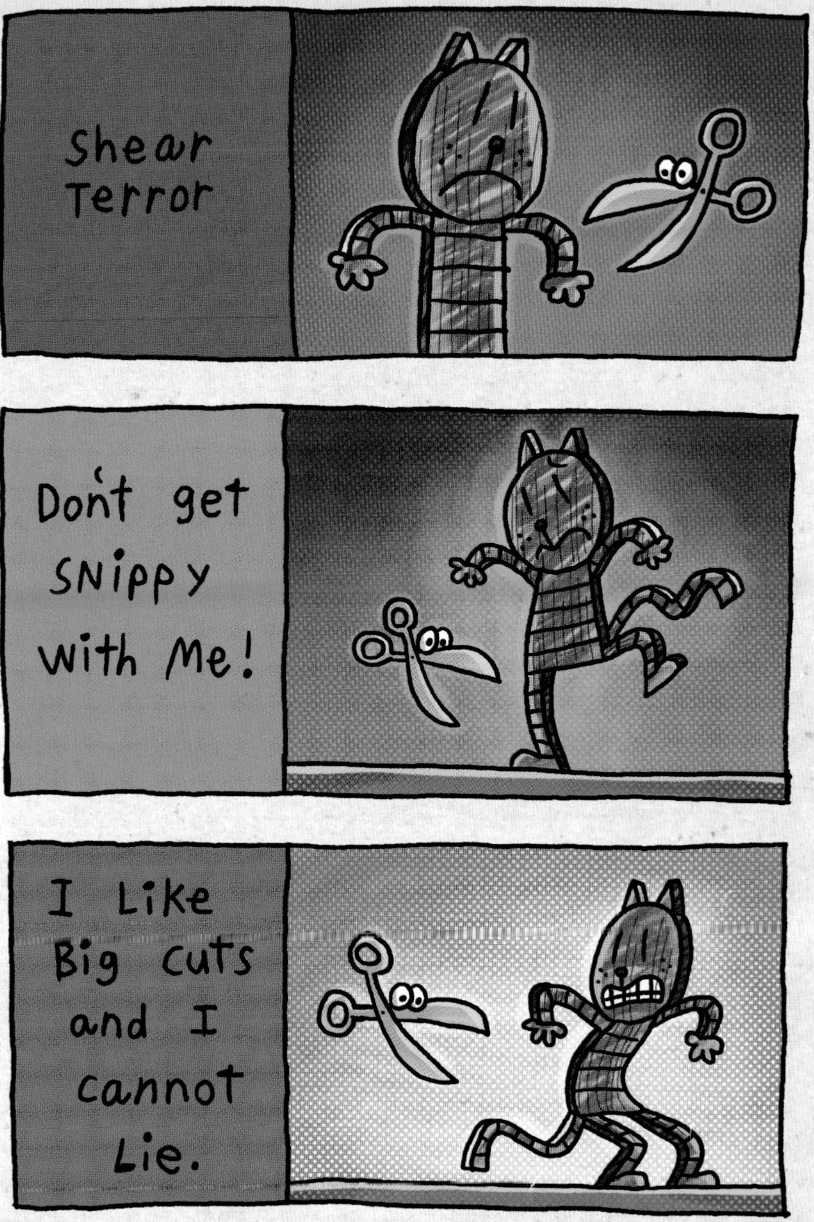
Shear Terror
Don't get SNIPPY with Me!
I Like Big cuts and I cannot Lie.

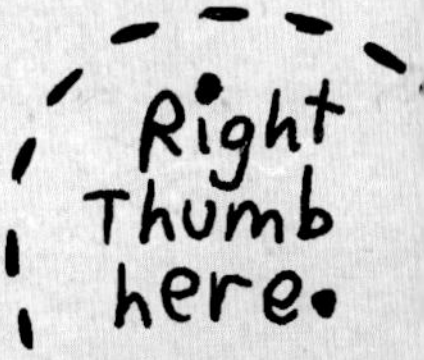
Right Thumb here.

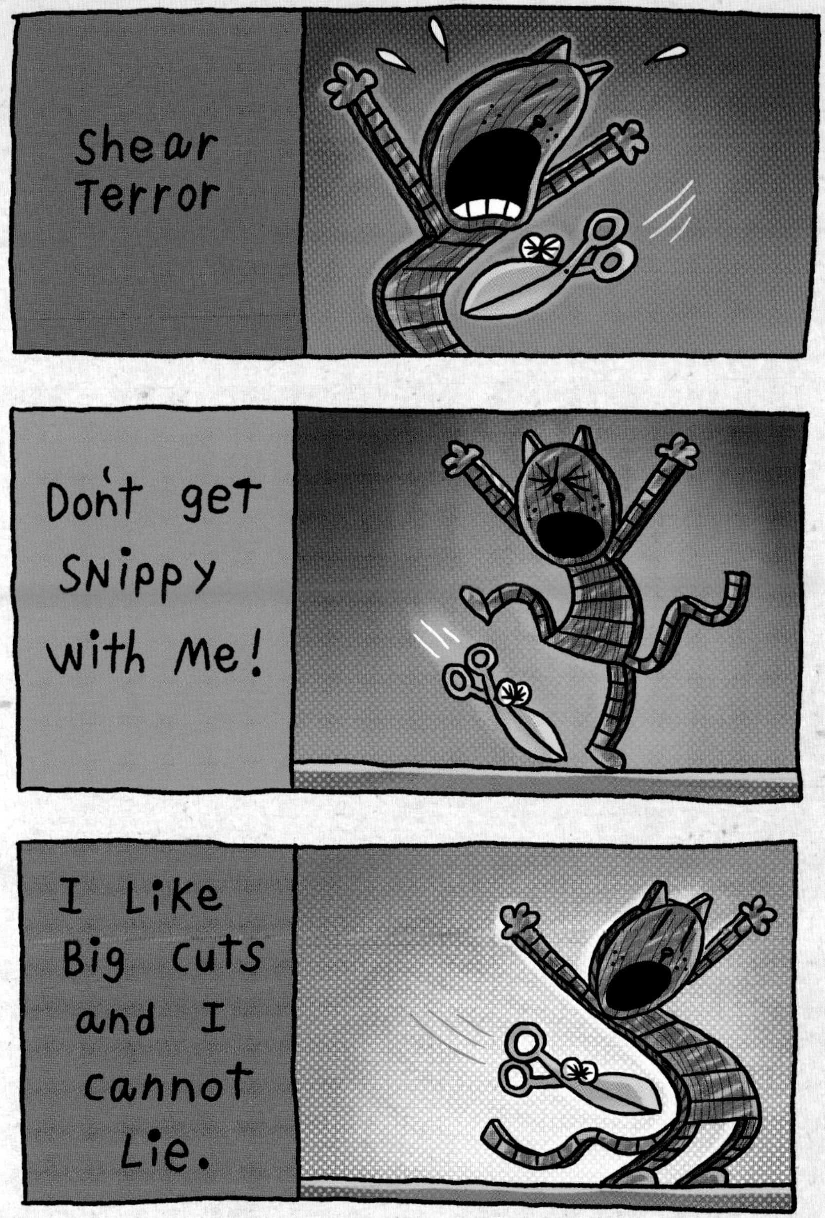
Shear Terror
Don't get SNIPPY with Me!
I Like Big cuts and I cannot Lie.

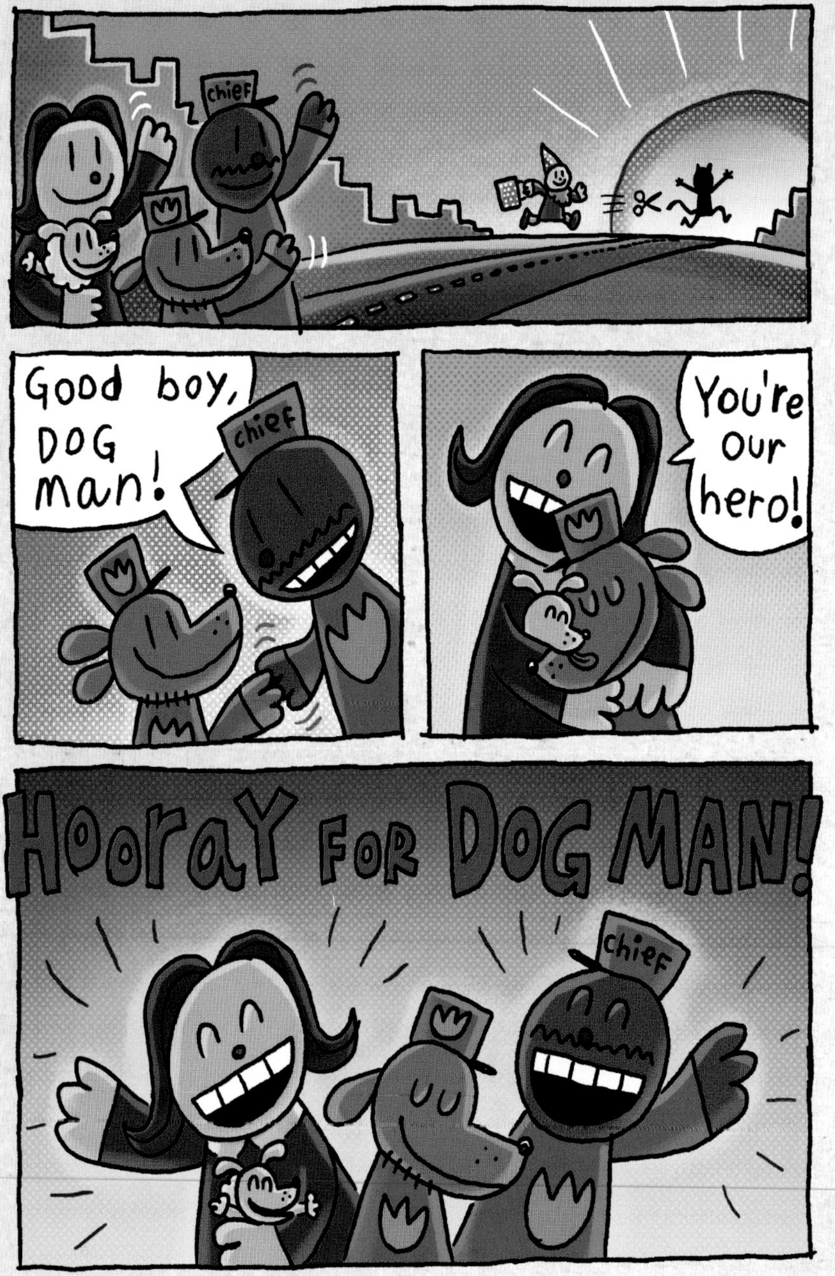
chief
Good boy, DOG man!
chief
You're our hero!
HOORAY FOR DOG MAN!
chief

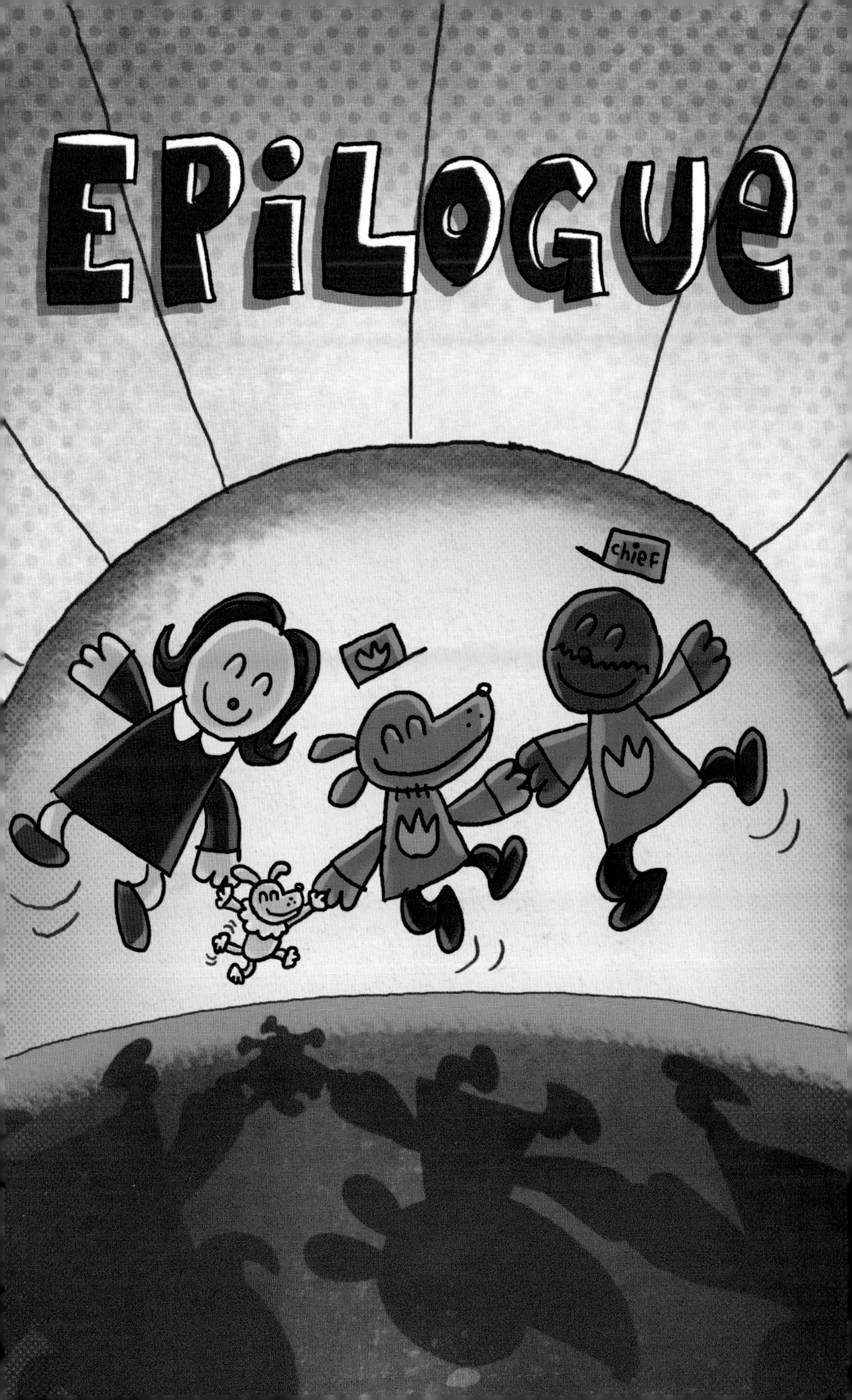
EPILOGUE
chief

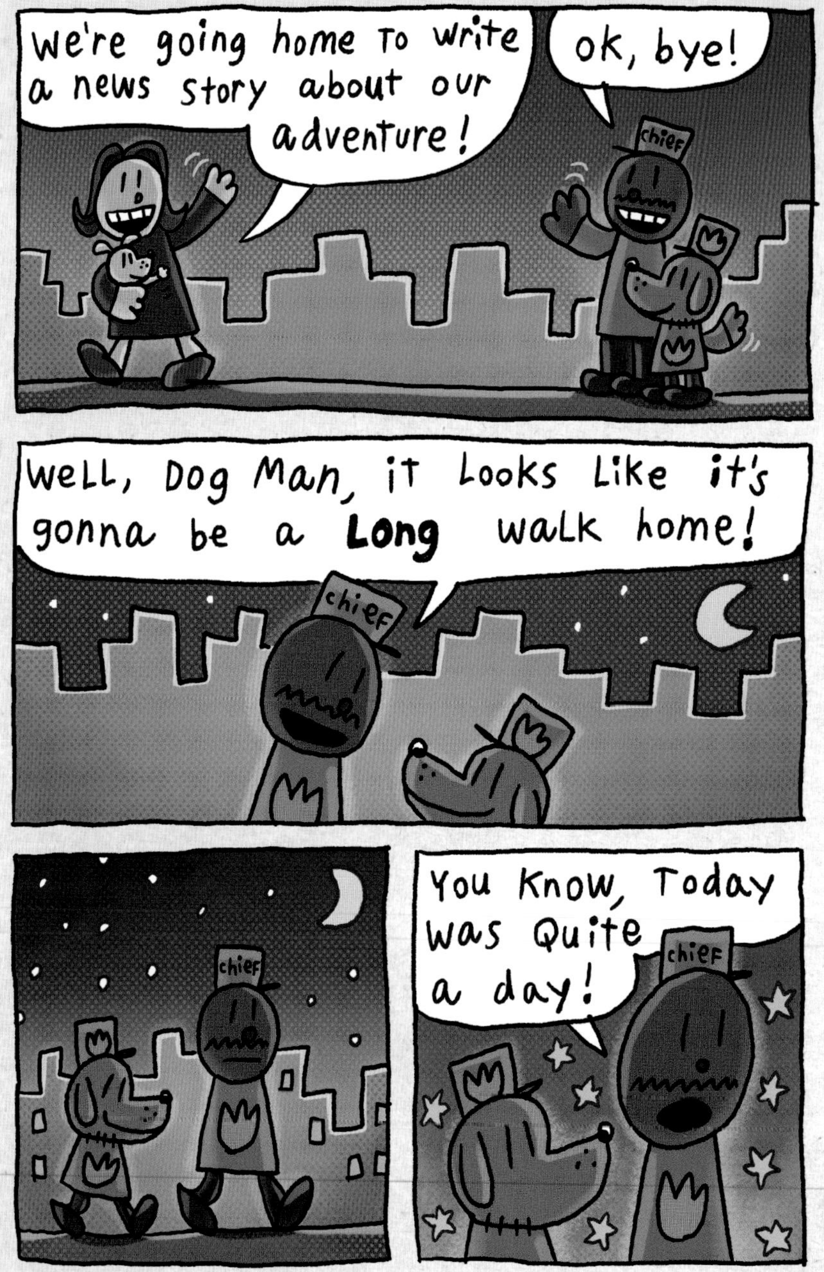
We're going home To write a news story about our adventure!
ok, bye!
chief
chief
WeLL, Dog Man, it Looks Like it's gonna be a **Long** walk home!
chief
You Know, Today was Quite a day!
chief

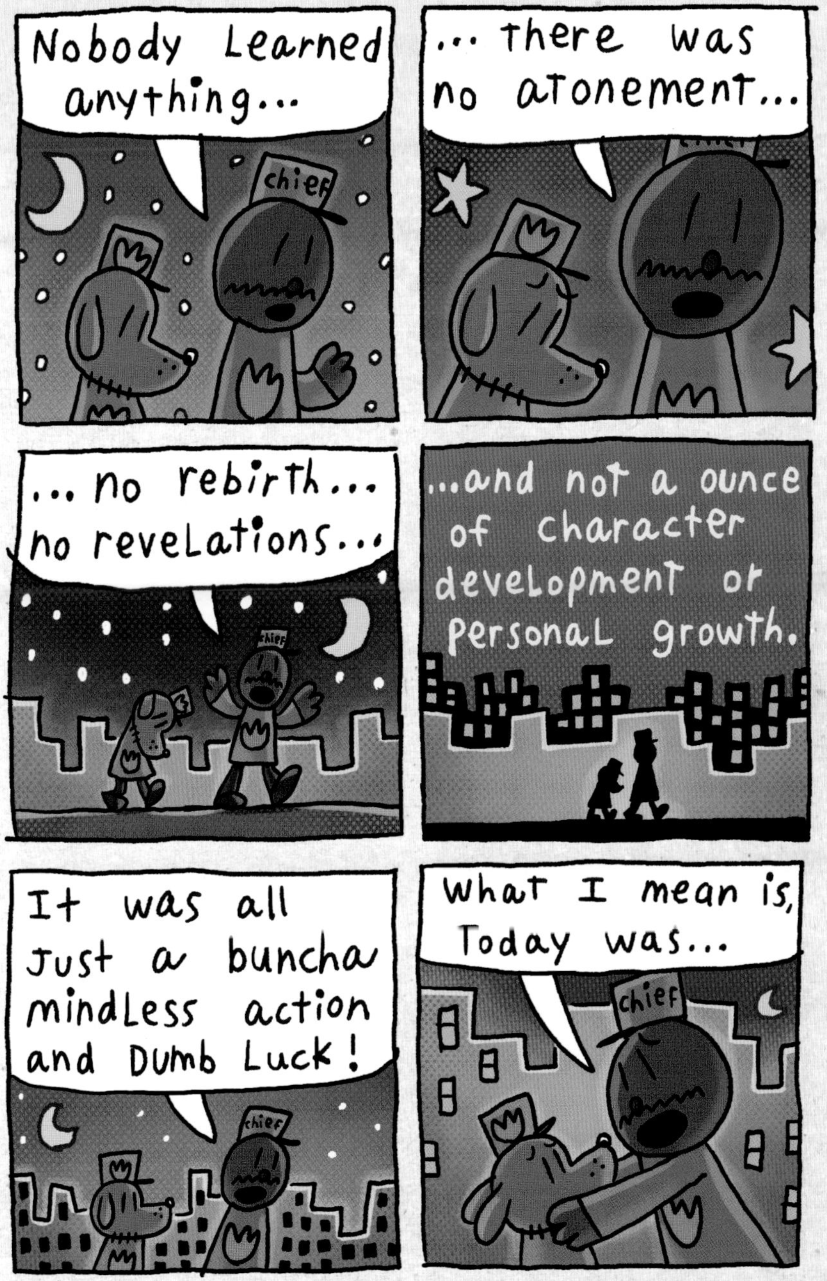
Nobody Learned anything...
... there was no atonement...
... no rebirth... no revelations...
...and not a ounce of character development or personal growth.
It was all Just a buncha mindless action and Dumb Luck!
What I mean is, Today was...

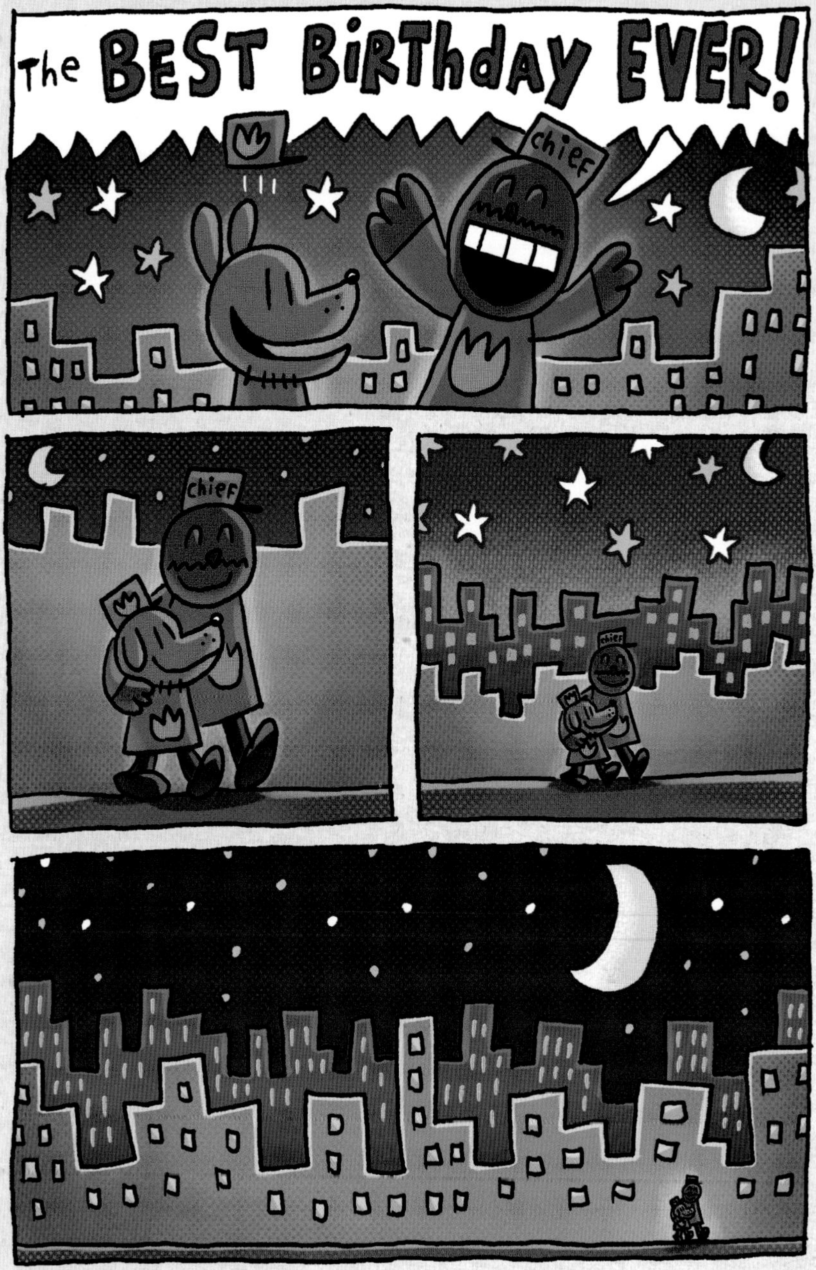
The BEST BiRThday EVER!
chief
chief
chief

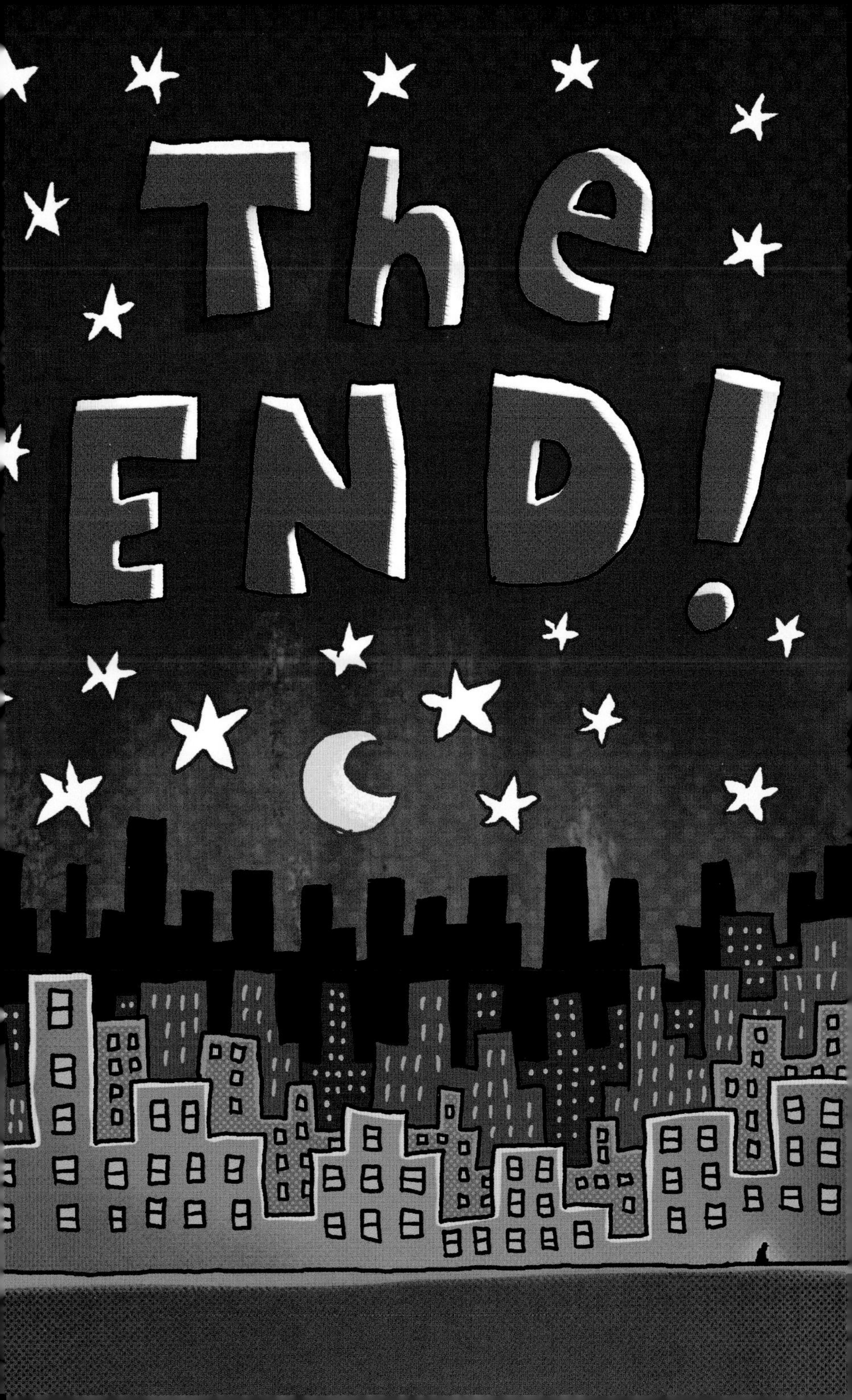
The END!

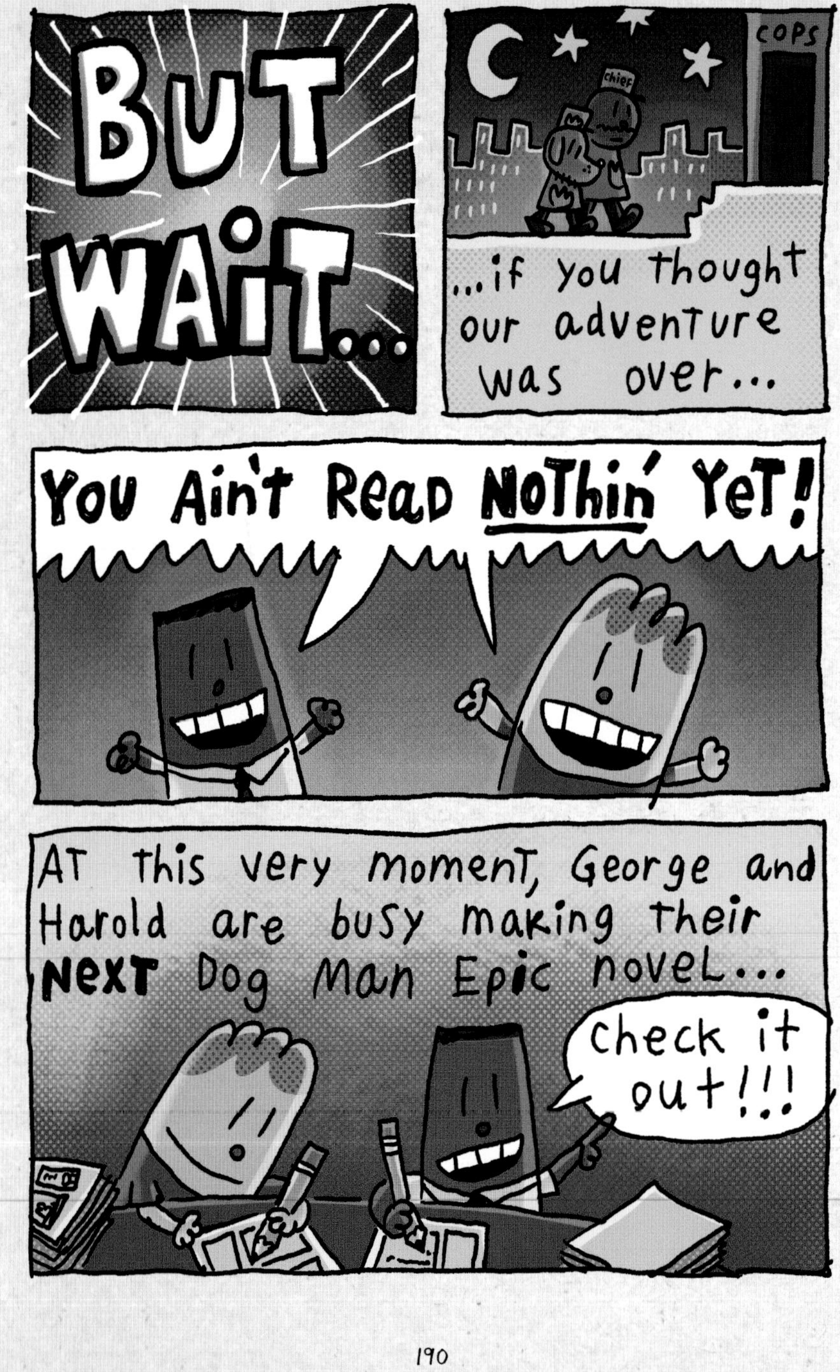
BUT WAIT...
COPS
Chief
...if you thought our adventure was over...
You Ain't Read NOThin' YeT!
AT this very moment, George and Harold are busy making their NEXT Dog Man Epic novel...
Check it out!!!

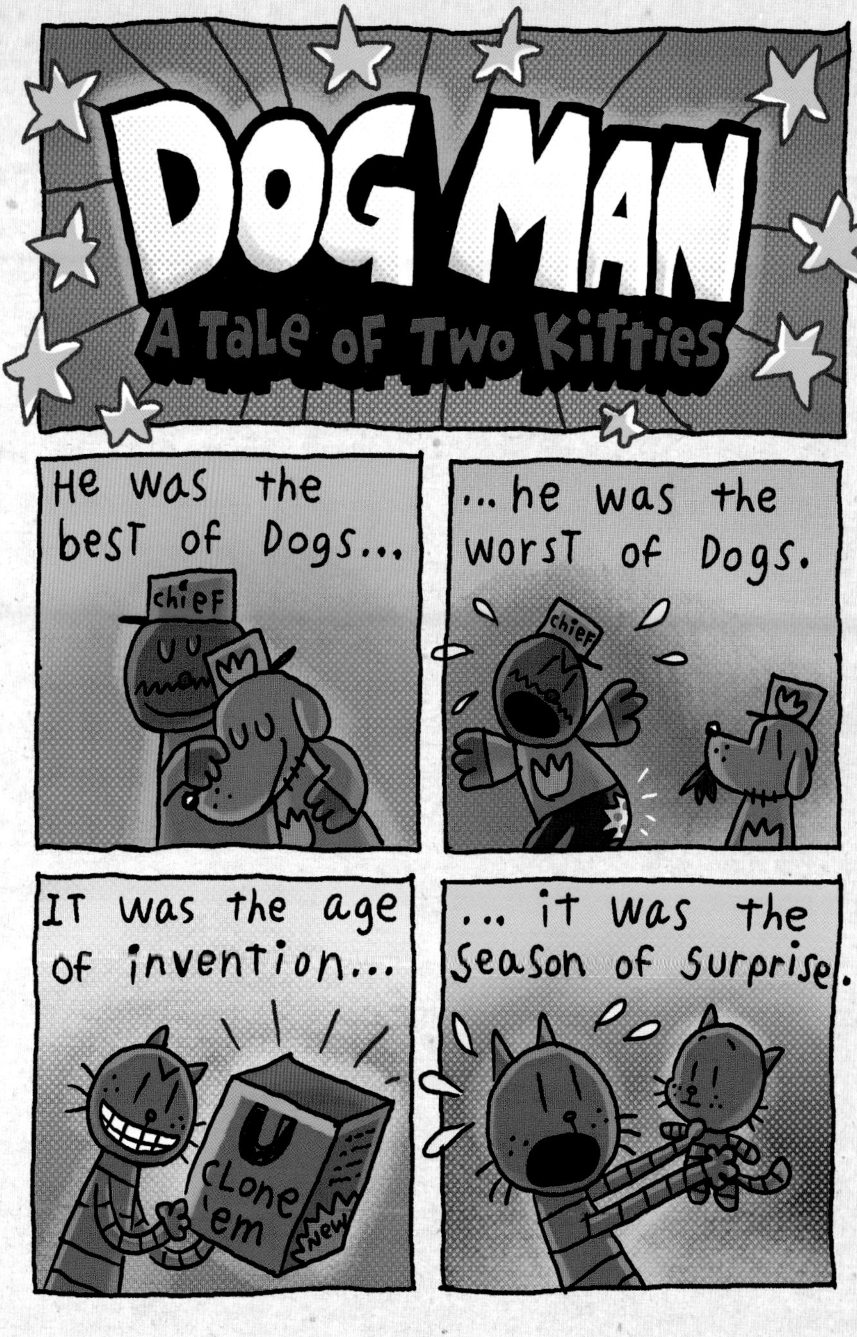
DOG MAN
A Tale of Two Kitties
He was the best of Dogs...
chief
...he was the worst of Dogs.
chief
IT was the age of invention...
U
CLone 'em
NEW
... it was the season of surprise.

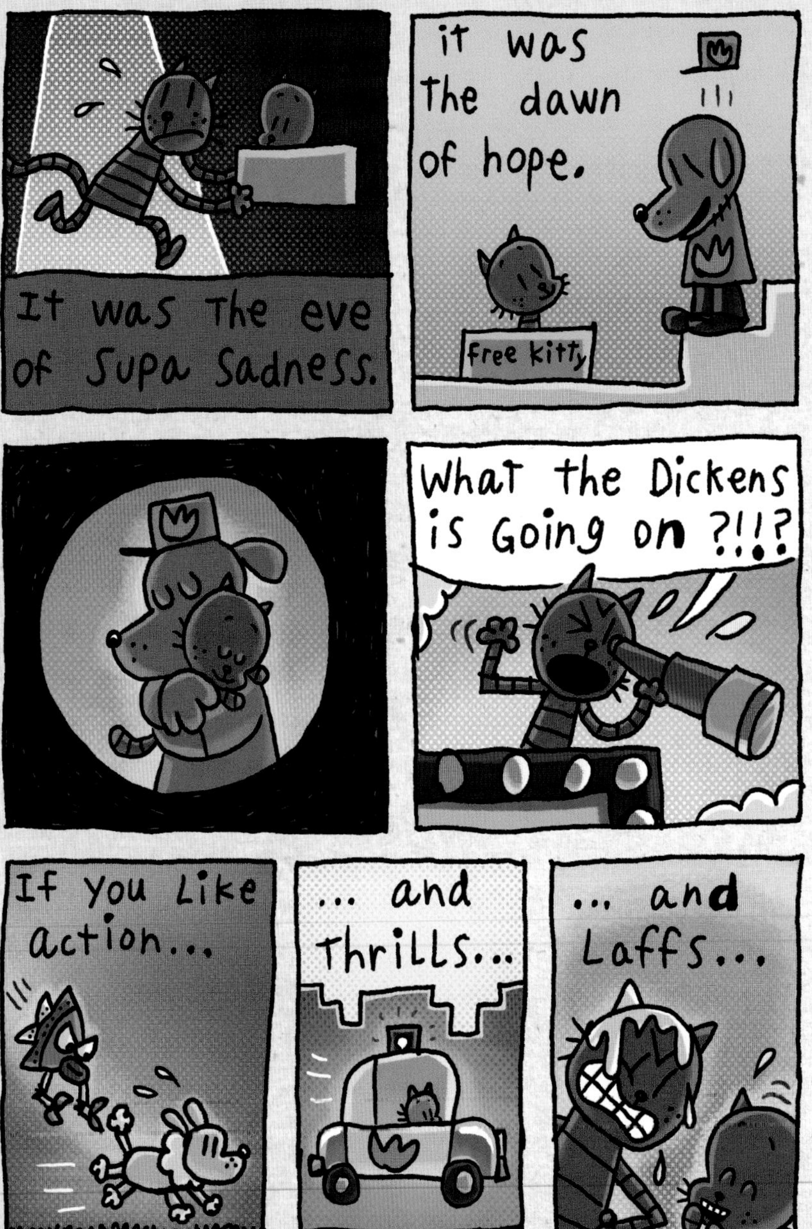
It was The eve of Supa Sadness.
it was The dawn of hope.
Free kitty
What the Dickens is Going on ?!!?
If you Like action...
... and ThrilLs...
... and Laffs...

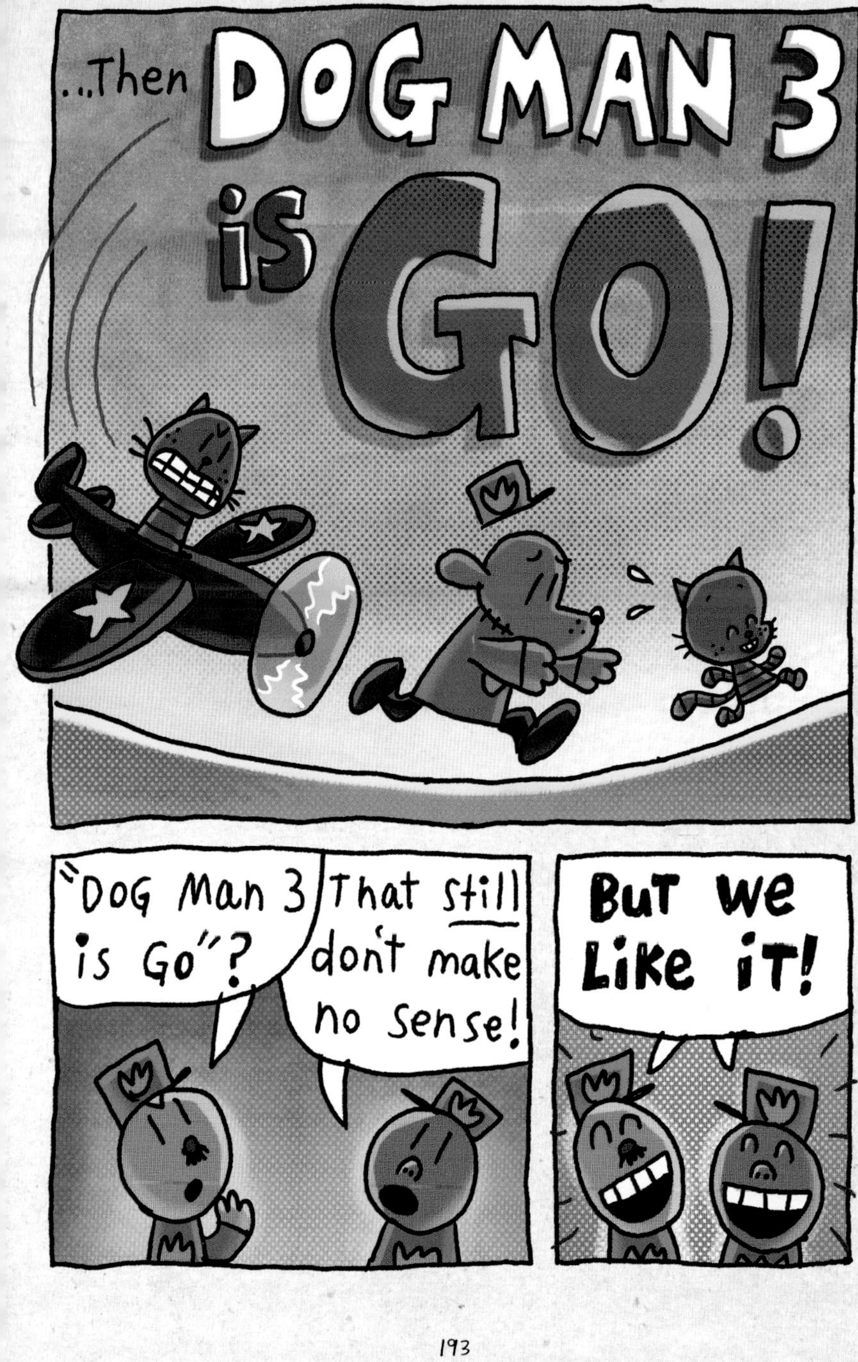
...Then DOG MAN 3 is GO!
"DOG Man 3 is Go"?
That still don't make no sense!
BUT WE LIKE IT!

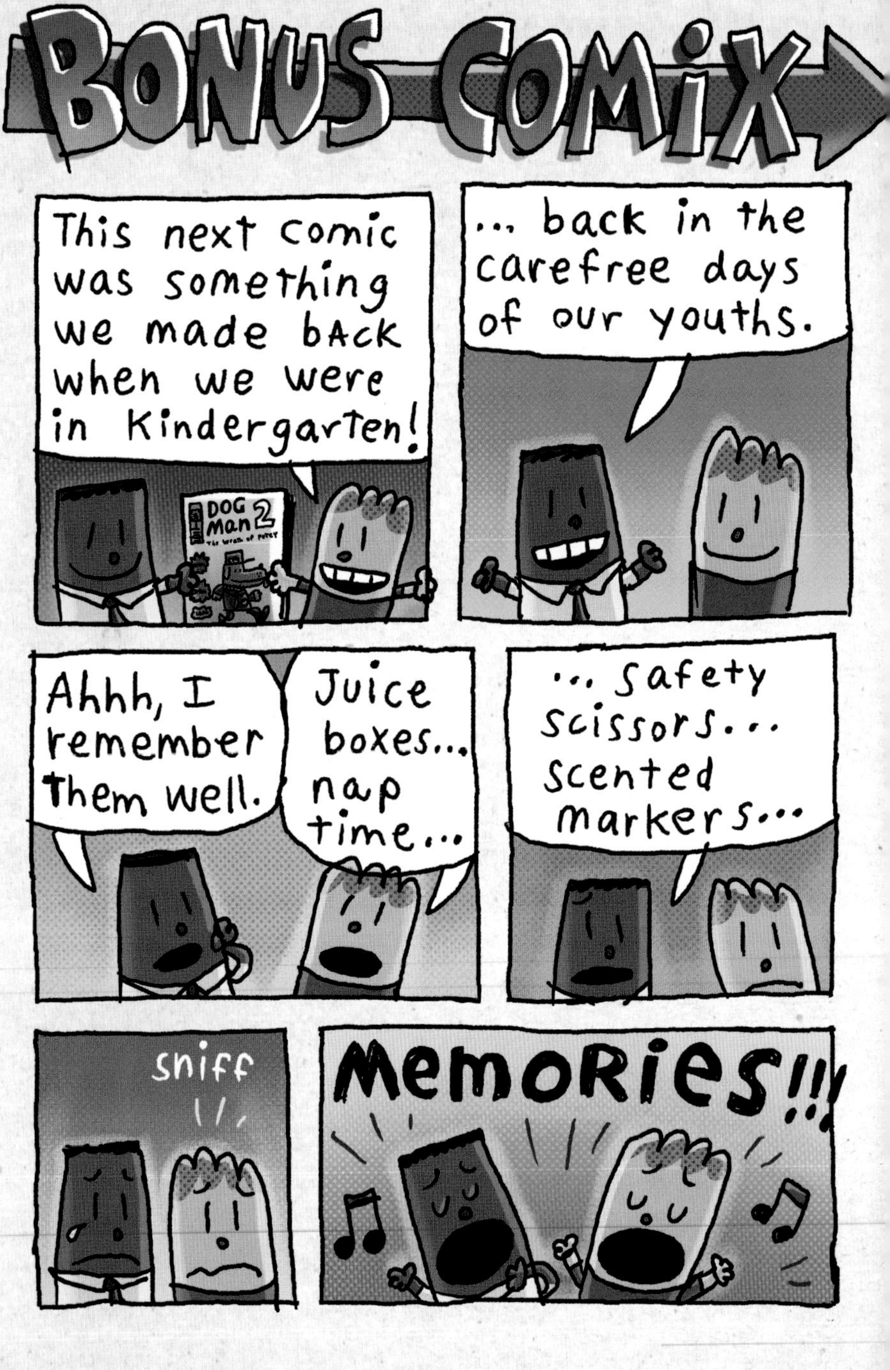
BONUS COMIX
This next comic was something we made back when we were in Kindergarten!
DOG Man 2
... back in the carefree days of our youths.
Ahhh, I remember them well.
Juice boxes... nap time...
... safety scissors... scented markers...
sniff
MEMORIES!!!

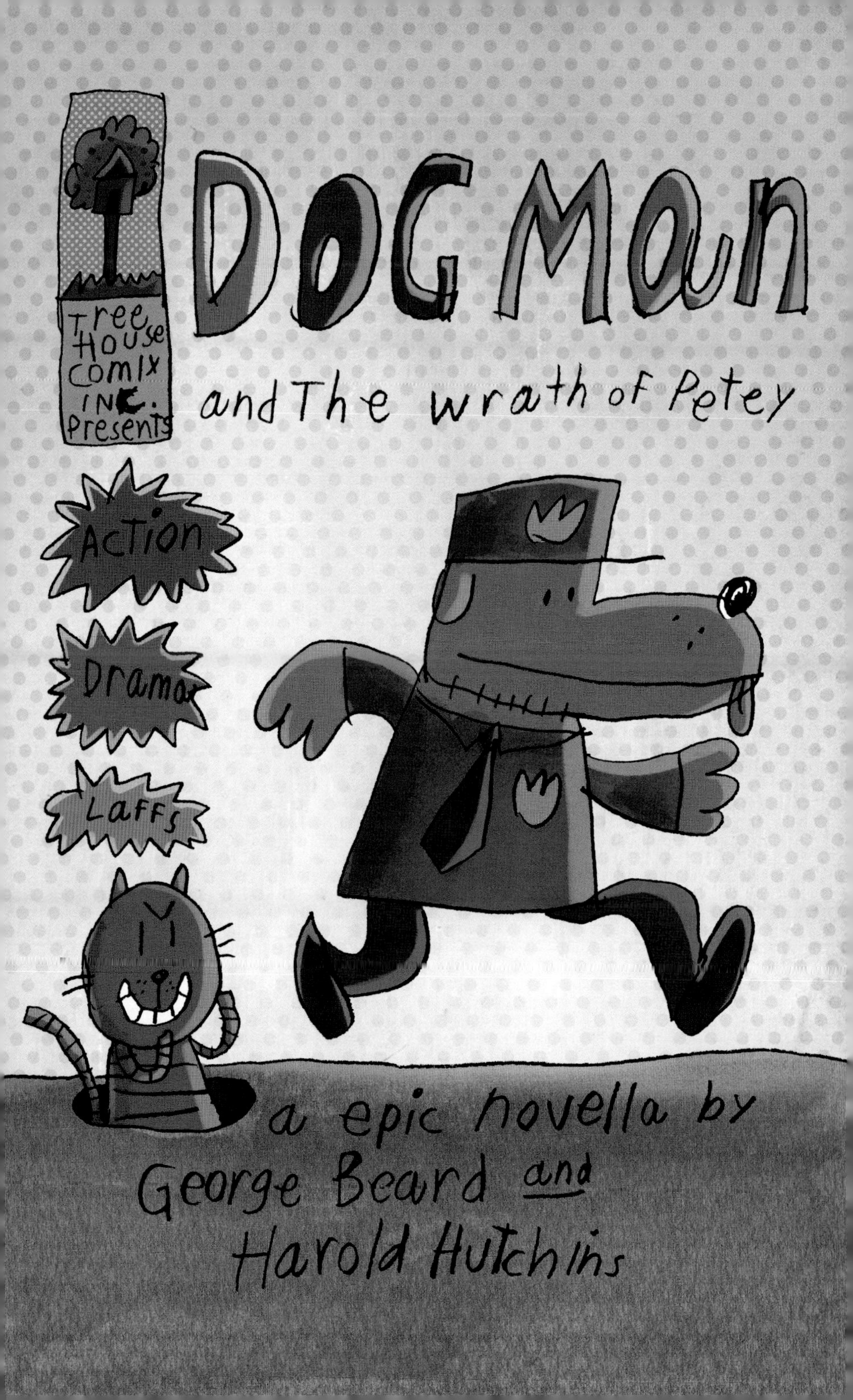

Tree House Comix Inc. Presents
DOG MAN
and The wrath of Petey
Action
Drama
Laffs
a epic novella by
George Beard and
Harold Hutchins

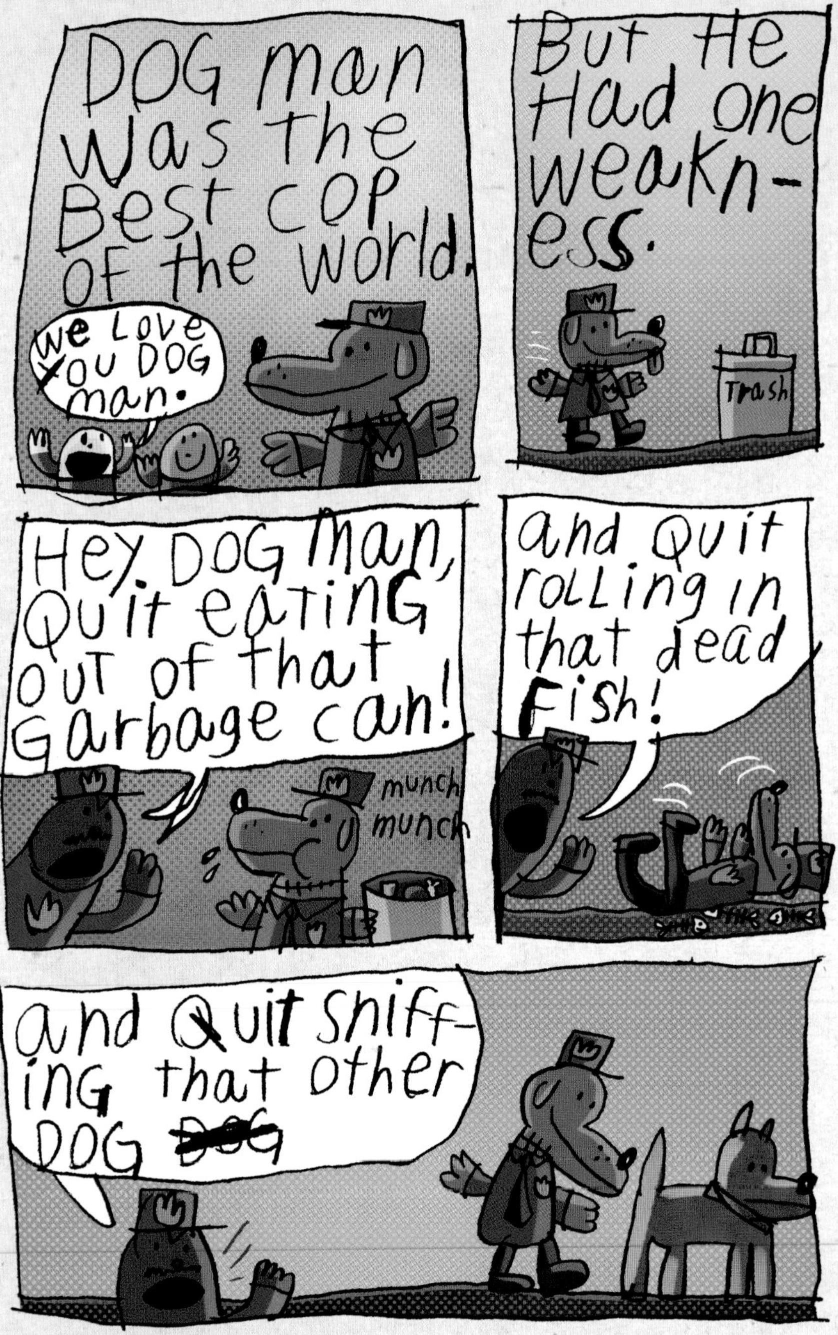
DOG man Was the Best cop of the world.
We Love you DOG man.
But He Had one weakn-ess.
Trash
Hey DOG man, Quit eating out of that Garbage can!
munch munch
and Quit rolling in that dead Fish!
and Quit sniff-ing that other DOG ~~DOG~~

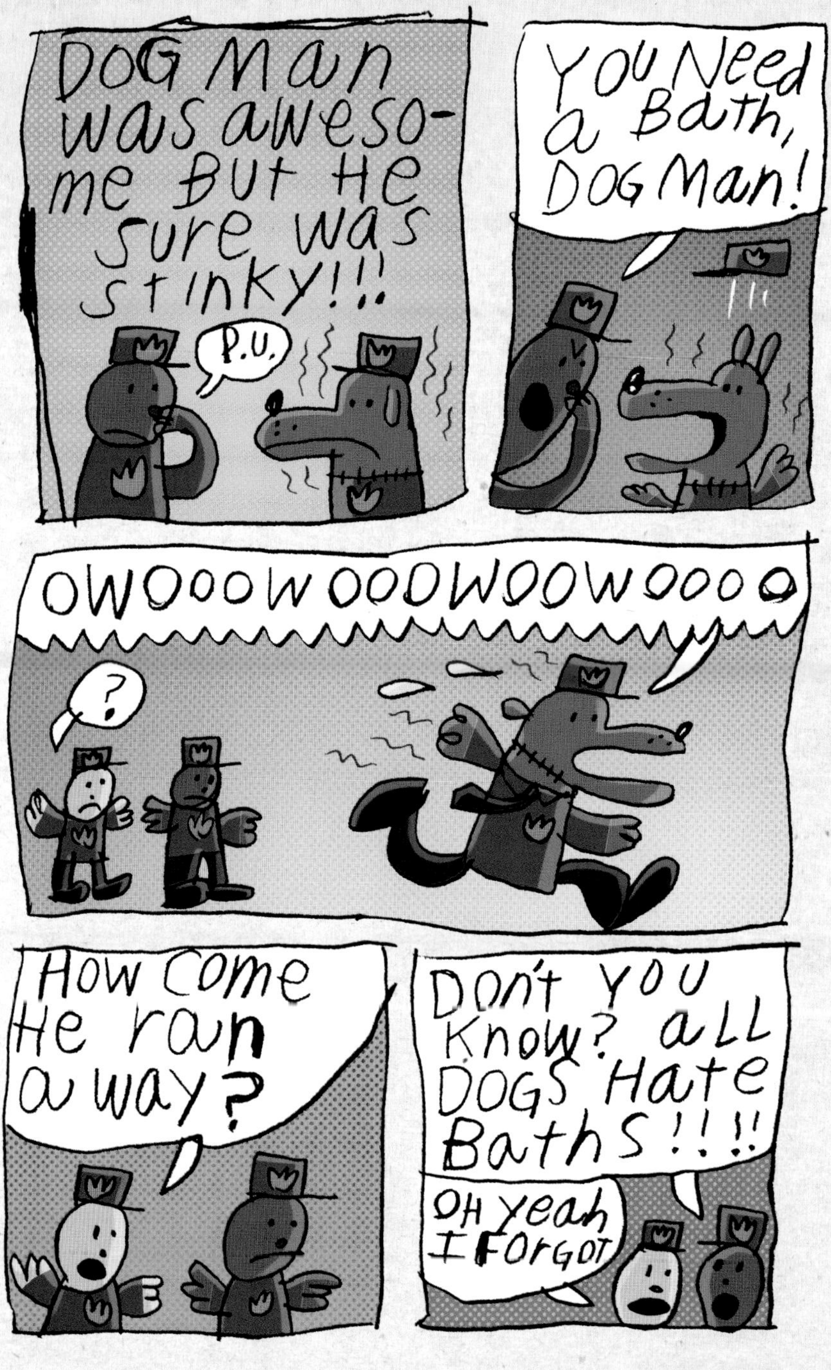
DOG Man was awesome BUT He sure was stinky!!!
P.U.
You Need a Bath, DOG Man!
OWOOOWOOOWOOWOOOO
?
How come He ran away?
Don't You Know? all DOGS Hate Baths!!!!
OH yeah I FOrGOT

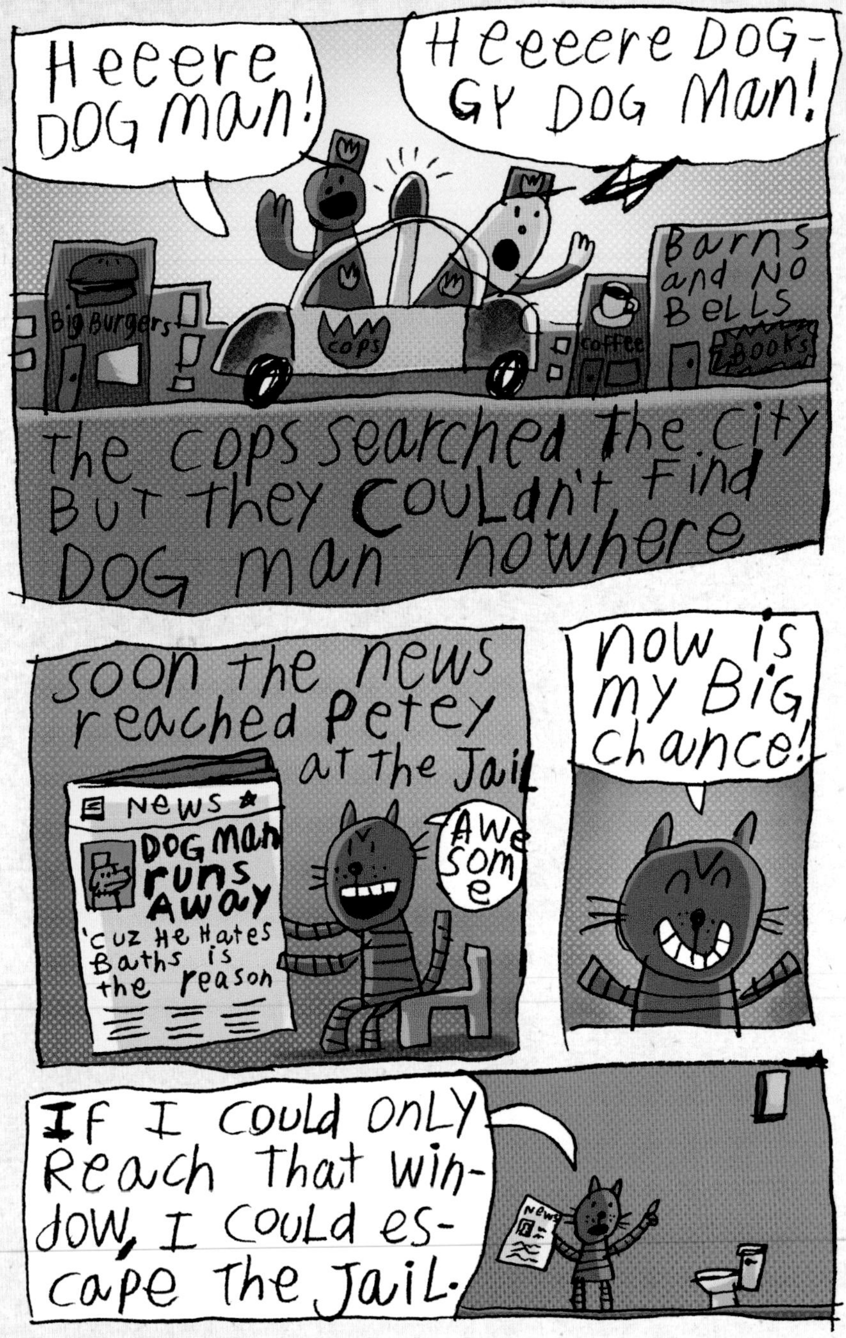
Heeere DOG Man!
Heeeere DOG-GY DOG Man!
Big Burgers
cops
coffee
Barns and No BeLLS
BOOKS
The cops searched the city But they CouLdn't Find DOG man nowhere
soon the news reached Petey at the JaiL
NEWS
DOG Man runs AWay
'cuz He Hates Baths is the reason
AWesome
now is my BIG chance!
IF I could onLY Reach That win-dow, I could es-cape The JaiL.
NEWS

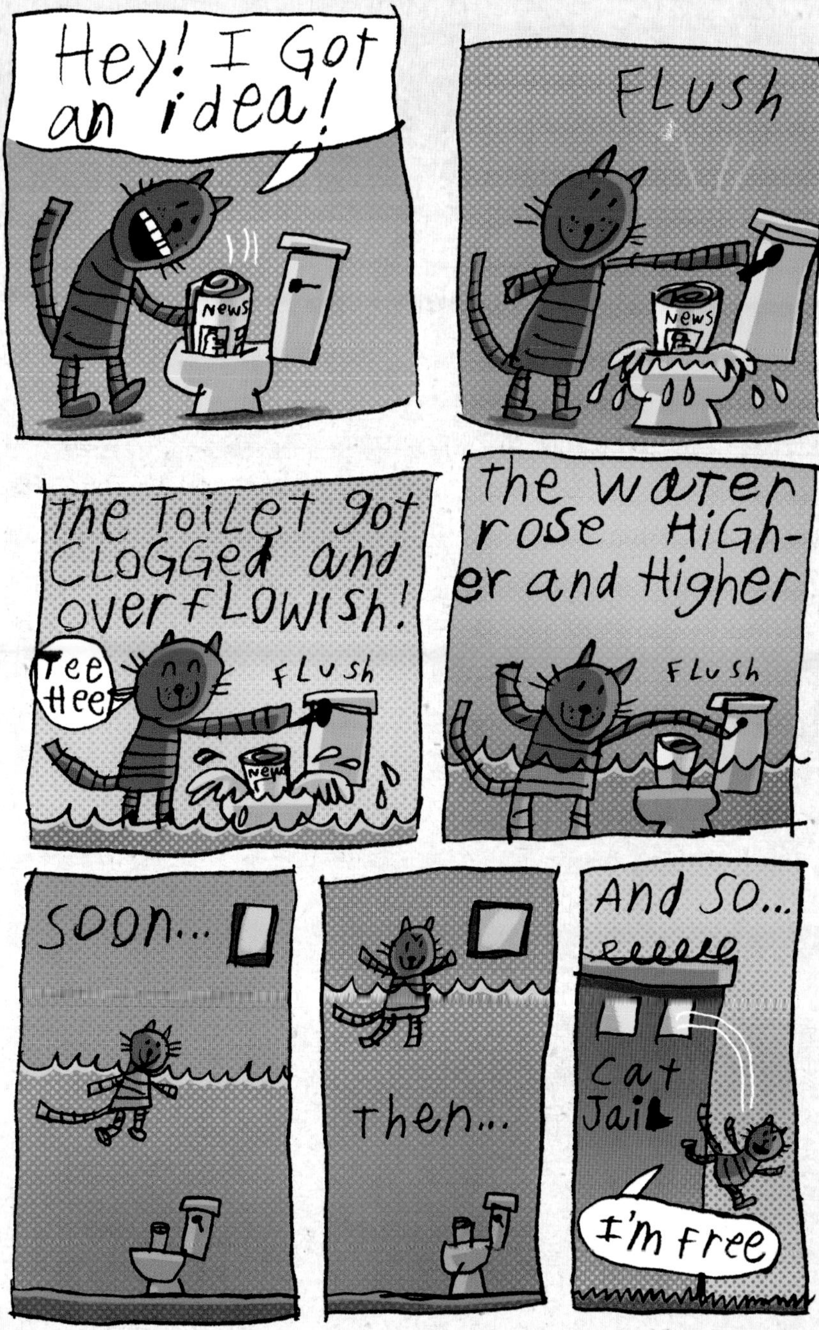
Hey! I Got an idea!
NEWS
FLUSH
NEWS
the ToiLet got CLoGGed and overFLOWISh!
Tee Hee
FLUSH
the water rose HiGher and Higher
FLUSH
soon...
then...
And so...
cat Jail
I'm Free

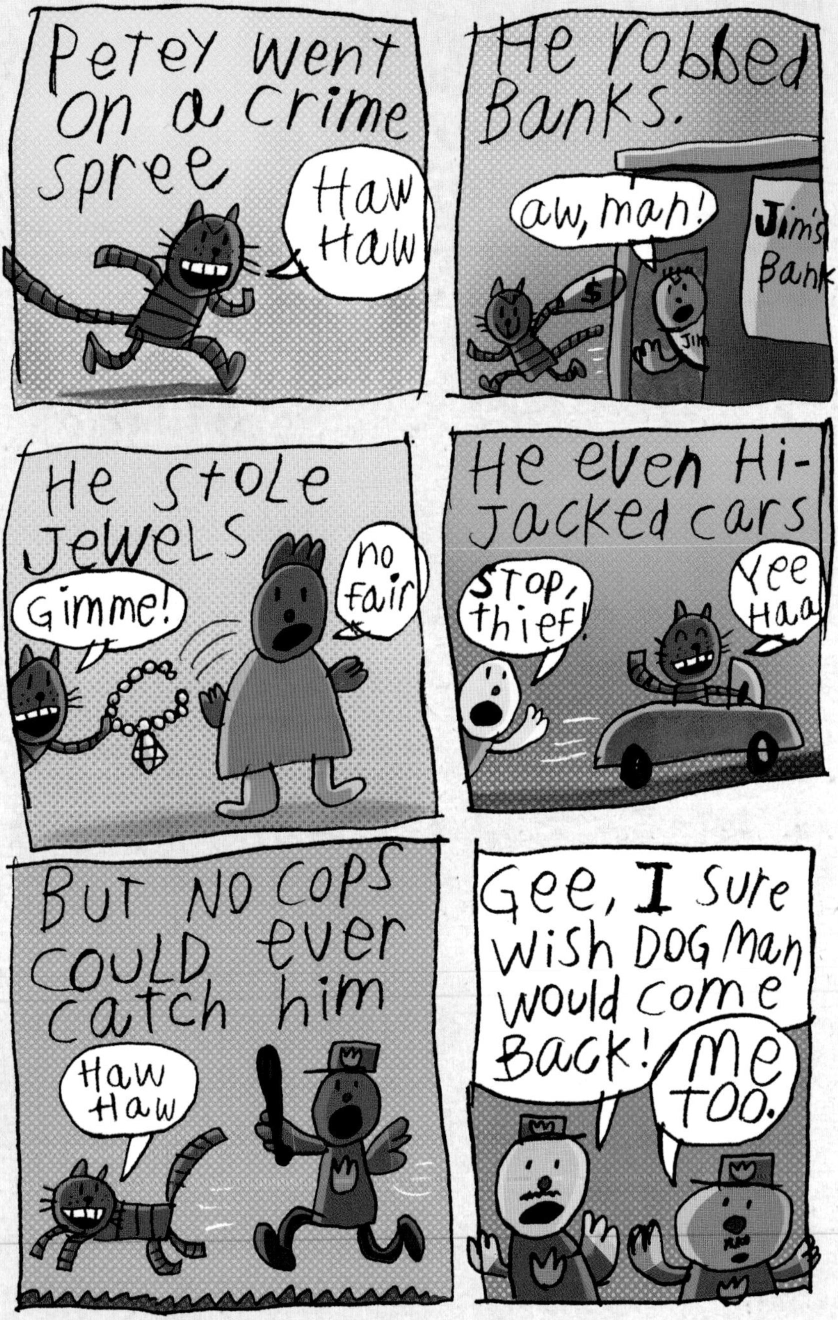
Petey went on a crime spree
Haw Haw
He robbed Banks.
aw, man!
Jim's Bank
Jim
He stole Jewels
Gimme!
no fair
He even Hi-Jacked cars
Stop, thief!
Yee Haa
But no cops could ever catch him
Haw Haw
Gee, I sure wish Dog Man would come Back!
Me too.

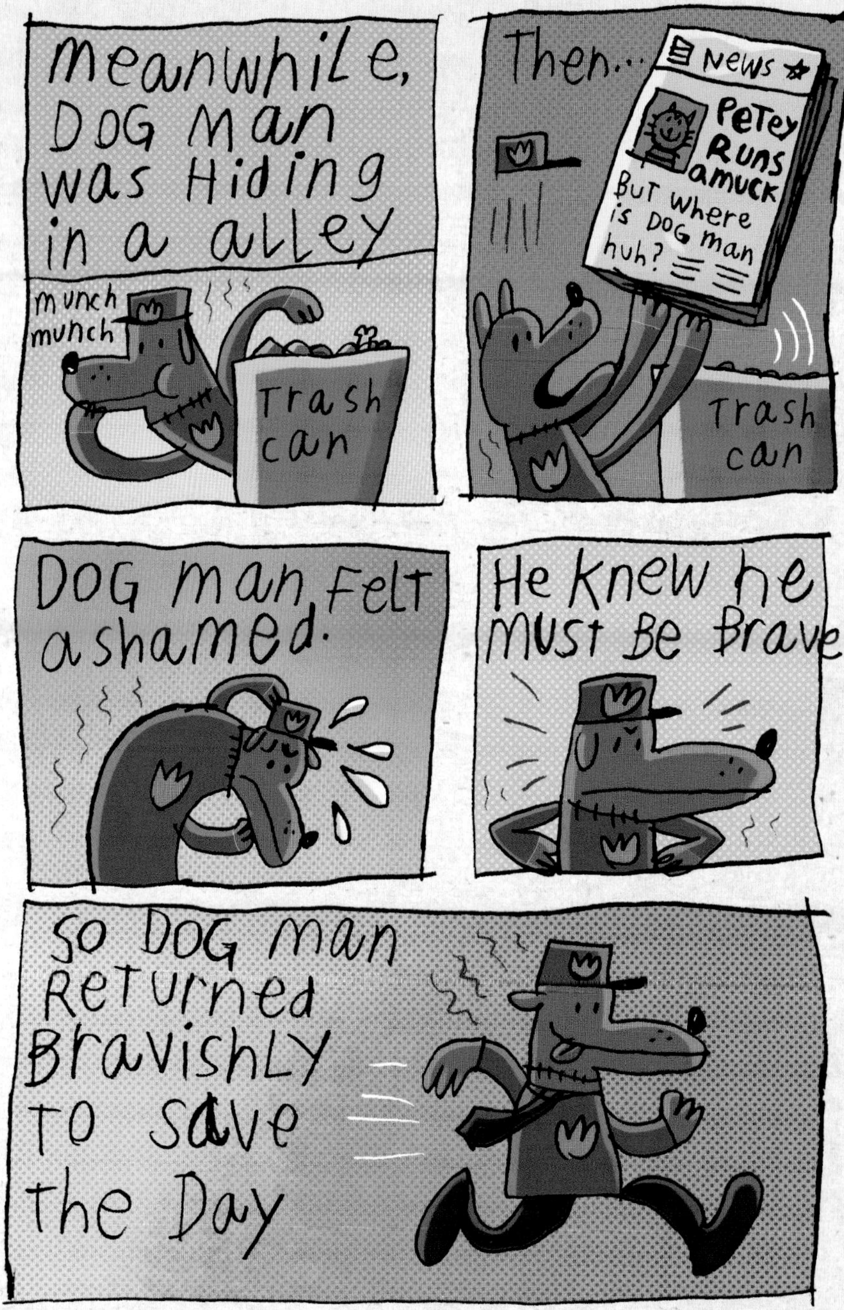
meanwhile, DOG man was Hiding in a alley
munch munch
Trash can
Then...
NEWS
PeTey Runs amuck
BuT where is DOG man huh?
Trash can
DOG man FelT ashamed.
He knew he must Be Brave
So DOG man ReTurned BravishLY TO save the Day

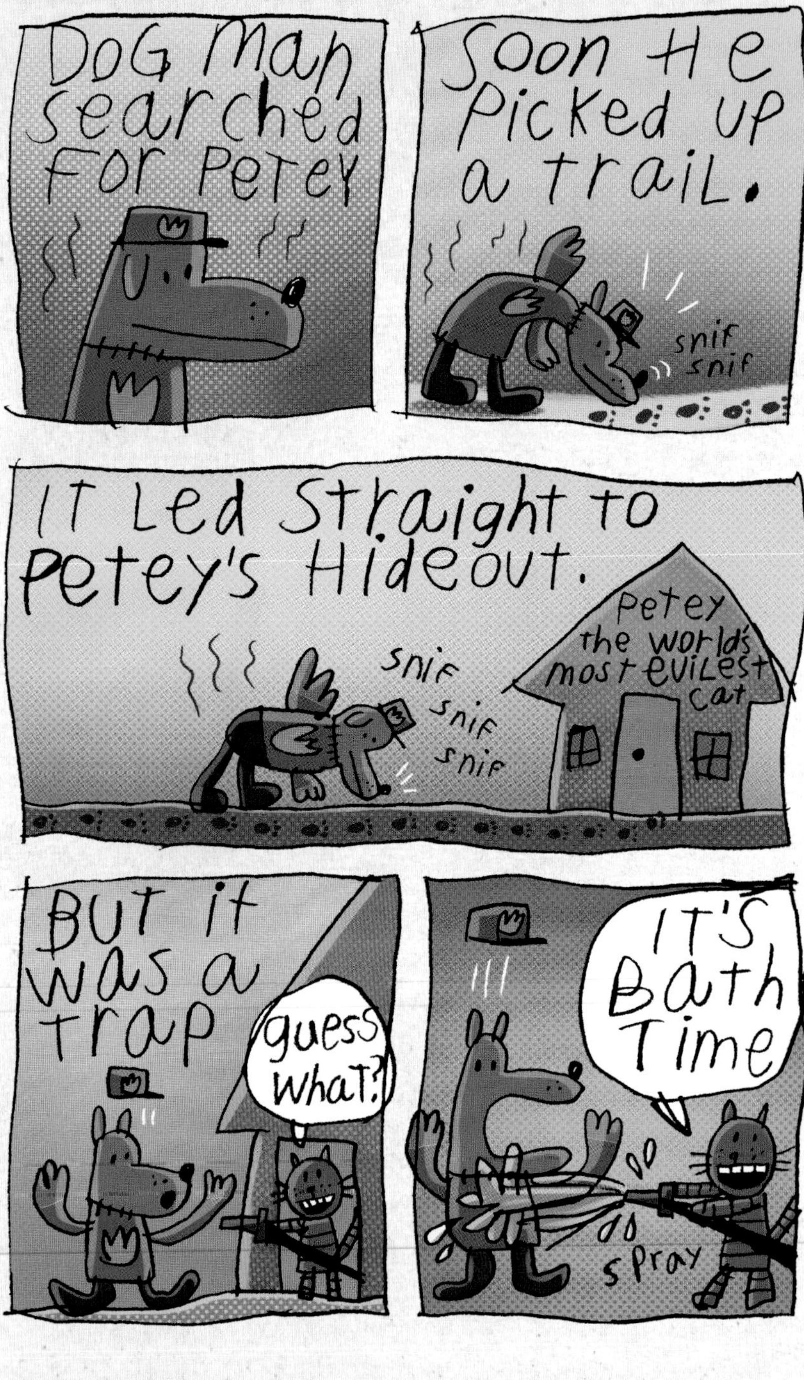
DoG Man searched For Petey
Soon He Picked up a trail.
snif snif
IT Led Straight to Petey's Hideout.
snif snif snif
Petey the world's most eviLest cat
But it was a trap
guess what?
IT'S Bath Time
spray

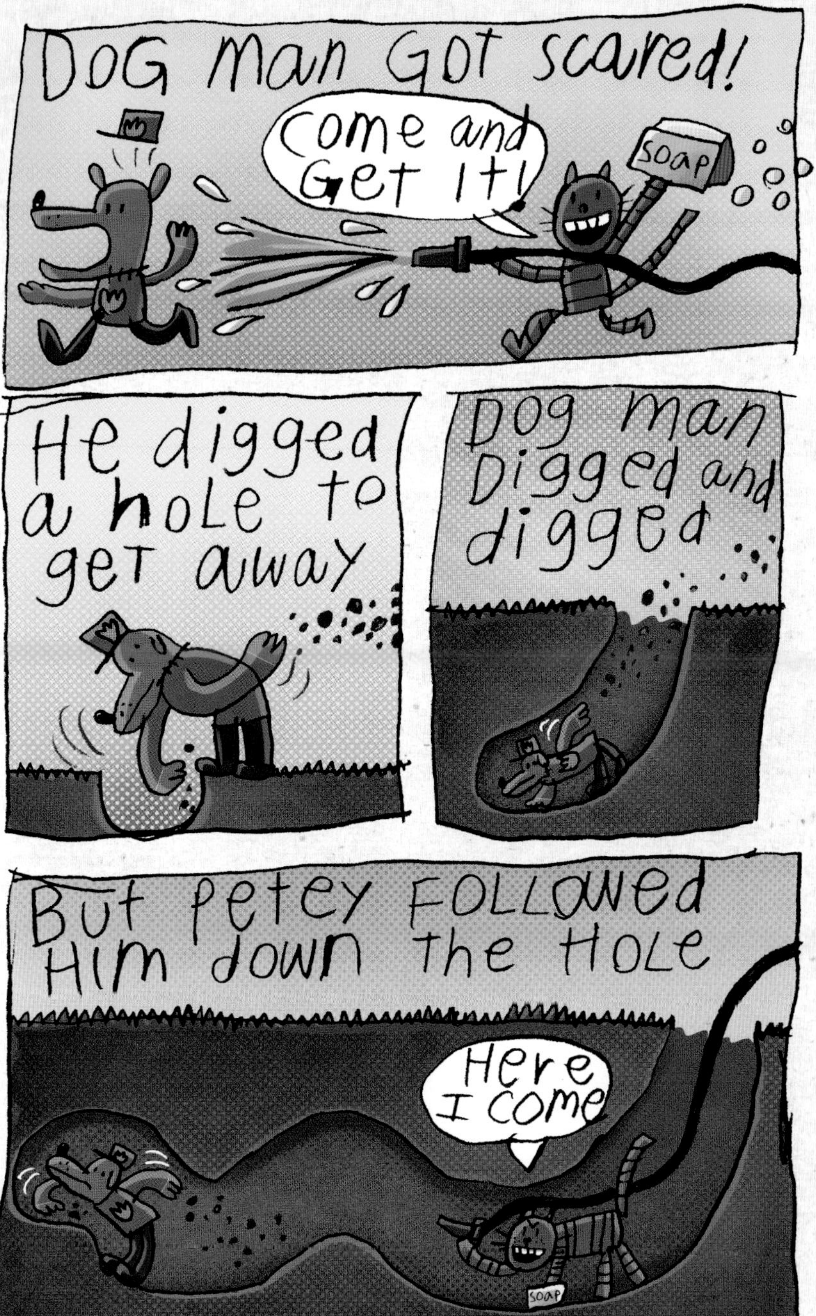
Dog Man Got scared!
Come and Get It!
SOAP
He digged a hole to get away
Dog Man Digged and digged
But Petey FOLLOWED Him down the Hole
Here I come
SOAP

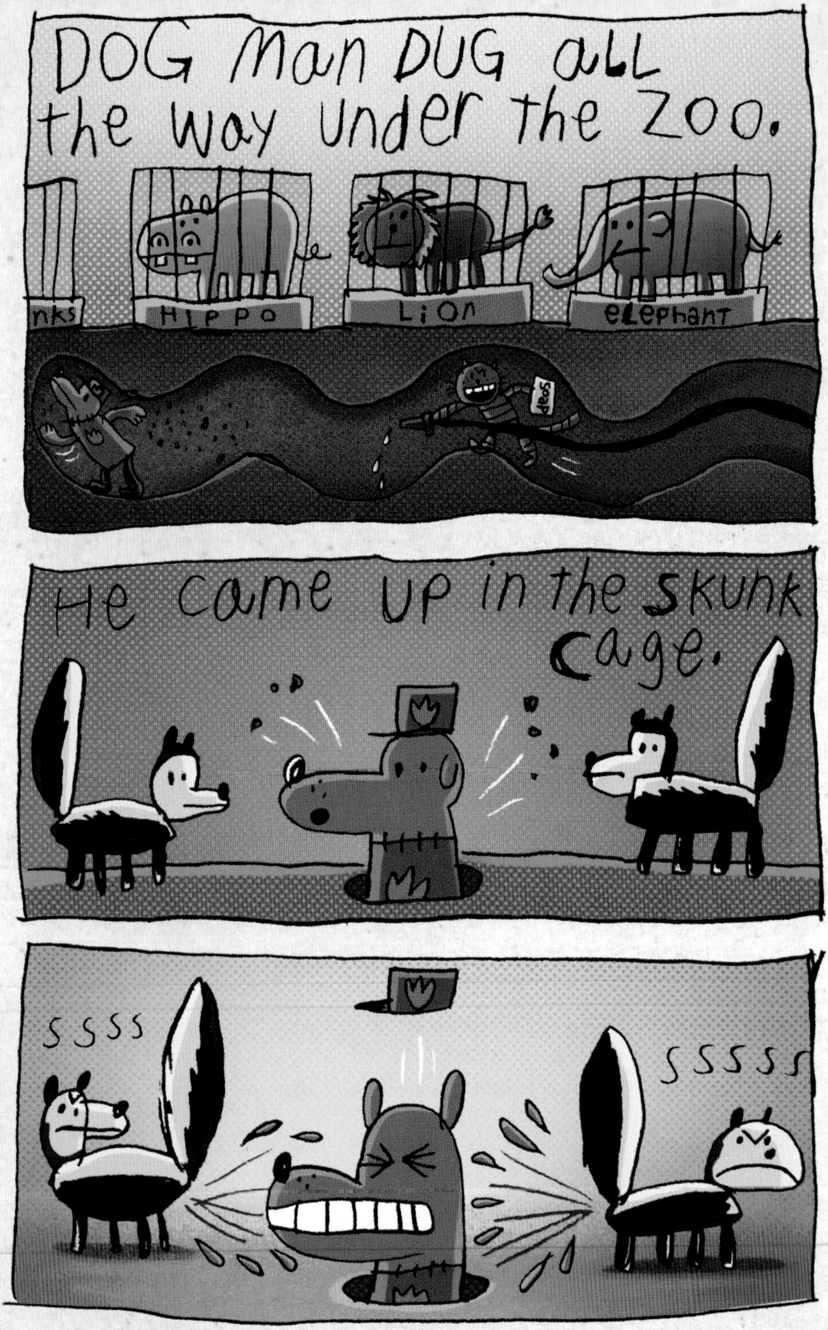
DOG Man DUG all the way under the Zoo.
nks
HIPPO
LiOn
eLephant
Soap
He came up in the skunk cage.
SSSS
SSSSS

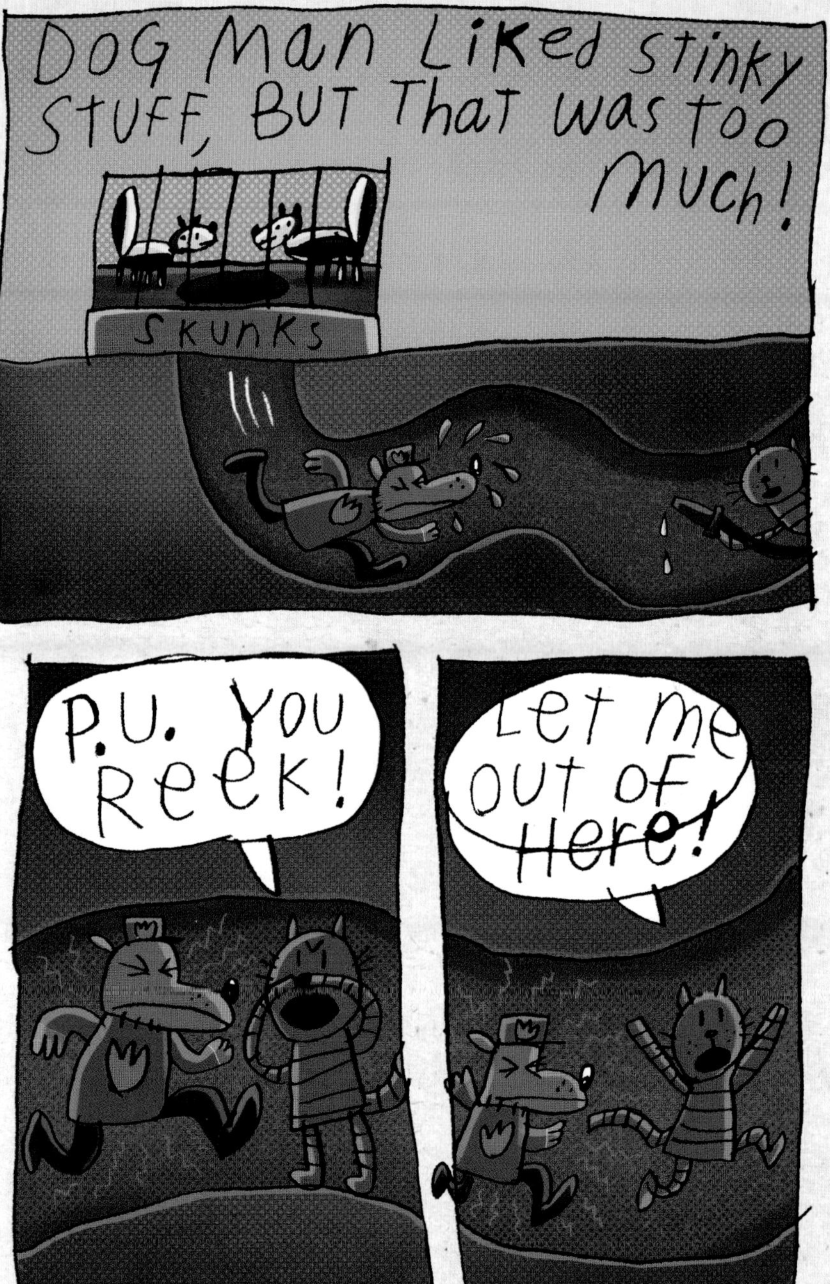
Dog Man Liked stinky stuff, but that was too much!
Skunks
P.U. You Reek!
Let me out of here!

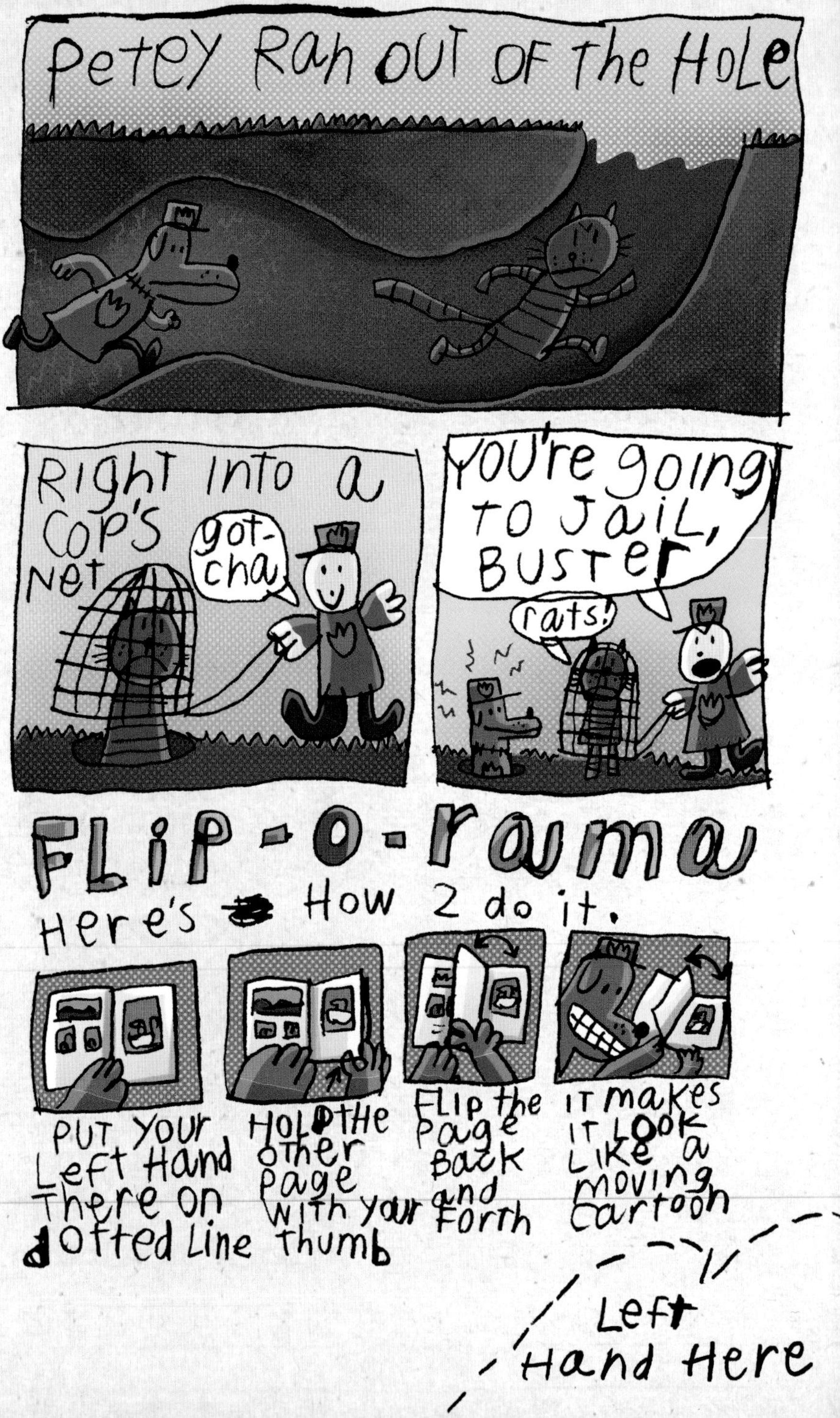
Petey Ran OUT OF The HoLe
Right into a Cop's net
got-cha
You're going TO Jail, BUSTer
rats!
FLip-o-rama
Here's How 2 do it.
PUT YOUR Left Hand There on dotted Line
HOLD THE other Page with your thumb
FLIP the Page Back and Forth
IT makes IT LOOK Like a moving Cartoon
Left Hand Here

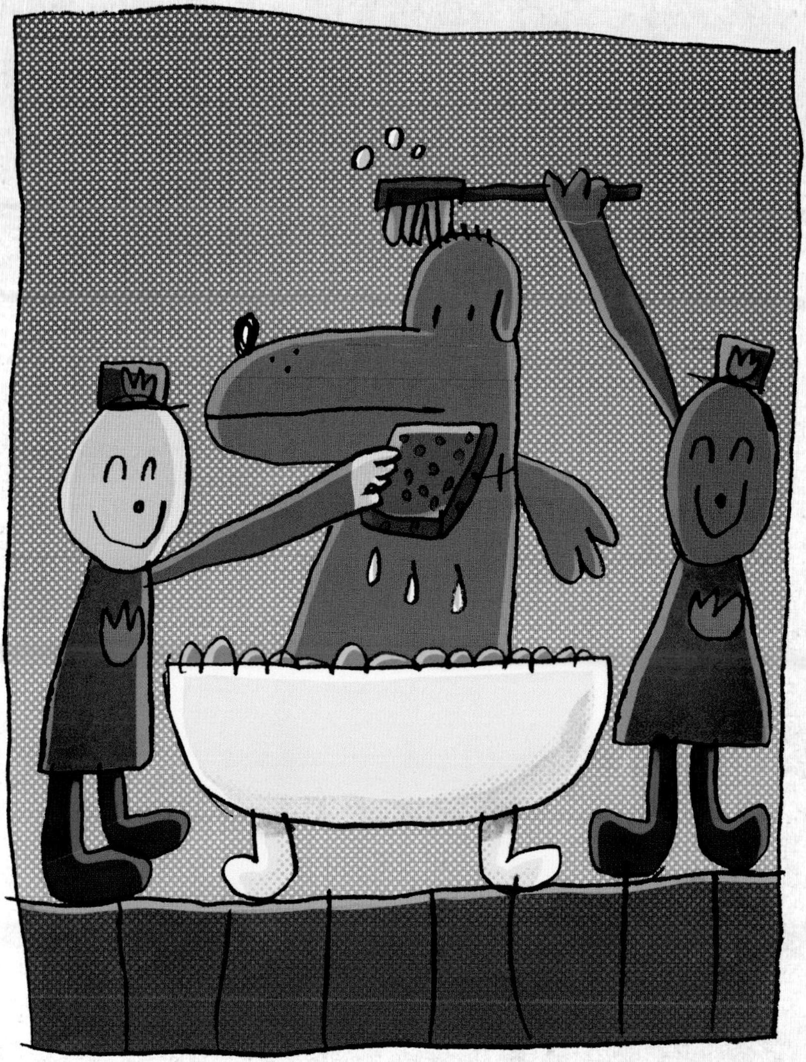

Bathtime for Dog Man

RIGHT THUMB Here

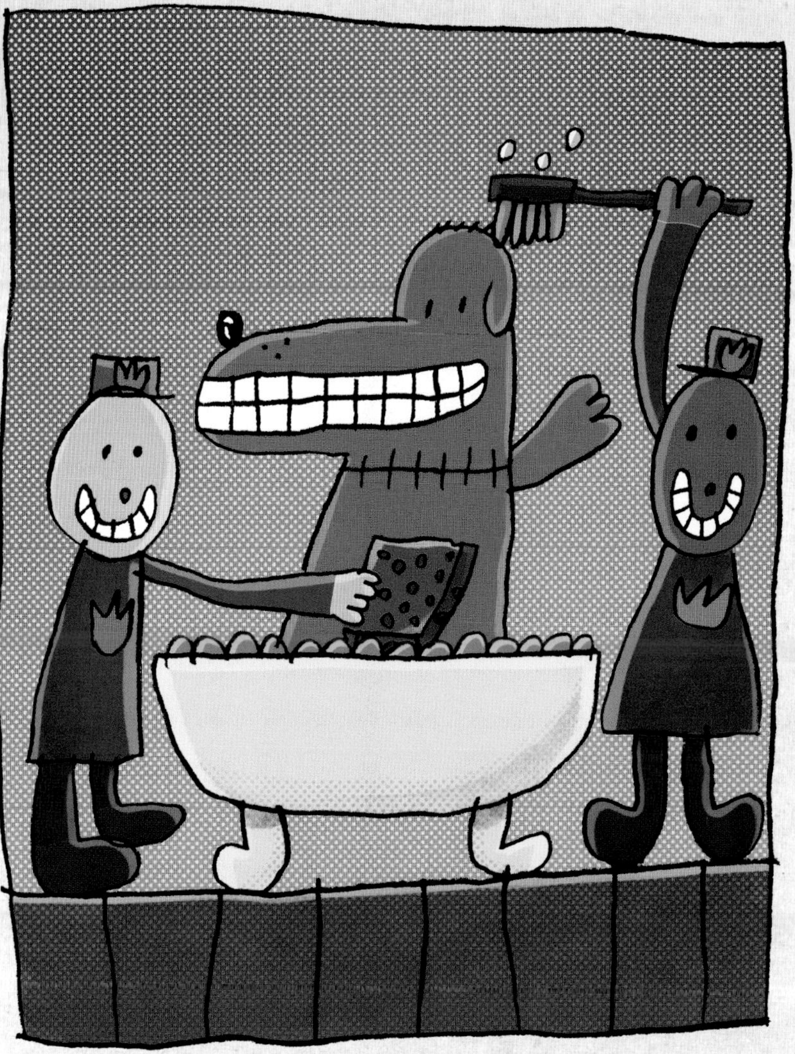

Bathtime for Dog Man

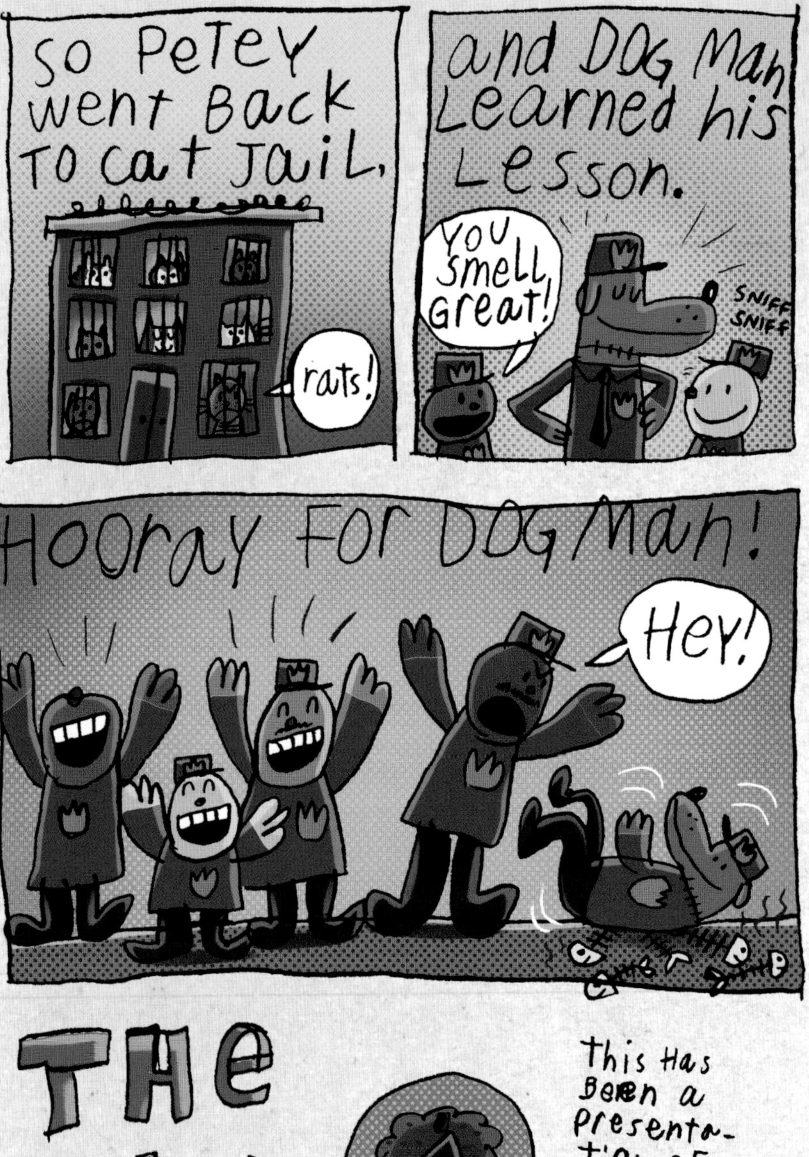
So Petey went back to cat jail,
rats!
and Dog Man learned his lesson.
You smell great!
SNIFF SNIFF
Hooray for Dog Man!
Hey!
THE END
This has been a presentation of tree house comix inc. All rights reserved

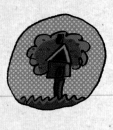

HOW 2 DRAW DOG MAN

in 41 Ridiculously easy Steps!

1
2
3
4
5
6
7
8
9
10
11
12
13

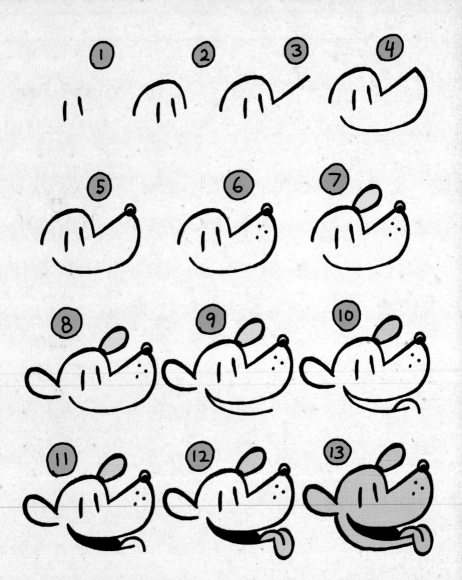

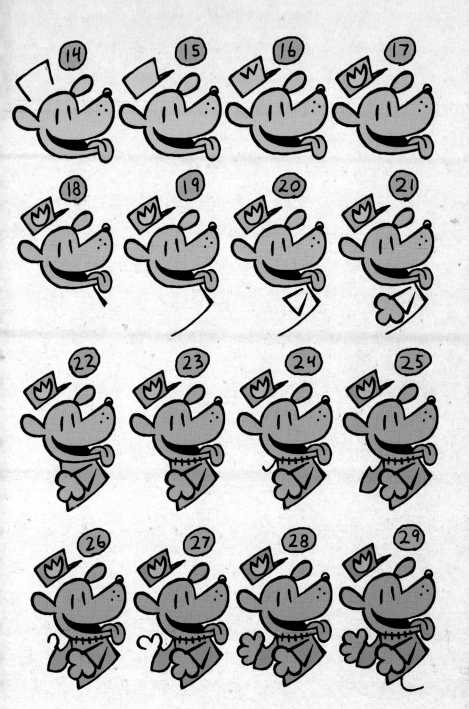

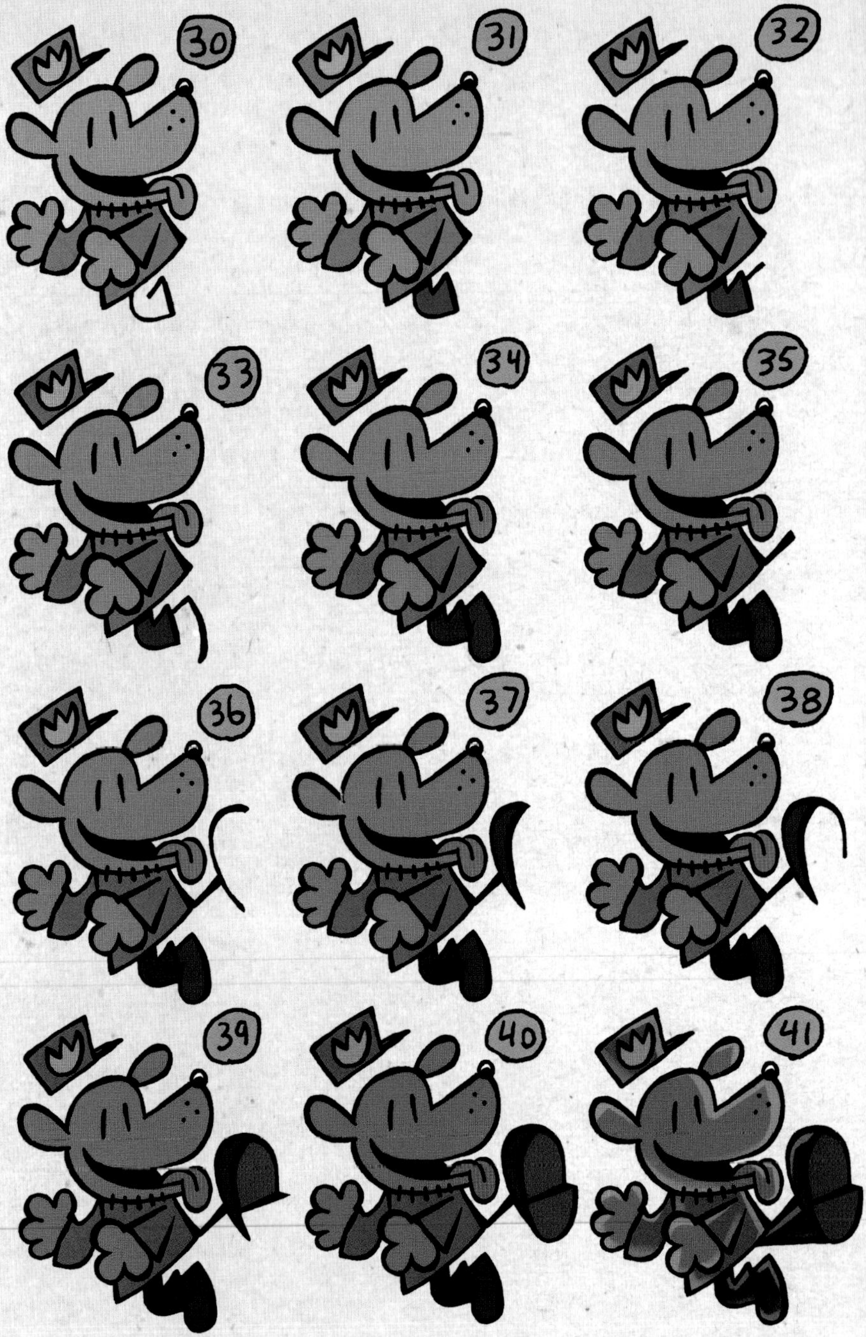
30
31
32
33
34
35
36
37
38
39
40
41

HOW 2 DRAW Petey

in 28 Ridiculously easy steps!

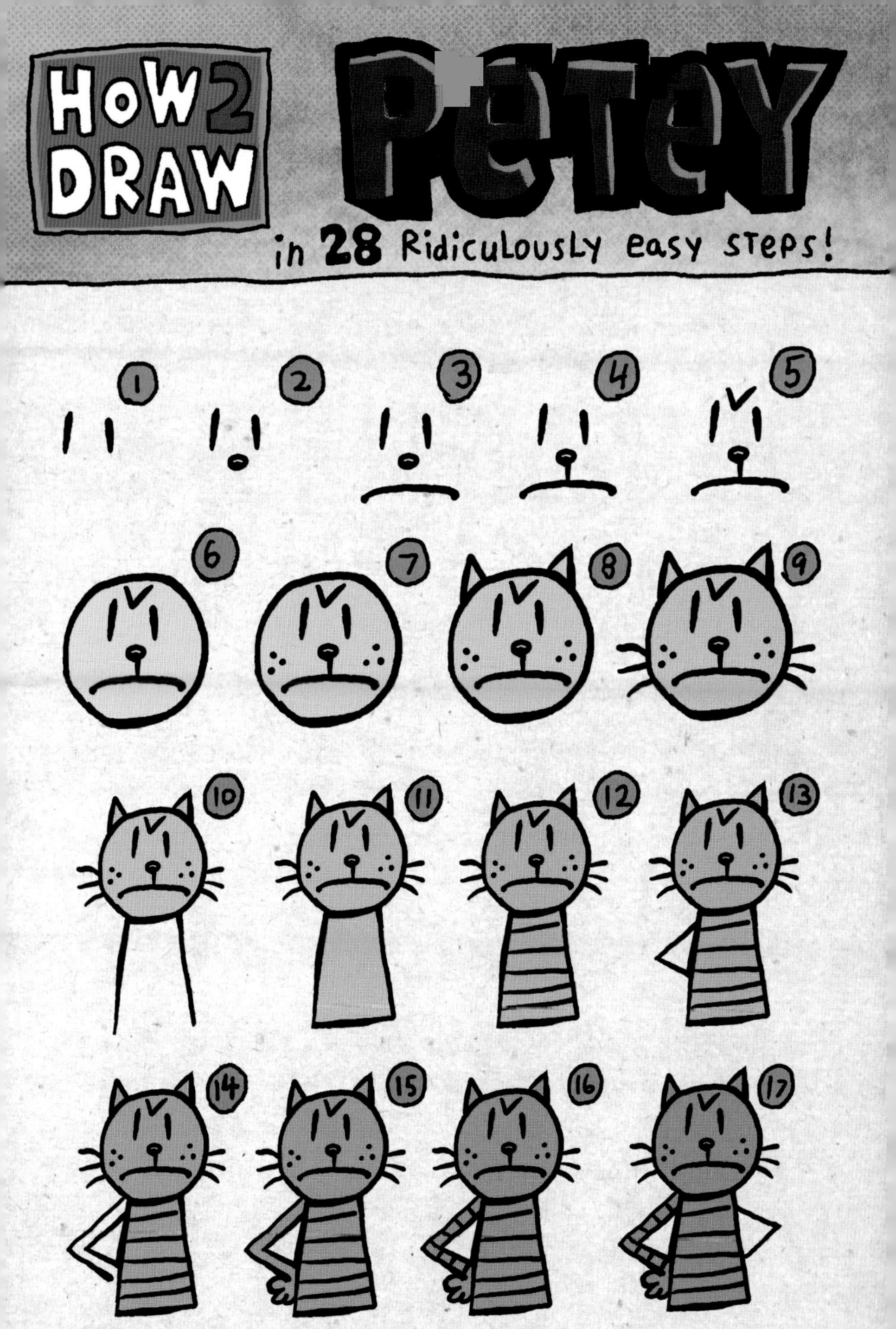
1
2
3
4
5
6
7
8
9
10
11
12
13
14
15
16
17

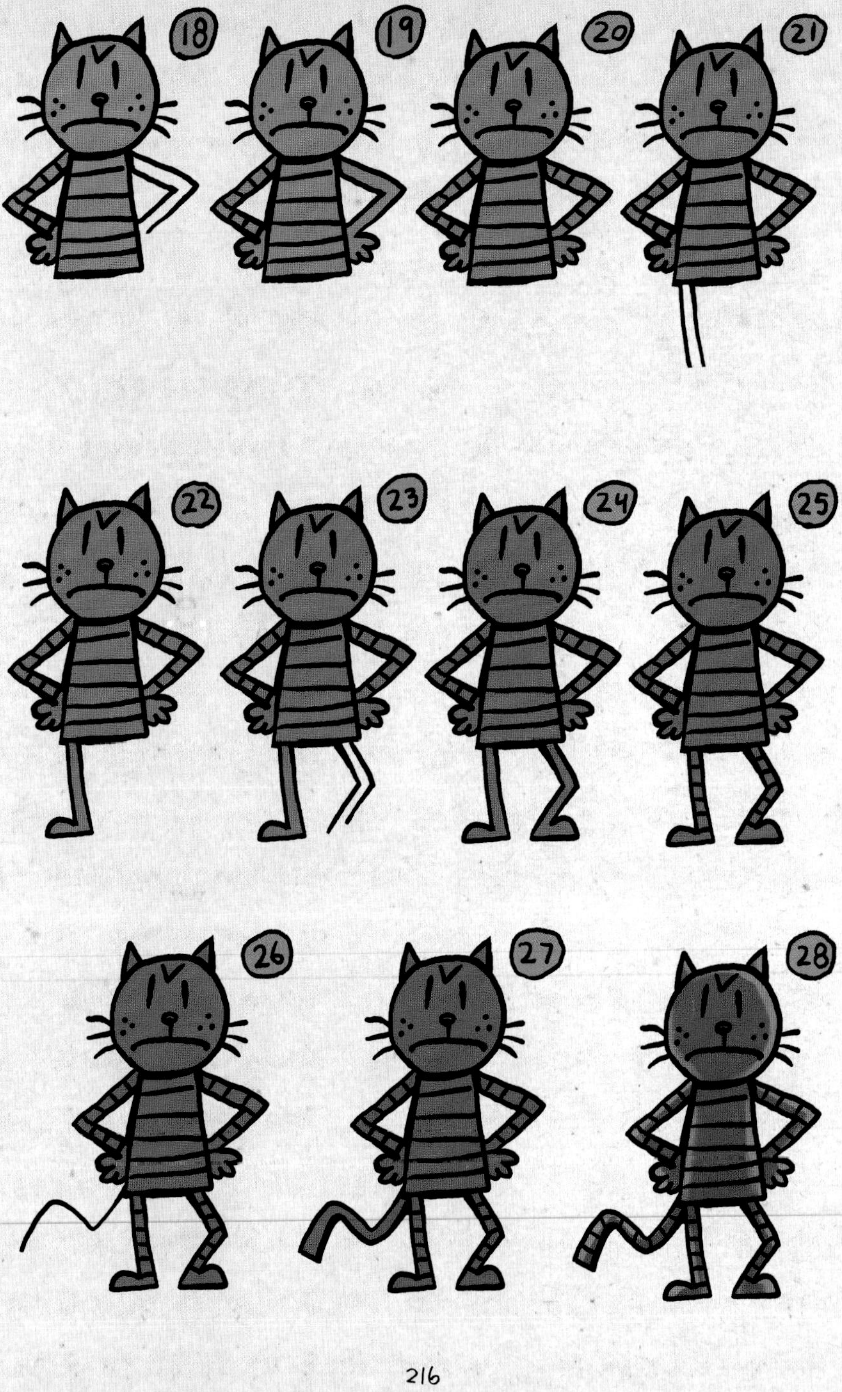
18
19
20
21
22
23
24
25
26
27
28

HOW 2 DRAW FLAT PETEY

...in 8 more Ridiculously easy steps!

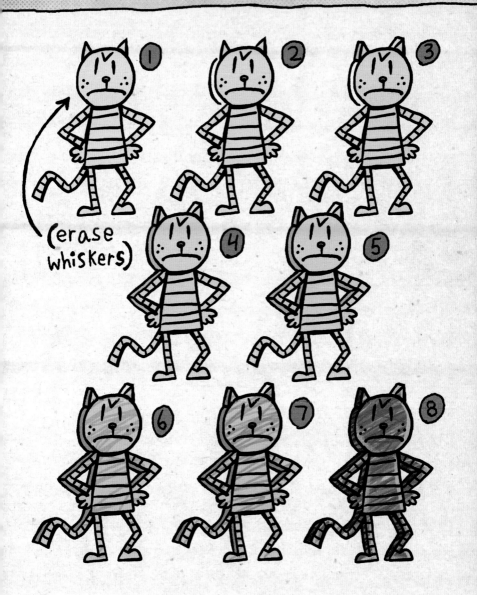

(erase whiskers)

HOW 2 DRAW FLIPPY

in 16 Ridiculously easy Steps!

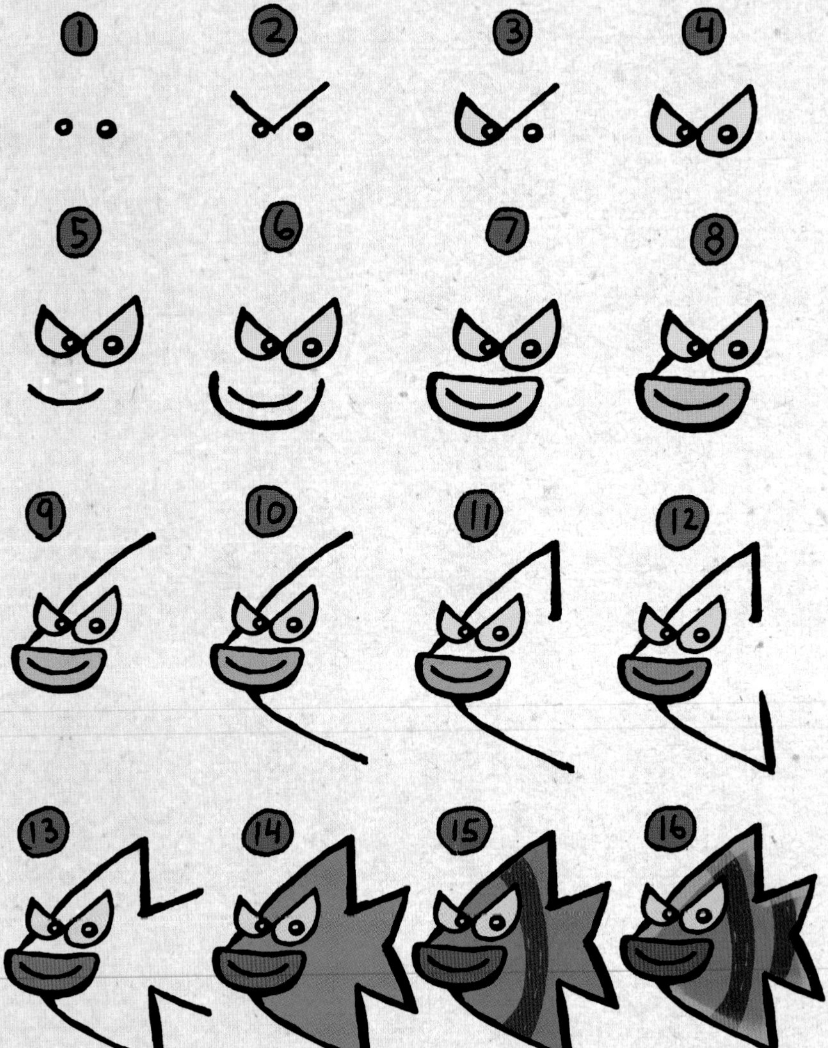
1
2
3
4
5
6
7
8
9
10
11
12
13
14
15
16

HOW 2 DRAW ZUZU

in **24** Ridiculously easy steps!

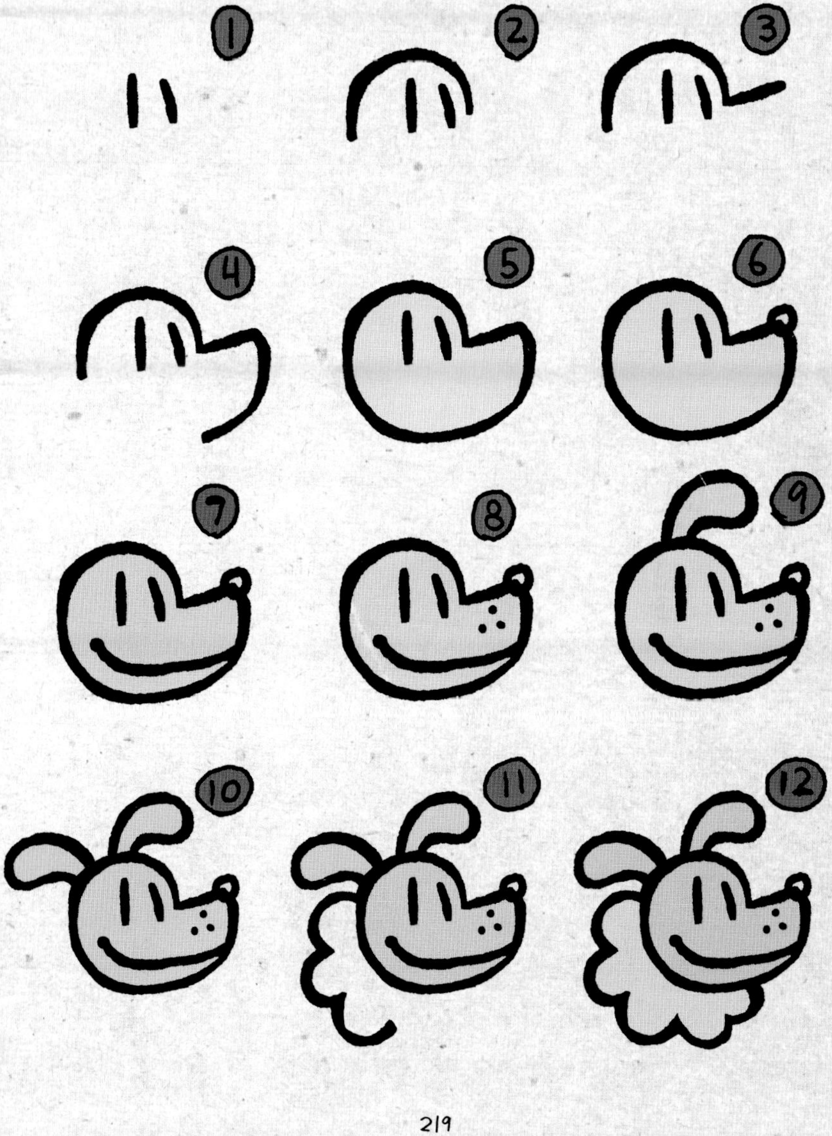
1
2
3
4
5
6
7
8
9
10
11
12

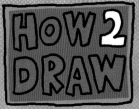

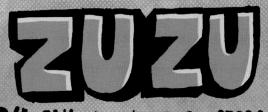

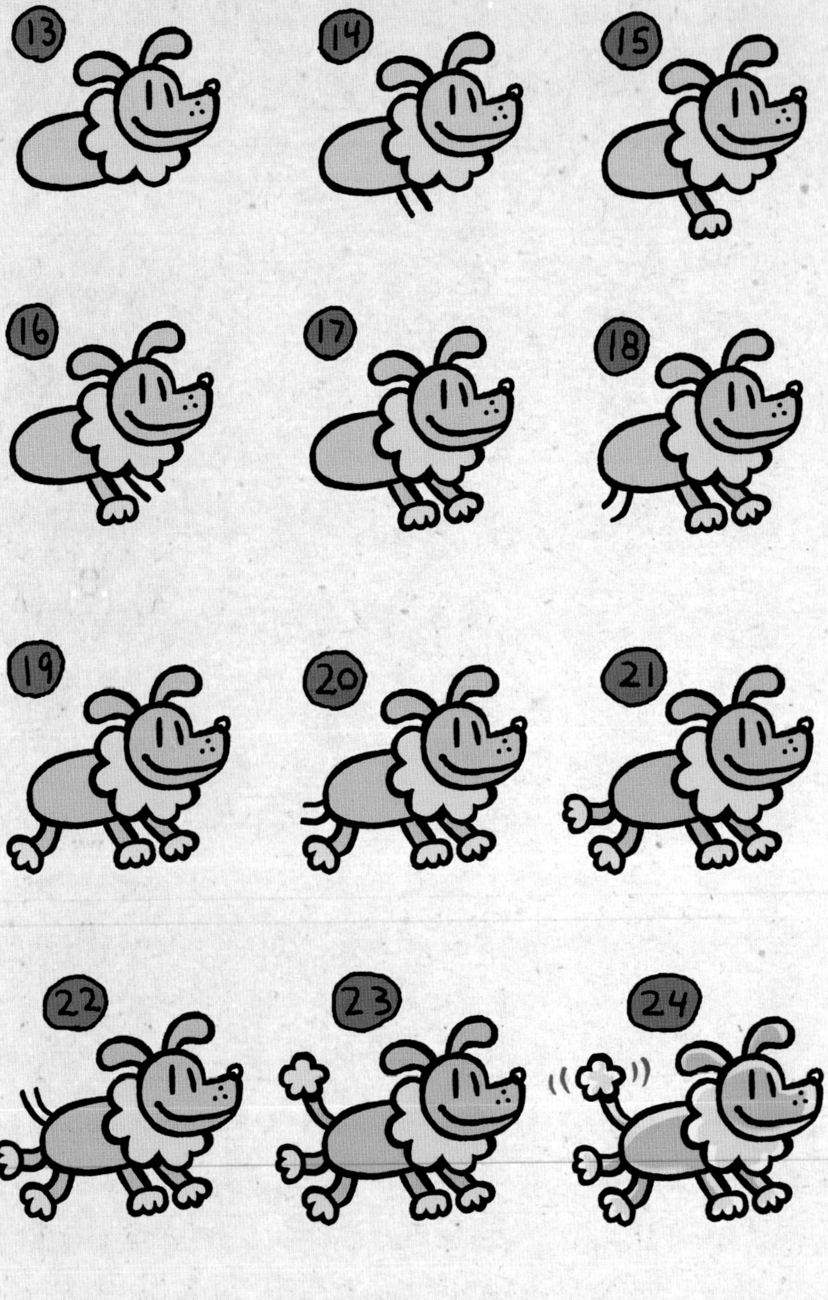
13
14
15
16
17
18
19
20
21
22
23
24

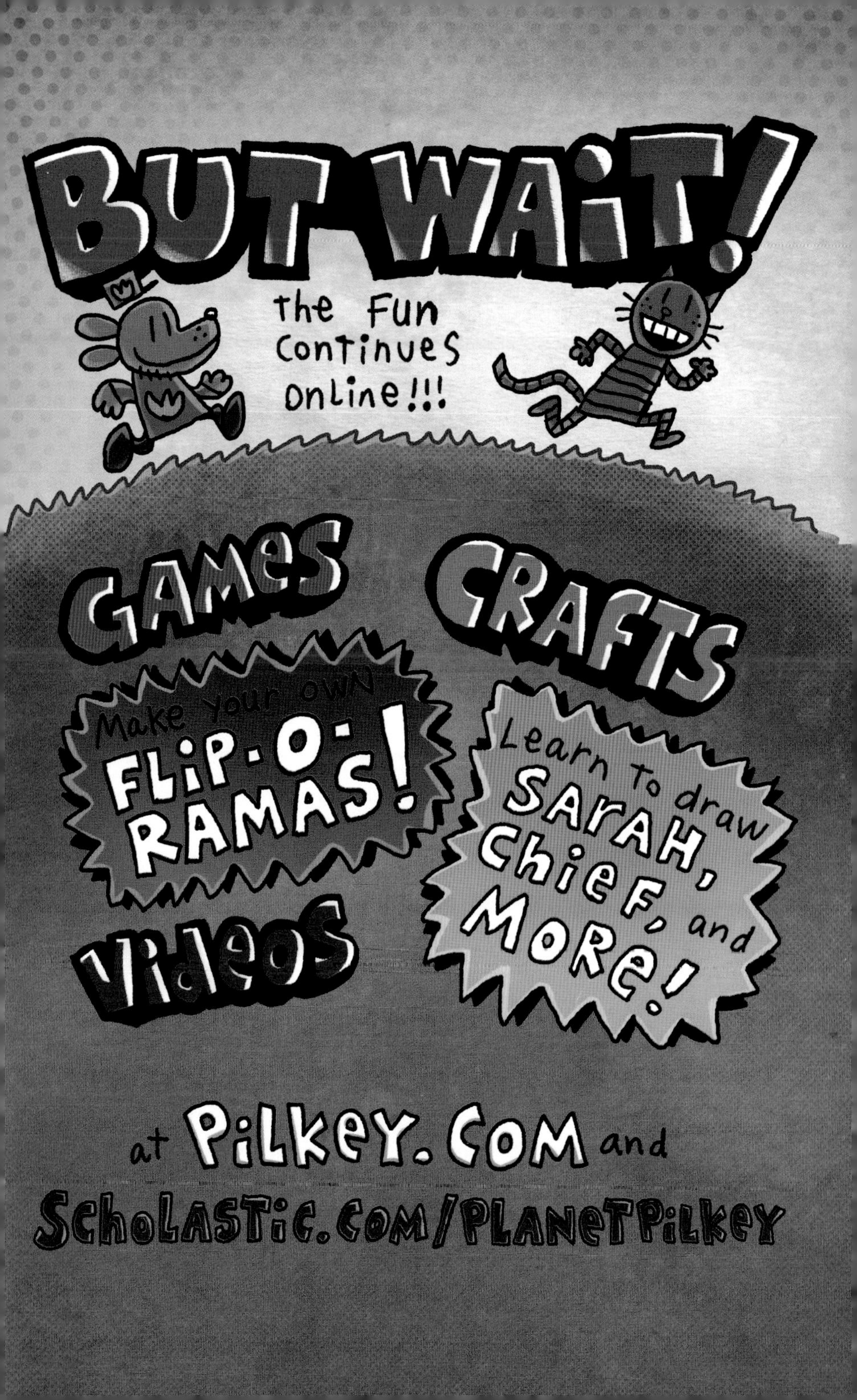

BUT WAIT!
the Fun continues online!!!
GAMES
CRAFTS
Make your own FLIP-O-RAMAS!
Learn to draw SARAH, Chief, and MORE!
videos
at PiLKEY.COM and
SCHOLASTIC.COM/PLANETPILKEY

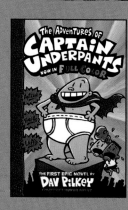

ABOUT THE AUTHOR-ILLUSTRATOR

When Dav Pilkey was a kid, he suffered from ADHD, dyslexia, and behavioral problems. Dav was so disruptive in class that his teachers made him sit out in the hall every day. Luckily, Dav loved to draw and make up stories. He spent his time in the hallway creating his own original comic books.

In the second grade, Dav Pilkey created a comic book about a superhero named Captain Underpants. His teacher ripped it up and told him he couldn't spend the rest of his life making silly books.

Fortunately, Dav was not a very good listener.

ABOUT THE COLORIST

Jose Garibaldi grew up on the South Side of Chicago. As a kid, he was a daydreamer and a doodler, and now it's his full-time job to do both. Jose is a professional illustrator, painter, and cartoonist who has created work for Dark Horse Comics, Disney, Nickelodeon, MAD Magazine, and many more. He lives in Los Angeles, California, with his wife and their cats.

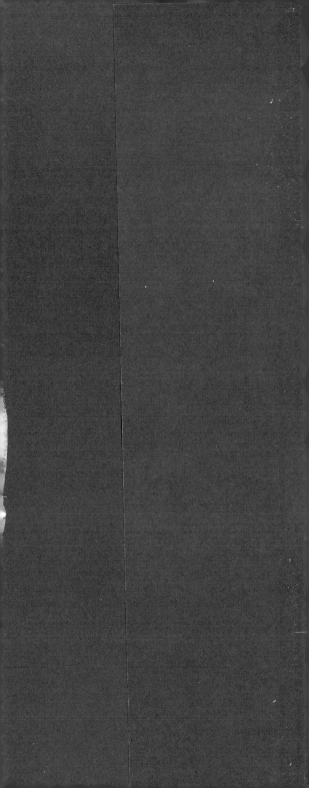